BUT GOD!
I WRITE SONGS

Emmy's Story, Part 13

By
Kenneth Lee McGee

For Harper and Luna.

You will always be loved.

A special thanks to Sue Midlock for creating the cover. She is so talented. I prefer my book covers to be rather simple and she does a great job. If you want to see more of her covers, check out her Facebook page Your Book Cover. There are examples of covers where she lets her talent shine.

I would like to thank Denise and Stephanie for their support and for pushing me to get my books published.

I want to thank the people from my church who have graciously allowed me to include fragments of their lives as inspirations.

I want to thank my wife Sheila for being my toughest critic.

Prologue

On the morning of her thirty-third birthday Emmy Colasanti-Colwell sat behind the recording console in the basement studio of the home she shared with Kenny Colwell and listened to a newly recorded vocal track. *I need to redo that line.* She listened to the end of the track and then closed her eyes. She waited for a moment and then began to pray out loud. "Lord, thank you for your many blessings." She prayed for the people on her prayer list, the church and then asked for direction for her life. "Lord, guide me. Show me if there is anything I need to change." Then she paused. She cleared her mind and listened for the Holy Spirit to talk to her heart, just like Pastor Tyler taught people at church. She felt her heart slow down as she took deep breaths. For four minutes she sat with her eyes closed and her mind clear without making a sound. Then suddenly she opened her eyes and sat up. She put her feet on the floor and grabbed the arms of the recliner.

"But God! I write songs! Are you sure? I don't know if I can do that." She paused again and listened. "Okay," she thought about one of her favorite verses. "In Psalms 28:7, it says 'The Lord is my strength and my shield; my heart trusts in him and he helps me. My heart leaps for joy, and with my song I praise him.' My song, Lord. That's what I do. I write songs, not what you are telling me." She closed her eyes and tried to fight back the tears. "Songs, I write songs," she wept until Philippians 4:13 popped into her head. "I can do all this through him who gives me strength." She sighed and took a deep breath. "Fine! I won't fight you because you always win."

At that moment Kenny entered the control room. "You okay, Em. I thought I heard something."

"That was me fighting against God."

"Did you win?"

"Of course not," she said. "But this is crazy."

He tilted his head. "What? And why would you fight God?"

"Because I'm stubborn and because of what He wants me to do," she said biting her lip.

7

"What is He asking you to do?"

She raised her hands. "The Holy Spirit told me to write a book."

"A book? Are you sure? You write songs." He pulled her out of the chair and held her hands.

She looked up at Kenny, and he saw the sparkle in her eyes. "That's what I tried to tell Him, but He won't listen."

Kenny let go of her hands. "What will you do?"

She shrugged. "I'll do what He told me to. I don't know what good it will do, but I'll do it. I'll write a book about my life. Like anyone will want to read that," she said and then laughed. "This is crazy. Where in the world would I start?"

Kenny kissed her cheek. "I'm sure you will figure it out, m'lady."

She looked up at her dorky, rock star husband with the funny ears that stuck out. "Should I start at the beginning?"

"Do you mean in the alley?" Kenny rubbed his jaw and felt his two-day-old beard.

"Sure! Why not? I might not open the book with that, but I would want whoever might be silly enough to read a story about me to know how we met."

"Makes sense. Did you eat yet?"

"No, are you going to make breakfast?" Emmy asked.

"What would you like for your birthday?"

She grinned, "Could I have some blueberry pancakes, m'lord?"

Chapter One

"Mommy! Mommy! We're gonna write a book, too." Heather Rose announced as she and her twin sister ran into the den toward Emmy. Isabella Marie emphatically nodded her head in agreement.

"What are you going to write about?" Emmy turned her chair around to face them. They stared at each other, and then Isabella said, "We're gonna write a story about..." Isabella bit her lip and looked back at Heather. "...a story about you and Daddy and how much you wuv each other."

Heather grinned and said, "And how you always kiss each other."

Emmy laughed as Sofia Talford, the kids' nanny, entered the room. "I do like to kiss your daddy."

"Come with me, girls. Mommy has to work."

Emmy watched as the twins ran out of the room, both giggling. *I can't believe they're seven and a half years old already.*

"I'll keep them busy, Emmy."

"Thanks, Sofia. I need to spend a couple of hours on this."

Emmy closed her eyes and said a quick little prayer of thanks as she thought about the twins and her son Kevin Michael. *For someone who was never supposed to have babies, I have been blessed with three adorable ones.* "Okay, enough daydreaming. I need to get serious about this book." She opened the document on her computer and began to read.

I never intended to become a singer in a band. I enjoyed singing as a kid, but I never thought of it as a career. God chose it for me. I gave my heart to Jesus in the summer of 2001 and began attending Crest Ridge United Nazarene. I kept feeling the Holy Spirit leading me to use my God-given talent. My voice. Eventually, I overcame my fear and tried out for the worship band. I should explain that I was rather shy and quiet, so when I auditioned for the band in January of 2002, it was a big deal. Wow! That's over eleven years ago. I knew I could sing background. I'd been singing with Kenny since I was a little girl. I never expected to be the featured singer, or lead a worship service, but that's how it worked out. Once I realized God was in control, I decided to use my voice, and my dancing (I can't stand still when I'm singing) to spread the Word to teens. I thought I could reach teenage girls. Kenny always says it's because I looked like a teenager. He's so sweet, but he probably needs glasses.

My name is Emily Olivia Colasanti Colwell, but everyone calls me Emmy. I still go by Emmy Colasanti in my *professional* life. Kenny insisted so I would have a bit of privacy in our personal lives. I was born in South Hampshire at St. Bart's on July eighth. I was a *surprise* baby. Kenny told me I didn't have to put what year, but I don't mind. I was born in 1980, so I'm thirty-three. Wow! That sounds so old. All my friends tease me about acting like a teenager. I don't always act like that, but I guess sometimes I do act a little immature. Which is the opposite of my best friend, Kristen. She is a pampered princess who has always dressed in the latest fashion. She's got a closet full of pretty dresses. Me, on the other hand, I like to wear jeans and t-shirts. Shorts in the summer. I was a tomboy as a kid, and I guess I still am to a certain degree. I love football and tried never to miss a Bears game when Tony still played for the team. Oh, more about Tony later. I *do* wear dresses to church most of the time. Kenny is always telling me how pretty I look in a dress, but he's kinda biased.

In case you don't know, I'm married to Kenny Colwell, who is in the Guinness Book of World Records. He's considered the dorkiest rock star of all time! He's gonna get after me for saying that, but it's true. Not the Guinness book thing, but the dorkiness. He's known all over the world because of Fridays At Five and people think of him as a celebrity. Boy! Would they be surprised if they could spend a week with him. He's the most down-to-earth guy I know. If he's not performing, he's as normal as Tony or John. Wait! Did I just call Tony normal?

10

I take that back. Kenny is super talented, and I think he writes some great songs, but he's not into the rock star thing at all. I'm talking about the lifestyle some of them have. He's never trashed a hotel room, or any of those other things that make the tabloids. He's never done drugs and rarely drinks alcohol. He loves to play his music, and the other guys in the band feel the same. They are all family men and music just happens to be their career. You might not believe this, but it's true. Back in 1998, he bought a Honda Civic. He drove that car until last January when I convinced him to buy a new car. So what did he do? He bought another Civic. I rest my case, your honor. Our former nanny, Mary, used it when she attended North Park College, but she gave it back to Kenny after she graduated. You should have seen the look on his face. He was ecstatic. He loves his new Civic just as much. Oh, two years ago for my birthday, Kenny bought me a new car to replace the GMC Envoy I had been driving. I just happened to comment on a SUV I saw one day, so he bought one for me. If you know me at all, you realize that I still check the sales papers for bargains and I still clip coupons for groceries. I can't help it. That's how I grew up. So he bought me a BMW X3. I about died! It's loaded with all kinds of technology and stuff. He told me he wanted me to be safe. He really loves me, and I love him so much. Don't get me wrong, I really like my X3, but I'd be just as happy in a used Honda, or maybe my Civic Si. When Kenny bought his new Civic, I did something I almost never do. I made an impulse buy. I saw this blue Civic and drove it. I didn't need it, but I bought it anyway. I could rationalize that it gets better gas mileage than the X3, but honestly, I just wanted a faster car. Not faster, but more fun to drive.

Emmy's cell phone rang, and she checked the caller ID. "What's up, Mom? I'm working."

"It's about time you got a job," Patricia Colasanti said. "I can't find the remote for the TV, and I want to watch my shows.

Would you come over here and help me?"

"Mom, you have people there to do that. Just push the button."

"What button? How am I supposed to know which button to push?" Mom paced around her apartment. "I just want to watch the TV." She swore under her breath but Emmy heard.

"Mom, do you see that thing around your neck? It hangs down in front of you," Emmy said patiently.

Mom looked down and saw the call button. "What do I do with this?"

"If you press it, your care partner will come and take care of you." *Am I going to have to remind you every day?*

"They better get here soon. My shows are starting."

"I will talk to you later, Mom." Emmy sighed and ended the call. She sat back and closed her eyes. *At least she still knows how to use a phone.*

Emmy sat up and returned her attention to her computer.

When I did my first tour, Kenny bought me a journal, so I could keep a diary of my adventures on the road. I've kept up that tradition. Whenever I went on tour, I wrote in a journal. I kept track of where we played, the size of the crowd and other boring stuff because Dad Colwell always did that for FAF. Most of what I wrote in the journals was more like a diary. They weren't supposed to be read by anyone other than maybe Kristen, because there's a lot of personal stuff in them. Some stuff that I never want Kenny to read. It's not really bad stuff. Nothing like some of the things written about movie stars. It's not about my sex life because that's too boring. Not the sex, but writing about it. Shoot! I hope I have a good editor if this ever gets published.

After I felt the Holy Spirit convicting me to write a book, I told Kenny. He and his father are writing one about Fridays At Five, but he won't let me read any of it, yet. I'm putting some of the personal stuff in the book, but not everything. I hope you understand. I need to have some secrets. Kenny and I tried writing together in the den, but that didn't work. Neither one of us could write with anyone else in the room. So he's using the basement and I get to use this room.

If I had to sum up my book in a few words, hmmm, let me think. Okay. My book is about my travels as a Christian singer in a worship band. His book is about a decadent rock band. I'm kidding because... the dorkiness thing remember. I'm going to include some personal stuff here and there, but don't believe anything he writes about me in his book. He just wants to embarrass me. So here goes.

Emmy sat back and sighed. She closed her eyes and began praying out loud. "Lord, do you really want me to do this? I know how to write songs, but this is kinda weird. No one will ever want to read about me." She was interrupted by a voice over the intercom.

"Emmy, I'm sorry to bother you, but Kevin Michael skinned his arm and needs you," Sofia said.

"I'll be right there." Emmy saved her manuscript and got up. "How will I ever find time to write a book? I have three kids and a dorky husband to take care of." She shook her head and headed upstairs to the playroom.

"Mommy! Kevin is bleeding. He needs stitches and a big Bandaid." Isabella pointed to the playroom where Kevin wailed.

"Let me take a look, Kevin." Emmy inspected the cut. "I think you'll live. Let me find a Bandaid. *This is what I do, Lord. I take care of my kids. A book? You must be crazy except that you're God and know everything.*

She led Kevin Michael into the bathroom, cleaned his wound and put a colorful bandage on the scratch.

"I think I might need a special treat for being so brave," Kevin said as he inspected the Bandaid.

"You think so, huh?" Emmy shook her head.

Chapter Two

Emmy finished adding the Italian sausage to the mostaccioli and stirred the pot of corn. She peeked into the oven to check on the garlic bread. She reset the timer for five minutes and opened the fridge. She pulled out the salad. *I'm glad I made this beforehand.*

"Is dinner about ready?" Kenny looked over Emmy's shoulder.

"Five minutes. Would you set the table and call the kids, please?"

"Will do." He grinned and kissed her cheek.

Ten minutes later Emmy said the prayer and asked, "How was your day, girls?"

"We went swimming with Dany and Daddy," Heather said with a mouthful of mostaccioli.

"Please, don't talk with your mouth full," Emmy said. *I've told you that a million times, Heather.* "I thought you were working on your book?" She looked at Kenny.

He held up a finger as he chewed his Caesar salad. "I did get a few pages written, but the girls wanted to swim. Dany called and I mentioned going swimming, so she came over."

"I forgot Tuesday is her day off. Did she say anything about Liz and the baby?" Emmy asked while cutting the Italian sausage into smaller pieces for Kevin Michael.

"Not really. Liz isn't due until around December, right?" Kenny asked.

"I need more milk." Kevin held up his empty glass.

"Pastor Tyler said her official due date is now November fifteenth." Emmy shook a finger at Kevin. "No more milk. Eat your dinner."

"Mommy, when Miss Liz has her baby will Avery and Dillan and Liam still live with them?" Isabella asked about the foster children who lived with Tyler and Liz Hammond.

"Probably, but we won't know for certain, Isa."

"I don't like Dillan, but I hope Avery can stay," Heather said as she munched on her garlic bread.

"Did you get any work done, Em?" Kenny asked.

"I have a rough draft of the second chapter. I don't have a clue what to write about. I read my journal about that first tour and wrote about that. Do you think I should add hot Italian sausage to the mostaccioli? This tastes a little bland."

"I like spicy sausage," Kenny said.

"Me, too!" Kevin agreed with his father.

"Are you going to let me read any of your story?" Kenny asked and then took a sip of water. "I'd like to read it."

Emmy shook her head. "Not a chance, buster. If it ever gets published, which would be a large miracle, you have to buy your own copy."

Kenny grinned then said, "Must be some good gossip in it."

"I'll never tell."

Emmy put the leftover mostaccioli in a Tupperware container and placed it and the salad back in the fridge.

By nine o'clock the kids were asleep.

"I'm going to be in the den reading if you need me," Emmy said to Kenny, who sat in his recliner in the family room listening to a CD.

"Do you need any help?"

"No, and don't try sneaking a look at my computer. That sounds pretty good. Who is it?"

Kenny pointed to the jewel case on the end table. "Katie Hollins Band. Just came out. You can listen if you let me read..."

"Forget it. I'll be up late, so make sure you check on the kids. I need to read what I wrote."

"Don't you remember?" Kenny grinned.

Emmy stuck out her tongue and headed to the den. She closed the door and plopped down into her comfy leather recliner, booted up her laptop and began to read.

I pulled the wireless Shure SM58 microphone from its stand and looked out into the sanctuary of the New Life Church in Westminster, a city in the northern suburbs of Chicago. Although the lights were bright, I could see that the large crowd consisted mostly of teenagers. I

15

could also hear the clapping and hollering. It was Tuesday, March 4, 2003, the first night of the five-day-long tour. I hope this doesn't confuse everyone too much, but I'm putting conversations in quotes. They may not necessarily be word-for-word, but you get the gist.

"Hi, everyone. My name is Emmy Colasanti, and we are the Crest Ridge Worship Band. We want to thank you for inviting us here tonight. I'd like to pray before we get started if you don't mind."

I paused, and the crowd became quiet and still.

I need to fill you in on some stuff. I've sung in front of 50,000 people before at Fridays At Five shows, but only with Kenny at my side. That never bothered, or scared me. I'd been singing with him since the age of fourteen. This night was different. I was fronting the worship band by myself. I didn't have him to lean on, but I had Jesus. I had gotten used to singing in church and though I still got butterflies in my belly, I felt safe and secure in my home church. I knew my church family loved me. Now I was in a different church and didn't know if the audience would like us or not. I felt insecure and more nervous than ever before. For a split second I thought about running off the stage and forgetting about ever singing in front of people again. But I didn't. I knew this was where God wanted me to be, so I sucked it up and did what came naturally. I prayed. Well, it comes naturally now. That wasn't always the case. Certainly not when I was a kid.

"Lord, we thank you for this time together. We pray that your name will be exalted tonight. That is the reason we are here. We pray that your love will flow through everyone present. In thy precious name we pray."

I signaled the band with a slight movement of my hand, and they started the first song. For the next seventy minutes I led the band as we worshiped. At the end of the program, Chase Hillman took over for me. He was the worship leader at Crest Ridge United Nazarene, our home base. He talked to the crowd for a few minutes and opened the altar to anyone who needed to pray. A

16

large group of teens made their way forward. The staff of New Life Church took over. Chase joined me on the piano bench. He played quietly for the next fifteen minutes. Then I led the congregation as we sang a Chris Tomlin song to close out the service. Chase and Yvonne left our church back in February. He accepted a position in Toledo, Ohio. That's where they're originally from. (My editor is going to kill me for bouncing around all over the place!)

Okay, so shortly after I joined the worship band, Chase Hillman, my boss at church, wanted to record a service. I happened to mention that I knew a guy who might be willing to help produce it. None of the guys in the worship band really knew about my relationship with Kenny back then. Some of them thought Tony was my boyfriend. Kenny had the time, so he agreed to produce the project. We recorded two Sunday morning services and had enough material for a CD. Steward Music Group released it in September of 2002. Mr. Kesson, the owner of the company, wanted the band to do some touring to support the CD, but he understood we would be limited because the guys had families and jobs. We arranged to tour for three weeks in March of 2003. I don't know why I ever agreed to do that because I was getting married on April fifth. I'll include more details about that later, but now back to the first tour.

The rest of the band went to the foyer where we had a table of merchandise set up. We had our live CD for sale now. We also had t-shirts and photos of the group, but more importantly, we had free New Testaments for anyone who needed one. We also gave away a devotional book written by Dr. Herb Ausland, the retired pastor of our church. He's not retired anymore because he's on the staff, but he will probably retire again soon.

"Oh, jeez, that is so confusing. I'm jumping back and forth in time. How in the world will a reader ever figure out what I mean? Why did I ever agree to do this?" Emmy paused for a moment, but then she kept writing.

I remained in the sanctuary to talk to the many teens who gathered around. They were almost all girls. I posed for pictures and took the time to answer all their questions. A lot of the questions were about makeup and other girl stuff. I even signed a few autographs. I have never felt comfortable signing an autograph. I certainly don't see myself as a celebrity. I don't even picture Kenny as a celebrity.

I remember saying, "Please understand. I am just someone who sings songs. I should ask for your autographs. Remember to keep your focus on Him." I tried to explain my feelings as best I could, but I knew they weren't listening and I felt kinda dorky.

The crowd thinned out, and I looked toward the back of the sanctuary where there was a small group of people. I saw Tony. Then I saw Kenny. I couldn't believe it. Although I was in church, I ran back to where my fiancee and my close friends were standing. Remember, we weren't married yet.

"You didn't tell me you were gonna be here." I hugged Kenny and almost knocked him over.

"Did you really think we wouldn't be here, Em?" He said and then he kissed me right there in the church. "I didn't want to miss your first gig, but I didn't want you to feel nervous knowing we were here. We arrived just before you started and sat in the back."

I explained how nervous I felt as I took the stage.

"We wanted to surprise you, Emmy." Tony put his arm around my shoulders. Kristen and John were there, and so were Cam and Lindsey. Paul and Lynette had made the trip, too. I'll explain more about these people as I go on. I talked to them for twenty minutes, but then they had to head home. They let Kenny and me have a couple minutes to ourselves. Kristen made sure the guys didn't hang around too long. I kissed Kenny a few times even though we were in church. You have to remember this was just before we got married, and my feelings and hormones were... well, you know.

Eventually, I joined the rest of the guys and helped pack up the merchandise. The crew loaded out the gear to the waiting truck. Everyone pitched in to do whatever needed to get done. An hour and a half later, we were on the road. My life on the road officially began. The next night we would be in Columbus, Ohio. There were eight people in the leased bus. There were bunks for eight and a bedroom in the back. Since I was the only girl, I got the bedroom. Everyone stayed up for an hour or so to unwind after the concert. I got sleepy and told everyone good night. I retired to the bedroom and fell asleep to the sound of the highway. That's kinda how my first night went on the road with the worship band.

Emmy sat back in the recliner and closed her eyes. *I should delete everything and forget about it. There's no way I can write a decent book about myself. God, are you sure this is what you want? I should read my journal again. There has to be something in them that would be more interesting.* She picked up her journal and read it again. *Shoot! This is more boring than what I just wrote. Of course, it was never written to be read by anyone other than me. I'm going to delete everything and start over.* She placed a finger on the delete key. *I'm sorry, God. I tried. I really did.* She bit her lip and paused for a moment. *I can't disobey you, Lord.* She moved her finger and saved her work. *Maybe this will be something for the girls and Kevin Michael to read after they grow up. I can write it like that and maybe no one else will ever read it. No one in their right mind will want to read it.*

Chapter Three

"What are you working on?" Kenny sat next to Emmy near the rear of Mr. Robertson's 737.

She snapped her laptop shut and frowned at him. "I'm working on my book. That's why I'm sitting back here by myself. I need some privacy."

"Sorry, Em. I didn't mean to disturb you. I'll go back up front and bother Andy."

"Don't be like that. You know I planned to work on my book. That's why we left the kids at home with Sofia and Niles. I want to go over the chapters I have. Did I tell you that the biggest part of writing a book is the rewriting?"

"You might have mentioned something along those lines."

"Well, that's what Denise said, and she should know since she's a pro."

"Okay, I'll talk to you later. Should I see if I can get another room at the hotel?"

"Don't even think about that. I won't be working on my book all night. Now go away and let me work." She waved a hand to dismiss Kenny. She waited until he headed back toward the front of the plane and then opened her laptop.

Our small caravan arrived in Columbus, Ohio, in the early morning hours. We had no trouble locating the Living Water Church where we would be playing that evening. The bus and truck both had GPS units. Kenny made sure of that because of something that happened one night with Fridays. They got lost in the mountains and almost didn't make it to a gig. We parked in the rear of the building. The drivers did. We used real drivers just like Kenny and the guys. I always tried to talk one of them into letting me drive the bus for a while, but they wouldn't. They teased me about being too young to have a driver's license.

I woke up slowly and thought about Kenny as I looked at the ring on my finger. Kenny and I were engaged and the wedding was exactly one month away. I couldn't wait to get married. Maybe I shouldn't tell you this, but, what the heck. I was a virgin and couldn't wait to sleep with my husband. Looking back, I'm not sure how I managed to wait. It took every bit of strength I had. I got out of bed and used the private bathroom in the bedroom to get ready for the day. Everyone else had to share a bathroom in the middle of the bus. Being the only girl had its privileges.

"Good morning, Chase. Did you sleep all right?"

"Hi, Emmy. I got enough sleep I guess. You?"

"I slept just fine. I still feel a little guilty that I have a nice comfortable bed and everyone else has to sleep in those bunks."

"You know we leased this specific bus so you would have a bedroom all to yourself. The guys understand."

"I'll start the coffee. Are we going to eat on the bus?"

"I think today we can eat at the Denny's since it's right across the street."

Chase Hillman would have been called the tour manager if he worked for Fridays At Five. He was an ordained minister, as well as a husband and father of two young daughters. He played keyboards and led the band. He did most of the arrangements, with a little help from me, and even wrote some of our material.

One by one the rest of the group emerged from their cocoon-like bunks. Hank Lysenko popped up next. Hank had been playing bass at the church for over twenty years. He was the oldest member of the group by far. Well, not like thirty years or something, but he was the oldest. He recently became a grandfather. He had a grandson to spoil. This was his first opportunity to be part of a touring band.

"Morning, Grandpa! Did you sleep all right?" I greeted him enthusiastically.

"I need my coffee. Is it ready?"

"I have a cup ready for you right here."

"Thank you, Emmy. You know just how to take care of me."

"I work for Robertson Industries and have to take care of the team members, so I'm used to it."

I didn't mind doing little things for the guys. After all, I wouldn't be singing if not for them.

Emmy sighed and looked out the window. *Maybe I shouldn't worry too much about this. It's just a first draft. Denise told me to get it down on paper and not worry about editing it.* She watched as the plane flew through some clouds before turning back to her computer.

The rest of the guys emerged over the next hour. Though I was the youngest member of the group, I acted like a mother hen at times. Steve Van Zant played lead guitar for the band. Martin Case played acoustic and electric guitar. Everyone called him Dixie. He replaced John Patterson in the touring band since John couldn't travel because of his job. Martin earned his living as a professional musician and had been with other Christian bands. He was thirty-two and single. Born in the small town of Russelville, Alabama, he still lived with his parents when not on the road. He had a strong southern accent and the girls flocked around him, since he was the best looking guy in the band. Our regular drummer, Skip Mason, was still in school, so he couldn't travel. Chase replaced him with Alan Vicini, who had been the drummer for The Notable Exceptions until they broke up the previous fall. Alan had only recently started attending the church. He was the perfect drummer to join the touring band since he owned a music store and was able to travel. His wife, Stephanie, and college-age son Adam ran the store in his absence. Stuart Lederer worked as a technician and recording engineer for Steward Music. He was divorced with two sons. He was responsible for both house and stage sound. A veteran of many years of touring with groups of all genres, Stuart was the only member of the group who did not attend our church. I remember he was quiet and kept to himself much of the time. There were three drivers along. Larry Twilley was in charge of transportation. His father, Leonard, was a driver for Fridays At Five and a legend in the business. I know that because Leonard told me so. He would tell stories about Fridays on the road, but I promised Kenny he could use them in his book. I'll only use them if I need to fill in some space. Larry was assisted by his cousin Buck Twilley and his brother-in-law Cecil Parrmeister. Nothing like keeping it in the family. The other two guys were brothers, Jess and Joe Zawaski. They were jacks-of-all-trades. Their main responsibility was loading and unloading the gear. They slept in the sleeper section of the truck cabin since there weren't enough bunks in the bus. They didn't mind. They amused the group with stories from their youth in Europe as members of a traveling family circus. No one could tell exactly how old they were. Chase wasn't sure but thought they were in their mid-forties. They could be as old as sixty, though. I was never brave enough to ask. Those two were tireless workers who shared a small apartment in SoHam. They were never without their Bible, which was written in a foreign language. Chase thought it might be Romanian but wasn't positive and the brothers never said.

Whoa! What the heck was that? Emmy lifted up in her seat as the plane flew through some turbulence. The captain announced he would attempt to climb out of the rough air, so Emmy waited a few minutes before continuing to work.

Chase assembled us for a time of devotions and prayer. After that we headed over to Denny's for breakfast. We met the drivers who were now heading to bed for a few hours sleep. Somehow they managed to get by on about five hours of sleep a day. Of course they took naps as often as they could. Chase had arranged to meet the pastor of the church for breakfast.

23

"How many?" the hostess asked.

"There will be ten of us." Chase smiled at her.

"Give me a couple minutes, and I'll make room."

A man in a sport coat walked over to Chase. "Hi, I'm Pastor Dan Eaton. Are you Chase?"

"Hello, Dan. I'm Chase, and this is our group. Thanks for meeting us."

"Did you have a safe trip?"

"No problems. We parked in the back of the lot. I hope that's all right."

"Sure. You can park wherever you need. I assume you will want to pull your truck up close to unload later."

"Yes. Perhaps after breakfast you can show us where we need to unload."

We were seated and for the next hour chaos reigned. It took two waitresses to handle our group. It was a treat for the group to be able to eat together in a restaurant. Normally, we would grab whatever we could on the bus. Kenny has teased me for years about my choice for breakfast. If it's on the menu, I always have blueberry pancakes. I love them, and I'll tell you why. At Christmas one year when I was a kid, I ate breakfast with Kenny and his mom and dad. Mom Colwell made blueberry pancakes and they were so yummy. I had never had them before.

"How long do you think you will need to get set up, Chase?" Pastor Eaton asked.

"We should be ready for a soundcheck within two hours. We're not using any lights. Just our PA."

We didn't have any lights of our own at this point. We didn't feel we needed them since our concerts were more like a church service than a rock show.

"We have a decent setup for lights in our tech booth."

"Would you mind if we use your lights?" Chase asked Pastor Dan.

"No, of course not. My son will be here this afternoon. He's our lighting guru. If you tell him what you

24

need, I'm sure he can help you out."

"Thanks, Dan."

"We will open doors at six and our local worship team is going to start at seven. You should be able to go on at eight as per plan."

"I'm looking forward to listening to your group."

Pastor Dan noticed me, even though I was sitting at the other end of the table. The guys were teasing me, and I was giggling like a teenager. Just a note about these guys. They were older and more serious than the younger guys who became The Only Hope, but Dixie teased me a lot. The other guys not so much.

Pastor Dan leaned close to Chase. "I thought that Emmy Colasanti was... how can I put this. I thought she was..."

"Older and more mature!" Chase grinned as he looked at me.

"Her biography on your website mentions she is in her early twenties. She looks like a high school student."

"Yes, she is twenty-two and engaged to be married next month. I know she looks like a teenager and usually acts like one. Would you like to meet her?"

"Yes. I would like to talk to her. My son listens to her CD all the time. I mean your CD."

Chase hollered down to the other end of the table, "Emmy!"

The other end of the table got quiet because they assumed I was in trouble for goofing around.

"Emmy! Would you come here please?"

Dixie said, "You're in trouble now, Emmy."

I sat by Chase who grabbed a chair for me.

"I'm sorry. We were just having fun. The guys were teasing me about the bus." I tried not to sound like a kid, but I probably did.

"It's okay, Emmy. You're not in trouble, but they might be." Chase glared at the guys.

"This is Pastor Dan Eaton. Dan, this is Emmy Colasanti."

"It's nice to meet you, Emmy," he said with a smile. "Is it all right if I call you Emmy?"

"Yes, sir. No one calls me Emily except my grandmother."

Grandma Isabel was the only person who ever consistently called me Emily. Grandma lived to be a hundred just like she promised. She passed away in July of 2010. A couple of months after she turned one hundred. Just wanted to put that in here.

"Em, I think Dan was going to call you Ms. Colasanti."

"Oh, sorry." I giggled and the guys laughed at me, so I did what came naturally. I stuck out my tongue and made a face.

Pastor Dan looked at me as we talked. He told me later he had a hard time believing I was twenty-two. To him I looked about eighteen at the most. I didn't help matters by acting like a kid.

"My son listens to your CD all the time."

I smiled shyly back. "Thank you, Pastor Dan. We appreciate the support and prayers from all the places we visit."

At this point we had played in front of exactly one congregation other than our own church. I turned red and felt like a doofus because I was trying to act like I thought the pastor of the church would want. Maybe I was hanging around Kenny too much.

"He might be helping with the lights for tonight's service," Pastor Dan said picking up a strip of bacon.

"That would be great. I hope I have a chance to meet him." At this point I didn't know Darren at all, so I really wasn't sure if I wanted to meet him or not. He could be a total dweeb.

"I know he's been looking forward to meeting you."

I talked to Pastor Dan for a few minutes and tried not to sound like an immature teenager. Since my natural speaking voice is kinda high, I usually sound like a kid no matter how hard I try. Then I went back to sit with the guys. Dixie teased me again. I soon learned to put up with the teasing. Everyone finished their breakfast and it was time to get to work.

Larry Twilley maneuvered the truck into position. Pastor Dan watched as everyone pitched in to unload the truck. Everyone had their job and responsibility—even me. Hank and I started unloading some of the merchandise. Pastor Dan showed us a good location to set up the table. His son arrived earlier than expected.

"Emmy, this is my son, Darren. Darren, this is Emmy Colasanti."

"Hi, Emmy. I just want to say that I really enjoy your music. I'm a big fan of the band."

"Why, thank you, Darren. Your father told me that you might help us with lights tonight." I might have touched his arm. FYI, he wasn't a dweeb. He looked hot.

"I program the lights for our services. I could show you our board."

"Maybe you could show Stuart Lederer. He does our sound. He's over there in that red baseball cap."

"Okay, I will. Do you need any help now?"

"If you wouldn't mind. We need to move all these boxes inside."

I smiled at Darren, and he took over moving the merchandise.

"Emmy, you should be ashamed of yourself. Flirting with that boy to get him to do our work," Hank said.

"I wasn't flirting! I was just being friendly."

"Yeah sure."

I hate to admit it, but Hank was partially right. Okay. Mostly right. Darren was rather handsome, and I didn't think I was flirting too much. But I was flirting to get him to help me.

In less than an hour the truck was emptied, and the gear moved inside. In another seventy-five minutes everything was up and running. We got our stuff ready for a quick soundcheck just to make sure everything was working. Stuart tweaked the sound a little to fit the acoustics of the sanctuary. He could do that because of his experience in the studio and on the road with real bands. Plus he had some electronic gear to do that stuff. It was very similar to our home church. Chase called me up to the platform and we ran through a few songs. Darren showed Chase and Stuart a few settings for lights. After the soundcheck, Darren and Stuart talked more about lights. Stuart went over the set list and Darren programmed a few cues into the board and would manually fill in with other lighting effects.

"Okay, we're all set. It's almost one now. Let's meet back here at five. The church is providing some food and beverages," Chase informed us.

"Yeah! Free food." The Zawaski brothers were always excited by the prospect of free food.

"We will need to do a final soundcheck before the doors are open. Any questions?"

"Are we going to hang around after the service?" Steve asked.

"Emmy and I are going to stay and meet with people. Anyone who wants to join us is welcome. I don't think we need to be in a super hurry to get out of here tonight. We are only going to Louisville. Should take four hours."

Pastor Dan told Chase, "The church has decided to order food for you guys after the service. I hope everyone likes pizza."

Everyone tried to thank Dan at once. Jess and Joe Zawaski were thrilled.

"The church has two vans that you may use this afternoon. Darren is available to guide you. He knows his way around Columbus."

Several of the guys heard Pastor Eaton's offer and jumped at the chance to get away. Darren asked me if I wanted to go. I was going to go, but Hank frowned at me. I declined the offer because I didn't want to upset Hank The guys had Darren drive them around. Some of the guys hit the sack to get a little rest.

"Chase, if you want to lie down on the bed go ahead. I'm going to check email and call home. Then I think I will go for a walk."

"Thanks, Emmy. I could use a nap."

"I just need to use the bathroom, then it's all yours."

Chase waited while I used the bedroom.

"See you later. Have a nice nap. Should I make sure you're up by any certain time?"

"If I'm still in there at four have one of the guys wake me up. I need time to get ready."

"If you're still in there at four, I will toss you out myself. I need time to prepare for tonight myself."

Emmy closed her laptop as Micah Hurst, her band's rhythm guitarist, sat next to her.

"What's up, Micah?"

"The guys want to know if you're mad at us about something. Are you?"

Emmy wrinkled her nose and shook her head a bit. "I'm not mad at you guys. I'm working on my book."

"That's what I tried to tell them, but they don't listen. Oh, did you make any changes to the set list?"

"I didn't make any changes. To be honest, I haven't even thought about it much. Do you think we need to change anything?"

"Not really. The lighting guys have the set really dialed in. I'll let everyone know about the set list and to leave you alone."

"Are you going to tell them I'm being a diva?"

"Nah! They already know that," Micah teased as he got up and returned to his seat.

She stuck out her tongue, laughed and then returned to her laptop.

In a group this size there were many different types of personalities. Despite that everyone got along well. Some of the guys liked to roam around and see the city. Others were content to hang around the bus and read. I liked to stay active. I get bored if I'm not busy. I saw Martin Case watching TV in the lounge area.

"Hey, Dixie! I'm going for a walk. Wanna join me?"

"Sure. I was just killing time. Where do you want to go?"

"No place in particular. I just want to be outside and get some fresh air."

"Give me a minute, and I'll go with you."

"I'll meet you outside."

I'm sure that's pretty close to what we said. Dixie met me outside, and we walked to the front of the church. I looked up and down the street and shrugged.

"Which way should we go?"

"Does it really matter?" Dixie was easy to get along with.

"Probably not. Let's go this way." I started walking to the right and Dixie followed along. "So, Dixie, how long have you been playing in bands?"

"Since high school. I started at church, and after I graduated I went on tour with a local band. One thing led to another and I ended up with... well you know the rest. How about you? Did you always want to be a singer?"

"I don't think I ever wanted to be a singer. Maybe God did, but I never had a great desire to sing. Kenny always knew he wanted to be a musician."

"Is it true that you used to sing with him at churches when you were a kid?"

"Yeah, I did. I sang with the band a few times." We kept walking, and I checked out the area. It didn't look any different than parts of SoHam. I could see some of the same businesses. Fast food joints, strip malls, that sort of stuff.

"You know you have a beautiful voice, Emmy. I don't mean like some opera singer, or that you have... like some awesome vocal range but you sound... I don't know how to describe it. You seem so sincere. I probably shouldn't say this, but you are very pretty, too."

I think I turned bright red. "Thank you, Dixie. It's

okay to say that. You know I'm engaged, and I just look the way I look."

"You are different. You are so humble and don't even realize how much your fans adore you."

"You're being silly. I don't have fans. Kenny has fans. Millions of them." I couldn't picture anyone being a fan of me.

"The teenage girls who come to see us are really here to see you. Don't think that the boys don't notice you either. They are captivated by your smile."

"Oh, Dixie! That's not why I do this at all. I don't want them to see me. I want them to see Christ through me. If I didn't think that was our goal, then I would quit right now."

"I know that's why we do what we do, but there are some people who come to the *shows* for just that. A show."

"Well if that's the case, sorry." I thought about it as we walked. "I didn't mean that, Mr. Case. It's our job to show them the love of Jesus and if we do that by entertaining them, I guess it's all right."

"You do entertain them by just being who you are," Dixie said.

I didn't know what he meant.

"You sing and dance and it's obvious you are having a good time. You don't put on an act like I've seen other groups do."

Emmy sighed and closed her eyes. *It's a good thing Denise will fix this for me because that was horrible. I sound like I'm preachy and full of baloney. Do fans really see me as just another entertainer out to make a buck? I don't need the money. Maybe I shouldn't charge anything for my shows. Of course, I have to pay the band and the crew and all that. That's all I can handle for today. I need to get my mind on tonight's show. Crap! Why do I think of it as a show? It's supposed to be more than that.*

31

Emmy didn't reopen her manuscript until she boarded the plane the next morning. She talked to her friends for a time before settling into her seat near the back. *Maybe it got better overnight.* She hoped as she turned on her laptop.

We walked around for an hour before returning to the bus. I checked my room and saw Chase sleeping on the bed. I didn't disturb him. I joined Martin and Hank in the lounge.

"I'm bored. All this waiting around kinda sucks."

"What would you be doing if you were home, Emmy?"

"I would be taking care of Kenny."

"Oooh! Taking care of your husband-to-be, huh?"

I blushed a little. "Well, I would be if he was home. He's very demanding."

He's not really. He's laid back and extremely low maintenance.

"I bet he is!" Martin and Hank both teased me.

"Maybe you should get married, Dixie."

"I will someday when I meet the right girl."

"Make sure you are looking in the right places."

"You mean at church?"

"I think that's the best place to look."

Chase finally woke up, and I had my bedroom back. I got ready for tonight, but I didn't change into the clothes I would wear for the service yet. I would do that later. By five everyone was back and ready to go over to the church and eat. First we did a quick soundcheck. After Chase and Stuart were satisfied with the sound, we headed to the cafeteria area. Though we were not really a professional touring band, like Kenny and the guys, we did everything we could to present ourselves in a professional manner. We used top-of-the-line gear and made sure the sound was right. Some members of the church had brought food for the band and crew. Pastor

Dan offered thanks and we dug in. Darren sat next to me. I smiled at him and then saw Dixie looking at me. I tried not to flirt, but I might have just a little.

"Did you have fun showing the guys around Columbus?" I asked.

"I had a good time. Those foreign guys are hilarious. I laughed until I was almost crying. They would talk to everyone. They met a guy from their old country and started talking to him in some language."

"They are really something. I don't know how they get by sometimes. I know they have jobs, but they are always at the church working on whatever needs to be done."

After we finished eating, Chase and I went with Pastor Dan to meet the local worship team. We spent a few minutes talking and then Dan needed to organize the volunteers. The church was taking up a freewill offering so there were no tickets for the service. The doors opened at six and there were about a hundred teenagers waiting to come into the building. Steve Van Zant and Alan Vicini were manning the merchandise booth before the service. Some of the teens grabbed front row seats in the sanctuary while others were interested in the CD and t-shirts. Alan was talking to a group of girls who were buying CDs. He told me later what they said.

"Could we get Emmy Colasanti to autograph our CDs?"

"Please! We want to meet her."

"Can we meet her please?"

Alan wasn't sure what to tell the girls, but he asked Steve, "Do you know where Emmy is now?"

"I think she is with Chase. There she is."

I was on my way out to the bus when Steve spotted me. He waved and got my attention.

"Emmy, these girls wanted to meet you. I know you're busy, but do you have a couple minutes?"

"Of course I do." I saw the girls waiting and walked over. "Hi, I'm Emmy. How are you? Are you from the local teen group?" Something like that, but I was sincere. Really!

One of the girls answered for everyone. "This is our church. We've all grown up here."

I asked each girl her name as I personalized each CD with their name and a Bible verse.

"Thank you so much, Emmy."

"You're welcome. I hope you enjoy the service."

"Are you really in your twenties, Emmy? We thought you were a teenager from your picture."

"I'm not a teenager anymore." I giggled and wasn't sure if they believed me.

"How old are you, Emmy?"

"Sandy, how can you ask such a personal question?"

"It's all right. I'm twenty-two. It's on the website."

"I thought it was a mistake. You don't look nearly that old."

"You still look like a teenager if you ask me."

"Yeah, and you're so tiny!"

"You sure have a pretty voice."

"And a pretty face! What kind of makeup do you use?"

I grinned and giggled with the girls. They were thrilled to discover that I still acted like a teenager at times. I felt like a teenager even though I was engaged. I made my way out to the bus to get ready for the service. I refused to think of it as a show, or even a concert. To me it was a worship service. Later, I learned it was all right to entertain people. Some people expect it.

I was alone in the bus getting ready. I had time to call home and talk to Kristen for a few minutes.

"Hey, Em. How are you doing? Where are you today?"

"We're in Columbus, Ohio. I'm in the bus about ready to go back inside to get started."

"How was it riding the bus with all the guys? Did they treat you okay?"

34

"They like to tease me, but I don't mind. They are such good guys, though. Jess and Joe still call me Miss Emmy, and they treat me like a princess."

"Have you ever known them to say an unkind word about anyone?"

"No, they somehow see the good in everyone they meet. I need to get going. I want to listen to the other band. I love you, and I'll call again when I can."

"I love you, too, Em. Have a good service tonight."

I met Kristen Keasling at a high school dance when we were juniors. I actually ran into her, literally, in a restroom. I was running away from another kid and crying. Within five minutes Kristen and I became best friends and have been ever since.

It was nearly seven when I made my way back into the sanctuary. I joined Chase and Pastor Dan on the front row off to the side. Pastor Dan was about to make his way to the platform to open the service. I looked around and noticed the sanctuary was filled to capacity. I nudged Chase as I spotted the Zawaski brothers.

"Look! Jess and Joe are wearing their suits."

"How do they manage to look so good every night. They look like slobs all day and work so hard. Yet they somehow manage to get cleaned up and look like that for every service," Chase wondered.

I grinned. "Maybe there are four of them."

"Yeah, and we never see them all together."

The brothers looked at me, and I smiled back.

Pastor Dan was ready to open the service. The audience stood as Dan led in prayer. They remained standing as he led them in a song. Then he introduced the local worship team. They sang for thirty minutes. They were pretty good. A little rough with some of the harmonies, but better than most.

Pastor Dan got back up. "We are going to take a break, then the Crest Ridge Worship Team will play for us. We will get started right at eight, so you have a few minutes to visit."

As soon as he finished, some of the teens noticed me and came over to talk. Chase asked Hank to stay with me, almost as a bodyguard, because he noticed some teenage boys hanging around. I knew why Chase asked Hank to stay. I smiled up at him.

"I'll be all right, Hank, if you want to go."

"I don't have anywhere else to be, little lady."

"Thanks."

I did notice some of the guys staring at me. It almost made me wonder if I had dirt on my face or something. I refused to believe they might be interested in me as a *female*. I was still rather naïve about men. That plus the fact I would be marrying my best friend in a month.

Just before eight the guys made their way to the platform to tune up and get ready. After they were set to go, we gathered for a quick prayer. Most of the crowd was back in their seats as Pastor Dan stepped up to the microphone.

"I know many of you have heard this group's CD, and I know a couple of the teens have even seen them perform before back in Illinois. I know you will enjoy them tonight. Please welcome Emmy Colasanti and the Crest Ridge Worship Team!"

The band started playing softly as I made my way to the center of the stage. I took the wireless microphone out of the stand and began with a prayer.

"Lord, we are here tonight to praise you. I love you with all my heart, and if there be anyone here tonight that doesn't know you, I pray that you will make your presence known to them through our music. In thy precious name we pray. Amen!" I looked out at the crowd and smiled. "All right! We are going to have fun singing our praises for the next hour or so. If you know the songs and want to sing along, that will be great. I see the words are on the screen already. Stand up if you want. Clap along. This song is called 'You Rescued Me' and it goes like this!"

36

Chase had the band ready and as soon as I finished, they kicked it off. The audience rose to their feet and were clapping along as I sang. I love it when the audience sings along. I feed off of their energy. I suppose all singers do. I know Kenny does. Some people say I change from the shy person I really am and become a totally different person when I sing. I just allow God to use me. I usually dance around, as long as I have the room. I bounce from one guy to another as I sing. I can't help it. It's not something that's choreographed or anything. At times I don't even realize it. About midway through the set, I had everyone sit down.

"This next song is about a young girl I knew..."

I found out that nearly everyone in the audience had heard 'Yolanda's Song' before and most of them knew the story. I met Yolanda Garcia at a teen service at our church in March of 2002. I was sharing my story with the teens, and she accepted Christ that night. We talked afterward and shared phone numbers and stuff. Then in July I met her sister Juanita. Juanita told me Yolanda had been killed by a drunk driver in Mexico City. I learned the accident had happened only seventeen days after I met her at the church. Krissy and I prayed with Juanita and after she left, Krissy and I sat back down with everyone. I noticed Kenny scribbling words on a bunch of napkins. It is hard to believe, but without ever meeting Yolanda, he wrote the words to the song. He even included the words seventeen days without knowing the circumstances. Kenny didn't write the song, and he admits it. It was the Holy Spirit guiding his hand. Otherwise the song wouldn't be the same. If at all possible we tried to use the church's video screen to show the presentation that was put together by Steward Music. It was just like a music video. The video ends with a photograph taken that night at the teen service of Yolanda and me hugging and smiling into the camera.

Darren Eaton dimmed all the house lights as we played the song. He had a soft light on me as I sang about the girl I only knew for a brief time. The song Kenny Colwell wrote was on its to becoming a big hit across the country. It usually took all of my professionalism to make it through the song without crying. Tonight that didn't work. I managed to sing the song but could not control the tears flowing down my face. I closed my eyes and muddled through somehow. The audience saw the tears, and they knew how real this song was to me. As I finished, the crowd rose to their feet as one. I heard the applause.

"Thank you. I'm sorry I started crying. I know I should be more professional, but I'm not. I'm just a girl that can sing a little with the help of God. Are there any tissues around?"

I looked for a box of tissues. A young girl in the front row saw a box of tissues by the altar and brought it up to me.

"Thank you so much."

"You're welcome, Emmy."

I hugged her before she took her seat, then I took a few seconds to compose myself.

"I'm ready now, Chase."

Chase started the next song and we continued. We ended the service with 'Glorified.' After we finished Chase came to the front, talked for a few minutes and then led everyone in prayer. Pastor Dan took over and some members of the church came to the front. Chase and I took seats near the front. The rest of the band left to take care of their assigned duties. Stuart played some appropriate music on the PA in the background. Hank and Martin were in charge of the merchandise table with help from some local kids. As soon as it was appropriate, the Zawaski brothers left and changed clothes. They returned ready to work. Stuart shut down our PA, and Darren used the church's system to keep playing the background music.

After everyone at the altar had left, the guys began working. Stuart was responsible for all the cables. He disconnected everything and Jess and Joe packed and loaded out the gear. Within an hour the truck was loaded and ready to roll. Chase and I joined the rest of the guys by the merchandise table. I graciously signed autographs for everyone who asked—at least I pray I was gracious. A few kids wanted all the guys to sign autographs. Most of the kids just wanted to talk to me and get my autograph. I still felt embarrassed by all the attention. I knew the guys would tease me later. Pastor Dan had Darren pick up the pizzas. Dan took Chase and me into his office and presented Chase with a check. The church guaranteed two thousand dollars for the band and there was more than that in the offering.

"I can't thank you guys enough for coming tonight. I know how difficult it is to travel and be away from your families."

"We all feel that this is God's will for us. Hopefully the teens who accepted Christ tonight will come back to your church, or maybe they attend somewhere else, but the important thing is they receive follow-through."

"We will do our best in that regard. Darren should be back with the pizzas. Are you hungry?"

"Starving!" I grinned.

Pastor Dan smiled. "How soon do you guys need to leave for Louisville?"

"I'm not sure. It's only three and a half hours to Louisville. I'll see what everyone wants to do. We might wait until morning to leave. I'll have to ask Larry. He's in charge of the drivers," Chase answered as I thought about the pizza and my rumbling stomach.

"If you want to stay overnight here at the church, you are welcome. There are locker rooms by the gym with showers. There aren't any beds but there are a couple couches in the teen room."

"Thanks, Dan. I'll let you know in a few minutes what we decide to do," Chase answered.

Chase talked to Larry and Hank. Larry wanted to take the truck on to Louisville that night. He would take

39

the Zawaski brothers with him. Buck and Cecil would stay with the bus. This way everyone could sleep on the bus and get a good night of rest.

Chase informed Pastor Eaton. "Dan, we are going to send the truck on ahead, but the bus will stay here. Would it be possible to use the showers in the morning?"

"Certainly! I will be here by seven and open the building. I'll call the local police, and let them know your bus will be here overnight. They will keep an eye on you guys. You'll be safe enough."

"Thanks again for everything."

"If you guys want to come back sometime, we would be glad to have you."

I saw Darren walk in with the pizzas, so I ran over to him. I really was starving, and I wanted to be first in line. We got everything set out on a table in the kitchen. I smiled at him and then noticed Hank and Steve shaking their heads at me. I stuck out my tongue and grabbed a slice of pizza before Pastor Dan said the prayer. As soon as he finished, I took a bite.

"Where are you gonna sit, Emmy?" Darren asked.

I could feel Hank and Steve glaring at me as I led Darren to a table. I made sure Darren saw my ring several times. I didn't want him to get the wrong idea. He understood and showed me a photo of his girlfriend Jody King. We kept in touch for a few years, and he even invited Kenny and me to his wedding. He married Jody. Unfortunately, we were in Europe at the time and couldn't go. He worked as an associate pastor at a church in Hillsdale, Michigan. The same church that Liz Hammond and her family attend. Tyler, too. Then in 2011, he joined the staff of our church. He came to SoHam at the same time Pastor Tyler took over as senior pastor. When I saw him again, I wondered if he would remember how I flirted. Okay, I admit it. I did flirt just a bit to get him to help us, and we did spend some time in the teen room.

Chapter Five

Natalie Hammond raced her three-year-old brother Grayson to the front door. Dillan and Liam Curry arrived a second later.

"Uncle Jason!" Natalie screamed. "You're finally here! We've been waiting all morning."

Jason Kimmerle opened the storm door and allowed his wife, Michelle, to enter first.

"Who are you?" Soon-to-be-six Dillan looked up at Jason.

Just-turned-five Liam stood by his taller brother. "Do we know you? Wanna see how fast I can run?" Liam sprinted away.

Jason swept Natalie into his arms, and Michelle picked up Grayson.

"I haven't seen you for so long, Uncle Jay."

Derby bounded into the house from her trip outside with Tyler and nearly knocked Dillan off of his feet.

"Down, Derby!" Tyler ordered.

Derby barked at Jason and wagged her tail back and forth at close to the speed of light. Liam dashed through the room again and then disappeared down the hall.

"I see you met the boys," Liz Hammond entered carrying Avery, Dillan and Liam's twenty-month-old sister.

Grayson scrambled down from Michelle's arms and chased Derby out of the room.

Natalie scooted down and walked up to her mother. "That's Avery, Uncle Jay. She likes Daddy the best."

Jason walked up to his older sister and smiled. "Hello, Avery. That is a pretty dress. Is it new?"

Avery clung to Liz for a moment before holding out her arms. "Uppie!"

Jason took Avery.

"It appears you have been replaced, Tyler," Liz said and then patted her baby bump.

"Avery, who's got you?" Tyler chuckled.

Dillan chased after Liam. Grayson reappeared with one of Derby's chew toys.

"Don't put that in your mouth, Grayson. It's yucky," Natalie said. "Derby slobbers all over it."

"Look at those blue eyes." Jason ran a finger through Avery's fine, blonde hair. "You are such a doll.

"Avery, that's my uncle Jay. He can be your uncle, too," Natalie said before heading for the safety of the kitchen.

Avery grinned at Jason. "Jay-Jay," she said softly and Jason fell in love.

Jason walked up to Liz fifteen minutes later. "She won't let go of me."

Liz finished combing Natalie's hair. "You're good to go. We need to leave in five minutes."

"Yes, Mommy."

Liz tried to take Avery from Jason, but she squirmed and held on tight. "She was the same way with Tyler at first. Now she's your friend for life."

"Boys! We have to leave for church. Front and center," Tyler said sternly with a trace of affection.

Dillan, Liam and Grayson appeared in that order.

"Is this Sunday already?" Dillan tilted his head.

"Yes, and what do we do on Sundays?"

Liam raised a hand and bounced on his toes. "We sing songs and listen to you talk for a hundred hours."

Tyler rolled his eyes. "I'll do my best to keep it under five hours today."

Dany Kimmerle followed Emmy into the kitchen. "What time did you guys get back?"

Emmy looked at the microwave clock. "Three thirty or so. I got my butt out of bed, but Kenny is being a stinker. He said he will be there for the second service, but I don't want to miss my Sunday School class. Girls, did you wash your hands and brush your teeth?"

Heather and Isabella rushed up to Emmy, held up their hands and pulled back their lips to show their pearly white teeth. "All clean, Mommy. Are you going with us, Dany?" Heather asked.

"Do you mind if I ride with you this morning?" Dany knelt

to talk to the twins. "Is your brother ready?"

Heather turned around and shouted, "Kevin Michael, get your butt in here right now!"

"Heather Rose! That is no way to call your brother," Emmy said.

"That's what you say, Mommy." Heather grinned at Dany.

"Out to the Odyssey right now. March!" Emmy pointed to the mudroom. "Where did you park, Dany?"

"I walked over. I hate to use the car when I can walk here in a couple of minutes." Dany checked Kevin Michael's appearance. "You look pretty sharp today."

"Don't tell, Mom, but I'm bringing a police car," he whispered.

"It will be our secret." Dany zipped her mouth and threw away the key.

Emmy rolled her eyes. "Like I don't know."

Emmy turned the corner and pulled into the parking lot of Crest Ridge United Nazarene. She directed the minivan into a space and slammed on the brakes. "If you tell Kenny how I drive, I will raise your rent to a reasonable amount," Emmy said and then grinned.

"I'm sure he knows you drive like a NASCAR racer." Dany glanced at the kids who appeared oblivious to Emmy's driving.

"You should ride with me in my Civic Si. I can really make that baby move." Emmy jumped out and helped Kevin Michael out of his car seat.

Heather and Isabella climbed out of their booster seats and stood beside Dany.

Heather tilted her head. "Why is Miss Liz so much taller than you if you are sisters?"

"Heather!" Isabella rolled her eyes in a perfect imitation of Emmy. "Don't you know anything. It's because Miss Liz is older. It's like Aunt Diane and Mommy. Aunt Diane is older, so she's taller than Mommy."

"Mom, does that mean when I get older I will be a lot taller than Isa because I was born first?"

"You are only a few minutes older, so I don't think you will

43

be much taller than Isa. Sorry." Emmy held Kevin Michael's hand until they got close to the front doors. "No running!" Emmy shouted to no avail.

"I looked, Mom, but I saw Ben and Taylor."

Tony Bertucci snuck up behind Emmy and grabbed her shoulders. "Guess who?"

"I heard you coming, creep. You are about as stealthy as a herd of elephants chasing a Sherman tank."

"Good morning, Dany. Did you risk your life riding with this brat?" Tony asked.

"She's a good driver," Dany insisted.

"Yeah, and so was Jimmy Doyle."

Emmy shrugged at Dany. Dany shrugged back.

"You got us there, Tony," Emmy said.

"Gene Hackman's character in *The French Connection*," Tony explained. "The big car chase scene."

"Whatever. Where's Sloane and the rest of your tribe?" Emmy asked.

"I dropped them off and parked the van like a good husband. Where's Kenny?"

"Still sleeping. He's being lazy. I didn't get back any earlier, and I made it to church on time. You hear anything about the new sanctuary? You guys are going to bid on it, right?"

"Sure, why not? The Bertucci and Keasling Construction Company has a fine record when it comes to building churches."

"So this would be the first, right?"

Tony tugged on Emmy's hair. *I still miss the ponytail.* "For your information our company has built three churches in the last ten years." Tony expressed pride in the company founded by his late father and his uncle, Daniel Keasling, over fifty years ago.

"Any of them still standing?" Emmy asked.

Dany grinned. "I love the way you guys tease each other like brother and sister. I know you're not really, but you act like it."

"Oh, gross, Dany. How can you even think I could be related to this creature. He's barely human."

"Dany, did I ever tell you about the time Emmy was at my house, and I started acting like a gorilla?"

44

"What do you mean acting? Mama said you always acted that way." Emmy tried to walk faster but Tony stayed right behind her. "Stop following me. I'm going to have you kicked out of the neighborhood. I have a connection with the developer. Just you, though. Mama and Sloane and the kids can stay."

"Your generosity is overwhelming," Tony teased. *Yeah, I know how much you guys contribute to the church.*

Dany noticed a couple entering the building. "Hey! That's Jason and Michelle. I didn't know they were here." Dany hurried to catch up to the younger of her two brothers and his wife.

"Creep," Emmy hissed.

"Brat," Tony chuckled.

"How is Mama feeling? I talked to her earlier this week, and she complained about her hip. You know it has to be killing her to even mention it. She said it was like a dull toothache which means you would rate the pain as a twenty on on a scale of one-to-ten."

"Are you forgetting I played football from the time I could run until recently?"

"Yes, but you have no brain, so you are incapable of feeling pain."

Tony opened the door for Emmy out of habit.

"Thank you, Tony," she said equally out of habit. "You better make her see her doctor, or else I will."

"Yes, boss lady."

Emmy shook her head. "I'll see you later in class. Save me a seat next to Kristen, please. I want to talk to Jason and Michelle." Emmy joined Dany and listened to Jason talking about Avery.

"She literally would not let go." Jason held his hands to his chest. "Tyler had to pry her away from me so they could get to church. Hi, Emmy. I thought you guys were on tour."

"Hi back. We are, but we rush home after Saturday's show. What have you guys been up to? I don't think I've seen you since the wedding."

"Working and trying to organize the apartment," Jason answered.

"Are you still living in Hillsdale?"

45

Michelle nodded. "I'm working as a legal secretary, and Jay is working as a substitute teacher."

Jason shrugged. "Jobs are scarce right now."

"How long are you staying? And why didn't you tell me you were here?" Dany held onto Jason's arm. "I am still your favorite sister, right?"

"Of course you are."

"Did you meet the boys?" Emmy used air quotes.

"Briefly, but they never stopped running long enough for us to get a good look at them," Jason said and then laughed.

"I call them the Streak and the Blur," Emmy said and then giggled. "But I have to admit they behave a lot better than when they first arrived. Tyler must have the patience of the Dalai Lama or some monk guy."

"Maybe Jesus?" Dany asked with a grin.

Emmy laughed. "I wouldn't go that far. I've played tennis against him, and he kicked my butt and was pleased about it. He hated to lose a single point."

"He's always been competitive," Dany said. "You can imagine the ping pong games between Tyler and Jason."

"I've witnessed them in action." Emmy hit an imaginary ping pong ball at Jason.

He slammed it back at her.

Sofia called Monday morning as they ate breakfast. "I'm sorry, Emmy, but I have to take my mother to the doctor this morning."

"That's okay. I'll see if I can convince Kenny to watch the kids. I really need to work on my book. He's not doing anything with that book he's supposedly writing with his father. He's being lazy until time to fly wherever the band is playing. At least I am doing something productive."

"I gotta run, Emmy. I'll be there around noon, or shortly after. Thanks for being so understanding. You're a great boss."

Emmy stared at the phone for a second. *Is that all you think I am? Do I treat you differently than Mary. Mary was, and still is, a part of the family. I never thought of her as an employee.* Emmy turned to Kenny and bit her lip. *I need to reevaluate how I treat Sofia.*

"Who was on the phone, Mommy?" Heather asked with a mouthful of oatmeal.

Emmy didn't bother to correct her. "Sofia. She won't be here until noon. Kenny, will you watch the kids, please? I really need to work on my book."

"Who wants to go swimming?" he asked.

The kids raised their hands and shouted their approval.

"Make sure you wait thirty minutes, please." Emmy filled her coffee mug and headed to the den. "I'm putting up my do-not-disturb sign." She closed and locked the door, grabbed her laptop and plopped into her recliner. She kicked off her untied sneakers and sighed. *Let's see how bad this looks now.*

It was midnight when Larry pulled out with Jess and Joe. I said goodbye and the Zawaski brothers kissed my hand. I giggled every time they did that. Everyone was on the bus hanging out in the lounge area. Most of them were too wound up for sleep. Hank headed off to bed first, and eventually everyone else did, too. Dixie and I were the last ones up.

"What were you and Darren doing?" Dixie asked.

"Playing ping pong in the teen room. Why?"

"Just wonderin'," Dixie said and then laughed.

I made a face at Dixie. The look on his face said he didn't buy my story. We did play ping pong, but we also listened to some music and maybe danced a little. Then Darren surprised me with a kiss. I guess if you want to get technical, I kissed him back, but that's it. Then I said something about being engaged and we both felt guilty. Enough about that night.

"Did it make us look like amateurs when I started crying tonight?" I asked to change the subject.

"Not at all, Emmy. It made you look sincere," Dixie answered.

"I can usually make it through that song, but I just

couldn't tonight. I was thinking about Yolanda and Juanita."

"It's okay to show your emotions during the service. You don't apologize for being happy, so you don't need to apologize for crying, either."

"Thanks, Dixie. I'm going out for a run in the morning. Wanna go with me?"

"Sure. What time?"

"I'll probably be up around seven."

"See you then. Good night, Emmy. See you in the morning."

"Night, Dixie."

I got ready for bed and spent a few minutes reading my Bible. I was studying the book of James at the time. I tried to make a habit of reading a few minutes every night before bed, and a few minutes in the morning. I don't want to make it sound like a ritual or something that I did as a routine. It helped me to stay focused because, after all, I am a flawed human being like everyone else.

Pastor Dan arrived a few minutes before seven and opened the church. I know because I was up and saw him out the window. Shortly after that the guys started waking up. They used the showers and then headed over to Denny's for breakfast. Dixie woke up, and he and I went for a run. Steve Van Zant was the last one out of bed. This meant he would be teased all day for being lazy. That was one of the things we did to break up the tedium of traveling. Kinda silly, but good for a few laughs. He made it over to Denny's and immediately the guys start harassing him. I know this because Chase filled me in on everything later.

"Hey, look who finally crawled out of his bunk."

"What about Emmy and Dixie?" Steve asked.

"They were up early and went out for a run. You were the last one out of his bunk today."

"Fine! I'm going to sleep on the couch from now on."

Dixie and I finished our run and returned to the bus. We showered and dressed. I figured everyone was over at Denny's eating breakfast, so Dixie and I headed over there. We saw Pastor Dan and invited him to breakfast.

"I would join you, but I need to run over to the hospital. One of my members is having surgery this morning."

"I will pray that everything turns out okay."

"One of my older members, Mrs. Byrnes, is having a hip replaced."

I didn't use those exact words. At least I hope not because they sound dorky. I've been around Kenny too long. I did quietly say a quick prayer for her as we walked over to eat. Dixie was not quite used to me praying so much, or so often. He asked why.

"I pray right away because otherwise I would forget. I have so much on my mind with the wedding coming up."

"I understand now, and I think that's a very good habit. I should do that, too."

"Are you teasing me, Dixie?"

"Not at all, Emmy. I meant what I said."

I still wasn't sure if he was teasing me or not.

Later, Chase got a call from Larry. "Just wanted to let you know we are in a truck stop outside of Louisville. We will head over to the church. Should be there by ten."

"I'll call the church and see if anyone is there. We'll be there around three, I think. We'll help you unload then."

"See you later, Chase."

Larry knew the Zawaskis would have the truck unloaded and everything in the church before the bus arrived.

Chase gathered everyone in the lounge before we left for Louisville.

I apologized to the guys. "I'm sorry I messed up last night guys. I will do better tonight."

49

"What did you mess up, Emmy?" Alan asked.

"I started crying during 'Yolanda's Song'. I won't do that again."

Chase told me, "Emmy, you can cry every night if you need to. I know that song means a lot to you, and, if you cry like a baby, we don't care. You don't ever need to feel ashamed for having genuine emotions."

Chase hugged me and I blushed, but I didn't cry. By eleven Buck pulled out of the parking lot and we headed to Louisville, Kentucky.

It was just a few minutes after three when Buck pulled into the parking lot of Louisville First United Nazarene. Buck saw the truck parked at the rear of the lot. He had a suspicion it was empty. Buck stopped to let everyone out. Chase walked into the building and was greeted by the church secretary.

"Pastor Dillon is in the building somewhere. I'll see if I can find him for you."

"Thanks. I'm Chase Hillman, by the way, and this is the rest of the guys."

"I'm Nancy. Oh, there's Pastor Dillon now."

Chase saw him coming to greet us.

"Hello! I'm Chris Dillon. You must be Chase Hillman."

"I am and this is our group. We should start unloading the truck."

"Oh, I thought those two guys had finished unloading."

"What?" Chase asked, and I started giggling. I knew Jess and Joe would be laughing, too.

"There were two guys unloading the truck earlier. I'm sorry but I couldn't help but laugh at them. They were working so hard and kept laughing and carrying on. They were talking in a foreign language, so I couldn't understand them. I talked to Larry the driver, and he told me that the guys wanted to surprise you by having the truck unloaded. Oh, I hope I didn't spoil the surprise. I need to learn to keep my mouth shut sometimes."

I saw Jess and Joe laughing, so I hollered at them, "Jess! Joe! You two get over here right now!"

They thought they were in trouble at first. They walked over to me with their hats in their hand and looked like two kids about to be yelled at by the school principal.

"Did you two unload the truck all by yourself?" I knew the answer, but I couldn't help tease them.

"No, Miss Emmy. We had help." They laughed because they knew I would say something.

"Who helped you?"

"Larry did."

"What did Larry unload?" I knew the guys well enough to know that Larry couldn't lift anything heavy.

"Larry helped unload the..." Jess and Joe started grinning again. "Larry unloaded the sleeping bags for us."

I couldn't help myself. I laughed and smiled at the guys. "You guys are something else. You did all this work for us."

I hugged the guys and embarrassed them.

"You don't need to hug us, Miss Emmy. We're all sweaty and dusty."

"I don't care! I love you guys so much. You are both so sweet."

This embarrassed them even more.

"We love you, too, Miss Emmy, and we love Mr. Kenny, too."

Chase and Stuart Lederer noticed all the gear was just where it needed to be except for the cables. Even the drums were set up and ready to go. The Zawaskis knew that Stuart didn't want anyone to touch the cables. They placed the two large cases of cables on the platform. Though the brothers may seem simple-minded to some people, they are actually very intelligent and knowledgeable. They could have set everything up without any help from Stuart, but didn't want to disobey him or break his rules.

Chase shook hands with Jess and Joe. "Thank you

both for all your work. We appreciate it very much. You guys can go get cleaned up if you want. We'll see you at five, okay?"

"Yes, Pastor Chase. We hope you don't mind that we unloaded the truck already."

"We don't mind at all." Chase somehow kept a straight face.

By five o'clock we had finished our soundcheck and were ready to eat. Pastor Chris Dillon used the church's large van to take us to a nearby restaurant. Everyone was along except for Larry, who was sleeping in the truck. Chase talked to Pastor Dillon about the service. There was no opening act tonight, but the local worship leader would lead the crowd in a few songs to begin the service. Pastor Dillon looked to be in his mid-to-late fifties and admitted he was not real familiar with our music. His kids were the reason the church invited us to be here tonight.

"Our regular music is a mixture of old and new. We have some older members who still like to hear and sing the old hymns."

"We will mix in some hymns tonight," Chase assured him as I listened from the other end of the table.

"I'll be honest with you, Chase. We had a Christian group come to the church last year and it wasn't... how can I put this... it wasn't a success. We had a large group in attendance. The place was full. But they seemed to be more like rock stars or something. You wouldn't believe the language they used. They were just interested in performing and getting paid. You guys seem to be more interested in doing what God wants you to."

"We're definitely not rock stars by any stretch of the imagination. Don't get me wrong, though. These guys are top notch musicians and we sound professional. We are only here because we all feel this is God's will for us. Emmy is thrilled to be traveling, but the guys would certainly rather be home."

"Who is Emmy? Is that the young girl at the end of the table?"

"Yes. Emmy is our lead singer. She's engaged to be married next month."

"Oh my! I thought she was a teenager. Please don't tell her what I said."

"It's all right. She's used to that. She looks so much younger than her real age. I think that's why so many teens like her. They think she's one of them."

"You said she's engaged."

"Yeah, have you ever heard of Fridays At Five?"

"Yes, I've heard the kids mention them before."

"Emmy's fiancee is the guitar player and singer for that band. He's also a Christian. He and Emmy grew up together. It's a long story." Chase laughed.

"I see," Pastor Dillon said.

I think he wondered if I was for real or not. I put that in here because it happened almost everywhere we went. People would take me for a kid. I got used to it.

Anyway, the service started at seven. After a prayer and a few songs to warm up the crowd, the band began to play. I noticed more older folks in the crowd tonight, so we started out with a hymn instead of our usual opening song. This seemed to be a good choice and soon even the older people were standing and singing along to their normal worship songs. 'Yolanda's Song' was especially well received by the crowd. After a shorter altar service than last night, I started talking to people. One grandmotherly-looking lady approached me.

"I want to tell you how much I enjoyed your music tonight. When I saw all those guitars and drums, I didn't think I would like it, but you were really good. It was too loud, of course, but everyone plays that way. I liked the fact that you sang some older songs for us more seasoned people. Too many teenagers don't know the older hymns. I'm glad you do. Your parents must be very proud of you. Is your father part of the band?"

I realized that this kind old lady thought I was a teenager. "Thank you very much. My parents are back at home in South Hampshire, Illinois. These guys take good care of me when we travel."

"Good! A young girl like you needs to watch out. Too many crazy people in the world today."

"I agree with you." I giggled as I looked at Dixie, who was making faces at me.

"I'm going to buy a CD for my granddaughter. I think she will like the music. She doesn't go to church."

"Well, I trust that will change. Maybe our music will be a good influence on her. That's why we sing."

"Good luck to you as you grow up. Did I mention that I turned eighty-three a few days ago?"

"You didn't mention that, and you certainly look very good for eighty-three. I hope you had a nice birthday."

"It was very nice. My kids took me out to eat at that buffet restaurant that I like."

By ten thirty the truck was loaded, and we were ready to hit the road. Since this church didn't have any facilities for us to stay overnight Chase wanted to get to the Nashville area tonight. Larry knew a truck stop just outside of Nashville where we could spend the night. It wouldn't take too long to get there. Just over three hours later the truck and bus pulled into the truck stop.

Emmy sat back and stared at the ceiling. *Shoot! I need to dust the ceiling fan.* Her reverie was interrupted by someone pounding on the door.

"Mommy! Mommy! Kevin Michael swam under the water all the way from end to end," Isabella announced.

Emmy closed her laptop, stood up and opened the door. "Good job, Kevin Michael." She put her hands on her hips and frowned. "Why are you dripping water everywhere? Go back to the kitchen and dry off before you ruin the floor." Emmy shook her head as the twins scampered away.

54

Chapter Six

Dany Kimmerle opened the front door of the guesthouse and smiled.

"Do I get to come in?" Darian Michaelis smiled back.

"Do I get a kiss first?"

Darian leaned forward, kissed her cheek and scooted past her into the house.

Dany rolled her eyes. "Where are we going for dinner? I'm famished." She closed the door and took a few steps toward Darian.

"I took the liberty of making a reservation at Ciao Bella. I hope that's all right."

"What time?"

"The earliest I could get was seven thirty. Will you survive until then?" Darian moved close to Dany, put his hands on her shoulders and kissed her again. "Was that better?"

"Getting better."

He kissed her again. Even longer.

"I think you're getting pretty good, but we still need to practice." She led him to the couch. "What time should we leave?"

"I thought we could leave around six thirty. We can park by the river and walk over to Ciao Bella since it's a beautiful night. You up for that?"

"I guess I won't wear my high-heels then," Dany joked.

"Hmmm. If you wear six-inch heels, you would only be two feet shorter than me." He grabbed her foot and grinned.

"I wouldn't be able to stand. What did you do today? Anything special?"

He continued to massage her foot. "Did some yard work for Ma. Caught up on emails. Nothing special. You?"

"I went over to the big house. The kids are home with Sofia, so I went swimming with them. Sofia doesn't like to swim unless she has to. I need to be careful because the water dries out my hair."

Darian shifted his hand to Dany's shoulder-length brown hair. "How can water dry out your hair?"

55

"The chemicals, you goof." She ruffled his neatly combed hair. "Should I wear anything special tonight?"

"What do you mean?" Darian thought about the small box in the car.

"Well, I'm not wearing shorts and a t-shirt to Ciao Bella."

"They don't have a dress code, and you said Emmy wore a t-shirt the last time you were there."

"It was for lunch with the kids. This is a Saturday night. I'll wear nice jeans and a top, since you're wearing nice jeans."

"You have lots of pretty dresses," Darian told her. *And I love looking at your legs.*

"Are you requesting I wear a dress, or does it matter?" Dany stood up and faced him.

"It's your choice obviously."

"I'll see if my good jeans are clean. If not, I'll find a dress." She headed to her bedroom.

Darian sat on the couch and drummed his fingers on his knees. He stretched his legs out and clenched his jaw. He practiced taking deep breaths to keep his heart calm. He glanced around the room. *You've put up some new photos. Those look like you and your brothers and Liz. I wonder how old you were. Maybe eight or nine.* He tried to stretch out the collar of the t-shirt under his dress shirt. He fidgeted on the couch for ten minutes until Dany returned.

"How do I look?" She twirled for him.

He jumped to his feet. "You look so fantastic, Dany."

"Thank you. Are we ready to go?"

Darian stared.

"Darian? Did you hear me?" She nudged him. "Are we ready to go?"

"Oh, sorry. Yes, I'm ready."

"I'll grab my purse."

"Right."

Dany glanced up at him. "You okay? You're acting kinda spacey."

"I'm fine. Just thinking."

Dany grabbed her purse, keys and turned off the lights. She closed the door and walked with Darian to his car.

"Thank you, Darian," Dany said after he opened the door for her.

Darian stood there with a silly smile.

"You can close the door now." Dany rolled her eyes. *Something is definitely up with you tonight. You've never been this much of a doofus.*

Darian closed the door, ran around to the driver's side, got in and backed out of the drive. He didn't speak until they left Bristol Ridge.

"Did you have any trouble getting past security?" Dany asked.

"Not really. The guard made a big deal about checking his list, but I knew my name was there. Have you got a taste for anything special?"

"I like their spinach ravioli, but I wonder what the specials might be."

"Everything is good, but I like the chicken parmigiana. Other stuff, too."

Darian parked in the new lot along the river and scrambled out of the car, ran around to the passenger side and opened the door for Dany.

"Thank you, Darian." She looked up at him. *You are being so polite tonight, and it's weirding me out a bit.*

They walked the few blocks to Ciao Bella and Darian opened the door for her.

"Good evening, Mr. Michaelis and Ms. Kimmerle. It's so good to see you both." Mr. Sabatino shook hands with Darian and smiled graciously at Dany. "Your table is ready. If you would please follow me." He led them to a table along the side with a bit of privacy. "Will this be satisfactory?"

"Yes, sir," Darian answered.

Mr. Sabatino pulled out the chair for Dany. "Melissa will be taking care of you this evening. Please ask if you need anything."

Melissa Sabatino took their drink order and pointed out the specials. Dany ordered the salmon ravioli and Darian stuck to his favorite. Later, they shared a tiramasu. Darian paid the check and left a generous tip.

"Was everything perfectly satisfactory?" Mr. Sabatino asked.

Dany smiled. "Absolutely scrumptious."

"Please come again soon, and tell Emmy I haven't seen her for too long of a time."

"I will get on her case for you, Mr. Sabatino," Dany said as she laughed.

They headed back to the car.

"Does he know you're living in the guesthouse?" Darian stepped around a couple heading toward the restaurant.

"Emmy told him, and she asked him to make sure he remembered me," Dany explained.

Darian opened the door for her again, and then ran around the car to get in.

"It's still early. Would you like to go for a walk?" Darian asked.

"Sure. That way I can work off some of the calories."

"Have you ever seen the waterfall?"

"No, but Emmy told me about it. I'd like to see it," Dany said.

Darian drove to the state park, and they walked over to the waterfall.

Dany pointed to the steps leading down. "Emmy said she would get as close as she could to feel the spray of the water."

"We can do that," Darian said. "I might toss you in the river."

"You could try." Dany skipped down the concrete steps and ran to the railing. She climbed onto the lowest rung.

Darian walked up behind her and put his hands on her trim waist. "The river must be low because you would usually get wet standing here."

They spent a few minutes by the waterfall and then headed back up the steps.

"Which way should we go?" Dany asked.

Darian looked both directions. "That way would take us to the college."

"Let's go that way then."

58

They saw a few other people walking ahead of them. A biker passed them, and they met an older couple walking their dog.

Darian spotted a bench and edged Dany toward it. "Can we sit for a moment?"

Dany grinned. "Are you tired already? I thought you were in better shape than this."

"I'm not out of shape. I need to talk to you."

Dany sat and Darian joined her. He pulled at his collar and rubbed his hands together to get rid of the sweat.

"What would you like to talk about?" Dany looked and listened to the river flowing past only a few feet away.

"Uh... How do you like living out by Kenny and Emmy?"

"You know I love living there." She put a hand on his arm. *I've never seen you this nervous. Did something happen at work?*

"Yeah, I guess you do." He nodded at another couple walking a tiny dog that strained at its leash to escape.

"It's such a beautiful night. Not too humid or hot."

Darian stared into Dany's expressive brown eyes. *Well, here goes.* He reached into his pocket and pulled out a small jewelry box. He dropped to a knee and watched Dany put a hand to her mouth. "Danielle Kathryn Kimmerle, will you marry me? I love you so much, and can't imagine my life without you. What do you think?"

Dany's eyes filled with tears as she wrapped her arms around his neck and kissed him.

"Is that a yes?" Darian asked while still kissing her.

Dany broke off the kiss only long enough to say yes.

The couple with the small, yapping dog returned and watched Dany and Darian kissing for a moment before walking away.

Dany released her hold on Darian and sat back. "Do you actually have a ring in there, or it is just an empty box?"

"Oh, right. You want to see the ring, huh?"

"I do believe that would be appropriate," Dany said.

He opened the box and handed it to her. "Mary helped me pick it out, but I could exchange it if you don't like it."

Dany shook her head. "I love it!"

"Do you want to see if it fits? Mary thought it would be real close."

"Yes."

Darian took the ring out of the box and slipped it on her finger. "Is it too big?"

"Maybe just a bit, but that can be fixed. Oh, Darian, now I know why you've been so nervous and goofy all night. I was afraid it might be something bad, but now this is a perfect night. I have to call home."

"I thought you might want to call Liz first."

"I'll call her next." She pulled her cell phone from her purse and called home.

"Hi, Dany, I was just thinking about you," Mom Kimmerle said. "Are you planning to come home anytime soon? I have some sheets you might be able to use."

"I'll come home soon, Mom, but I have some news. Are you sitting down?"

"What is it? Are you all right?"

"I'm engaged, Mom! Darian asked me to marry him, and I said yes."

"Dusty! Get on the phone. It's Dany," Mom shouted. "When did he ask? I want to hear all about it."

"We're on a bench by the Riverwalk. He just asked a moment ago."

"Hello, what's going on, Dany?" Dad asked with a sly smile.

"Daddy! Darian just proposed and I said yes!"

"He did? That was quick."

Karen looked at Dusty who had walked into the room. "What do you mean by that."

"Yes, Daddy. What does that mean?" Dany scooted closer to Darian and looked at him.

"I suppose it's all right to tell you now, but he stopped by the office yesterday and asked permission to ask for your hand."

"Get out! Did he really?" Dany pushed her shoulder into Darian.

"That is so romantic," Mom said.

60

"I didn't realize he would ask you tonight. I think he's pretty serious about you, Dany."

"I should hope so," Mom said as she rolled her eyes.

"He took me to Caio Bella for dinner, and he's been acting weird all night. Now I know why. I should let you go, so I can call Lizzie."

"We are very happy for you, Dany. Bring him home with you the next time you come."

"I will, Mom. I'll talk to you soon."

After kissing for a couple of minutes, Dany called Liz.

"Hey, Dany, hang on a second. Dillan! Do not grab Derby's tail. She will bite if you hurt her." Liz sighed. "Okay. It's been a zoo around here today. Liam hit Avery, and Grayson tried to hit Liam. I don't know why they are behaving like this tonight. So, what's going on?"

"Nothing too much. Darian took me to Caio Bella, and then we decided to go for a walk along the river. We stopped at a bench and he kissed me then he proposed and I said..."

"Dillan! That's it! Sit on your chair and do not move until I tell you."

"Lizzie, did you hear me?"

"I'm sorry. I heard something about the river."

"Darian asked me to marry him," Dany repeated.

"No way! For real?"

Dany nodded.

"I can't see you, but I bet you're nodding. Oh, Dany, I'm so happy for you. Did you know he was going to propose?"

"No, but I'm glad he did. It explains the way he was acting."

"You should call Mom."

"Just did."

"Tyler, Dany is engaged," Liz said as Tyler walked into the room carrying Avery.

"She is. Who to?"

"I heard that, Tyler," Dany laughed.

Liz shook her head. "Can you be serious for a moment?"

"When did this happen?" Tyler asked.

61

"Just now," Liz answered.

"Good. Now I have another tennis opponent in the family."

Liz shook her head. "You need to talk to Dillan about his choices."

Tyler handed Avery to Liz and left to talk to Dillan.

"I know he just asked, but did he have a ring? When do you think you'll set a date? Will you get married here, or back home?"

"Liz! We haven't had time to talk about that, but he did have a ring. I love it, but it needs to be tightened. I'll show you tomorrow."

"Have you called anyone else? You should call Grandma."

"I'll call her tomorrow. She's probably in bed already. I should call Emmy. She is always the last one to hear about engagements, so this time she will be one of the first."

"Good idea. You guys could come over if you want. I want to see the ring."

"Would you mind if we don't? You'll see us in the morning."

"But I'm pregnant. This is like a craving," Liz pleaded.

"That only works on Tyler. You can be patient for one night."

"If I have to, but you better not stop and see Emmy on the way home."

"We won't. Kiss the kids for me. See you tomorrow."

Dany waited while Darian called his parents and then Mary.

"What did they say?" Dany asked.

"Ma and Mary started crying. Dahlia screamed. Eli and Da took it in stride. They said I made an excellent choice."

"Do you mind if I call Emmy?"

"Go ahead, but I wish I could see her face when you tell her."

"We could wait until the morning," Dany suggested.

"I know you want to tell her now. Go ahead. Bet you a hundred dollars she cries."

Dany shook her head. "That's like betting the sun will come up in the east." Dany called Emmy.

"Hey, Dany. How was Caio Bella? What did you eat?"

62

Dany told Emmy about their dinner.

"Did Mr. Sabatino treat you like a queen?"

"Yes, and he said you better come back soon."

"We should do lunch again. Are you home already? Did you guys go anywhere after Caio Bella?" Emmy asked as she plopped into her recliner in the family room. "The kids are asleep. You guys could come over if you want. We could play Ticket To Ride or something."

"Thanks, but not tonight. We're sitting at a bench on the Riverwalk."

"Are you close to the waterfall? You should see it. It's really cool."

"We did already, and then we went for a walk. We sat on this bench and talked..."

"And kissed, I bet," Emmy said and then giggled.

"We kissed, but then Darian pulled out a box and got on his knee..."

"Dany!" Emmy screamed loud enough to be heard across the street. "Did he propose? Are you engaged? Tell me! I have to know!"

"Yes! Yes! Yes! We are engaged, and you're not the last one to know."

Emmy bolted out of her recliner and jumped on Kenny, as he read a book on the couch. "Dany's engaged!"

"Really? Since when?"

"Since a few minutes ago," Emmy bit her lip to try and stop her tears from forming, but it didn't help.

"Emmy! Are you still there?" Dany asked.

Kenny picked up the phone. "Congratulations, Dany. Emmy needs a moment. She's crying."

"I knew it!" Dany high-fived Darian.

Emmy grabbed the phone from Kenny. "I can't help it. I'm so happy for you guys."

"I'll show you and Liz the ring at church. She wanted to see it tonight and used being pregnant as an excuse. I told her to be patient."

"I'll be patient if I have to, but I want to see it first thing at church. The ring I mean."

"I promise," Dany said and then ended the call.

Emmy straddled Kenny and kissed him. "Did you know already?"

"Nope. For once you know before everyone else."

"About time. The girls will be so excited."

"You aren't going to wake them and tell them tonight, are you?"

"I would if they were older. I won't even call Krissy."

"No texts, either," Kenny warned.

"Party pooper," Emmy complained but then kissed him again with more urgency.

"If you girls are quiet and eat your breakfast, I have some good news for you." Emmy sat at the breakfast nook table with a cup of coffee and a blueberry muffin.

"We're eating, Mommy. What's the news?" Isabella asked.

"Dany and Darian are going to get married," Emmy said as she grinned. "Isn't that great?"

Isabella looked at Heather, and they both looked at Emmy without saying a word.

"What's the matter? I thought you would be happy. You look sad. Why?"

"If Dany marries Darian, will she have to move away like Mary did?" Heather asked.

"We don't want Dany to move away," Isabella said and then crossed her arms over her chest.

Emmy looked at Kenny, who was cutting a stack of pancakes for Kevin Michael. Kenny shrugged.

"I don't want her to move, either. Should we make sure she knows she can keep living in the guesthouse?"

"Do you think Darian will mind living there?" Kenny poured more syrup on the pancakes and handed the plate to Kevin.

"It might be closer to work for him. I suppose eventually they will want their own place, but maybe not for several years."

"Mommy, please don't let Dany leave. We will miss her too much," Isabella said.

"We won't have to worry about it for several months, Isa."

"Are they going to get married today?" Heather asked. "Does Dany have a princess dress already?"

"Not yet, Heather. It will be a while before they get married." Emmy checked her phone. "Dany texted that Darian is going to pick her up. She doesn't need a ride today."

Later, Emmy and Liz waited in the foyer for Dany and Darian to arrive at the church.

"There they are!" Emmy pointed as Dany and Darian entered through the other set of doors. She and Liz hurried through the crowd and met Dany before anyone else.

Liz grabbed Dany's hand and said, "You're coming with us."

Emmy smiled at Darian. "We will bring Dany back after we're finished."

Darian laughed and said, "We expected this."

Emmy followed Liz and Dany into the main church office.

"We need more privacy," Emmy said. "There are too many people in here."

They pulled Dany deeper into the suite of offices.

"We can use Tyler's office. He's never in here," Liz said as Emmy closed the door.

Dany smiled and stuck out her hand. "I know you want to see the ring."

Liz and Emmy oohed and awed over the yellow gold ring with a diamond that sparkled as much as the ladies' eyes.

"Where were you when he proposed?" Emmy asked.

Dany explained.

"I knew it!" Emmy exclaimed.

"What? Tell us," Liz insisted.

"That has to be the same bench where Cam proposed to Lindsey except he did it in the winter. I wonder if even more couples have gotten engaged there."

"Maybe," Liz said. "Tyler and I have stopped at that bench. It is a romantic spot. There's a great view of the river."

"I'm going to call Denise. She works at the *SoHam Herald*. This might be worth a story."

65

After grilling Dany for details for ten minutes, Liz and Emmy released her and escorted her back to Darian.

"You may have her back now, but you better be ready to be bombarded by your friends," Liz said.

Emmy called Denise Bartell that afternoon.

"Have you been working on the book?" Denise asked.

"I didn't have a chance yesterday, but I'll work on it this afternoon."

"What's going on otherwise?"

Emmy explained about Dany and Lindsey.

"That might make a good story. I'll put out some feelers, and see if I can locate other couples. Thanks for the tip, Emmy. Get some more chapters written."

"I will. Promise."

Emmy got Kevin Michael to take a nap, and Kenny took the girls across the street to play with Dotty and Noemi Bertucci. She used the den to work on the story. *Now where did I leave off?* She opened the folder and scrolled to the line of red X's she used to mark her place. Here it is. She read her journal for a few minutes to remember the day in question and then began typing.

Cecil stopped and let everyone off the bus at the restaurant. After they filled the truck and bus with fuel, Larry and Cecil parked the vehicles and joined everyone inside. Dixie told me later that it wasn't until then that Chase finally realized I wasn't with them.

"Where is Emmy? I thought she was with you, Dixie."

"She went to bed, Chase. I guess she's still sleeping."

"I don't want her to be on the bus by herself. Someone needs to stay with her."

Hank volunteered to go back to the bus.

"I'm not that hungry, and I could use the sleep. I'll go back."

"Thanks, Hank. Do you want us to bring you anything?" Chase asked.

66

"No, just make sure I have my coffee in the morning."

The group hung out at the twenty-four-hour restaurant until they got tired enough to go to sleep. I slept later than usual and didn't wake up until eight o'clock. I got out of bed and listened to hear if anyone else was awake. The bus was quiet except for the sound of the diesel motor. I got dressed and opened my bedroom door. I walked past the bunks and heard some snoring from Hank's bunk. No one was up yet, so I returned to my room and read my Bible and devotional book for a time. I said my morning prayers and turned on my laptop. I was able to Skype with Kenny for an hour. Kenny and the guys were preparing for a short tour of Australia and New Zealand. I tried to convince him to come with me until they had to leave, but he wouldn't. He didn't want to become a distraction. He was right. Had he been along, it might have taken away from our real reason for touring. Not that it would have been his fault, but it's like Michael Jordan showing up at his son's basketball games. Kenny didn't want that to happen to us.

I said goodbye to Kenny and caught up on emails about our wedding. I was so fortunate to have great friends who handled a lot of the details for me and Kenny. I'll never regret hiring Paula Kratzsky as our wedding planner. She would have been worth twice what she charged. We sure didn't want to move the wedding to a later date. My friends know why. S-e-x! I heard some of the guys getting up. I hurried to the small kitchen area and made coffee for Hank. Chase bought some donuts from the truck stop store and they were gone as quick as a flash. Alan was the last guy out of his bunk today. Steve was glad it wasn't him for once. Alan swore that he wasn't the last one out of his bunk, but it's in my journal. That proves it.

"What do you guys want to do?" Chase asked. "We can eat here, then find the church, or we could find the

67

church first and see what's around it."

Most of the guys wanted to get to the church, so that's what we did. It didn't take too long to find the Belmont Church. Larry and Cecil pulled the vehicles into a parking area. Chase hopped off the bus and Rob Durham greeted him. Rob was one of the worship leaders at the church and a recording artist as well. He showed Chase where to park the bus and where the truck needed to go.

"Thanks, Rob. It's so good to see you. How are Beth and the kids?"

"They're doing fine. You will get to see them later. How are Yvonne and the girls? I know Beth talked to them a couple of days ago."

"They are doing great, and the girls are growing like weeds."

"I should tell you that we sold all the tickets for tonight. The place will be packed."

"That's good to know. I'll admit I was worried because you guys have so many groups in here to play."

"I should thank you again for letting me open for you guys."

"Don't be silly. We should be opening for you. Is Beth going to sing with you?"

"On a couple tunes."

Rob had arranged for some help unloading the gear. The Zawaski brothers were surprised, but grateful. They were actually tired from all their hard work the day before. The truck was unloaded and the gear set up in no time. Larry moved the truck out of the way. Hank and I set up the merchandising table.

"Hank, we might need to order more CDs. We're running low." I reminded him as I counted our inventory.

"There is another case in the bus," he said.

Chase brought Rob over to introduce him to me, since he hadn't done that earlier. "Emmy, this is Rob Durham. Rob, this is Emmy."

"Hello, Emmy. It's nice to meet you. I've been enjoying your music. I have the CD in the car."

"Wow! Thanks, Rob. I've got some of your CDs at home."

"Oh, Emmy, I talked to Denny Dottery last night. He's coming tonight."

"Are you kidding me?"

If you don't know, Denny is the singer and guitar player in The Lyricon. Both Kenny and I love their music. We've got all their CDs.

"What's wrong, Emmy?"

"I should have brought my CDs so he could autograph them for me."

"I think they will want to buy your CD and get your autograph, Emmy," Rob teased.

"I'll have to see if I can call Kenny and let him know where we are."

Rob looked at Chase as I tried calling Kenny on his cell phone. I left a message when he didn't answer.

Now, you need to realize that I had no clue about what would happen later. I'll tell you now, but keep in mind that I was clueless at the time. I can picture Kenny saying that I'm still clueless, so I'm sticking out my tongue even though he's not in the room. You'll understand. This is what happened behind my back.

Rob took Chase to the side. "Kenny's coming to town, Chase. I talked to him yesterday. He wants to surprise Emmy."

"She will flip out. You do know they are engaged, right? She and Kenny have been friends since she was a little girl."

"Yes, I know. Kenny told me they are getting ready to fly to Australia, but he wanted to see Emmy before they left."

"Oh, I can't wait to see this." Chase rubbed his hands together. I can picture him doing that because he did it a lot. And I can see the devilish look on his face. He could be rather devious at times.

Rob continued, "Denny is going to meet Kenny at the airport and take him out to eat. When they get back,

I'll just have to keep them out of sight until you guys are on stage."

"I'll try to keep Emmy busy. She will want to listen to your set."

Rob nodded. "I'll make sure Kenny and Denny stay out of sight."

"I can't wait to see the look on her face. This will be priceless. I've got an idea. Let's move 'Yolanda's Song' up in the set and Kenny can come out on stage and join her."

I mentioned this to Chase the other day, and he laughed. He told me all the details about how they conspired to keep me away from Kenny. I'll never forgive them for that, but it does make for good memories.

Emmy heard someone knock on the door, so she paused. "Who's there?"

"Mommy, I woke up. I'm hungry. I need something special," Kevin said as he tried to open the door.

"Give me a second, and we can have some ice cream." Emmy saved her work and closed her laptop.

"My belly needs some chocolate sauce, too."

Emmy smiled as she walked to the door. She opened it and rubbed her stomach. "I think my tummy needs some special chocolate sauce. Will you help me make it?"

"I can help if you want, but I really just want to eat it, Mommy."

Emmy ruffled his hair as they headed to the kitchen.

Chapter Seven

"Emmy, I can help with breakfast. You don't have to do it by yourself," Mom Colwell offered.

"It's all right, Mom. I have to make some pancakes, and the rest is almost finished." Emmy stirred the sausage and gravy and lowered the heat. She checked the biscuits in the oven. Closed the oven door with her hip and dribbled some water on the grill section to make sure it was hot enough to start the pancakes.

"Ellie, let Emmy take care of breakfast," Dad Colwell said and then pointed to a barstool. "Sit down and relax."

"Carter, I like to help. I don't just sit down and expect everything to be done for me."

"I never do that, do I?" he asked.

Ellie and Emmy laughed together.

"She's got you there, Dad," Emmy said as she poured the pancake batter onto the griddle.

Kenny walked into the kitchen, greeted his parents and then patted Emmy's backside. "Should I get the kids ready to eat?"

"Yes, but make sure they wash their hands first." Emmy stood on tiptoes and kissed Kenny. "You need to shave."

Emmy finished the pancakes by the time Kenny brought the kids downstairs.

"Me-maw, when did you get here?" Heather rushed up to her grandmother.

"A few minutes ago, Heather. Do I get a hug?"

Heather hugged Me-maw as Isabella showed Gra a book she was reading.

"You can read to me after breakfast, okay?"

"Everyone find a seat and we can eat." Emmy set the food on the breakfast nook table.

The kids scrambled into their seats.

"You should sit by me, Gra," Isabella said.

"I think I will, Isa." He sat between the girls.

"Can we say the prayer, Mommy?" Heather asked.

"You can say it together."

"I'll start, Heather."

The kids said the prayer, and then Emmy and Me-maw filled plates.

"I don't like biscuits and gravy." Kevin pushed his plate away.

"You cleaned your whole plate the last time I made it," Emmy reminded him.

"Did I really?" He stared at the food and then sniffed it. "I think I might like it, but I don't know for sure."

"There is an easy way to find out," Me-maw said. "You take a bite and chew it up slowly. Like this."

Kevin Michael saw his sisters eating without fussing, so he took a bite. He chewed it and then took another bite. "I remember now. It was something else I didn't like."

Kenny grinned at his son. "Maybe it was rutabagas."

"Yuck! Rooterbagas are so gross." Heather made a face.

"You've never eaten a rutabaga," Emmy said. "My mother tried to make us eat some once, and it made me sick. Mom said her grandmother would make rutabagas and squash all the time in the winter."

"Gra, do you have a grandmother?" Isabella asked.

Gra finished chewing a piece of sausage. "I did at one time, Isa, but she's is no longer living."

"Is she in heaven with Jesus?" Heather asked.

"I believe she is."

"What was her name? Was it Grandma, or did she have a real name like you and Me-maw?"

"Let's see. Elly, do you remember?"

"Carter, can't you remember your grandmother's name?"

"She passed away a long time ago. Oh, I remember. Her name was Martha Eunice Weaver before she married my grandfather."

"Eunice? Really?" Kenny asked. "That's not a name you forget."

"I probably only saw her a few times before she passed."

Heather took another bite of pancakes. "How did she die? Was she really old like Grandma Isabel? Grandma Isabel was over a hundred years old."

72

"I'm sorry, but I don't know, Heather, but she was not real old. Maybe in her fifties."

"Where is your grandpa?" Isabella asked.

"He's buried next to my grandmother now. His name was Robert Wilson Colwell and my father's name was Robert Travis Colwell. My real name is Carter Robert Colwell and one of your father's names is Robert."

Isabella and Heather looked at Kenny and then back at Gra.

"Didn't they know any other names?" Heather asked.

Me-maw shook a finger at Gra. "Do not explain. Let them finish breakfast before you give them a lesson in the family genealogy."

"Look! I finished all my biscuits and gravy," Kevin Michael said proudly.

"Good job. Now eat your pancake."

The kids cleaned their plates and helped Emmy carry the dishes to the kitchen.

"I'll rinse these off before I put them in the dishwasher," Me-maw said.

The girls followed Gra into the family room and sat next to him on the couch.

"Would you like to learn more about your family history?"

"Do you have any brothers or sisters, Gra?" Isabella asked.

"I don't have any sisters, but I have two younger brothers. Parker and Thomas."

"Where do they live?"

Emmy and Me-maw walked into the room and sat in the recliners facing the couch.

Kenny held Kevin Michael. "We are going outside to play in the sandbox. We have to build a new road, so Kevin needs his diggers."

"Don't let him eat any sand, please," Emmy said.

"Parker and Thomas live in Virginia. They live on farms and have horses."

"Real horses or pretend ones?"

"Real horses that people can ride on," Gra explained.

"Where is Virginia?" Isabella asked.

73

Gra explained in great detail as Emmy rolled her eyes.

"Mommy, can we go see the horses this afternoon?" Heather asked.

"It's too far away, Heather. It would take all day to drive there."

"But we could fly there, Mommy," Isabella said.

"Maybe someday, but not today." Emmy realized the girls were getting too used to traveling with the band.

"Do you have anymore grandmas or grandpas, Mommy?"

"No, sweetie. Grandma Isabel was the last one. All of my other grandparents died when I was a little girl just a bit older than you and Isa."

"Does that mean Gra and Me-maw will die soon? I don't want them to," Isabella said and began to cry.

Gra hugged her tightly. "We don't plan to die for a long, long time, Isa. We want to see you grow up and have kids of your own."

"Our other grandma is sick and has to live in a special place for people who can't remember anything. Right, Mommy?"

"Yes, dear." Emmy sat quietly.

"What are you thinking about, Emmy?" Me-maw asked.

"Just thinking about my grandparents. Grandma and Grandpa Colasanti died within a few months of each other when I was nine and then Grandpa Sandusky died when I was twelve."

"I remember, dear. Your grandmother passed in December, and you came over to play with Kenny in the snow."

"I don't remember much about their funerals," Emmy said. "I suppose I was there though."

"You were, but you didn't stay until the end of the wake. You came home with us and spent the night."

"Do you still have the music box?" Gra asked.

"Yes, it's in the safe. It will be a hundred years old soon."

"Do you have a real music box, Mommy?" Isabella asked.

"Yes, I do. Grandmother Mary gave it to me on my ninth birthday."

"Does it really play music like an iPod?" Heather asked.

Emmy laughed. "It only plays one song."

74

"Can we see it?"

"Haven't they ever seen it, Emmy?" Me-maw asked.

"Not really." Emmy bit her lip. "I know at some point I need to pass it along, but I don't know how I will ever choose who gets it."

"We want to see it, Mommy. Can we play with it?"

Emmy thought about it for a moment. "I will let you see it, and we can play the music, but you can never play with it. It's not a toy."

"Okay," Heather said and then shrugged. "What good is it if you can't play with it?"

"You will understand one day, Heather."

Me-maw and the girls followed Emmy into the den where Emmy opened a panel hiding a medium-sized wall safe. Emmy opened the safe and pulled out a metal container.

Heather tilted her head. "Is that it? It doesn't look like a music box. It looks like Uncle Rory's toolbox."

"The music box is inside. This metal thing protects it." Emmy opened the metal container, pulled the music box from the fabric padding inside and showed it to the girls.

"It looks old and yucky," Heather said.

Isabella put a hand to her mouth. "It looks like a magic box, Mommy."

"It is rather magical." Emmy pulled a short strand of leather with a single key attached from inside the metal container. She used the key to wind up the box, moved a small lever and the box began to play.

Isabella put both hands to her mouth. Heather rolled her eyes.

"Do you recognize this song?" Emmy asked.

"It's the song our piano teacher plays," Heather said. "Doesn't it play anything else?"

"I think that song is beautiful, Mommy," Isabella said.

Emmy let the song finish. "There is something else I should show you."

"What is it, Mommy?" Isabella stared at the music box with wide opened eyes.

Emmy took the key and inserted it into a tiny keyhole hidden in a dark spot of the polished wood. She turned the key ever so slightly and a drawer popped open without a sound.

"This is a secret compartment, and it can only be opened with this key." *Or anything else thin enough to press against the release.* "This key can never be lost, or else you can't open the box."

Isabella nodded while Heather rolled her eyes.

"When I was a little girl, I started putting my special treasures in the secret compartment." Emmy opened the drawer all the way and reached inside. She pulled out her treasures and held them up for the girls to see.

"Is that a CD?" Heather asked. "Is that what really plays the music?"

"No, this is an autographed CD that your father gave me. It's the first CD they ever made," Emmy explained. She held up the CD for the girls to see.

"Mom!" Heather sighed. "I have that CD upstairs. It's Daddy's old music."

Emmy showed them the second release by Fridays At Five, which didn't impress Heather at all. She pulled out a folded note written on faded purple stationery. "This was written by your father and given to me on my twentieth birthday. It's a story about a book he bought."

"Can we read the book, Mommy?" Isabella asked.

Emmy chuckled, "Only if you are fluent in Italian and want to read a very boring book."

"What else is in there?" Heather asked. "Anything fun?"

Emmy pulled out a piece of purple ribbon. "This is from Uncle Tony. He gave it to me on the day I met Mama Bertucci and his sister Heather."

"That's the Heather you are named for," Isabella reminded her sister. "Remember? We saw her name in the cemetery place."

Emmy bit her lip as she held the fragile ribbon in her hand.

"You wore that in your hair on your wedding day, didn't you, Emmy?" Mom Colwell hugged her.

"Yes, but it has a different meaning now. Back then it was

something borrowed and kinda blue." Emmy replaced the ribbon, note and CDs and then pulled out three small baggies. "This is the best treasure of all," Emmy said to the girls.

"It looks like hair," Heather said after inspecting the baggies.

"It is hair, but it's very special hair. It's a lock of hair from each of my most precious..." Emmy stopped.

"It's hair from Mommy's miracles," Mom Colwell continued. "It's the first hair cut from you girls and your brother."

"Oooh! That's my hair," Isabella read her name.

"I want to play my iPod. Can we go, Mommy?" Heather asked.

"Yes, you may go," Me-maw said.

Heather dashed away.

Isabella hugged Emmy. "I like your treasures, Mommy. Maybe I should find a secret place to put Doll Kitty because she's starting to fall apart again."

"That is a good idea, Isa. I will help you find something."

Isabella left to join her sister.

Mom Colwell hugged Emmy. "Is there any doubt now?"

Emmy managed a small smile.

Chapter Eight

"I have to spend most of the day on my book, you guys. Denise got on my case yesterday because I haven't written anything for a week," Emmy explained. "I'll make dinner, but you are on your own for lunch."

"Sofia and I will handle things, Em. You can have the day to work," Kenny offered.

"Thanks, I'll make it up later."

Emmy made breakfast for the kids and Kenny. She filled her coffee thermos and locked herself in the den.

"Where did I leave off that chapter about Nashville?" She checked her laptop and found the place she stopped. She read the beginning of the chapter and gathered her thoughts before continuing to write the rest of the chapter.

We, the band, went out to eat and returned to the church around six. We got ready for the concert, which started at seven. So far I hadn't seen Kenny or Denny. Denny picked him up and took him out for dinner. They didn't get back to the church until after Rob's set had started. Denny kept Kenny hidden as he looked out at the crowd. He saw me and Chase on the front row off to the side.

Rob finished his set, and they took a short break. By now everyone in the band knew Kenny was there. The guys got tuned up and a couple minutes after eight, we were introduced. We started off with our normal opening song. The crowd tonight was much younger and more enthusiastic than the night before. I noticed that Chase moved "Yolanda's Song" up in the set, but I didn't suspect anything. He often made little changes in the set list. After the fourth song, Chase introduced the band. I noticed this was earlier than usual. Chase was doing it now because this gave Kenny time to get ready. After the band introductions, the stage lights dimmed. There was a spotlight on me as I began to introduce the song. I heard a bit of commotion on the stage to my right and in the crowd. Chase had warned Stuart to be ready to mute my microphone in case I dropped it. I closed my eyes as I usually did to introduce the song. I said a quick prayer and then began. Kenny was on stage, and, as quietly as he could, he moved next to, and a little behind, me. He stayed out of the spotlight.

"Our next song was written by a dear friend of mine. It's about a girl who went to our church. She was taken home a while back."

My voice began to crack, and, at this point, Kenny began to strum his guitar. I heard the guitar and knew it wasn't Steve or Dixie. I turned to look and nearly dropped my microphone. Kenny stopped playing for a few seconds and set his guitar down. Steve and Dixie took over as Kenny and I hugged.

Chase said, "Please welcome Kenny Colwell the writer of 'Yolanda's Song.'"

The audience got extremely loud as they realized who was on the stage.

"Kenny and Emmy have been friends since she was a little girl, and she didn't know he was going to be here tonight. Please excuse us for surprising her like this. She can be a little emotional at times." Chase made a face at me. "Oh, by the way, I should mention they are getting married next month."

The crowd erupted again.

I looked over at Chase. "You are going to get it!" I managed to compose myself enough to start the song. "I'm sorry for crying like this, but it's just the way I am. If you give me a moment I will start again."

I paused and looked up at Kenny. I held the microphone at my side so Stuart knew to keep it muted. Kenny picked up his guitar, and I moved closer. I can't tell you everything I said to him as we hugged because it is too personal, but I will share what I said out loud.

"I'm happy to see you, but you're gonna get it after the service." I didn't mean it in a bad way.

79

He smiled and started playing the song. I turned back to face the audience.

"As I started to say before, this song..."

I managed to get through the song without crying since Kenny was with me. He stayed on stage for the rest of our set but switched to an electric guitar. We finished and I went backstage with him. Even though there were other people watching, I gave Kenny a long, and very passionate, kiss. I shoved my tongue down his throat.

"I'm so glad you're here. When did you get here? Where are you staying? How long are you gonna be here?"

"Slow down, Em! I just got here this evening. I just had to see you before we left for Australia. Are you mad?"

I kissed him again in case he didn't understand that I was far from mad at him.

"Denny met me and took me out for dinner. I'm sorry if I embarrassed you."

"You didn't embarrass me. Did I embarrass you by getting all emotional. I'm sorry I hugged you so hard."

"I'll survive. I think you only bruised my ribs. I don't think they're broken."

"I didn't see Denny. Is he still here?"

"He's with the guys. Do you want to see him?"

"Yes! I want his autograph."

I paused for a moment and then smacked Kenny's arm.

"You stinker! Chase told me Denny was going to be here, and I told him I wish I had known because I would have brought my CDs for him to sign."

"Why does that make me a stinker?"

"I don't know why, but it just does. Come on! Lets find Denny."

I took Kenny's hand, and we went to find Denny Dottery.

"There he is with Rob and Chase. Please stay with me. I'm too nervous to meet him by myself."

Some of the other people, who were backstage in

80

the church's fellowship hall, thought it was funny that a local guy like Denny Dottery could make me nervous when I was perfectly at ease with one of the biggest rock stars in the world.

"There you are, Emmy. Denny wants to meet you," Chase said.

I couldn't imagine why he would want to meet me.

Chase brought me over to talk to Denny. I bit my lip, and was almost to shy to even say hello. Kenny shook hands with Denny and teased me, "Emmy made me stay with her because she was too nervous to meet you by herself."

"Kenny!" I poked him in his ribs. "Did you have to say that?"

"I'm happy to meet you, Emmy. I'm a big fan of your music."

I smiled but was too tongue-tied to say anything.

"Please forgive my little friend, Denny. She's a bit shy around some people."

Denny looked at Kenny, then back at me. I moved close to Kenny and he put his arm on my shoulder.

"She's too shy to meet me. Incredible. Emmy, you do realize who's standing next to you?"

"This is just Kenny. He's my best friend in the world. I have never been shy around him."

"That's a fact."

"Did I mention we're getting married in a month?" I held up my hand to show off my engagement ring.

"Congratulations, Emmy." Denny smiled at me because I seemed to be acting like a teenager in love.

"Can I have your autograph? I'll find something for you to sign."

"I'll sign something for you if you sign my CD."

I giggled. "Sure! I'll sign something for you."

Later after everything had settled down, the crew started loading out the gear.

Hank told Chase, "We'll handle everything here. Why don't you take Kenny and Emmy and your friends out for dinner or something? We'll be ready to roll out of here when you get back."

"Are you sure, Hank? We've never done it this way before."

Everyone started laughing. Chase wondered why. "What's so funny?"

"You do know we're in Nashville right. Ever hear of Waylon Jennings?" Hank asked.

"Oh, yeah. I get I get it now. Ha! Ha!"

Chase found Rob and Beth. They took Kenny, Denny and me out to eat. I stayed close by Kenny and held his hand all the time. I didn't want to let him out of my sight. I smiled shyly at Denny while we ate. I hope he didn't think I was flirting.

"Will you take a picture for me, Kenny? You can use my phone."

"Sure, Emmy. Who do you want a picture of? As if I can't guess."

"Me with Denny. Do you mind? I want to email it to Kristen tonight."

"Of course I will, sweetie."

Kenny took a couple pictures for me, and he asked the waitress to take a shot of the whole group. She happily obliged because she knew it would mean a bigger tip.

We got back to the church and the truck was loaded and ready to roll.

"Thanks, guys. I'll make it up to you someday," Chase said to the guys, and then he walked over to where Kenny and I were holding hands and making eyes at each other. "Are you staying in Nashville tonight, Kenny?"

My ears perked up as I waited for his answer. I admit I was torn between doing the right thing and sharing a room with my fiancee. What difference would it make? We would be sharing a bed in less than a month.

He grinned at me. "Yes, I'm going to be here tonight and fly to St. Louis tomorrow. Why?"

"You're going to St. Louis? So are we," I said.

"I know, Em."

I whispered something to Kenny, and he whispered back.

Emmy paused and sat back. *Should I say what we said to each other? It's pretty personal. Of course, it wouldn't matter now since we're married.* She listened as the girls shouted at each other. *Kenny and Sofia can handle it.* She read the last paragraph again. *Denise will tell me to cut it unless I reveal what was said. I'll put in it for the time being.* She put a finger to her mouth and then began typing again.

No, I'm not telling you what we said. It's much too personal. I will admit that it concerned sex, but that's all I'm saying.

"What are you guys talking about?" Chase asked.

"Nothing," I answered, and I know I turned red. That answered Chase's question without me saying anything.

"Emmy, would you like to stay overnight with Kenny and fly into St. Louis in the morning?" Chase asked, as if I were his child.

"Can I?" I looked at Kenny and then at Chase. I didn't know how he would react to me staying overnight with Kenny since we weren't married yet. I bit my lip. I knew that no one would ever say anything. Kenny and I could share a room, and a bed, without anyone ever knowing other than the guys in the band. "Would you mind, Chase?"

"Not at all. As long as I get to use the bedroom on the bus!"

I giggled and then kissed Kenny. "Will you buy me a plane ticket?"

"We'll check the flights when we get back to the hotel."

I blushed as I looked around the room. "We are engaged," I whispered to Chase.

"I didn't say anything, Emmy," Chase said.

I looked at Kenny, "Did you already check into your room?"

"Yes, why?"

"Does it have two beds?"

"Two queen-size beds as a matter of fact."

I looked at Chase, "See, we can each have our own bed. We won't be sleeping together." I knew that would probably not be the case, but I tried to sell it to him.

"No one is judging you, Emmy."

"I want to be able to look you in the eye tomorrow with a clear conscience. That's all."

"It's all right, Emmy," Chase said and then walked over to the guys. I followed him. "Emmy is going to stay in Nashville tonight and fly into St. Louis with Kenny in the morning."

"Lucky girl! Who gets the bedroom tonight?" Dixie asked.

"I think it's only fair that Hank gets the bedroom since he is the oldest."

"I thought you wanted it, Chase," I reminded him.

"I was just saying that to tease you. Hank has trouble sleeping in the bunk, so he can have the bed."

"You're too good to us, Chase."

Jess and Joe walked over to me. "You were so special tonight, Miss Emmy. Better than ever. We'll see you tomorrow in St. Louis."

"Thank you so much. I'll see you in the morning."

I told everyone good night, and then I saw Dixie talking to Kenny. I walked over to listen to them.

"I'll see you tomorrow, Dixie." I held Kenny's hand as I looked up at Dixie. I knew he understood.

"Have a good time tonight, Emmy. Have a safe flight. Do you guys need a ride from the airport?"

"We'll just take a cab, Dixie. Thanks for the offer, though," Kenny answered.

"No problem. Let us know if you change your mind," Dixie said and then walked away.

Kenny and I watched as the bus and truck pulled

out. Rob and Beth dropped us off at the hotel, and we headed up to the room. I don't ever remember feeling like this before. I've wanted to sleep with Kenny for a long time, but it never seemed like it was going to happen as much as tonight. Kenny checked the flights into St. Louis and booked two seats on a flight into Lambert International. I stayed up for a while to talk with him. We were both prolonging the time before we went to bed. I was nervous because I was about to lose my virginity. Kenny acted nervously because it would be our first time together. That's a sly way to say he wasn't a virgin. After thirty minutes of talking and trying not to touch each other, I confronted him.

"Do you think it's wrong for us to even stay in the same hotel room? We know we aren't going to share a bed, but everyone else might think we are." I didn't believe a word of that, but I wanted to see his reaction. He looked disappointed.

"I suppose I could have gotten you a room of your own."

I giggled and then said, "I'm glad you didn't." I bit my lip as I rationalized. "In less than a month we will be married. Then we can sleep together every night. Will it really matter if we get a head start?"

"This will be your choice, Em, although I know how you feel."

"Nashville would be a good place to spend our honeymoon."

"But we already have reservations in Ireland," he reminded me.

"Lots of couples start early."

"So true."

Okay, to end the suspense, we kissed and held onto each other, but we didn't share a bed. Not all night, I mean. We did cuddle together for a while, but I fell asleep. Patience might be a virtue, but it's sure not an easy one to follow.

Emmy closed her eyes. *How did I ever have the strength to not sleep with him that night? I doubt I could go back in time and make the same choice.* She saved the chapter, set the laptop on the desk and walked out to the kitchen.

"Are you getting some work done, Emmy?" Kenny asked.

"Yes, I am. Do you remember that night when you surprised me in Nashville?" She poured out her cold coffee and opened the fridge to grab a bottle of water.

Kenny nodded. "Are you writing about that night?"

"Yes, but I didn't reveal what I said to you."

"That's good. You might need to be censored."

"Do you think it would have been wrong to go ahead and sleep together? We were engaged."

Kenny put his hands on her shoulders. "If you have to ask, then I think you know the answer."

"Denise will probably tell me to cut the chapter down."

"Mommy, Kevin Michael is bothering us. We want to play without him," Heather complained.

"Take it up with your father and Sofia. I'm working today." Emmy headed back to the den and started writing again.

I woke up and looked at the clock. It was after nine. I jumped out of bed and looked for Kenny. His bed was empty. I threw on some clothes, threw all my stuff in my bag and took a look around the room. I took the elevator downstairs and found Kenny having some coffee and a bagel.

"Sorry I overslept, but now I'm ready to go."

"Relax, Emmy. We don't have to be at the airport for another hour."

"Oh good. I was so worried I might miss the plane."

"Did you think I would leave without you?"

"No, I guess you wouldn't."

My phone rang and I looked to see who was calling.

"It's Tony. I should talk to him."

"Say hello for me."

"Hi, Tony, I thought about calling you last night,

but it was too late. You'll never guess who's with me."

"Hello to you, Emmy, and say hi to Kenny for me."

"Did you know he was coming to Nashville? Did Kristen know, too?"

"I'm sorry, we couldn't tell you. Were you surprised?"

"Totally surprised. I started bawling like a baby and almost dropped my microphone. It was so embarrassing, but so sweet. Chase had to keep things together until I could talk again. How are you doing?"

"I'm doing just fine. Mama says hi. She wants to know if you are getting enough to eat."

"I'm eating a lot of stuff. Everywhere we go, they feed us. I might gain fifty pounds before I get home. I'll never fit into my wedding dress."

"I doubt that."

"Do you miss me at all?" I asked.

"Are you gone?"

"Very funny."

I talked to Tony for a few minutes, but then we needed to get to the airport.

"I've got to run. I'll be home sometime in the early morning on Sunday or Saturday. You know what I mean."

"Will you want a ride to church?"

"Probably. I'll be too tired to drive."

On the way to the airport I got a text from Chase letting me know that everyone arrived safe and sound in St. Louis. Hank thanked me for the use of the bed. I laughed and wondered if Hank would let me have my bedroom back.

Kenny and I landed in St. Louis. Since we didn't check any bags, we made good time through the airport. Kenny hailed a taxi and gave the driver the address of New Horizon Methodist Church. The driver looked at Kenny and didn't say anything, but he took a long look at me.

"Excuse me, Miss, but you look a lot like this singer my daughter listens to all the time. Holy cow! It is you.

Jackie is going to see you tonight. It's all she has been talking about for the last week. You are Emmy Colasanti, aren't you?"

"Yes I am." I giggled because I couldn't believe what just happened. "Let me give you a note for your daughter. Tell her to come and see me before the service. I would like to meet her. What was her name again?"

"Her name is Jackie, Jackie Tomkins."

"Please give her my note okay."

"I'll do that, Miss Colasanti. She will be so amazed that I had you in my cab. Just think a real celebrity."

I giggled again and Kenny poked me in her ribs.

The cab driver looked back at us again. "A real celebrity. In my cab. Unbelievable!"

Chase met us when we got to the church. The driver asked if he could have a picture. Chase offered to take a picture of the driver with Kenny on one side and me on the other. He still didn't recognize Kenny. Chase used the driver's phone to take a couple pictures.

"Thanks for riding in my taxi."

"Thank you for the ride. How much do we owe you?"

"Nothing. I forgot to turn on the meter."

Kenny gave him forty dollars to cover the ride and tip. I handed him the note to give to his daughter.

"I'm off duty now. I can't wait to show this picture to my daughter."

"Don't forget to give her the note."

"I won't. I promise."

The driver left, and I started teasing Kenny. The cab driver must have been the only person in St. Louis who hadn't ever heard of Fridays At Five.

"I'm a celebrity. What was your name again? How do I know you?"

"Very funny, Em."

He tried to grab me, but I got away. He chased me around while the band watched wondering what was happening. I'm sure Dixie thought it was our way of

88

having foreplay. I know he thought we slept together because he asked me about it later. Anyway, I ran over to Hank and hid behind him.

Hank asked, "What is going on? Did you guys have a fight?"

I tried to explain. "The taxi driver recognized me, but not Kenny. His daughter is a fan of our band, and he thought I was a celebrity. He had Chase take a picture of us."

Chase was almost on his knees because he was laughing so hard. The other guys were listening, and they too were just dying with laughter.

"She is coming to the service, and I want to meet her. I gave her father a note so I would know who she is."

His daughter wrote me a letter a couple of months later and told me what happened. The taxi driver, Mr. Tomkins, made it home. He ran in the house yelling for his daughter.

"Jackie! Where are you? I need to show you something."

"I'm in the kitchen, Daddy. What do you want to show me?"

"You'll never believe who was in my cab."

"I don't know. Who, or do I have to stand here and guess all night?"

"Emmy Colasanti."

"Get out! Why would she be in your cab?"

"She flew into Lambert, and I took her and a friend to the church where they are playing tonight. I had someone take a picture of me with Emmy and the guy with her. I'll show you. Oh, and she gave me this note. She wants to meet you before the show. Here! Look at the picture."

Jackie looked at the picture and saw that it was indeed me. She took another look at the picture and fainted. She fell to the floor.

"Jackie! Are you all right? Mother, come here quick! Jackie fainted." Or words to that effect.

Her mother came running and held Jackie's head until she revived a few seconds later.

"Sweetheart, are you all right? What happened?"

"I was looking at the picture."

"I'm sorry, baby. I didn't realize seeing a picture of Emmy Colasanti would affect you so much."

"Daddy! Did you see who else is in the shot?"

"Of course. One of her friends. Some guy. I never got his name."

"Oh! My! God! Daddy! Are you kidding me?"

Jackie ran to her room and returned in a few seconds holding a CD in her hand.

"Look at this picture on the back of this CD."

She showed her father a picture of Kenny Colwell. He looked at the CD for a few seconds and then at Jackie.

"That looks like the guy who was with Emmy today."

"That happens to be Kenny Colwell of Fridays At Five! You have heard of them, right?"

"Sure. I took you to see them last year. Are you telling me that I had him in my cab and didn't even know it?"

"Yes!"

"I need to sit down before I faint."

I made Kenny promise not to include this story in his book. I think it's funny and selfishly wanted it for mine. He can use the sex part in his book. He's the rock star after all.

Meanwhile, back at the church, Kenny and I were talking. "What time do you have to leave?"

"I need to leave right after your concert."

"Service," I corrected him.

"I need to leave right after your service. We're flying out real early. I'm cutting it pretty close by waiting until after the service, but I want to hear you once more before we're married."

"You're so sweet. I should marry you or something." I loved to tease him.

Just before the service started a young girl slowly approached me. I saw her and suspected it might be the cab driver's daughter.

"Jackie, is that you?"

"Hi. Yes, I'm Jackie Tomkins. I'm sorry to bother you, but my father gave me this note to give to you so you would know who I am."

"I'm happy to meet you, Jackie."

I looked at the note I had written in the cab and then I tugged on Kenny's arm. He had his back turned while he was talking to Chase. Kenny turned around to see what I needed.

"Jackie, this is my fiancee and friend, Kenny Colwell."

"Hello, Jackie. I'm glad to meet you."

Kenny offered his hand, but Jackie stood stone still and couldn't seem to speak.

"Jackie, are you okay? Do you need to sit down? Do you need a glass of water?"

Jackie was finally able to speak after a few seconds. "I'll be alright. It's really you."

"Why don't you sit down for a moment?" I grabbed a bottle of water from the stage and handed it to Jackie. "Have a drink, Jackie. You look so pale."

"I'm okay. I just couldn't believe it. Daddy showed me the picture with both of you, and I fainted."

"Does that happen often?" I was sincerely concerned about her health.

"Never before. I think it was just the shock of seeing the two of you with my father. I've been a Fridays fan since I got your first CD. I was just a kid, but I loved the music. I have all your CDs and yours, too, Emmy. Oh! I sound like a dork. Please don't laugh at me."

"Why would we do that?" Kenny asked.

"You should know that we are just regular people who happen to sing. We aren't anything special. Well, I'm not anyway. I guess Kenny is."

"I'm not either. Don't believe her, Jackie."

91

"I know you have been friends forever. I read that on your website. And you're getting married, too."

"We have been friends for a very long time. Are you here with friends? Where are you sitting?"

"I'm here with one of my girlfriends. Our seats are over there about halfway back."

"Please come and see me after the service and bring your friend. I'd like to meet her and talk to you some more."

"Thank you, Miss Colasanti."

"It's Emmy. Please call me Emmy."

"Okay. Naomi is not going to believe this is really happening."

Jackie went back to her friend, and Kenny and I headed backstage.

"I could never do this at one of our shows, Em. The security is so tight that I almost never get to meet the fans anymore. Maybe I should join your band as a backup guitar player."

"Well, I would have to hear you play before I let you in the band."

"You stinker. You'll pay for that."

I teased Kenny and we ran backstage and right into Chase. "Are you guys goofing around again?"

"Sorry, Chase. Kenny was asking if he could join our band, and I told him I would have to hear him play first."

"You guys are goofy." Chase shook his head. He told me later that he wondered what it would be like to have Kenny in the band.

There was an altar call at the end of the service. I looked around to see if I could spot Jackie and her friends. I saw Jackie with her friend at the altar. Jackie had her arm on her shoulder and appeared to be praying with her. I walked over and knelt to pray with them. Jackie explained that her friend Naomi had just accepted Christ.

"Naomi, if you need one, please go back to our

table and pick up a New Testament and a copy of the devotional book. You should take one also, Jackie. I use it everyday, and I find it to be a great help."

"Thank you, Emmy. We will."

Naomi looked at me with tears still flowing down her face. "When you sang that song about the young girl I just knew that I needed to accept Jesus before I left here tonight. Thank you for coming to our church."

"Moments like this are why we do what we do. This makes everything worthwhile."

"We put our names on your email list. Jackie Tomkins and Naomi Belton."

"Good! I'll remember your names. We try to send out an email at least once a month. We send one out whenever we are going to be on tour in your area also. I try very hard to answer all the emails I receive, but it sometimes takes a while."

I hugged both girls and made Jackie promise to stay in touch. She did for several years, but then we kinda lost track of each other. I hope she's still going to church.

"Em, I really need to get back. I know you guys are heading home tonight, but I've gotta fly. I'll see you at the end of the month." We kissed for close to a whole minute and then Kenny had to go.

It was after midnight when the truck and bus hit the road for home. Chase and I were the only ones who had to work in the morning service although Chase expected everyone else to be in church. On the bus Chase had a moment to talk to Stuart Lederer, the sound guy. "You are always welcome to join us for service, Stuart."

"Thanks, Chase. I might just take you up on that. After seeing first hand what a difference Jesus makes in your lives, I think I want to be a part of that."

"You can be a part of it right now, Stuart. You don't have to wait another minute. You don't need to be in a church. Just ask Emmy where she and Tony were when they were saved."

"Okay. Will you help me?"

"Yes, we will all pray with you if you want."

Everyone on the bus had been listening quietly as Chase talked to Stuart. They all gathered around and began to pray with him. Stuart became the newest member of the family of God as he knelt on the bus.

When we were about a half hour away from the church, I called Kristen. She agreed to meet me. She arrived at the church a couple minutes before we did. I saw her as soon as I stepped off the bus. I dropped my bag, ran over to her and threw my arms around her. "Oh, Krissy, it's so good to be home."

"You owe me big time for getting out of bed and picking you up. I should have made you walk home," Kristen said, but she wasn't serious.

"Thank you for being such a good friend, Krissy."

"Oh, I suppose you would have done the same thing for me."

"Not a chance. I wouldn't have gotten out of bed to pick you up," I teased.

The Zawaski brothers come over to say good night.

"Good night, Miss Emmy. Good night, Miss Kristen. We will see you in the morning.. Emmy did a great job."

By the time I got home, Kenny was in the air. It would take twenty-four hours to get to Sydney.

Emmy sat back and took a drink of water. *I wonder how hard it would be to track down some of the kids who were on the email list back in those days? We should have done a better job of following up. Maybe after the summer tour is over, I could have Jana and the ladies in the office cross check those old lists with current ones. Maybe even Facebook.* She put the cap back on the water and set it on the table next to her. *I should finish this chapter with that Sunday at church. Where did I put my journal?* She found it under a sales ad from Sainsbury's and spent several minutes reading about coming home that day. *I don't remember much about the ride home. I suppose I fell asleep right away.*

94

Although we were both tired, no one could tell as Chase and I led the worship team in the morning service. Chase shared a few of the details about the tour. I also recounted some of the highlights. I used Naomi and Jackie as examples of why we went on tour. We asked for continued prayer support since the worship team would be on the road again starting Tuesday morning.

When I got home after church, I was totally wiped out. Tony and John were at the house. They brought some food over that Mama had prepared because she knew I would be too tired to cook.

"Mama made some lasagna and a corn souffle. I picked up some bread and Kristen was supposed to put together a salad," Tony explained.

"Thanks, Tony. I'm almost too tired to even think about eating."

I made it through lunch and then fell asleep on the couch in the TV room.

"Tony, would you carry her upstairs and put her on her bed?" Kristen asked.

"I suppose I could carry her. Should I toss her on the bed, or lay her down gently?"

John and Kristen laughed. "She is so out of it, that I don't think it would matter. But maybe you should be gentle with her."

I think I slept for three hours before I woke up. I got out of bed and realized I didn't have my jeans on anymore. I saw them folded neatly on the dresser and slipped into them. I went downstairs and found Tony, John and Kristen in the TV room. I sat next to Tony.

"Did you have a long enough nap, Emmy?" Kristen asked.

"Yes, I feel much better now," I paused then continued, "I thought I had jeans on earlier, but when I woke up, I didn't. In fact, I don't remember going up to bed at all."

"You fell asleep down here and I carried you upstairs, Em. I put you on your bed."

"Did you take my jeans off, too? Did you look at me when you did that, you creep?" I punched his arm.

Kristen came to Tony's rescue. "He didn't take off your jeans, Em. I did, so don't be upset with him."

I looked at Tony and bit my lip. "I'm sorry for hitting you. Thanks for carrying me upstairs."

"Can you tell us about the tour now? Did you have fun?"

I spent twenty minutes going over some of the highlights of the tour.

"Did the old guys in the band tease you a lot?" Tony asked.

"Not as much as you would have, but they did a little. Dixie teased me more than anyone, I guess."

"He's the only one even close to your age, Em," John added.

"Yeah, what are you implying?"

"Nothing."

"He knows I'm engaged."

"I didn't mean anything, Emmy."

I wondered if there was something to what John said. Could it be possible that I had somehow given Dixie the wrong impression. I know I teased him. Maybe he took it as flirting. If that was the case, I would have to correct that immediately.

Emmy rested her chin in her hand. *Should I mention anything about my relationship with Tony?* She bit her lip for a moment. *I could always add something later if Denise thinks I should. Kenny knows most of what happened, but not everything. I'll think about it.* She saved her work and shut down her laptop.

96

Chapter Nine

Emmy walked into the Starbucks on Canton Lane. She glanced around, saw several women seated at a table laughing, smiled at a grandmother holding a young girl and then spotted Denise talking on the phone at a table in the back. Denise looked up, saw Emmy and waved to the chair opposite her. Emmy pointed to the counter to indicate she would buy something first.

"I don't care if he thinks his story doesn't need to be edited," Denise said angrily. "I think it sucks, and I have the final word. If he doesn't like that, tell him to take his story somewhere else." Denise lowered her head and sighed. She looked up as Emmy approached and said, "As soon as the kids are out of college, I will leave this behind me and concentrate on my fiction. How are you, Emmy? How are the kids? Are they still interrupting you every five minutes?"

"I'm doing all right, and Kenny and Sofia are taking care of the kids for the most part."

"What do you have to show me?" Denise took a long drink of her coffee.

Emmy pulled a hard copy of her first four chapters out of her canvas bag.

"Where did you get that? My daughter could use that for school."

"I think I got it at Sainsbury's," Emmy answered.

Denise reached across the table, pulled Emmy's copy in front of her and began to read. Emmy watched as Denise flipped through the pages at a rapid pace.

She must need to be a speed reader because of her job. Emmy took a sip of her White Chocolate Mocha Frappuccino.

"Okay, this isn't bad for a first draft. I want you to concentrate on making sure you show the reader more than just telling them. I'll give you an example..."

Denise pointed out several scenes and ways they could be improved.

"You want the scenes to jump off the page at the reader. You want them to feel the excitement in the air as you begin to sing. You want them to smell the dry ice and blink at the light show." Denise waved her hands around as she smiled. "I'm going to be swamped for the next month. Let's plan to meet in early October. Keep plugging away and don't be discouraged. You have an interesting story to tell, and I want to help make it happen. I gotta run. You can stay in touch via email or text me if you get stuck on something."

"Thanks, Denise." Emmy watched as Denise put on her wide-brimmed burgundy hat, grabbed her briefcase, gulped down the last of her coffee and swept out of the Starbucks like a one-woman-flotilla. Emmy put her hard copy back in her bag and took her Frappuccino back to the car. *I should use the library to work this morning.* She drove to the library, found an empty table in the back and pulled out her laptop.

I woke up early Tuesday morning, rolled over in bed and snuggled under the covers. I was savoring my last few moments before I needed to get up. Kristen walked into my room and sat on the edge of the bed.

"Are you gonna sleep all day?"

I smiled and asked, "No, I can tell it's still early. Did you have breakfast yet?"

"Not yet. I thought I would wake you up so you could make pancakes."

"I'll make pancakes. Give me a couple minutes to use the bathroom and throw on some clothes. Are the guys coming over this morning?"

"Not that I'm aware of. Why? Did you want to see them before you leave?"

"I guess not." I got out of bed and made my way downstairs. I made the pancakes as Kristen finished getting ready for work.

"These smell good. Do we have any maple syrup left?"

"On the second shelf, I think. Hey, Krissy..."

"Yeah, what?"

"Did the wedding invitations get mailed?"

"Yes, Emmy. They've all been sent."

"Thank you. You're the best friend in the whole world." I hugged Kristen. "Do you think Tony or John would be willing to give me a ride to the church this morning?"

"Oh, right, I forgot. Tony said he would, but it will cost you. His words, not mine."

Today the band and crew and I would be leaving for our third five-day tour. I skipped the second week because nothing out of the ordinary happened, and I know no one wants to read about every single show. This time we would be stopping in Milwaukee, Minneapolis, Des Moines, Kansas City and Carbondale. Since there would be more driving this week Chase added a fourth driver. Carl Twilley is another cousin to Larry and Buck Twilley. Dixie Case spent the weekend with Steve Van Zant rather than fly home to Alabama. He was thinking about moving into the area because he would have more job opportunities. He and Alan Vicini talked about putting a band together. Dixie would love the chance to front a band. I think he would be pretty good at it. The ladies would love him.

I had to be at the church by noon. Tonight's service started at seven and Chase wanted to be in Milwaukee by three. The guys loaded the truck in the morning with help from several men from the church. Jess and Joe Zawaski supervised the loading. Chase debated sending the truck on ahead but decided to have the truck and bus travel together for today. Shortly after eleven thirty the guys in the band started arriving at the church. The drivers pulled into the parking lot and inspected the truck and bus. Larry and Cecil would be driving the bus and Buck and Carl would handle the truck. Stuart Lederer was bringing his son, Ryan, on this trip since he was on break from college. Ryan would be helping his father while he was learning the business. Ryan had also been taking lessons on the guitar since he was twelve. For the last three years he had been taking bass guitar lessons. He knew all of

99

our songs, which came in handy later. Hank showed up, but in obvious pain. Chase tried to talk him into staying home but Hank wanted to give it a try. I was the last one to show up at the church. Tony gave me a ride as promised and hung around while everyone's gear was loaded.

The bus and truck pulled out of the church parking lot. Soon we were on Interstate 55 heading to Milwaukee. The guys sat in the lounge area talking about the last couple of days. Hank tried to get his back to relax, but his muscles were still tight and felt strained. I noticed and offered to help. Hank ended up using the bedroom and put a heating pad on his back. I said a prayer for Hank because unless he improved dramatically, I doubted he could play tonight.

By the time we arrived at Damascus Road Church in Milwaukee, Hank was up and feeling better. Chase instructed him to take it easy, and they would take care of his gear.

"I can still help with the merchandise table," Hank insisted.

"Okay, but don't be lifting anything. We need you to be able to play. We can take care of the other things, but we need you to play bass."

Hank took it easy, and everyone pitched in to help unload the truck and the bus. By five thirty everything was ready to go. We did a thorough soundcheck until Stuart and Chase were satisfied with the results.

Brian Compton was the senior pastor, and he took the group downstairs for a quick meal. "I trust this is enough to help you get through until afterward. We will have more food for after the concert."

"This is just perfect, Pastor Brian. It will take the edge of our appetites," Chase assured him. I wondered if it would be enough to feed the hungry guys.

"Where are you headed after here?"

"Minneapolis. Calvary Chapel to be exact. I've never been there, but I did check out the website."

"I have an old friend on staff there by the name of Willis Berringer. We went to college together. Would you tell him I said hi?"

"Certainly."

Shortly after six thirty everyone met with Pastor Brian in a small room behind the platform for prayer. We prayed for Hank's physical needs especially. Because of Hank's back problem he had a stool on stage in case he needed it. The service began at seven with a prayer and a few songs by the local worship leader, John Yeaney. He led the crowd in a few worship songs before introducing the band.

As I came out to the platform, I prayed for God's guidance. All of a sudden, I sensed an urgent need to pray for the teens of the church.

"Chase, can we wait just a moment, please?"

"Sure, Emmy. Is something wrong?"

"I just feel a need to pray for the teens."

"Hang on guys."

I said a quick prayer for the teens in the church, then they continued to their places on the platform.

"Hello everyone and thank you for being here tonight. We are the Crest Ridge Worship Team from SoHam. We're going to sing some songs that we hope you know. Please sing along if you want."

I still sensed that something was not quite right after the first three songs.

"Chase, I feel that we should do 'Yolanda's Song' now. I don't know why, but I just feel led to do it now instead of later."

"Then we should, Emmy."

Chase informed the other guys of the switch in the set. I introduced the song and began singing. Before I finished the first verse there were twenty teens at the altar. By the end of the song there were over a hundred teens at the front of the church. I didn't know what to do. I'd never seen this kind of reaction to anything. I glanced at Chase for guidance. He whispered to back off and let the local pastor take over. Pastor Brian came back to the platform and led an altar service. The youth leader, Graham Dancose, moved through the teens to pray with them. John Yeaney came over to talk with Chase and me, while we sat on the side of the platform.

"I'm sure you had no idea, but twelve days ago two of our teens were killed in a car accident."

I trembled as I closed my eyes. Chase put an arm around me for comfort.

"Emmy sensed something even before we began tonight. We are sorry for the church's loss."

"I think this service will go a long way in beginning the healing process for these kids."

For over thirty minutes Pastor Brian Compton, Graham Dancose and other church leaders prayed with the teens. When they were finished and everyone had returned to their seats, John talked to Graham about how I sensed the need for the teens to have a chance to pray. Please don't think I did anything special. I'm sure there were others who sensed the same need as I did.

Graham took a microphone. "I want to thank Miss Colasanti and the rest of the team for their willingness to follow where our Lord was leading them. They did not know of our loss. I don't know about the rest of you, but I think we should continue with the service. What do you think?"

The audience answered his question by standing and clapping. Graham looked over at Chase and me. "Are you willing to continue? I know you have a long trip ahead of you tonight."

To answer his question the band members took their places and Chase began to play "I Will Be True To You." I sang for the next hour. After the service, I was surrounded by teens. I took the time to talk to them, and I was pleasantly surprised that no one asked for an autograph. I did have my picture taken with some of the teens, though.

After the crowd left, the band members and the

crew loaded out the gear. Only after that had been completed did we have an opportunity to relax and eat. The guys tried to make a big deal out of what I did, but I wasn't taking any credit. I got all over them.

"Will you guys knock it off! I didn't do anything that any of you wouldn't have done."

Chase waved his hand at me. "Hold on, Em. The guys know you are more sensitive to the Holy Spirit than the rest of us. Tonight was just another example of that."

Before we left Pastor Brian handed Chase a check.

"I can't thank you enough for tonight. Hopefully this will help with your expenses."

"Thank you, Pastor Compton. You know we don't do this for the money."

I know it seems like we say that every night and people might think it gets to be a routine, but it's truly how we feel. Sure, we need to pay the expenses, but none of the guys are doing this because they need the money. Actually, because of the structure of the group, no one got paid nearly as much as you might think.

"I know, but it takes money to be able to go on the road," Chase said.

Only then did Chase look at the check. It was for five thousand dollars.

We left Milwaukee and an hour later Hank's back problem flared up again. He was in obvious pain. I knew the bunks couldn't be very comfortable, so I did what I thought I should.

"Hank, you should take the bedroom. I can sleep in a bunk. You need the space more than I do."

"Emmy, I couldn't. You need the privacy." He waved his hands in a negative gesture and even that movement hurt his back.

"Don't be silly. I can sleep in the bunk and no one will see me. We can both use the bathroom in back. Not at the same time of course."

"Some of the guys snore."

Chase heard this comment and answered. "No one

snores any louder than you, Hank. It will be a lot quieter if you sleep in the back. I'm sure Emmy doesn't snore. I'm just assuming that of course."

"Kristen has never mentioned that I do," I said.

After being convinced I would be all right in a bunk, Hank used the bedroom. He headed to bed as soon as I got my pajamas and stuff out. Everyone else stayed up for a while to unwind. They didn't say much about it, but I could tell they were all kinda proud of what we did that night.

"Now we need to remember that we have a lady with us tonight," Chase reminded the guys.

"Where? What lady? All I see is us guys and Emmy," Dixie teased.

"Very funny, Dixie." I stuck my tongue out and looked for something to throw. Then I realized he might take this as flirting again, so I stopped.

"Let's try to behave like gentlemen."

"You might want to fumigate Hank's bunk, Emmy."

"Make sure you change the sheets."

They continued to tease me about sleeping in Hank's bunk.

"You guys are pigs. Ryan will think you are a bunch of immature frat guys."

Ryan smiled at me. He was enjoying his first trip on the bus, even with his father on board.

"Emmy, do you want to use the bathroom first to get ready for bed? You should because it can be a little rank after these guys are finished."

"Maybe I should get ready now, even though I'm not yet sleepy."

I used the bathroom to get into my sleepwear. A t-shirt and running shorts. I had a robe to wear, also. While I was in the bathroom Chase talked to the guys. He didn't think I could hear him, but I could.

"Please remember that Emmy is up here with us. I know everyone is used to some time in the morning to get ready, and we all need to make adjustments."

I finished in the bathroom and rejoined the guys in the lounge. They didn't seem to pay me much attention as they watched a movie. Soon the guys started getting ready for bed and slipping into their bunks. Dixie, Ryan and I were the last ones in the lounge.

"Are we gonna run in the morning, Emmy?" Dixie asked.

"I'd like to. Would you like to join us for a run, Ryan?"

"Would you guys mind if I do?"

"Of course not. We usually do a couple miles. Not too fast a pace. I'm sure you can keep up."

"Okay. What time?"

"Six thirty. Is that all right?"

"I'll see you guys then. Night, Dixie. Good night, Emmy."

"Night, Ryan."

Dixie and I talked for a little while longer before I called it a night. I climbed into the bunk that Hank used. I was right below Dixie's bunk.

Emmy stopped typing and took a moment to read. She bit her lip. *Shoot! This doesn't seem any better than the last chapter. I don't know how to show stuff like Denise wants.* She checked the time. *I need to get home. I've got to get the laundry done before we leave on Friday. The kids are excited about going with us this weekend.* She saved her work and put her laptop away.

She drove home, walked into the kitchen where Heather met her with her hands on her hips.

"Mommy, do we have to take Kevin Michael with us this weekend. Can't we leave him home alone?"

Emmy set her bag on the island. "Why would we do that? Has he been bothering you?"

"Isa and I are learning a new song, and he keeps trying to sing with us, but he ruins it. He can't remember the words, and he sings way too loud." Heather raised her hands over her head to indicate how loud he sang.

"I'm sorry, Heather, but we can't leave him home. That's not what Jesus would want us to do."

"But Jesus could take care of him. You always say he protects us."

Emmy chuckled. "He does, but he's not a babysitter."

Kenny walked into the kitchen carrying a basket of dirty laundry. "How did it go with Denise?"

"All right. She read my stuff in like a minute and then gave me some suggestions. She wants to meet in October. Did you know Heather and Isa are learning a new song?"

"Yes, I heard them practicing. They sound pretty good." Kenny continued into the laundry room.

Emmy followed. "I was going to take care of that."

"I thought I would help get it started. Should I use bleach on the white stuff?"

"Not on any of my stuff," Emmy said. "Let me sort it for you, and then you can take it from there." She sorted the clothes as Kenny watched. "Denise says my scenes need to pop more. She wants to be able to feel the excitement of the concerts and smell the pot in the air. Oh, wait, that's your shows."

"Ha! Ha! I can't help if people smoke. You aren't going to give up, are you?"

"Never! I'm going to finish my first draft and then start going through it. I decided that I will end the book before the kids are born."

"Why then?"

Emmy shrugged. "It has to end somewhere. I'd rather it end then. The kids need to have a private life, and I don't think being in a book would necessarily help that."

"I could help if you want."

Emmy shook her head. "You can help with the laundry, but you aren't going to see my book until you buy a copy, buster."

The landline rang and Emmy walked into the kitchen to check the caller ID. "Yes, this is the Vatican. Would you like to talk to the Pope?" She hopped onto the countertop.

"And you think I'm going to hell," Father James said sternly. "How are you doing with that sex laden book you are writing? Are you spilling all of your filthy secrets?"

"Just the most perverted ones," Emmy answered and then giggled. "How are you?"

"I need to see my little sister and my nieces and nephew."

"You know how to get here. You don't have to wait for an invitation."

"I hate to show up unannounced. Who knows what my tender eyes might see."

"If you're thinking I'm going to let you read my book, forget it. I won't let Kenny read it either."

"I'm not interested in learning about the early sex life of my angelic little sister."

"Aren't you a little bit interested?" She jumped down and retrieved a can of Dr Pepper from the fridge.

"Only if you're willing to come to confession. Where are you going to be this weekend?"

"Two nights in Boston. We're taking the kids with us. You wanna get away for a decadent weekend of sex, drugs and rock and roll?"

"No, I did that last weekend. I checked out the new worship band at St Cecil's. What a bunch of losers."

"You are so supportive."

"Should I bring lunch, or can you feed me?"

"I wouldn't turn down some food from Darby's," Emmy said as she checked the washer to make sure Kenny added soap.

"I have taken a vow of poverty," Father James insisted.

"You are so full of it. I bet you have a hundred bucks in your wallet right now, and besides, Danny never makes you pay for anything. He treats you like you're the Bishop or The Cardinal of SoHam."

"Now that's a promotion I would accept."

"I'll talk to Pope Whatever the Fifth and put in a good word."

"What should I get if I stop at Darby's?"

"Should I call in the order, so it's ready when you arrive?"

"Bless you, my child. That would be lovely. I'll be at your shack as soon as I can. Don't forget to include onions on my dog."

"Yes, Father."

Father James picked up the order from Darby's, and Danny Darby wouldn't let him pay for the food.

"You know the rules, Father James."

"But this is a rather large order, Danny," Father James said. "You have to pay for the parking lot repairs somehow."

Danny shook his head. "Say hi to Emmy and everyone for me. I added three slices of chocolate cake. She will have to figure out how to split them up."

"You are a saint, Danny."

Father James arrived at Emmy's and walked into the kitchen with the two large sacks of food. He set them on the island and hollered. "I hope you have something to wash these fries down with."

Heather and Isabella raced into the kitchen. "We didn't know you were coming over, Father James."

"I wanted to surprise my favorite nieces. Where is your mother?"

"She was upstairs packing clothes for us." Heather pointed. "We're going to fly to Boston with Daddy's band."

"We know a new song. Wanna hear it?" Isabella asked.

"Yes, indeed." He sat on one of the barstools and dug out some fries and his chili dog.

Emmy walked into the kitchen as the girls began singing. "I hope that's not my chili dog." She put her arms around him and kissed his cheek. "Oh, is it a sin to kiss a priest? I forgot."

"I'll cut you some slack since you know the Pope so well."

Kenny and Kevin Micheal appeared. Emmy passed around the food and told the kids to eat at the breakfast table.

"What do you have for a parched throat?" Father James asked.

Emmy pointed toward the garage. "The beer's out there. You know where we keep it. You can help yourself."

"I didn't want to take one without asking."

"Yeah, right." Emmy stuffed three fries into her mouth.

"You guys want one?"

Kenny shook his head.

Emmy nodded.

Father James grinned, "Wait a second. Aren't you members of that Nazarene church now? I believe they frown on the consumption of alcohol."

"Could I have one if I promise to confess to you later," Emmy used her childlike voice.

"You could, but I doubt if your confession would be sincere." Father James left and returned with two bottles of Sam Adams. "I counted my fries before I left."

"Fine! I'll confess to being a fry thief, too."

"How is your mother doing these days?"

"She's not getting any better. How about your parents?" Emmy asked about her half-brother's adoptive parents, Josef and Helen Boyanov.

"They are doing well. Mom called me a few days ago. They were on one of those senior citizen tours in Las Vegas. She said she won fifty bucks."

"What a high roller," Emmy teased.

"She does all right for eighty-two."

"If they ever come to SoHam, I want to meet them," Emmy said and then took a drink.

"I'll let them know."

They finished their lunch and Father James stuck around for a couple of hours to play with the kids.

"I'm going home. They have officially worn me out."

"Thank you for stopping by, and for bringing Darby's," Emmy said and then hugged him.

"It was my pleasure. Now I have to stop at my chiropractor's office for an adjustment."

Chapter Ten

"We have to leave in five minutes," Emmy said after checking the clock on the microwave. She clapped her hands. "Finish your breakfast and wash your face and hands."

"But I'm not finished with my cereal," Heather complained.

"You've had enough time to eat. Take one more bite and then get ready."

"But..."

"Listen to your mother, Heather," Kenny insisted. "Do you have to pick up Carson and Caden?" Kenny moved behind Emmy and squeezed her shoulders.

Emmy turned to face him. "Diane is taking them today, but I will the rest of the week. Are you going to pick them up? Today is just a half day."

"I can do that." He kissed her. "Hustle up, kids. You don't want to be late on the first day of school."

Emmy dropped the kids off and parked her BMW X3. She entered the school and spotted Mary Galves standing outside of her kindergarten classroom.

"Hi, Emmy, I can't believe the summer is over." Mary guided some kids into the classroom where one of the assistants helped get them situated.

"Are you ready for this?" Emmy peeked into the room and spotted Kevin Michael playing with Benjamin Bertucci.

"A better question is are the children ready to have school all day," Mary said.

Emmy waved at Kristen Randolph and Grace, who were talking to Natalie Hammond. "I hope you can get them to take naps in the afternoon, Mary."

"I don't think that will be a problem."

"I'll talk to you later. I want to see how the girls are doing with Miss Redmon. I don't really know her."

"Vera is very nice. The twins will love her," Mary said. "She just graduated from Olivet. This is her first year of teaching."

Emmy walked down the hall to one of the second grade classrooms and peeked inside.

"Hello, Mrs. Colasanti-Colwell, I'm Vera Redmon."

Emmy grinned at the tall, slender teacher and immediately noticed her flaming red hair. "Please, call me Emmy."

"Emmy it is. Please, call me Vera. I appear to have a group of students from Bristol Ridge." Vera glanced over her shoulder.

Emmy pointed at the children. "My girls are there, and those three are Zachary, Noemi and Caden. They think they are all cousins, but they aren't really."

"Do you have any suggestions for telling the twins apart?"

Emmy laughed. "If you listen to them it will become apparent. They have totally different personalities, but Heather still has a birthmark on her right elbow."

"I'm a bit nervous, but looking forward to the challenge."

"There are lots of parents who are willing to help. You will be fine. I'll see you later." Emmy headed down the hall and waved to Sloane Bertucci.

"Hi, Emmy," Sloane said and then paused for a moment. "Can you believe all of my kids are here except for Coby? Taylor Beckett is starting pre-K. They are growing up so fast."

"Is Mama watching Coby for you guys?"

"Yes, and she will keep busy. Taylor will be home in the afternoons. I will see you later." Sloane headed upstairs.

Emmy met Sofia Talford later for lunch at Robbins Old Fashioned Ice Cream Parlor to discuss Sofia's schedule.

"I totally understand you guys having to cut back my hours." Sofia led the way to a table in the corner. "They are in school all day, and you and Kenny are home most of the time."

"Will you be all right financially, or will you need to look for another position?"

Sofia shook her head. "Niles just got promoted, and we are talking about starting a family of our own. I do not want to work at all if we can afford it. At least until the children are in school."

"You will make a great mother. If you can survive my kids, you can handle anything," Emmy said with a grin.

After dropping the kids at school the next morning and getting Kenny to agree to pick them up after school, Emmy headed to the den to work on her book. *I need to spent six hours working on this.* She opened her laptop and settled back in her recliner.

It was just after six thirty when Larry pulled into the huge parking lot at Calvary Chapel on the southern edge of Minneapolis. Buck pulled in right behind the bus. Dixie, Ryan and I were up and ready for our run. Chase was awake and talked to Larry. Now I wasn't there, but Chase filled me in on what they talked about. This is the general gist of their conversation.

Larry remarked, "I saw a pancake house three blocks back down the road. I think that's where we're headed."

"Let me give you some money. I don't think the rest of the guys will be ready for breakfast for quite a while."

"Thanks, Chase. I'll bring back a receipt."

"I'll see you guys later. I'm supposed to meet Pastor Lou Alcus here at eight. He is supposed to take us out for breakfast. The bus should be empty by nine so you guys can sleep. We will try to unload around three. Jess can move the truck into position so you guys can sleep as late as you want."

At this time Chase was responsible for just about everything related to the tour. He kept track of the money, our daily schedule and all the other stuff. Yvonne handled many of the details about the travel and accommodations. The record company did offer some support, but not nearly as much as they do now. Of course, it's nothing like a Fridays At Five tour. Those are a completely different animal.

Pastor Alcus arrived a couple minutes early and took Chase into the church to his office.

"Thank you for meeting me so early."

"This isn't early for me. I'm usually up by six and here by seven. I actually got to sleep in today. How was your trip?"

"Uneventful."

112

"I take it that is good news."

"Yes indeed. We had a wonderful service last night, and everyone should be well rested and ready to go tonight."

"I actually got an email from Pastor Compton about last night. He wanted me to thank you again. I wish I could have been there. I would like to meet Miss Colasanti. Would that be possible? She sounds like the most wonderful person in the world."

I hope you realize he didn't really say that. I'm just goofing around.

"Of course. I think she might surprise you."

"How so?"

"You will understand when you see her. Right now she is out for her morning run." Chase looked at his watch. "I take that back. She is probably back by now. She is an early riser most of the time and likes to go for a run to organize her thoughts. At least that's what she tells me. I think she likes to run because she is still a tomboy at heart."

I like to run because it keeps me in shape. It takes a lot of energy to sing and dance around on stage. The fact that I've always been a tomboy is irreverent, or irrelevant. Doesn't matter.

"Surely she is not alone on these runs."

"Dixie usually goes with her, and I think Ryan ran this morning, also. I think we will be ready to go around nine. Will that be all right?"

"Yes. Is there any place in particular you would like to go?"

"Larry, one of our drivers, noticed a pancake house just down the street."

"I've eaten there many times. The food is good, and the prices are reasonable."

"Sounds good to me. We will pay for our own breakfast and lunch."

"No way! We are paying for all your meals while you are with us. We will have food for everyone both before the service and afterward. I have arranged for a crew of ten young men to be at your disposal for unloading this afternoon and even more for after the service to help load up."

"That is more than we expected, Pastor Alcus."

"We can have more men this afternoon if you need them."

"Ten men will be more than enough. Thank you."

"You asked about our lights in your email. Our leader of technology will be here at three. He can do just about anything you might need. I don't know much about the operation of the light desk, but we have a good setup," Pastor Alcus added.

"Thank you. We don't need anything too fancy. We're not putting on a show. We're here to praise the Lord and minister to whoever might be in need."

Just so you know, Chase actually talked like that. He could be rather formal and stuffy when dealing with clergy and stuff. In real life he's funny and just as capable as me when it comes to having fun.

"That is refreshing to hear, Pastor Alcus said. "We've had services before where that was not the case. I listened to your CD and really enjoyed the music. Well, I should let you get back. You probably need to get ready. I will be here in my office or else in the sanctuary. We can use one, or two, of the vans to take you wherever you need to go during the day."

"You are too kind. I will try to have everyone here by nine."

I had Chase check this for accuracy. He read it and laughed.

"Emmy, you make us sound like a couple of old fogeys."

"Should I change it? Should I make you sound like the truck drivers?"

"Don't do that. I need to keep my job."

The drivers were usually very careful of their language when I was around, but they slipped up

114

occasionally. I assured them I had heard that language before. I grew up hearing it, and I admit I did occasionally slip up myself.

Chase returned to the bus and discovered everyone was up and in the process of getting ready. I was in the bedroom getting ready. Hank wasn't in the bedroom with me while I was getting ready. They were in the lounge area. I just wanted to make sure Kenny knows that.

"How is your back this morning, Hank?" Chase asked.

"It feels better than yesterday. I think I can return to my bunk tonight. I don't want to inconvenience Emmy again."

"Let's see how it goes today. I don't think Emmy really minds using the bunk. I think she had fun last night hanging out with all the guys."

I really did. I wanted to be treated like everyone else, and that wasn't the case when I used the bedroom. These guys were all older than me. Dixie being the youngest, and I think he was in his early thirties, but he would never tell us when he was born. I'm not counting Ryan because he wasn't really in the band. He was just along because of his father. The other guys were old enough to be my father. Except for Chase. He's like ten years older than me. Ten or maybe a little more. Why are guys so secretive about their ages? I thought it was only women who did that.

At 8:55 everyone was ready to go. Chase led the way to Pastor Alcus' office, but he was not there. We found him in the sanctuary pacing the aisles as he prayed. He stopped as he sensed our presence.

"I'm sorry. We didn't mean to interrupt you prayer."

"That's all right. I will just pick up where I left off later. I have been accused of wearing out the carpet in here with my pacing. I just find it the best way for me to pray for my people."

Chase introduced all the guys and saved me for last. Pastor Alcus was indeed surprised when he met me.

"Chase told me I would be surprised when I met you. You look like a teenager."

I smiled shyly.

"We treat her like a teenager most of the time. She usually acts like a kid," Dixie teased, and I poked him in the side and then made a face at him. I'm sure that made me look immature.

We loaded into the church vans and headed down the street to the pancake house. Chase looked around to see if the drivers were still there but didn't see them. Chase sat next to Pastor Alcus. I sat between Dixie and Ryan at the opposite end of the table. Pastor Alcus told me later that I acted like a miniature version of his daughter as I joked around with Ryan and Dixie. I can't remember for sure, but the guys were probably teasing me about being engaged. Dixie did that a lot. He was always asking about my sex life, but not in a creepy way.

Chase overheard our conversation. "She has a large voice though. I don't mean loud. Just... well, you have heard her on the CD. She is more amazing in person. She is very attuned to the direction of the Holy Spirit. Last night was a perfect example of that."

"She seems so shy and quiet."

"She is until she starts singing."

"I can hear you. I'm right here, guys," I said as I looked up at them. Why did they always talk like I wasn't there?

Emmy paused, saved her work and headed to the kitchen.

"Are you getting stuff done?" Kenny asked.

"Yes, but I can't tell you what. Are you hungry?"

"I could eat a sandwich, but I'm not starving."

"Good. Could you make one for me, too. We have some roast beef and a thing of potato salad." Emmy grinned because she had roped Kenny into making lunch.

Kenny made the sandwiches and fixed a plate of potato salad and cottage cheese.

Emmy made a face at the cottage cheese. "What's this for?

Are we on diets?"

"It was in the fridge, so I thought we should eat it before it goes bad."

Emmy took a bite of her sandwich. "I talked to Sofia about her schedule."

"Really, Heather." Kenny stared at Emmy.

Emmy stared back.

"You are always getting after Heather for talking with food in her mouth," Kenny explained.

Emmy rolled her eyes. "She said she understands, and they are thinking about starting a family. We might need to hire a new nanny in the near future."

They finished lunch and Emmy put the dishes into the dishwasher before grabbing a bottle of water and returning to the den to work again.

We returned to the church after breakfast. Some of the guys wanted to do some sightseeing and others were content to simply hangout and relax. Pastor Alcus had one of the church members act as a guide for the guys who wanted to see the city. They used one of the vans. Pastor Alcus showed the ones who stayed at the church where the library and teen room were located. I saw a ping pong table in the teen room.

"Would it be all right if we use the ping pong table?" I asked kind of shyly.

"Of course you may. Just make yourself at home."

"Thank you so much."

Pastor shook his head. "You are so much like my daughter."

I guess he might have thought I would be like a star, but I surprised him by being so down to earth and unassuming. Boring really. I really am, Kenny. Stop laughing at me. I spent time in the teen room with Ryan playing ping pong and air hockey. We listened to some of the CDs in the teen collection. Pastor Alcus heard us having fun and popped his head in a couple of times. He mentioned something about us acting like siblings and that he would have assumed Ryan to be the older sibling. Ryan laughed at me, so I did what came naturally, I made a face and stuck out my tongue.

No one seemed to be interested in lunch. The guys, who went sightseeing, just grabbed some fast food. Some of the guys grabbed some light snacks from the bus. I hung out in the lounge and read. I listened to some tunes through my headphones because the drivers snored as they slept. Pastor Alcus took Chase on a hospital visit. Everyone met back at the church office shortly before three. True to his word, there was a group of twelve strong-looking young men ready to work. I looked at them and then glanced at Dixie. I knew I had to behave, or else he would tease me about flirting with the guys. Jess Zawaski moved the truck into position. Joe and Stuart Lederer supervised the unloading. Steve Van Zant and Dixie Case stayed in the sanctuary to show the guys where to place the gear. I kinda wandered around and tried not to get in the way. I was not checking out the guys, Kenny, but I did catch some of them smiling at me. Chase met with Toby Fitzpatrick, the tech-team leader, and they went over some basic lighting needs. Toby knew all of our songs and had a good grasp of what Chase would like. I helped Ryan unload the merchandise from under the bus. We continued to goof around with each other until Chase had to get after us.

"Emmy! Will you knock it off and behave. You guys don't have all afternoon to get set up."

"Sorry, Pastor Hillman. It was my fault," Ryan apologized.

I kept teasing Ryan. Chase shook his head and gave up. He muttered something about Kenny going nuts trying to put up with me. Hank helped set up some of the merchandise, but we didn't allow him to do any lifting.

"Don't you be lifting anything now, Hank. You're not a young man anymore," I teased.

"I'm not that old, Emmy. I just have a bad back."

"Yeah, and you stole my bed because of it."

"You can have it back. I'm feeling better now."

"No, you can use it again tonight. I had fun hanging out with the guys, especially Dixie and Ryan. Though Ryan is a total dork." I took off running with Ryan chasing me.

I heard Chase hollering, "Emmy! You come back here." But I didn't pay him any attention. I think some of the local guys thought I might be Ryan's girlfriend.

By three thirty everything was unloaded and hooked up. Stuart did a quick test to make sure everything worked properly. That's doing a line check. I know some of the technical stuff now, but back then I just did what Mr. Lederer told me. I didn't goof around during soundchecks. I knew when to be serious. He had trouble with my wireless microphone and dug out the spare receiver. It worked fine. Chase gave all the guys who helped their choice of either a CD, t-shirt or whatever they wanted.

One of the guys asked, "Could I have my picture taken with Emmy? I already have the CD."

"Sure! Let me find her." Chase found me goofing around with Ryan. "Emmy! Would you come with me?"

"Okay. Am I in trouble?" I figured I better cool it with Ryan and start behaving like a mature young lady.

"Yes! Big trouble, little lady."

I knew he was teasing me.

"Some of the guys who helped us unload would like to have their picture taken with you."

"Really?"

"Yes. They seem to think you are pretty or something."

I was a little embarrassed since I looked rather sweaty and a general mess. Just the way I usually look being the tomboy that I am or was. Did you catch that sarcasm? I took pictures with everyone and even signed whatever they had. I reminded them I was just doing what God had led me to do. I heard a couple of them comment about me looking pretty. I looked in the mirror later. My face was sweaty and I had a streak on dirt on my right cheek. My hair looked like a total disaster. They still thought I was pretty, though. I suppose they didn't know any better. No one seemed to know about my engagement to Kenny, which seemed strange.

The soundcheck went well and by five thirty everyone gathered in the fellowship hall for the pre-service meal. Calvary Chapel was accustomed to putting on concerts, and they had a well organized group of volunteers. They had sold tickets to tonight's concert and the large sanctuary was nearly sold out. This was the largest church we had been to so far. I learned later it held over two thousand.

After an opening prayer, the worship leader led the crowd in a few songs. Pastor Alcus introduced us, and we took the stage. The pastor watched as I transformed from a shy teenager into an amazing singer who seemed to know just how to both entertain and lead the crowd in worship. Those are his words, not mine. I used the entire platform to dance around. We sang for an hour and a half. Well, almost. Some of the time we testified or talked about what the songs meant to us. Chase took over at the end and again there were a number of teens who came forward. Pastor Alcus and his team prayed with the teens. Chase and I waited respectfully off to one side of the platform. The rest of the band and crew attended to their assignments.

After everyone had left the altar area, the crew started the load-out. As promised there were plenty of young men to help. Stuart Lederer took care of the mics and cables while Jess and Joe supervised the volunteers. They knew exactly how to load the truck so everything came off in an organized way. Have I mentioned how the gear was packed in the same kind of heavy-duty cases that Fridays At Five used? The cases are on wheels and are easy to move even though they're heavy. They are pretty much indestructible, and I thought it was cool to have the name of the band stenciled on the sides. I thought it made us look like a real band.

The truck was soon loaded and once again the volunteers were offered their choice of merchandise. Again many of them wanted to meet me. At least this time I didn't have dirt on my face. And again I couldn't believe they thought of me in that manner. Naive virgin thing again. I certainly didn't think of them like that. I posed for pictures and signed autographs for anyone who asked even though I knew I would pay for this fan adulation later. The guys would tease me all the way to Des Moines. There was pizza and other food in the fellowship hall for the band and crew and also all the volunteers. Ryan hung out with me to keep me company. Several of the kids asked Ryan if he was my boyfriend. He would shake his head no. I embarrassed him by holding his hand. I wasn't wearing my engagement ring because Kristen had gotten on my case about losing it, or having it stolen. I left it at home for this trip. I hoped Kenny wouldn't be upset when he found out. I did tell him, and he understood. Eventually we were ready to head to Des Moines. I boarded the bus expecting to be razzed by the guys but they were strangely quiet. No one teased me at all. They didn't quite ignore me, but they acted strange for some reason I couldn't figure out. Hank used the bedroom again. By one thirty everyone was in their bunks. The bus seemed eerily quiet.

Emmy put a finger to her mouth and checked the time. *That's enough for today. The kids will be back any minute. I want to hear about school. Oh, I need to email Denise with my last chapters. I better do that now before I forget.* She sent the email, saved her work and walked into the kitchen just as Heather and Isabella raced into the room.

"How was school?" Emmy asked.

"Miss Redmon is so cool!" Heather announced. "She let us sing songs after lunch."

"I need a snack." Kevin Michael dragged his backpack

121

along the floor. "I am so tired. I didn't know school would be so long."

"You can have some fruit, but then maybe you should take a nap," Emmy said.

Kevin opened the fridge and grabbed some pudding. "Can I have this?"

Emmy nodded.

"I don't need a nap," he said. "I'm going to play outside in the woods with Ben. We are going to hunt for spiders."

"Okay, but don't bring any spiders or other bugs into the house."

"But, Mom, I need to keep some spiders to study them. I am going to be a bug scientist when I grow up."

Emmy sighed and shrugged. *Last week you still wanted to be a fireman and a police officer. Who knows what you will be interested in a month from now?*

Sofia arrived early the next morning and helped with breakfast and packed the kids' lunches. "Where are you guys going to be this weekend?" Sofia wrote the names on the paper bags.

Emmy shrugged. "You know I can't remember. I think we're going to be in North Carolina, but I could be wrong. I'm glad all we have to do is show up and take the plane to wherever. We will be home on Sunday morning sometime."

"I will make sure the children are ready for church. Niles will pick us up, so you and Kenny can sleep later if you want."

"I don't even know if I'm scheduled to sing on Sunday. Even though we're only gone two days a week, this tour is occupying more of my time than it should."

After sending the kids to school, Emmy retreated to the den to work. She checked her email and saw that Denise had replied. As Emmy read the reply her shoulders slumped. *Crap! I thought the story was getting better.* She turned at the sound of someone knocking.

"Em, can I come in for a second?" Kenny asked.

"Yeah, I haven't started working."

Kenny entered. "Sorry, but I need the checkbook and I left

122

in in the desk." He grabbed the checkbook and turned to leave. He glanced at Emmy and stopped. "Are you okay? You look upset."

"I'm never going to be a writer. I suck at it."

Kenny sat on the arm of her recliner. "What happened?"

Emmy explained about the email. "Denise says I'm rambling, and I need to write more about me. My feelings and my motivations and stuff like that."

"Isn't that what you've been doing?"

"I thought so, but I guess not. I've been writing about what goes on during a tour."

"Do you want me to take a look at it?" Kenny asked.

"No! You can't see it," Emmy answered. She pushed him off of the recliner. "Sorry. I didn't mean to snap at you. Would you get upset if I write about us a little?"

Kenny grinned and said, "Not as long as you don't call me a dork."

Emmy laughed. "But you are a dork. Go away and let me work. I'll figure something out."

Kenny kissed the top of her head and left.

Emmy moved into a comfortable position, ran a hand through her hair for a moment and then smiled. "I know what to write about. I'm not sure where to put it in the story, but I can figure that out later."

I met Kenny Colwell when I was seven. He was ten, and we fell head over heels in love. That's how it would have happened in fiction, but since this is supposed to be reality, it didn't. Not until a few years later.

Kenny's parents live in this gorgeous old house that's been in their family for around 120 or 130 years. My parents bought a small house three doors away. Kenny and I met in the alley. That sounds weird, but it's true. Diane and I were walking to school and he introduced himself. We've been best friends ever since. Wow! That means I've known him for twenty-six years. Is that right? I'm no good at math. Anyway, I'll skip ahead a little. Kenny used the carriage house next to the alley to practice. When I was fourteen, I would sing with him. Wait! We used to sing together before that, but I'm talking about after Fridays At Five started. They used the carriage house to rehearse for several months, and I would hang out with them. They let me sing harmony and kinda tolerated my presence since I was Kenny's friend. I loved being a small part of the band, but I knew it wouldn't last. They started touring and since I was a kid, I couldn't travel with them. I did sing on stage at local gigs, but I never envisioned making music a career like Kenny did.

Kenny graduated, did a year in college and then the band started touring full-time. I was still in high school. I got good grades, but didn't socialize much. My parents wouldn't let me go to games or dances by myself. Diane was allowed to do whatever she wanted. I didn't realize it at the time, but I was bullied by some of the older kids in school. Kids would push me in the hallways. There was a lot of verbal abuse. I was petite and didn't look old enough to be at Roosevelt. I also suffered because of my sister's reputation. She was hot and didn't try to hide it. I was a late bloomer if you get my drift.

Sometimes I wish I could go back and do high school all over. I wouldn't be so shy. I would be more active. I'm not talking about boys. I could have been a cheerleader. I was athletic and loved to dance though I didn't have many chances to show it. I could have tried out for the theater club. Stuff like that. But we can't go back. When my girls are in high school, I will encourage them to be more active.

Emmy paused and read for a moment. "Maybe this is more like Denise wants. I'll work on it and see if I can fit in in somewhere. It can't be any worse than the other chapters."

Chapter Eleven

"Liz, is it true there's a board meeting tomorrow to talk about the plans for the new sanctuary?" Emmy asked as they left their Sunday School class.

"I'm pretty sure that is the highest priority item on the agenda," Liz answered.

"Did you know Carl Tomanek designed our house and most of the others in Bristol Ridge?"

"You mentioned he was your architect, but doesn't he do mostly larger buildings?" Liz put a hand on her baby bump. "Settle down. You're kicking me."

"Usually, but we're very happy with his work, and we hope he gets the contract to design the new sanctuary."

"Tyler claims he's not worried about the prospect of building a new sanctuary, but I know better. At least he has Pastor Ausland and Dr. Behren to talk to. They've been through a building program."

"I'll talk to you later, Liz. I need to find Kenny."

Grayson Hammond walked up to his mother with Coby Bertucci in tow. Grayson put a hand on Liz's baby bump. "Baby's getting bigger, Coby." Grayson laughed and he and Coby dashed away to resume playing.

After lunch Emmy grabbed her keys and said, "Kenny, I'm going to take the kids over to see Mona and Bill. They called earlier and complained about not seeing them very often." She hesitated and put her keys back. "I changed my mind. We're going to walk."

"Be careful if you go through the woods. I saw a gigantic bear the other day." Kenny held his hands far apart. "He was taller than the trees."

Kevin Michael waved his plastic sword around. "I'm not afraid of any bears. I will chop his head off."

"Oh, Daddy," Isabella said as she rolled her eyes. "There aren't any bears in the woods, but I did see a mommy deer with her baby a few days ago."

"We won't be gone too long." Emmy leaned over the

recliner and kissed the top of Kenny's head.

The kids followed Emmy out through the garage.

"Should we walk through the woods, or along the road?" Emmy asked.

"The woods!" Kevin shouted. "I want to kill the bear."

"We can take our path through the woods, Mommy." Heather pointed. "It's a shortcut."

Emmy followed the kids around the back of the house and saw the path Heather mentioned. "Do you take this path to get to Diane and Brady's house?"

"Come on, Mom. You have to be careful on the hills and look out for bugs and spiders."

"I saw a snake in the woods, but it ran away," Kevin said.

Heather and Kevin ran ahead, but Isabella stayed close to Emmy.

"Are there any poisonous snakes in the woods, Mommy? Carson said some snakes are poisonous and can bite you and make you sick."

"There are some poisonous snakes in Illinois, but I don't think any of them live in our woods. You should be careful though," Emmy cautioned. "I can remember when I was a little girl and me and your father found a small snake in his backyard. He caught it and we both held it, but then we let it go."

"Are you going to put that in your book?" Isabella stopped to look at a butterfly.

"Maybe," Emmy answered and then glanced ahead. "Heather! Wait for us, please."

"Hurry up! We want to get there before it gets dark."

A few minutes later they strode down the last hill before the road.

"Look both ways before you ever cross a road," Emmy said.

Heather sighed. "We know, Mommy. We aren't babies." She grabbed Kevin Michael's hand. They looked in both directions and raced across the road. "It's clear. You can cross the road, Mommy."

Emmy led them up the long driveway to the house.

126

"Is this the house from the *Gone With The Wind* movie?" Isabella asked.

"No, but it kinda looks similar." Emmy walked up the steps of the wide porch and knocked on the eight-foot-tall double doors.

"Why is there such a big roof?" Kevin looked up and pointed.

"It's called a portico," Emmy explained.

"That's another word for porch," Isabella whispered.

Mr. Robertson opened the door. "Who is here to see us?"

"I brought my sword so I could kill the big bad bear!" Kevin whipped the sword around and narrowly missed hitting Heather.

"Be careful, Kevin Michael. Maybe you should leave your sword outside."

"Okay, but I need it when we go home."

"Come inside and make yourself at home. Mona made some fresh cookies."

Heather led the way through the entryway and back to the kitchen. "Do you have cookies, Grandma Mona?"

"Yes, I do. Do you think it will be all right with your mother if I let you have some cookies and milk?"

"I want chocolate milk." Kevin Michael looked on the island and saw a plate of cookies.

"Did you ask politely?" Emmy helped Kevin onto one of the barstools.

"Can I have chocolate milk, please?"

"That's better."

"I happen to have some chocolate milk in the fridge," Mona said. "We have Weber's Dairy deliver it along with our regular milk. Carson and Caden have taught Lily to ask for chocolate milk. I love the way she tries to talk like them."

"She's starting to talk more. I think it helps to have older brothers or sisters. Carson is really good with her. He's so patient. A lot more than Diane ever was with me and we were a lot closer in age."

"Carson will be a big help to Diane when she has the baby. Has she ever talked about a name with you? Bill was wondering."

127

"We were talking about names last week. I think she likes Conor and Cullen, but I'm not sure if Brady likes those names."

"I like Conor and that would fit with the other boys." Mona passed out cookies and glasses of chocolate milk. "But I'm sure whatever name they choose will be just fine."

"I suggested Garrick Adler, but Diane said that would be a terrible name for a baby. It sounds like an old man."

"Where on earth did you come up with that name?" Mona chuckled.

"I saw it online. I think it was a law firm or something," Emmy admitted.

"I need more chocolate milk." Kevin held up his empty glass.

"One more glass but that's all," Emmy answered. "I need to talk to Mr. Robertson."

"Go ahead, dear. I'll watch the kids," Mona said.

Emmy found Mr. Robertson in the den and knocked on the open door. "Are you busy?"

"Not really. I was watching golf, but it's too boring without Tiger Woods. What's on your mind?"

She sat next to him on the leather couch. "Are you aware the church board is going to decide whether or not to build a new sanctuary?"

He muted the volume on the TV. "I have talked to Carl about that."

"Do you think the board will approve his plans?"

"I can't say it's a done deal, but I think they are very likely to approve the plans."

"Good," she said and then bit her lip for a moment before adding, "Kenny and I have talked about it, and we are willing to make a sizable contribution to the building fund. The church really needs the extra space, and Kenny said they don't have any mortgage, so they should get approval from whatever committee decides these things."

"That's very thoughtful and generous of you, Emmy."

She stared at him for a moment before asking, "Do you know how much it might cost to build the new building?"

128

"Carl did tell me what he thought it would cost," Mr. Robertson said without adding any more details.

She grabbed his elbow. "Tell me so we can decide how much to donate."

He rubbed his chin and then turned his head to face her. "That might not be necessary, Emmy."

"Why not? The church needs to raise the money somehow."

"True, but... you shouldn't worry about it."

She gazed into his eyes. "Are you trying to tell me something?"

"Well, Mona and I did discuss it for a while before deciding."

"Oh my God! You're donating the money to build it, aren't you?"

"It's not really all that much considering..."

"Considering the fact you guys are the most generous people in the world." Emmy moved closer and hugged Mr. Robertson.

Mona walked into the room and smiled. "Did you tell her about the donation?"

He nodded.

Emmy jumped up and wrapped her arms around Mrs. Robertson. "How will the church ever repay you guys?"

"They don't need to repay us, and we know that giving money to the church is not the way you get to heaven."

"That's right." Emmy wiped her eyes. "You can't buy your way to heaven."

"We do go to church occasionally when we travel," Mona said.

"You could start coming to our church all the time. I know you've said you think you might be a distraction. It would be like Michael Jordan or Bill Gates showing up or something, but the people would get used to it. Maybe the church could name the new building the Robertson Chapel or something."

Bill shook his head. "No, I made that a condition of the donation that my name wouldn't be attached in any way. The board knows, but we would like to keep it as anonymous as possible."

"I won't tell anyone." Emmy crossed her heart.

"Mommy, we are full of cookies and milk," Heather said as she rubbed her stomach. "Can we go outside and play?"

"We want to see if Aunt Diane and Lily are home," Isabella added.

"Okay, but come right back if Diane isn't home."

The girls and Kevin sprinted to the back door and ran outside.

"I suppose there are other things the church needs," Emmy said. "The school has a rather large budget."

"That is true," Mona said.

Emmy turned to Mr. Robertson, reached up and kissed his cheek. "Have I told you lately how much I love you guys?"

"Not that I can remember," he said and then chuckled.

Pastor Tyler called the board meeting to order at 6:32 on Monday evening. The group of twenty spent time praying, and Tyler led a short devotional time. They quickly worked their way through the various reports and finally got to the main subject of the meeting.

"Bill and the building committee have met with Mr. Tomanek several times," Tyler revealed. "Would you like to talk about the plans?"

William Griffith nodded. "The committee feels that Mr. Tomanek's plans meet every need of the church for future growth." He spent a few minutes going over details of the architectural plans.

"What about things like computers and video screens and sound gear? Has all that been taken into consideration?" Bob Cartwright asked.

"There is a separate plan for all of that," Mr. Griffith assured the board. "It will be state-of-the-art."

Jim Rosek and Roger Goldman added to Mr. Griffith's comments.

"Do we have a motion to accept the plans?" Pastor Tyler looked around the table after the questions stopped.

"I so move," Dylan Michaelis said.

Lenore Toth raised a hand. "I second the motion."

Tyler allowed for more time to discuss the plans and the finances.

"Is it true that someone has agreed to fund the entire project?" Marley Menconi, the newest member of the board, asked.

Pastor Tyler chuckled and then nodded. "That is correct."

"Do we need to keep their names anonymous?" Marley asked.

"If at all possible, the donors would like to remain anonymous, and they have requested that the church not name anything after them."

After another short discussion, Tyler called for a vote. The board unanimously voted to accept the plans.

"Thank you. Bill, how soon will we be ready to accept bids?" Tyler asked.

"I think we will have a decision within a month about who to award the contract. In my estimation, we could be ready to use the new building in about twelve months if nothing catastrophic happens."

Chapter Twelve

"How are you doing, Detroit?" Kenny shouted into his microphone after Fridays At Five had played three songs to open the show. "We're glad to be here tonight, and we're going to play a mix of songs. This one is 'Daybreak In Alabama.' Sing along if you know it."

Dave Persching counted off the song, and the guys continued the show. Emmy stood behind the side fill speakers and watched.

"Hey, Emmy, that was a great set tonight," Ty Dalicandro, the crew chief and tour manager, said.

"Thanks, Ty. We kinda changed the set list. I hope we didn't screw up the lighting guys too much."

"I didn't notice any screw-ups," he answered.

Ralph Glissman walked over and put an arm around Emmy's shoulders. "Nice job, Emmy."

Emmy said thanks and then tilted her head. *Was tonight really all that different? It must have been pretty good for Ralph to say something.* She watched as the man in charge of everything on the tour walked away. She turned back to Ty and yelled into his ear. "What's up with Ralph. He usually never says anything."

"It's probably because he's only got a couple of weeks left."

Emmy bit her lip. "Shoot! I totally forgot that he's retiring. Is the band and crew doing anything special after the final show?"

"They are, but they're keeping it hush hush. I've just been told to be ready to make sure he's at the side of the stage that night."

"Are you taking over for him?"

"I think I'm in the running for that position, but it might be a while before the band tours again," Ty answered.

"I hope they don't tour, but you could get a position with plenty of bands."

"True, but this organization is great to work with," Ty said.

"You better not let Andy hear you say that," Emmy said.

"I won't. He might cut my pay," Ty said with a smile.

On Saturday Fridays At Five took the stage in Seattle for the final show of the summer tour. After playing for an hour, Kenny looked to the side of the stage, saw Ty with a thumbs up and had the crowd sit down.

"I want to take a minute to take care of some business. This is the final show of the summer tour, but it's not our final show. Lord willing. However." Kenny raised a finger. "It is the final show for one of the company's most important members. There are many people who work behind the scenes to put on a show like this and many more to keep things organized. One of the first people we hired was Ralph Glissman. He's been the production manager for... well, as long as we've needed one. Over fifteen years, right?" Kenny glanced at Jeff.

"At least that long," Jeff said.

Ralph shook his head as Ty grabbed his elbow. "Come on, Mr. Glissman. This is your time to be in the spotlight." Ty led Ralph to the center of the stage.

"Ralph is retiring to spend more time with his family and especially his grandkids." Kenny put an arm around Ralph as Jeff, Dave, P.J. and Adam gathered around. "We want to thank you for your many years of hard work and dedication. You have made our lives so much easier. You've allowed us to live our our dreams of being musicians."

At that moment Andy Walker strolled onto the stage with a special guest.

"Ralph, I think Alice is glad you are retiring," Kenny whispered off-microphone.

Andy grabbed Kenny's microphone. "Look who I found backstage." He squinted into the bright lights. "This is Ralph's wife, Alice." Andy glanced over his shoulder and waved. "And some of you might remember this guy."

Jeremy Lenhart, the band's original keyboard player, waved to acknowledge the roar from the crowd.

"I guess they still remember you," Andy said with a chuckle.

Jeremy hugged Ralph and Alice as Emmy wandered onto the stage and stood behind Kenny.

133

"Hey, Em, what's up?" Kenny asked.

"The tech guys have Ralph's family online. They are going to put them on the screens."

Kenny looked out toward the tech guys in the back of the venue and waved. A couple of seconds later an image of Ralph's family appeared on all the large screens that dominated the sides of the stage.

"Hey, Ralph, I think someone wants to say hi." Andy turned Ralph and pointed up to the screens.

"Hey, Dad, we want to say thanks for taking an early retirement so you can babysit whenever we need one."

The guys in the band cracked up. Ralph put a hand over his face and tried not to become emotional. He didn't succeed.

Kenny took his microphone back from Andy. "Ralph has always had a favorite song we do, and I think we should do it now. Is that all right with you?" He was asking the tech guys, but the crowd roared their approval. "Ralph, we're going to dedicate 'I Will Be True To You' to you and Alice tonight."

The guys went back to their positions. Frankie Hanna brought out Kenny's Martin acoustic. Noah Belanger handed Emmy a wireless microphone. Jeremy moved next to Adam in front of the bank of keyboards.

"Which one are you going to play?" Adam grinned.

Jeremy laughed. "None of them. I'm going to stand here and pretend I'm playing. Do they really let you sing harmonies?"

"Yeah, and sometimes I take the melody if Kenny's voice is tired."

Emmy stood next to Kenny and pinched his elbow. "You didn't tell me I would have to sing with you."

"I must have forgotten. Do you want to sing the whole thing?"

"No, let's do it like we always have." She thought about the many times over the years she sang this as a duet with Kenny and smiled.

Andy led Ralph and Alice to the side of the stage where two chairs had mysteriously appeared. "You can enjoy the rest of the show from here. I guess you are officially retired as of now."

After the last encore the band headed downstairs where catering had prepared a special feast in honor of Ralph.

"Jeremy, it's so good to see you." Emmy hugged him. "How is everyone?"

"We are doing great. Jennifer's treatments are over for now. Her lymphoblastic leukemia is in remission."

"That is the best possible news. Are you thinking of making a comeback?"

Jeremy shook his head. "My days of touring extensively are over. I might make a guest appearance once and again, but that's it. I have been working on a solo project. I might need someone to do some high harmonies. Would you be interested?"

"If you twist my arm hard enough, I might help out."

A short time later, Andy made a toast to Ralph and Alice. "May you live long enough to see your great-grandchildren grow up."

Emmy rolled her eyes. "You're a goof, Andy.

A couple of Thursdays later Emmy dashed into the family room carrying her laptop. She plopped next to Kenny on the couch. "Have you checked your email today?"

"I haven't had time. Why?" he responded.

"There's an email from Tyler. He said the kids are leaving."

"What kids?" he asked absentmindedly.

Emmy waved her hands around. "The foster kids. The Curry kids. You know. Avery, Liam and Dillan."

"Where are they going? Another visit with their grandmother?"

Emmy shook her head. "No! They're being adopted."

"What? When? He never mentioned that the last time I talked to him. Who is adopting them?"

Emmy had his full attention now. She checked the email again. "He doesn't say specifically. They are moving to another family who are in the process of pre-adopting them. Whatever that means. According to the email Sunday morning will be the last time they will have them." She paused and looked at Kenny. "They can't give up Avery. I will miss her too much."

"It might be for the best, Em. It can't be easy to handle all those kids especially with Liz being pregnant. Isn't the goal to get the kids back to their own family anyway?"

"Their own parents, yeah, but according to this, they are being adopted by a different family. I need to call Liz. I have to get to the bottom of this." Emmy headed back to the den where she had been working on her book. She called Liz.

"We didn't know until Tuesday, so it was just as much of a surprise to us," Liz explained.

"Where are they going? Do you know these people?"

"It's a family from North Oswego. We met them yesterday and had dinner together with the kids. It was kind of weird. We didn't know if we should discipline the kids at dinner or let their new parents do that."

"What were they doing?" Emmy asked.

"Just the normal bickering. Dillan threw a fit because Tyler wanted him to eat his veggies. Nothing out of the ordinary."

"How did the kids react to the other couple? Did they call you and Tyler Mom and Dad?"

"They acted better than I would have thought. Avery was quiet and shy, but that's just her. The boys talked a lot to the other couple..."

"Don't you know their names?" Emmy interrupted.

"Yes, but I don't think we're supposed to let people know. Some kind of privacy thing. Dillan and Liam understand, but Avery doesn't."

Emmy bit her lip. "I would adopt her myself if I could. She's so adorable, but I know the kids need to be together. How did Natalie and Grayson react to the news?"

"Natty was a stinker. She said she was glad the boys were leaving, but she wanted to keep Avery. Grayson didn't say much, but he never does. He keeps his feelings hidden more than Natty."

"Diane's boys are that way, too. Especially Caden. Carson will open up more, but Caden keeps it all inside. You never know how he feels."

Liz laughed. "That's like you and Kenny. He keeps his emotion under check, and you couldn't do that to save your life."

"Yes, I could. I'm not as emotional as I used to be."

"If you say so, Emmy," Liz said and then chuckled.

"What did Dany say about all this?"

"She cried, but I'm not supposed to tell anyone." Liz waited for a response but there was only silence on the phone. "Emmy, are you crying?"

Emmy bit her lip. "I can't help it."

"You will have a chance to say goodbye on Sunday."

"Somehow that doesn't help right now," Emmy said. "I better let you go. I'll talk to you later. I have got to work on my book. That will keep my mind off of Avery and the boys."

"You can call me later if you need, Emmy."

Emmy started her laptop and found the place she stopped. She read for a moment. *Should I take out the part about bullying? If I leave it in, should I mention Todd Delaney? He's the guy who bullied me the most.* She bit her lip as she read though the section again. *I'm definitely not including anything about those two guys who touched me by the lockers. I never told Kenny or Rory about that.* She took a deep breath. *It stays for now.*

The bus and truck made the short trip into Des Monies without incident. The drivers found the church just before six o'clock and parked behind the building. The drivers walked nearly a mile before they found a place for breakfast. This was an omen for our stay in Des Moines.

I woke up at my usual time of six thirty and tried to get out of the bunk to use the bathroom. The curtain seemed to be stuck, though. After trying in vain to open it, I realized the guys had me trapped somehow. At first I didn't say anything. I lay on my back, but could not fall back asleep. After a few minutes, I could hear Ryan and Dixie laughing in the hallway. I banged on the bottom of the bunk above me where Dixie had slept.

I heard the guys get out of their bunks. They were trying not to laugh but couldn't help themselves. Even Chase was laughing.

"I need to get up. I have to pee!"

"What, Emmy? We can't hear you."

"I have to pee. Will you please let me out of this bunk before I have an accident." I shouted even louder.

"Why can't you get out of your bunk, Emmy?"

"Because you guys have done something so I can't move the curtain."

I heard all the guys asking each other if they did anything to the bunk. They all claimed to be innocent.

"No one seems to know what you're talking about, Emmy. Are you sure you can't open the curtain?"

"Please let me out. I really have to go."

The guys knew they had teased me long enough. They unhooked the curtain and let me out. I got out and ran to the bathroom without bothering to put on my robe. When I came out, the guys were all waiting for me.

"You guys are so mean to me." I tried to make them feel guilty, but they didn't buy my act. I realized they weren't going to let me slide.

"It wasn't my fault those guys said I was pretty."

As soon as the words left my mouth, I realized this was a mistake because the guys teased me mercilessly. I took the razzing like a good sport, but I vowed to get back at them somehow. I knew it would probably continue until we got back to SoHam. I didn't go for a run that morning because it was pouring cats and dogs. I didn't have a way to release my nervous energy until Ryan and I got into a wrestling match.

"Emmy, what on earth are you doing?"

I looked up at Chase as Ryan was holding me on the floor. "We're just having some fun."

"Have you forgotten you are engaged to be married in less than a month and it isn't to Ryan." Chase shook his head as I escaped from Ryan's hold and slugged him.

Chase threw his arms in the air. "Once a tomboy, always a tomboy."

After that, I ran in the mornings no matter what the weather.

Emmy sat back in her recliner and put a finger to her mouth. *Should I include the part about Ryan and me wrestling? It was just some innocent fun, but people might not understand. They might think I was fooling around.* Emmy had her finger on the delete key, but then changed her mind. *I'll see what Denise says. It happened, so maybe I should include it.* She took a sip of water and continued.

When we looked back at the tour in years to come, Des Moines was everyone's least favorite stop. I won't even mention the name of the church. I'm not sure it even exists today. This is what happened. No one met us at the church until two hours before the service. No volunteers arrived to help. We were not fed at all, which really upset the guys. We made do with the tuna sandwiches I put together. The sanctuary was less than half-filled. Still we did our best. In some ways it was the best we *performed* during the whole three weeks. It was not meant to be, though. We pulled out all the stops. I tried every trick I had ever learned from Kenny to energize the crowd. They sat on their hands the entire night with dazed looks and glassy eyes. We cut short the altar call when it became obvious there would be no response. We did sell a few CDs, but that was about it. We loaded-out, and when it became obvious there would not be any food, we left. I'm not sure we even got paid, but it didn't matter. We met on the bus and prayed for the church. Chase learned several months later that the senior pastor had left two weeks prior after being accused of adultery. The entire staff had been fired as well after it was discovered they had been covering for him. On the way out of town, we stopped at a twenty-four hour restaurant to eat and discuss what happened.

After eating, we made our way back onto the bus one at a time. Even Ryan and I were quiet as we sat on the couch watching a movie. The guys headed to bed. Hank used the bedroom because his back pain had flared up again. Ryan and I were the last ones up. Poor Ryan! I

139

fell asleep against his shoulder. He told me that he tried to wake me up, but I was totally zonked.

"Emmy," he whispered softly. I didn't react. "Emmy," he said a little louder. Still no reaction. He put a hand on my shoulder and gently woke me up.

I opened my eyes and realized I was leaning against Ryan. "What happened? Where is everyone?"

"They all went to bed. You fell asleep against my shoulder."

"How long have I been asleep?"

"About an hour, I guess."

"I'm sorry. Why didn't you wake me up?"

"I suppose I didn't want to disturb you."

"You're sweet, Ryan. Tony would have hung me from the ceiling or something."

Emmy hit save and laughed. *No way would Tony have ever let me sleep for an hour like that. He would have tossed me on the floor or something.* Emmy checked the time and walked out to the family room. "Are you going to get the kids, or do I have to?"

"I'll go if you're busy on your book," Kenny answered.

"I am working on it. Could you go, please. I'll make it up to you later."

"Promises, promises." Kenny laughed and then stood up. "Will you make dinner, or should I pick up something?"

"I'll make dinner. What would you like?"

"Would you have time to make chicken enchiladas?"

"I have the time, but we might need some fresh sour cream and cilantro. Could you stop at the store?"

"I will if you check to see what you need and text me. I don't want to make two trips."

She kissed his cheek. "I'll check now and let you know. You need to get going. It takes you a lot longer to get there than me."

"That's because I obey the traffic laws." Kenny grabbed his wallet and keys. "Text me, or else I will forget to stop."

Emmy checked the fridge and the pantry. She added green onions and corn taco shells to his list before returning to the den.

140

It was a short trip from Des Moines to Kansas City, Missouri. We arrived in the middle of the night and stopped at a truck stop on the outskirts of the city. Everyone was able to get a good night of rest. Even the drivers. Chase had emailed the church and made arrangements to meet someone at noon. We had a leisurely breakfast and by ten thirty everyone was ready to head to the church.

Faith Bible Church was a large congregation with a new building. It was similar to our own church in construction. This helped us feel at home and, after last night's disaster, we needed something positive. We pulled in at eleven thirty and were greeted enthusiastically by Pastor Erik Buehning. I forgot how to pronounce his name. Right away we knew that tonight would be different. There were five guys to help unload the truck. Stuart had everything up and running an hour later. We did a quick soundcheck and were taken to lunch.

"Our congregation is a real melting pot. We have young and old, many different nationalities and a mixture of economic backgrounds. We have two services on Sunday morning and average about four hundred for each service."

Chase and I were listening to Pastor Erik as we ate lunch.

"How long have you been pastor here?" Chase asked.

"Just over five years now. I was an associate pastor in St. Louis before we were called here."

Erik showed us pictures of his wife and young kids. Chase dug out pictures of his girls and proudly showed them to Erik. He looked at me, but didn't ask if I had any kids. I figured he thought it would be impolite to ask a teenager if she had kids.

"Our worship team is going to do a few songs to open the service tonight. You said that would be all right."

"Of course. We would like to meet them if that's possible."

"They will be here before six to practice. They will just use the house PA system."

"They are welcome to use ours if they would like."

"That's very generous, but they are used to our system and would probably feel more comfortable using it."

"Do you have a light desk?" Stuart Lederer asked.

"Unfortunately, our lighting is not state of the art, to put it mildly. We have been hoping to upgrade it next year, but we'll have to wait and see."

"We don't need anything special. What ever you normally use for a service will be fine with us."

"We aren't here to put on a show, Pastor Erik," I pointed out.

Pastor Erik looked at me with surprise. I think I startled him because I had been quiet up to that point. "Please don't hold anything back. Our congregation likes to be entertained as well as being spiritually fed."

"Emmy will entertain them. She can be very surprising at times," Chase told him as I blushed and bit my lip.

Pastor Erik told me later that he wasn't sure he believed Chase. He thought, "Are you trying to tell me that this shy teenager is going to entertain our crowd. I highly doubt it." Instead he said, "Good! We have sold a lot of tickets to the youth groups of other churches. I have a feeling there will be a lot of teens here tonight."

At six the local worship team gathered to practice. Chase and I met them first and one by one the other band members introduced themselves. The local team was comprised of two husband and wife teams of singers and four musicians. They sounded enthusiastic, but there were a few sour notes in the singing. We had a short prayer together before the doors were opened.

At seven Pastor Erik began the service with a prayer and the local worship team led everyone in a few songs. They did a couple original songs, and I thought they sounded much better than during practice. The

142

musicians were obviously amateurs, but they did a good job.

Pastor Erik introduced us as Emmy Colasanti and the Crest Ridge Worship Team. I didn't know if I should correct him or not. Chase told me not to say anything because it would seem rude in a way. I encouraged the crowd to sing along if they wanted. I noticed there were a lot of teens and many different ethnic groups in the sanctuary. I had never sung for such a diverse crowd. The crowd stood as soon as the band kicked off the first song. They actually remained standing for most of the service. To me it felt more like a concert than some of the other places, and I moved around more than usual. I do believe Pastor Erik was thoroughly and pleasantly surprised by the seemingly magical transformation of me from a shy teenager to a dynamic bundle of energy. That's what Chase told me. A dynamic bundle of energy? Get real! At the end Chase asked the crowd to sit down, and he began to pray. Almost immediately teens start coming forward. Pastor Erik and his team took over and prayed with everyone who had a need. He sought me out afterward and thanked me.

"I must confess that when I met you, I thought you would be too... how can I put this... too shy and quiet for our crowd. I thought our group would overwhelm a quiet teenager like yourself. Boy, was I ever wrong. You were simply amazing. You had the crowd eating out of your hand. Where on earth did you ever learn to do that?"

I giggled and answered, "First of all, I'm not a teenager anymore. I know I look like one, but I'm not. And I guess I learned a few tricks from my fiancee. He sings in a band."

Chase heard Pastor Erik talking to me. He knew I was not going to tell him who I was engaged to, so he did. "Have you ever heard of Fridays At Five, Pastor Erik?"

"Yes, of course. I've seen them in concert a couple times. They are absolutely fantastic."

"Emmy used to sing with them."

Pastor Erik looked at me and then back at Chase. "Are you pulling my leg?"

"No, Emmy and Kenny Colwell grew up together. He has mentioned to me that Emmy was the first, and best, singer in the band. In fact, they are engaged to be married in April. So, I guess some of his stage presence has rubbed off on our shy little girl here." Chase hugged me and laughed because I had turned as red as a fire engine.

After everything had been loaded onto the truck and the band and crew had been fed, we began the trip to Carbondale, Illinois. Chase and I talked on the bus.

"It seemed like a concert to me tonight, Chase. Like we were performing. More so than any other place we've ever been, but still at the end the kids responded."

"Maybe tonight was God's way of showing us that we don't have to be afraid of entertaining people as well as trying to minister to their needs. People like to be entertained and have a good time. We don't need to be ashamed of enjoying ourselves."

"It felt good to just be able to have fun singing and dancing. The crowd really seemed to be having a good time."

Dixie had been listening. He told me, "There were several people who came up to me afterward and told me how much they liked the concert, Emmy."

"What did you say to them, Dixie?"

"I said 'thank you' and we would just talk."

"We have to remember that just because God wants us to mainly minister to teens, it doesn't mean we can't have fun while we're doing it," Chase reminded us.

The whole team learned a lesson that night in Kansas City.

Chapter Thirteen

"I would encourage you to take some photos with the kids," Tyler said after church on Sunday. Liz and Tyler hosted a going away party for the Curry kids. "I'm going to print them out, so the kids will have a picture to remember everyone. That should help ease the transition," Tyler explained.

"Are you going to email us copies?" Emmy asked.

"I can if you want," Tyler answered.

Emmy held Avery on her lap while the boys stood on either side.

Tyler got ready to take the shot. "Say cheese."

"Why?" Liam shrugged.

"Got it. Perfect shot." Tyler grinned.

"I want to see," Emmy insisted.

Tyler handed her his phone. "It's a perfect shot of you and Avery, and the boys are acting goofy like normal."

"Who is ready for cake and ice cream?" Allie Kimmerle and Dany Kimmerle began cutting the cake and scooping out the ice cream.

Isabella tugged on Emmy's arm. "Mommy, can we have some ice cream even though we haven't had our lunch yet?"

"Yes, but just because this is a special occasion," Emmy answered.

"I'm sorry we are serving cake and ice cream," Liz said apologetically. "But this was the only chance we had for the people of the church to say goodbye."

"It's all right, Liz. We can have an early dinner." Emmy walked over to the table with the cake and ice cream. "What flavor would you like?"

Heather looked at her choices. "Chocolate cake and vanilla ice cream."

Dany handed Heather the treats.

"Say thank you," Emmy reminded Heather.

"Thank you, Dany," Heather said and then grinned.

"May I please have yellow cake and vanilla ice cream?" Isabella asked politely.

Allie Kimmerle handed the plate to Isabella.

"Thank you, Miss Allie," Isabella said. "Are you going to have another baby? Lorraine needs a baby sister, or maybe a baby brother. Miss Liz is having a baby, and you should have one too."

"We have been thinking about it, Isabella," Allie said.

Dany looked at her sister-in-law. "Are you expecting?"

"Not yet, but we aren't preventing it." Allie handed a slice of chocolate cake to one of the older church ladies. "Have you and Darian decided on a date yet?"

"We are looking at dates in June. Mom said we could use the timeshare in Hawaii if we want." Dany cut a few more slices of cake. "We talked about where to have the wedding, and Darian agreed it should be in Hillsdale."

"Is Tyler going to marry you?"

"No, he's already married to Liz." Dany grinned and handed a slice of cake to Peter Bertucci. "Is that your second piece?"

Allie rolled her eyes.

"No, this is for Coby."

"It's all right if you want a second slice. We have plenty." Dany handed Peter another slice and added some ice cream to the cake. "Tyler agreed to officiate the ceremony, but we need to talk to the new pastor in Hillsdale. Mom suggested we ask him to be a part of the wedding."

"That's probably wise since you are using his church," Allie said. "Have you decided about the wedding party?"

"We know Liz will be my matron-of-honor and Eli will be Darian's best man, but other than that we haven't decided on a final number. He's got three close friends from college he wants to use. I've got my friends from Olivet and some cousins. There's you, and there are people like Emmy. It's not going to be easy to choose."

"Dany, I won't feel slighted if you don't choose me." Allie scooped out some more ice cream for guests. "I might even be several months pregnant by then."

"We will have to make a decision soon." Dany flipped her long hair over her shoulder.

"Can you help me record some Christmas songs?" Emmy

146

asked Kenny after she returned from taking the kids to school. "I want to record some for the kids."

"Sure, I can do that." Kenny tossed the Sweetwater catalog at the coffee table. "Do you have some tunes picked out?"

"I made a list of some old ones, but I kinda wrote a few new ones."

They headed downstairs to the recording studio, and Kenny listened to the new songs as Emmy played a keyboard.

"Those are pretty good, Em. When did you write them?"

"Here and there over the last couple months. The girls sing Christmas songs all year long, so they kinda got me in the mood."

After spending most of the day in the studio, Kenny saved the recordings and got ready to pick up the kids. "You might want to think about recording these songs for a real CD."

Emmy tilted her head.

"You know what I mean. Everyone releases Christmas CDs with old songs and maybe one or two new ones. You've got five originals songs that are awesome. Let's rethink this. I could get the guys together and we could knock out enough songs in a week."

"Can I use my guys?" Emmy followed Kenny up the stairs. "Or maybe we could see who's available."

"Dave and P.J. are on vacation. They took the kids out of school for the week."

"I'll make some calls, and see who is willing to come over."

After dinner Emmy began calling the guys in her band. Christian Becton had returned to Los Angeles, but Micah Hurst, Quinten Matthews, Miles Goossens and Bobby O'Connor agreed to help. Kenny talked Will Consoli into engineering the sessions. Jeff Rawlings and Adam Vicini agreed to show up the next afternoon.

"I still need someone to play lead guitar," Emmy hinted. "Do you know anyone competent enough to play my songs?"

Kenny pulled her onto his lap. "You're a stinker."

"If you're thinking about trying to play on my CD, you better practice. I want some fresh new riffs. Not those old guitar licks you use for your band's songs."

He tickled her behind her knees.

"Fine! I'll let you play, but I might have to erase your tracks

147

and wait for Christian to get back." She sat up quickly. "Maybe I could see if Freddie and Marshall Bender are busy." She mentioned two of the guys from the church's worship band.

"You could ask, but they do have real jobs, Em."

Late Friday afternoon Kenny added a final guitar part to the title track "Christmas All Year Long" and smiled at Emmy. "That's it. I think you've got a fantastic CD for this Christmas."

"Do you think we can get it ready in time to release it this holiday?"

"No doubt," Kenny said and then grinned. "What do you think, Will?"

"It can be ready. I really like it, Emmy. I'm not usually one to listen to Christmas CDs, but this one is different."

"Thank you, Will. I appreciate your help."

"My pleasure. I gotta run. Call me if you need help with the mixing or anything," Will said to Kenny and then headed home.

"I have a photo in mind for the cover," Emmy said. "It's on my laptop. I'll run up and get it for you." She returned a couple of minutes later and showed it to Kenny. "What do you think?"

"It will be perfect. Did you take it?"

"Yeah, we were downtown and the girls wanted to see the Christmas store. I took this as they faced that window with the decorated Christmas tree and the fake snow. It was in the eighties that day, so they wore shorts and little tops. I think it works great with the title."

"I agree, Em. I'm glad it shows the girls from the back. They can maintain a little bit of privacy that way."

Chapter Fourteen

After visiting with Gra and Me-maw on the weekend, Emmy settled into her routine of taking the kids to school and then working in the den. She pulled out her journal and began to read. Kenny walked in and she snapped the journal closed.

"Sorry, I didn't mean to pry, but I need the checkbook. What are you reading about, or can't I ask?"

"Do you remember that festival in Carbondale?"

"Yeah, that was back in 2003, right? Seems like something happened shortly after that." Kenny rubbed his jaw. "Can't remember offhand, but I know there was something."

"You're a dork," she said as she shook her head.

"I remember now. We got hitched."

"Go away and don't bother me. Don't forget to pick up the kids."

Emmy waited until he left the room before opening her journal. She read the account she wrote at the time and then began working on her laptop. She wrote for a solid two hours before going to the kitchen for a Dr Pepper. She returned and checked her work.

Carbondale was a different situation for the worship team. We were part of an indoor, day-long festival at the Shryock Auditorium on the campus of Southern Illinois University. Vine & Harvest Productions promoted the event that included seven artists and three speakers. We were scheduled to go on at six o'clock just before the two main headliners. We were contracted for an hour long set. Since there would be other bands and a speaker after us tonight, we would not have an altar call. This was usually the main focus of our concerts, but last night God revealed to us in a special way that it was all right for us to entertain people as well as minister to them. Tonight we would be entertaining.

We pulled into Carbondale a few minutes after eight o'clock after a seven hour trip from Kansas City.

149

Chase had directions to the auditorium. He called Mallory Knox, who was one half of Vine & Harvest Productions. Her partner was Iris Duronslet. Mallory was already at the auditorium and came outside to meet Chase.

"Hello, Chase. I'm Mallory and this is Mark Obregon. He's in charge of the production."

"It's nice to meet you both. I'm Chase Hillman, and this is Stuart Lederer our sound and tech guy."

"Maybe I should talk to Stuart while you and Mallory talk," Mark suggested.

Stuart and Mark talked as they headed toward the auditorium. Mark told Stuart about the company providing the sound and lights. He mentioned what kind of mixing board they had, and Stuart was familiar with it, but I can't remember what brand it was, and I didn't write it in the journal. It's probably not that important to most people. We used our own mics and our amps and stuff like that, but we didn't need to unload our PA gear. That made it a lot easier for our guys.

It didn't take long to unload the gear needed for today. The Zawaski brothers had arranged the truck in anticipation of today's needs. How they knew to do that was anyone's guess. The gear was unloaded and kept backstage for now. The headliners' crews were unloading and setting up their gear. At times it seemed like total chaos backstage and in the parking lot.

Chase returned to the bus with the passes for everyone. Most of the guys weren't too interested in meeting the other artists, but Ryan and I were. We were the first two in line for the passes. I wanted to know if there would be a chance to meet Aidan Cashell or Mark Haimes."

"I think that might be a slim possibility," Chase answered facetiously. He knew I would do whatever I could to meet them even if I had to sneak backstage.

"Are they here already?" Ryan asked.

"I know their crews are here, but I don't know if they are," Chase replied as he handed out the passes.

150

A little while later, Dixie and Ryan helped me set up the merchandise table. Once the doors opened, they would take turns along with Hank to be there to talk to anyone who stopped by.

There wasn't much to do until later. Most of the guys hung out on the bus. They checked their email and called home. They were anxious to get back to their families. Stuart Lederer talked to some of the tech guys from Hicks Brothers. They were impressed that he worked for Steward Music since it was now a world famous company. He arranged for one of the guys to run the monitor mixer during our set. Dixie asked me if I wanted to go for a run through the campus. I didn't want to hang out on the bus, so I agreed to go for a run.

Ryan saw me and asked, "I've been thinking about going to graduate school here, so I'm going to take a tour of the campus, Emmy. Wanna join me?"

"Dixie wants to go for a run. Why don't you join us for a run, then you and I can tour the campus. I doubt if Dixie is interested in that. He will probably want to check out the girls."

Ryan joined us for our run. We ran a couple miles before returning to the bus. Dixie did take some time to wander around checking out the girls. Ryan and I started walking around the campus.

"Where do you go to college?" I asked.

"I'm in my last semester at Lewiston University."

"Where's that?" I asked.

"Lockport, Indiana. It's a small town. If I do go to graduate school, it will probably be there, but I did want to check out this campus."

I realized Ryan wanted to spend time with me. I didn't mind hanging out with him, since he was close to my age. He was also charming, intelligent and not hard to look at.

"Are you excited about your wedding, Emmy?"

"No, not really. I'm only getting married for the tax benefits."

151

Ryan stopped walking and stared at me. I couldn't keep a straight face any longer. "I'm kidding. I can't wait to get married."

"I went out with this girl for a couple years, but I'm not ready to settle down and get married."

We kept talking as we wandered around the campus. At times I would grab his arm. He told me humorous stories and I would laugh. I guess we looked like any other young college-age couple.

Oh, I should tell you about the meeting Chase and I had with Mallory and Iris. Mark Haimes was at the meeting, and I got to meet him. They discussed set times and other last minute changes. They closed the meeting with a prayer. I learned that Aidan Cashell would not be arriving until around six that evening.

I was heading back to the bus with Chase when a group of young girls saw me. They ran over and asked for autographs. Some of them had CDs for me to sign. Others just had a piece of paper. I patiently signed for everyone while Chase waited.

"I'm sorry, Chase. You didn't have to wait for me."

"It's okay, Emmy. I just wanted to make sure you were all right."

"Those kids weren't going to hurt me."

"I promised Kenny I would watch out for you. I want to make sure you get home safely."

"It's not like I'm a rock star and need a bodyguard."

"To some of these kids you are. They've seen your picture in magazines, or on the CDs, and they think of you as a star whether you want them to or not. They see you on a stage singing with a bunch of guys, so to them you are a performer."

"I don't want to be, Chase." I remember getting emotional.

"I know you don't, honey."

"If we ever lose sight of why you guys are leaving your families and our egos take over, it is all over for me."

"We will just have to remember Des Moines. That should deflate our egos."

"You're right about that."

Chase and I joined the other guys on the bus.

"What's the plan, boss?"

"We should be backstage by five thirty. The food tent opens at one. You need to wear your backstage passes at all times. If you want to hear the other bands or the speakers you can."

"I want to hear Jennifer Sinclaire, but I bet she's not half as good a singer as Emmy," Ryan said.

"Emmy, did you realize you and Jennifer Sinclaire will be the only females on stage today?" Dixie asked.

"I didn't even think about that."

I didn't want to hang out on the bus, so I asked Dixie if he wanted to go for a walk.

"Are you bored, Emmy?"

"Yes! It's too quiet on the bus."

"I'll walk around for a while, but then I want to check out some of the other groups."

I giggled and asked, "Do you mean the other groups of college girls?"

Dixie smiled, but didn't respond. We went for a walk to kill time. I wasn't bothered by anymore autograph seekers.

"If I tell you something will you promise not to tell the other guys?"

"Sure Emmy. What is it?"

"I miss Kenny."

"Of course you do. It's natural to miss him."

"I mean something different, Dixie."

Dixie looked at me. Looking back on it now, I realized he thought I was talking about sex. He made an assumption about my relationship with Kenny.

"I get it now, Emmy. I think I would miss that too if I was married."

"Have you ever...?"

"Before I was a Christian, I did."

153

"Do you miss it?"

"Sure! I'm still human, Emmy. I'm always looking at the pretty girls wondering if one of them might be the one for me." He glanced at a group of five students as they walked past. "Unfortunately, college girls are too young for me, but they are easy on the eyes."

"Do you think I'm pretty, Dixie?" I asked trying to embarrass him.

"Of course I do. Just because you're almost married doesn't mean you're not attractive. I'm not saying I would ever try anything with you. I would never do that with any married lady."

"I'm sure glad we're going home after tonight. I can't wait to... you know." I said as I thought about my wedding.

"You're really something, Emmy."

I realized Dixie thought I meant I was horny. I realized I was.

"Where is Kenny now?"

"He's in Australia, remember?"

"I know that. I was asking about which city."

"I'm pretty sure they're in Sydney this weekend."

I stopped walking and looked at Dixie. "I wish I knew more single women. You deserve a good Christian girl."

"Well, there's always ChristianGirls.Com."

"Is there really such a site?" I asked.

He grinned and shrugged, so I smacked his arm. We kept walking and talking about our life to each other. I learned that Dixie wanted to start his own band, or maybe I already knew that. I can't remember for sure.

"Kenny might be able to help you with that. He has a few connections."

"I've talked to Alan about it. I'm talking about a rock band, Emmy. I don't feel that just because I'm a Christian I have to play church music all the time. I mean, if I was a carpenter, I wouldn't be restricted to building only churches."

154

"I understand. Kenny is a good example although he was a musician before he totally surrendered his life to Christ. He was saved when he was a teenager, but he told me he always held something back." I didn't say anything to Dixie about Kenny's relationship with Becky. It was while he and Becky were dating, that he fully surrendered his life to Jesus.

"Exactly! So was I, Em. Kenny didn't stop playing his music when he was born again."

"You are a good singer, Dixie, and you can sure play that guitar. If you had your own band, the girls would be after you. Are you prepared to deal with that?"

"I'm mature enough to realize that those girls are not what I need."

By the time Dixie and I returned to the bus, the doors to the venue were open and it was about time for the festival to begin. Ryan was anxious to watch the other performers.

"Emmy, do you want to go with me? I want to see Jennifer Sinclaire."

"I'll go with you, Ryan, but isn't she on second?"

"I just want to get a good seat."

"You do realize that with your pass you can go backstage. You could probably watch her from the side of the stage."

"That would be so cool!"

"Yeah, just keep your cool and don't act like a dork," I teased.

I went with Ryan. We hung out backstage and Ryan talked to some of the crew members working behind the scenes. I stayed with Ryan and didn't say much. No one paid me any attention. I'm sure they thought I was just Ryan's shy girlfriend. The first artist, who neither of us had ever heard of, was just a singer with an acoustic guitar. That didn't excite either of us even though he had a good voice. I can't remember his name, so I'll have to check my journal to see if I even wrote it down. I might have forgotten.

When Jennifer Sinclaire came out on stage with her band, Ryan was very attentive. Jennifer's style was kinda country, but with a little rock added. She was twenty-three and single. I thought Ryan had a crush on her without even knowing her. Ryan listened to her whole set and couldn't take his eyes off of her. I noticed Jennifer smiled at him as she left the stage.

"I think she smiled at you, Ryan," I teased. I couldn't help myself.

"I think she was smiling at you, Emmy."

"Yeah, if you want to believe that, you're a doofus." I poked him in the ribs, then I grabbed his hand.

"She's really pretty. Don't you think?"

"What I think doesn't matter. It's what you think that counts."

The next act had more of a hard rock sound. They seemed to have trouble getting their sound just right. Ryan liked them, but I didn't much care for their sound, or their attitude. They whipped their long hair around like I had seen other hard rockers do while they were singing about Jesus. It didn't feel like worship to me, but the crowd liked it.

"I'm going back to the bus, Ryan. Don't forget to come back to get ready."

"I'll see you later, Emmy. I won't forget."

I couldn't resist teasing him. "I could tell you thought Jennifer Sinclaire was pretty."

Ryan kinda blushed and admitted, "She's pretty, but not a pretty as you. You're a better singer, too."

"Thanks, Ryan. Maybe you should find out if she's married, or has a boyfriend." I didn't know about her relationship status at that time, but I learned more about her later in the day.

"Yeah, maybe. I doubt if I ever see her again though," Ryan said.

I returned to the bus to get ready. By five everyone was ready when Ryan ran in to get changed. He was working as the guitar tech tonight.

156

The preceding act was almost done with their set when we arrived backstage. After that group finished, the Zawaski brothers, with help from the production crew, worked to get our gear ready. It didn't take too long, and we had time for a quick soundcheck. We were ready to go when the speaker finished. The curtain opened and Alan kicked off the first song. Right from the start the crowd rose to their feet. We didn't slow down until we did "Yolanda's Song." Other than for that song and one other quiet song, the crowd remained on their feet for the whole set. I saw that Ryan had noticed Jennifer Sinclaire watching and listening from the side of the stage. He walked over to her after we were finished.

"I didn't know you were part of the band." She must have recognized him from earlier.

"I'm not really in the band. I just help out when I can. My name is Ryan, by the way. My dad does the front of house sound."

"You guys are really good. I mean really, really good! I've heard your CD, so I knew Emmy Colasanti was a good singer, but she can really get a crowd going."

"Yeah! She's a pro. Did you know she used to sing with Kenny Colwell and Fridays At Five."

"Serious?"

"For real!"

"No wonder you guys are so good. Is it true that Kenny Colwell wrote that one song you guys do?"

"Yes, he wrote it on a couple napkins in a place called Darby's Dogs."

"That is such a beautiful song. I mean it's sad because the girl died, but it has such a beautiful message."

"Sometimes Emmy cries when she sings it."

"I can understand why. I cry every time I hear it."

"Do you want to meet her?"

"Sure! I don't want to bother her, though."

"Don't worry. Emmy is not like that. She is the sweetest girl ever." Ryan brought Jennifer over to where I

157

was talking to Dixie. I saw them coming as I glanced over my shoulder. I was happy that Ryan had the courage to talk to her. I had turned back to face Dixie by the time Ryan touched my shoulder. I turned around.

"Emmy, do you have a minute?"

I smiled at Ryan and Jennifer noticed. "Sure, Ryan. What's up?" I'm pretty sure she thought I sounded like his teenage girlfriend.

"Do you have a minute to talk to Jennifer?"

"Of course, Ryan. Anything for you." I bit my lip because I realized I was giving her the wrong impression about Ryan and me. "Jennifer, how are you? I listened to your set earlier. You have such a beautiful voice."

"Thank you. May I call you Emmy?"

I giggled and Jennifer and I talked for a few minutes.

"Ryan told me you are the sweetest girl and don't act like a diva at all. He's right. You seem like a little sister, and I've just met you."

"Thank you, Jennifer." I checked the time. "Shoot! I gotta run. I need to go take my turn at the table. Will you guys excuse me?"

"You mean you go out there and work at the merchandise table?" Jennifer asked.

"Sure. We all take turns. It wouldn't be fair otherwise." I waved goodbye to Jennifer and blew a kiss at Ryan as I slipped away.

Chapter Fifteen

"Kenny, could you stop at the store after you drop the kids at school?" Emmy asked the next morning. "We need milk and bread."

"Is that it?" he asked as he grabbed his keys and wallet.

Emmy nodded and picked up a banana from the island. "That will get us by until I can make a list."

"Okay, I'm going to stop and see my parents. I need to go over some financial stuff with Dad."

"Call me if you need anything. I'll be in the den working," Emmy said and then kissed him.

"See you later, Em."

She waved to the kids from the landing outside the mudroom, closed the garage door, headed to the den and opened her laptop. *Now where did I leave off? Right, Carbondale.*

I made my way to the large entrance area or foyer or whatever it was called where all the merchandise tables were set up. I slipped behind our table, but Steve and Alan told me they would cover for me. I thanked them and scooted behind the big backdrop at the back of our booth.

Mark Haimes was at the side of the stage talking to Chase before his set. "How am I supposed to follow that? You guys blew everyone away."

"Thanks, Mark. We were just having so much fun and the energy from the crowd was amazing."

Aidan Cashell had arrived in time to catch about half of our set, but I didn't know it. To be honest, I probably wouldn't have recognized him because he now had a beard. Anyway, he walked over to Chase and introduced himself.

"Hello, it's a pleasure to meet you. I'm Chase Hillman. I sing and play keyboards."

"I saw most of your set. Mark is right. You guys are amazing. Especially your singer."

"Her name is Emmy Colasanti. She is so good, but she doesn't know it."

They chatted for a few minutes until Mark had to do his set. Chase and Aidan walked around the back.

By this time I was busy at the merchandise table, but I happened to see this guy walking toward our table. Though I suspected he might be Aidan Cashell, he was largely ignored by the large crowd around our table. The kids were buying CDs like crazy. He managed to get close and got my attention. I stared at him for a moment, not sure if he was really who I thought he was. The beard threw me off.

"Hi, Emmy. I'm Aidan. Could I talk to you for a moment?"

"Sure. Do you want to come around to the back where it's a bit calmer?"

He followed me behind the backdrop where we could talk without having to yell.

"I was amazed by your set. You are really good."

I didn't know what to say. Kenny has told me the same thing many times, but I always thought he said that because he loved me and was a bit biased. "Thank you. We were having fun. It wasn't exactly like our normal set. We were concentrating on entertaining the audience instead of ministering to them."

We talked until he needed to get ready for his set. He was a really nice guy. I stayed with the guys at the merchandise table until around eight o'clock.

"Go ahead, Em. We can handle it now. Go have some fun," Hank said.

I headed backstage and saw Aidan talking to Mallory and Iris. Chase was there and he spotted me. He walked over and asked if I was all right. I said I was.

"Come on. I'm going to the bus to change clothes. We need to get packed up as soon as Aidan is finished."

I nodded. "Okay. I'll go with you. I don't think we have any CDs left. It's a good thing we're going home tonight."

160

I changed into jeans and a t-shirt so I could help the guys load the truck. I wore a baseball cap with my ponytail sticking out through the hole thing in the back, and Ryan told me I looked like a teenager. Dixie and Alan broke down the merchandise table after most of the crowd was gone. There wasn't much left to pack up. All the CDs were gone and so were all the devotional books, which pleased me even more. It didn't take very much longer to load out the gear. The Zawaski brothers had loaded most of the gear already.

They smiled at me. "Are you trying to look like a boy, Miss Emmy?"

"I was just wearing my comfortable clothes, so I could help you guys."

"We've got everything already loaded. It was easy."

When the truck was loaded and ready, Buck and Carl headed home. Jess went with the truck. It would be a couple of hours until the bus left.

I grabbed Ryan and asked, "Will you come with me? I want to go backstage and talk to people, but I don't want to go by myself."

"Sure, I'll go with you, Em. Why are you afraid to go by yourself?"

"I feel shy around these guys because they are famous musicians."

Ryan laughed, "And Kenny is just... what?"

I grinned and smacked his arm. I held onto his arm as we went backstage to say goodbye to some new friends. I was glad to be going home, but it had been a wonderful tour. I wondered how Kenny managed when they were on tour for months at a time. Many of the band members from the different groups were still hanging out backstage. I managed to remain unrecognized for a while, but then Jennifer saw me with Ryan and ran over.

"Hi, Emmy. Hasn't this been a great day. I had so much fun. I've never played in front of so many people."

I'm pretty sure Jennifer assumed Ryan was my boyfriend since I was holding onto him.

161

"It was fun. I liked playing with a bunch of other bands." I looked up at Ryan and continued, "We've been on the road, but we're heading home tonight. I can't wait to sleep in my own bed." I leaned into Ryan and he put his arm around my shoulder to steady me. I'm sure it left Jennifer with the wrong impression. I did that a lot back then. I know better now.

Some of the guys from the bands wondered who Jennifer was talking to and they finally recognized me.

Aidan came over. "It was a pleasure to meet you ladies. Maybe we will run into each other again somewhere."

I grinned, but didn't say anything. I hate to mention this, but a few months later I learned that Aidan's wife filed for a divorce. Apparently, he had a few affairs while on the road. I know that happens, and it's a real shame.

Anyway, Ryan and I hung out with Jennifer as we wandered around backstage for thirty minutes. Ryan told me he liked Jennifer's southern accent. Finally, it was time to leave. Ryan and I headed out to the bus, but before we could get on board I was attacked with Super Soaker water pistols by Dixie and Joe. I was totally soaked by the powerful water guns. I was surprised but had a smile on my face. Larry handed me a fully loaded Super Soaker, so I began to fire at the guys. Joe gave his to Ryan. We chased each other around the buses and were having a blast. I was getting hit more often than I managed to hit the guys, but I didn't care. Eventually we all ran out of water. The guys all hugged me for being such a good sport.

Joe was very apologetic. "I'm sorry, Miss Emmy, but the guys made me do it."

"It's okay, Joe. It was fun. Where did you guys find these water guns?"

"Larry bought them the other day. He told me that Leonard always has some on the Fridays bus."

"I should have known it was Larry's idea."

Dixie came over to me and smiled. "Did you have fun, Emmy?"

"Yes! I wish we had these before tonight. We could have been having water wars all week. It would have been a blast!"

"Next time we go on a tour, we will have to make sure we have them along."

"I'm going to ask Larry where he got these. I'm going to buy some for home."

"You are really soaked, Em."

"I know! I'm soaked all the way through."

Dixie smiled and admitted, "I confess. I was the guy aiming at you the most."

"Naughty boy! Now my underwear is all wet."

"I've still got some ammo left. Should I use it on you?"

"Where are you going to shoot me?" I realized I was flirting with Dixie and stopped.

Just then Ryan came around the bus and began firing at me. I squealed as the cold water hit me in the back. Dixie shot at Ryan as I moved behind him. Ryan ran around the corner of the bus to safety, then stuck his head around the corner. Dixie was there but not me. I had taken Dixie's gun and was running around to get behind Ryan. I came around the corner of the bus just as Ryan realized where I must be. We fired at almost point blank range at each other. I turned and ran around the bus and straight into the arms of Jennifer Sinclaire. Ryan chased me and began firing but ran out of water. Jennifer laughed at us because we were having so much fun.

Jennifer asked, "Do you guys always have water fights?"

"We haven't before tonight, but we will from now on. Ryan soaked me."

"I might have to buy some of those to use on the guys in my band."

Ryan stood behind me. He held his gun over my head and let the remaining water drip down onto my hair.

163

I smiled and said, "You're gonna get it later, you stinker."

"I've gotta run. You guys have a fun trip home." Jennifer turned to look at the old minivan she and the guys from her band used for traveling. "It must be nice to travel in a large touring bus," she said to Chase.

"We have a lot of support from our record company and the church."

Ryan and I were alone. "Have you cooled off now, Emmy?"

"That was fun. We should bring these every time we go somewhere. I should change into dry clothes."

I changed clothes, came back out to the lounge and sat next to Ryan.

Chase wanted to talk to everyone before we left. "I want to thank everyone for the great job the last three weeks. We have had some different experiences, especially this week. Some lows and some highs. I think it has certainly been worth the effort. I hope everyone can get a good rest tonight because we are on the schedule for the morning service. Does anyone else want to say anything?"

"I'd like to say something if I may," I said.

"No! We don't want to hear it, Emmy."

My jaw dropped.

"I'm just kidding! You should know that by now," Dixie teased.

"I just want to say how much I appreciate the way you guys treated me this week. I know it was different with me in the bunk instead of in the back."

"Anyone got any ammo left in their Super Soaker?" Dixie asked.

I squealed and tried to hide behind Ryan.

"You know how much we love you, Emmy, and without you we wouldn't be doing this," Chase said.

"Come on, guys! There are plenty of good singers in our church alone."

"That's true, but none of them could do what you

do. None of them could have done what you did in Milwaukee."

I remembered that night and began to cry softly. Ryan noticed and put an arm around me.

Hank spoke up, "Chase is right, Emmy. You have a special gift and a calling to do this. Just because someone might be a good singer does not mean they could do what you do."

"Thank you, Hank. I do feel a calling to sing for the teens especially."

The bus was ready to leave Carbondale for the trip home. Some of the guys were too wound up to go to sleep so they stayed up. I was getting sleepy and started to yawn.

"I'm going to go to bed. I'll see you guys in the morning."

"Night, Emmy. We'll try to be quiet."

"You can make all the noise you want. I'm so tired I wouldn't wake up if you started playing your guitars at full volume."

I retrieved my pajamas from my suitcase and stepped into the bathroom. I showered and put on my pajamas. Only then did I realize I had forgotten my robe. I slipped quietly out of the bathroom and into my bunk. Thankfully, no one paid any attention to me as I did. Not that my pajamas were sexy or anything. Trust me, they weren't.

One by one the guys got ready for bed until only Dixie, Steve Van Zant and Alan were left. I could hear them talking about putting together a rock band. Finally, they headed to their bunks.

Emmy heard the kids hollering and realized she had worked without taking a break for lunch. She saved her work, closed the laptop and headed to the kitchen.

Chapter Sixteen

Emmy slowly opened her eyes and realized the sound she heard was her cell phone on the nightstand. She reached out, saw who was calling and answered.

"I'm sorry. Did I wake you up?"

"You're not sorry, but you did wake me up."

"Did you forget to take the kids to school?" Father James asked.

"No, Kenny took them." She brushed her hair out of her eyes and glanced at the clock. "Shoot! I need to get my butt out of bed. What are you up to today?"

"I have the day off, and it's been a while since I've seen my favorite little sister... named Emily."

"Have I ever told you you're my least favorite brother?"

"You might have mentioned it, but I know you're joking. You got any plans for the day?"

"I was going to work on my book, but I could wait until after dinner if you've got a better offer."

"Would you be interested in a round of golf?"

Emmy sat up, swung her legs over the edge of the bed and shrugged. "Not really. The only golf I've ever played was at Sandusky's. Is that what you mean?"

"I meant real golf. I've been invited to play at the Barclay Country Club, and I need a caddy."

"Are you yanking my chain? I don't know how to caddy, and I'm not about to carry a heavy golf bag all around the place."

Father James laughed and said, "All you have to do is ride in the cart with me and keep me company."

"Isn't it too cold for golf? It is October."

"If you'd get out of bed, you'd realize it is sunny and over seventy degrees. What do you say?"

"I just have to ride in the cart, huh?"

"And keep score."

"Who are you playing with?"

"Oh, did I forget to mention that?"

"Yeah," Emmy said slowly.

"I'm playing with John Randolph and some guy named Bertucci."

Emmy's eyes brightened. "You're playing with Tony and John? I didn't know they played golf."

"John is a decent golfer, but Tony's just learning."

Emmy jumped off the bed and raced to the bathroom. "Why didn't you say so in the first place. I wouldn't miss this for anything. Has he ever played before?"

"He did hit a few buckets at the range, but this will be his first real round."

"Will you pick me up?"

Father James held the phone away from his ear for a moment and then asked, "Are you in the bathroom?"

"I'm getting in the shower. Why?"

Father James shook his head. "Just be ready in fifteen minutes. Tony will pick you up at your house."

Emmy made it downstairs in time to grab a banana and gulp down some orange juice before Tony, John and Father James walked into the mudroom.

"Are you ready, Em?" Tony asked.

She set the glass in the sink and hurried around the island. "I'm ready. Do I need to bring anything?"

"Not really," Father James answered while standing in the doorway.

"Can I bring my cell phone?" she asked.

"Sure, why wouldn't you?"

"Not sure if they allowed photos." She stuffed her phone in her back pocket.

"Is that what you're wearing?" Father James asked.

Emmy looked down at her faded jeans and Fridays At Five t-shirt. "Yeah, why? Do they have a dress code?"

"Men have to wear shirts with a collar," Tony answered.

"And that matters to me because?" Emmy asked slowly.

"It might be a little cool for just a t-shirt. You should take a light jacket," Father James suggested.

Emmy sat in the middle row of Tony's van with Father James on the way to the country club.

167

"Are you a good golfer?" she asked Father James. "You've never mentioned it before."

"I used to play a lot more in Kansas, and I would shoot in the low eighties. Now I settle for breaking ninety."

"How about you, John?"

"I can break a hundred."

She tapped Tony's shoulder and asked, "What made you decide to become the next Tiger Woods?"

"It's a way to meet more people."

"You could hang out at the mall and meet people," she teased.

"I meant influential people, brat."

"I thought you had to be a member to play here?" Emmy asked as they arrived.

"We are members," John answered.

She looked at Father James.

He shrugged. "The Bishop is a member, and I've been here as his guest. He likes to bring me along when he wants to hustle some new members." He raised a hand and added, "Just to raise money for the church, mind you."

Twenty minutes later, they were on the first tee.

"You can have the honors, Father James," John said.

Father James drove his tee shot over two hundred and twenty yards down the middle of the fairway. John's drive was farther but just into the first cut of the rough.

"Okay, Tony, it's your turn," Emmy said. "Don't be nervous just because we're all watching."

Tony walked up, stuck his tee in the ground, took a practice swing, got ready, took a deep breath and let it rip.

Emmy, John and Father James watched as Tony's tee shot soared high into the sky and over some trees about two hundred yards away.

"Nice shot, Tony," Emmy said. "But how come yours went that way if the green is over there?" She pointed to the right.

Tony's shoulders slumped. He turned to face Emmy and handed her his driver. "I'm taking a shortcut."

She grinned as she carried his club back to the cart.

On the fourth green Emmy waited quietly as Tony lined up a three foot putt.

"The greens are a bit slow today," Father James said.

Tony took a deep breath and stroked the ball right at the hole, but it ended up two inches short.

"What was your score for that hole?" Emmy asked as she walked back to the carts with Father James.

"I parred it and John had a six."

Emmy wrote down the scores and then asked, "What did you get, Tony?"

He mumbled a number.

"What?"

He jammed his putter into his bag, turned to face Emmy and said, "I got a twelve, okay?"

Emmy wrote it down, got into the cart with Father James, quickly added up the scores and said, "Tony, you're ahead by twenty shots."

"You do know the lowest scores wins, right?" Father James asked.

"I know, but Tony's getting more practice than you guys."

On the eighth green Tony sank a fifteen foot putt.

"All right!" Emmy high-fived him. "You got a six. Way to go!"

"Em, it was a par three hole," Tony said.

"So. You're getting better. That's only two times over par."

Along the way, Father James offered some tips to Tony, and on the back nine, Tony started to improve.

"Nice drive, creep," Emmy said after Tony's drive landed in the middle of the fairway even farther than Father James' shot.

Tony turned, smiled and said, "Thanks, brat, but I want to see you try to hit a golf ball."

"I can hit it. Maybe not as far, but I bet I could hit it straight."

"Put your money where your mouth is," Tony said.

"Duh! I don't have any clubs."

"You can use one of mine," Tony offered. He handed her his nine iron. "Go ahead. There's no one behind us."

"Yeah, the only other group out here passed us an hour ago," Emmy said. She took the club and John tossed her a ball.

"Keep your left arm straight," Father James said.

Emmy set her feet, took a slow backswing and followed through with her head down. The ball shot into the air and landed in the middle of the fairway.

"Nice shot, Emmy," John said. "Right down the middle."

"I didn't see where it landed," Emmy said as she looked for it.

Tony walked up to her and pointed. "It went about twenty yards, Em."

She poked his side. "Well, I knew it wouldn't go very far."

Since there wasn't a group behind them, Father James let Emmy hit a couple shots.

"Not bad since my clubs are a bit long for you," he said after Emmy hit the ball close to the green.

"Beginner's luck," Tony said.

"Where did your ball go, creep?"

"It's in those trees over there," Tony said and then pointed. "I wanted to hit it there so I could take a leak."

Emmy rolled her eyes. "Such a lame excuse. Do you want me to give you a few lessons?"

Tony found his ball on the edge of the tree line. His next shot landed on the green and rolled within five feet of the hole. His best shot of the day.

"Nice shot." John high-fived Tony as they walked onto the green and marked their balls.

"You're up, Emmy," Father James said as he handed her his wedge. "Slow backswing and follow through."

Emmy nodded, took a practice swing and set her feet. She lofted the ball higher than expected. "Oh, crap!"

The ball landed two feet in front of the hole, took one bounce, hit the metal flag shaft and dropped straight down into the cup. Tony and John looked at each other and sighed.

"Oh, I guess I hit it right after all," Emmy said as she walked up, took the flag out, handed it to Tony, reached down, grabbed her ball and smirked at the guys. "Golf isn't so hard."

Tony three-putted from five feet.

Emmy added up the scores after the eighteenth hole.

"Do you guys want to hear the bad news?"

"Sure," John said.

"Okay, Father James shot an eighty-six. Not bad for someone his age. John almost broke a hundred. Just eight shots over it." She looked at Tony, smiled and said, "You had an eighty-five... on the front nine, but you improved to a sixty-one on the backside."

"Nice improvement," John said.

"I'm buying," Father James said. He put his putter in the bag and slid onto the seat.

"This was fun. I can't wait to send these photos to all my friends," Emmy said as she hopped onto the cart and floored it. "If I was a regular golfer, I would want a faster cart. This thing's too slow."

At the dinner table that evening Emmy recounted her adventures to the kids and Kenny.

"Did Uncle John really hit the ball in the pond?" Isabella asked. "Did he have to go swimming to find it?"

"Can we play golf in the woods like Uncle Tony?" Heather asked.

"He wasn't always in the woods, but more than the other guys."

"I want to take my gun in the woods and shoot some golfs," Kevin said.

By eight thirty Emmy was in the den sitting in her recliner with her laptop.

It was three minutes after six when the bus pulled into the church parking lot. I woke up as soon as the bus stopped. I pulled on a pair of shorts and a sweatshirt and jumped out of the bunk. I ran to the bathroom, took care of business, then ran to the front of the bus. Larry opened the door and I stepped out into the rather chilly morning air. Tony was leaning on the driver's door of his GMC Envoy waiting for me.

171

"Emmy! I'm over here."

I heard his voice and ran over to him. "I thought Kristen was picking me up. Why are you here instead?"

"She wasn't feeling all that great last night, so I volunteered to be here."

"That was sweet of you," I hugged him and then poked him in his ribs.

"Do you need help with your stuff?"

"Yes, please."

We walked over to the bus. By now everyone was up, dressed and semi-awake.

"I need my coffee! Is there any coffee ready?" Hank complained.

"I'll fix your coffee, Hank. Just give me a couple minutes."

"Where are the bagels I bought yesterday?" Steve asked as he searched through the cupboard.

"They're gone. You guys ate them all."

"Is this milk still okay, Emmy?"

"Does it smell okay, Ryan?"

He opened the carton and sniffed it. He made a face. "It smells funny."

"Then dump it out. Have some water instead."

"Emmy, have you seen my book?"

"I put in on your bunk, Steve. Did you look there?"

"I found it. Thanks, Emmy."

All the guys were looking for something to eat or drink. They started gathering up their belongings as Tony watched. It seemed rather chaotic to him, but to the guys it was routine. I started the coffee and then grabbed my suitcase. I handed it to Tony and grabbed my dresses from the small closet.

"Will you take these out to the truck for me? I need to make sure the guys have their coffee and don't leave anything behind. We have to return the bus this morning."

"I'll be waiting outside, Em. Take your time."

"It shouldn't take too long."

"Yeah, whatever you say, Em." He laughed at me,

172

so I stuck out my tongue. I gathered the few remaining items from the bunk and stuffed them in my backpack. "Don't forget to strip the bunks. Toss all the bed sheets in a pile by the couch." I somehow managed to slip in and out of the guys as they scurried about. I stopped and bent over to pick up a newspaper from the floor and was run over by Alan.

"I'm sorry, Emmy! Are you okay?"

"I'm all right. Is this your paper?"

"Not mine! I think it was Carl's."

For the next thirty minutes I played the role of mother to all the guys. I made sure they had everything that belonged to them. I inspected all the bunks and the back bedroom. Finally, the bus was ready for Larry to return it to the leasing company. The truck and trailer belonged to Larry and his father, Leonard. It would be unloaded later and taken home by Larry. The guys gathered around outside and shared some hugs.

"Thank you for letting me use the bedroom, Emmy. I really appreciate it. My back feels a lot better now."

"You're welcome, Hank. It wasn't too bad being with the guys. They were careful and gave me enough privacy."

Chase told everyone, "I know I don't have to remind you about this morning's service, but I will anyway. We need to meet at eight in the music room."

He heard a collective groan from everyone but he knew they would all be there in a couple hours.

"Also, we are playing May 24 in Elgin at the Hemmens Auditorium. I've been there before and it's a great place to see a concert. That's a Saturday night. I know the promoters. Earl and Rose Wheeling. Their company is M&R Productions, and they always do a good job of promoting their events and they treat the artists extremely well. We are going to use the truck but we won't have the bus. We will make carpool arrangements later. See you in a couple hours. Thanks again for a great tour."

173

Fifteen minutes after leaving the church, Tony pulled into my driveway.

"That was quick."

"There's no traffic on Sunday mornings," he answered.

"Are you going home, or are you hanging out here until church?"

"I brought clothes with me, so I guess I will hang out here. You don't mind, do you?"

"No, will you help me carry my stuff inside, please?"

Tony grabbed my suitcases while I unlocked the back door. I ran upstairs to see if Kristen was awake. I peeked in Kristen's room, but she appeared to be asleep. I was about to walk away when Kristen said, "I'm kinda awake, Emmy. Come and sit by me. I know you want to tell me all about your week." Kristen sat up and I jumped onto the bed and lay next to her. For fifteen minutes I talked about my week.

We got ready for church and arrived just before eight. Kristen and I ran to the music room. Chase went over the service schedule. All six songs were ones we knew well. We ran through the songs quickly and had some time before our Sunday School class started.

Even though some of the worship team members were tired, we had a wonderful service. Tony gave Kristen and me a ride home and waited for us to change clothes. We picked up John at his apartment and headed over to Tony's house. Mama had been preparing a meal to celebrate my return. Kristen and I helped Mama get everything ready. Daniel and Karla Keasling, Kristen's parents, arrived with even more food. I stood next to Kristen as she talked to her parents.

"Mom, you didn't have to bring anything."

"I know, dear, but I told Mama I would bring a salad and a dessert. You should talk to your father. He is being more stubborn than usual."

"What is Daddy doing?" Kristen asked.

"It's what he's not doing. He is supposed to go to see his doctor, but he won't. His hip has been bothering him again. He has trouble just getting out of bed in the mornings."

Kristen's father had been putting off seeing his doctor because he needed hip replacement surgery. Kristen saw her father talking to John and Tony. She went over and hugged him while I followed along. "Daddy, I need to talk to you. Mom told me that you need to see your doctor, and you aren't going. Will you go see the doctor as a favor for me? If your hip is hurting too much, you won't be able to enjoy any grandkids you might have one of these days."

"Are you trying to tell me something, Kristen?"

"No, of course not. I meant that you might have grandkids in the future. Will you please see the doctor?"

"I can't take the time away from work."

"Yes, you can! You are basically retired now. Why don't you just make it official. The company will survive if you retire."

Daniel Keasling had a hard time ever saying no to Kristen. "All right. I'll go see the doctor."

"Thank you, Daddy. I love you."

"I love you, too, sweetie."

"Dinner is ready. Let's eat," Tony announced.

Emmy checked the stats. *That's a long chapter. I might have to shorten it. I could cut the last part because it's not really all that relevant, but I'll wait until I talk to Denise again.* Emmy saved her work and closed her eyes and dozed off for a moment. She woke up to the sound of Heather and Isabella singing one of her new Christmas songs and smiled.

Chapter Seventeen

Emmy walked into Starbucks and spotted Denise sitting at the same table as the last time they met. Denise sipped her coffee while holding her phone to her ear. She waved at Emmy.

Emmy moved past the line of customers at the counter. *Do you ever relax, Denise? I bet not.* Emmy sat across from Denise and opened her laptop.

"How are you? It's good to see you again. Thank you for emailing me the updated story. I read it over the last two days, and I am impressed by the improvement. I did correct some obvious mistakes, and I made some suggestions." Denise paused and shrugged as her phone rang again.

"I saw your email this morning. I like how your suggestions are in different colors. That makes them easy to spot."

Denise listened to her call for a time before rolling her eyes. "No! That's final. Deal with it." She ended the call. "You would think kids old enough to be in college could make some decisions on their own. Now, have you decided on the end of the book? Are you going to continue it to the present, or will that be another story?"

Emmy took a sip from her bottle of water. "I think I will have to end it earlier otherwise it will be a thousand pages long. I know I will have to cut some stuff because no one wants to read about every single night on our tours."

"True. You need to write about the highlights. I want you to pick moments and events that were either funny, sad, spiritually uplifting, or memorable for some reason." Denise lifted a hand and touched a finger for each point. "They don't have to be all about the band. Your readers want to know about you. What makes you tick. What your favorite color is. It's purple, I know. Share some intimacy with the reader. I don't mean you have to share intimate details about your sex life, but you could if they are funny." Denise chuckled and waved her coffee mug around without spilling a drop. "Do you see where I'm going?"

Emmy nodded. "I was kinda saving some of that for later chapters."

"That's fine, but you need to keep your reader interested from the start. Add a few details that entice the reader to keep turning the pages. Tell them something about Kenny."

"I could remind the readers how much of a dork he is." Emmy grinned as Denise's phone rang again.

Denise took the call and talked for a couple of minutes. "I'm sorry, but I need to get back to the office. Keep writing and don't be discouraged. This is going to be a good read." Denise stuffed her phone into her large canvas bag, shoved her wide-brimmed hat on, flipped her long black hair over her shoulders, took a final sip of coffee, stood up and drifted out of the Starbucks like a breeze floating through a crowded grove of trees.

Emmy sat for a moment and thought about her book. *I'm going to keep writing, and we can always reorganize the chapters after I finish the first draft.* She moved to the other side of the table so she could watch people and began to work.

I thought about skipping ahead to May after we got back from our honeymoon, but I changed my mind. So about the wedding, it was absolutely perfect! Of course I cried during the ceremony. We booked the Lincoln Hotel for the reception even though it cost a small fortune. By the end of the night, I was exhausted. Kenny took me to the carriage house and carried me up the stairs. I was so sleepy that he had to undress me. I don't think he minded. I'm not sure if I should include this, but what the heck. I fell asleep, and it wasn't until a couple of hours later that we finally made love. My first time, and it was better than I ever dreamed. We went to Ireland and England for our honeymoon, and we did do some sightseeing. Enough about that.

At band practice on Thursday Hank's back was bothering him so much that he couldn't play. He had been to his doctor earlier that day. Now he had to tell Chase that he might need surgery. He definitely wouldn't be able to play on Saturday in Elgin. I stood beside him as he told Chase the news.

"Hank, you need to take care of your back and not worry about us. We can use either Ryan or John Patterson. I know Ryan would love to play. He knows all the songs."

"I'm really sorry, Chase. Maybe you should find a permanent replacement for me. I would like to continue, but it's just too hard on my back. After I recover from the surgery, maybe I can still play on Sunday mornings."

"Hank, you have given the church many years of faithful service. You deserve a break. I'm sorry it's because of your back, but you will recover, I'm sure."

I was too afraid to even hug him for fear of hurting him.

Chase informed everyone about Hank's back issues. "We need to keep Hank in our prayers. I asked Ryan if he feels ready to play Saturday, and he assured me he was ready and willing. I know he is capable." Chase went over the Sunday morning service and then the touring band rehearsed. Alan Vicini took over for Skip Mason on drums and Dixie Case joined on guitar. John Patterson would also be playing since Elgin was fairly close. Kristen was going to sing harmonies with me. I was excited to have Kristen with me for this concert. Jeff Morrissey agreed to run lights and Bruce Sutherland was going to take care of the monitors. Stuart Lederer would be mixing the front of house. After the rehearsal, Chase talked to the tech crew about the facilities at Hemmens.

"I think we can use our PA gear and their lighting desk. It is very similar to ours, Jeff. You won't have any trouble with it. You know our songs and we don't need a rock show just the usual suspects."

"Will there be volunteers for the spotlights?"

"Yes! Good point. Yvonne will be in charge of directing the light show if you want to call it that. They have a good communication system that we can use."

"Sounds like a plan, Chase."

Chase then talked to Stuart and Bruce. "Do you guys have any questions?"

178

Stuart and Bruce were both pros and didn't anticipate any problems.

"I just have one question. Is Emmy going to use her IEMs?"

"I think so. She likes the in-ear-monitors."

"I think that everyone should start using IEMs. It would help cut down on stage volume."

"I'm not sure we can afford it right now."

"I think we might have a way to get around that."

"They would make a big difference."

Chase arranged for everyone to travel up to Elgin in three large vans. Larry Twilley was going to drive the truck. The Zawaski brothers were going to load it on Friday. They would travel with Larry in the truck. So far everything was going according to plan. Chase wondered if he was forgetting anything.

Emmy closed her laptop and got the attention of the two ladies sitting at the next table. "Are you going to be here for a few minutes?"

"Would you mind watching my laptop for a minute? I really need to, you know." She pointed to the restroom.

"No problem, honey."

Emmy used the facilities and returned. "Thanks."

"No problem. You look familiar for some reason. Do we know you?"

"Probably not unless you go to Crest Ridge United Nazarene," Emmy said as she sat back down.

"No, but you look familiar for some reason."

Emmy shrugged and opened her laptop.

Shortly after noon on Saturday, the worship team and I left the parking lot of Crest Ridge United Nazarene on Canton Lane in Crest Ridge. Kenny was going with us, but he didn't plan on playing. He just wanted to be a spectator. The caravan of three vans and an eighteen-wheeler headed for Elgin and the Hemmens Auditorium.

179

Earl and Rose Wheeling met us upon our arrival. Earl and Chase were old friends and they hugged each other. Yvonne Hillman and Rose Wheeling had attended the same college and had even lived on the same floor of their dorm. They spent some time catching up on news about other friends.

Larry backed the truck up to the loading dock. Earl had hired six guys to help unload tonight. M&R Productions had a large staff of loyal volunteers to help handle the crowd along with the regular Hemmens employees. The doors were scheduled to open at six and the concert would begin at seven.

By five o'clock we were ready for the concert. We were hanging out in the green room preparing. The soundcheck went smoothly. Jeff Morrissey was using his laptop to program the lights. Tonight would be more like a rock show than any of our previous events, with the exception of the festival show in Carbondale. Chase had given the go ahead to Jeff to pull out all his tricks. Kenny and I were staying close to Kristen. This was Kristen's first time singing with the team in a place other than church. She had sung with The Notable Exceptions in front of thirty thousand people at the SoHam Memorial Stadium, though.

"Emmy, I think I'm more nervous tonight than ever before. What if I screw up?"

"If you do, then I will hit a sour note, too."

"You never hit a wrong note, Emmy."

"You won't either, Krissy."

"The guys don't seem nervous at all."

"They have butterflies just like we do but they don't let it show as much. Dixie told me he is nervous until he hits the first chord, then he is okay."

Our pre-concert food was ready and brought into the rehearsal room next to the green room. Chase prayed for the food and we dug in. I filled a plate with fresh fruit and had tea with honey to drink. This seemed to help my voice. Kristen and I sat at a table with Ryan and Kenny.

"Are you nervous about tonight, Ryan?" I asked even though I knew the answer.

"Not really. I've been to lots of shows with my dad, so I'm used to it."

"Yeah, but this time you will be on stage and not behind the scenes."

"Are you trying to scare me, Emmy?"

I giggled. "Maybe a little. I know you will be all right. I have confidence in you."

"Thanks, if I screw up, I'll blame you," he joked.

Some of the other guys were going through the food line.

"Hey, Dixie, are you going to leave any food for the rest of us?" Alan asked.

"I left a couple chicken legs for you. Isn't that enough?" Dixie answered back.

"Come on! You know I don't like legs."

He added something else, but I'm not going to include it here. You can use your imagination to figure out what he said.

The guys were hungry and filled their plates. I saw Boyd Goldman and Perry Johnstone grabbing some food. They had just finished their first year of college, I think, and were working as guitar techs tonight. Boyd was responsible for Steve's guitars and Perry was taking care of Dixie and John Patterson. Part of their job was to make sure the guitars were in the right spot in the rack and tuned correctly. Both guys were talented guitarists themselves. They were playing with the teen worship band on Wednesday nights. They were singers, also.

After everyone had finished eating, Boyd and Perry headed to the backstage area. They had work to do. Steve Van Zant joined them a few minutes later. "Are you guys finished? All the guitars are tuned correctly?"

"Yes, Mr. Van Zant. Tuned, wiped down and all ready to go."

"Do you remember which guitar I need for each song?"

"I have my list," Boyd answered.

"Don't lose it."

Steve was teasing Boyd. He knew how much this opportunity meant to him. Perry was talking to Dixie and John. Dixie had four guitars for tonight, but John was only using two. His were both Gibson acoustics. Dixie used Fender guitars exclusively. He had a collection of over twenty guitars, but didn't bring all of them on the road. Boyd and Perry would also take care of any needs Ryan might have. Ryan used the same bass guitar for every song, so he didn't require much attention. He did have Hank's bass as a backup if needed. Alan Vicini used Tama drums and hardware. His son Adam was with him tonight and was working as his drum tech. Adam was also part of the teen band. He played keyboards and sang. The teen band was very talented, and they dreamed about recording a CD in the near future just like the older guys. Bobby O'Connor was the drummer and Ryan played bass for the teen group. Bobby was the only one who didn't sing with the group. They didn't have a name for their band yet, but were narrowing down the choices. In case those names sound familiar, they should be. But I'll get into that later.

Kenny finished eating and stood up. "Em, I'll see you at home. I'm going to find my parents."

"You're going to ride home with them, right?"

"Yeah, we'll leave as soon as you finish. I know you'll be busy afterward, and I don't want to interfere."

"I'm glad you're here."

I kissed him and we hugged for a moment. Not too long because that might have caused a reaction if you get my drift. We had only been married for less than two months, and we were definitely making up for lost time.

Kenny headed out to look for his parents. He was going to sit with them for the concert. I felt a little nervous just knowing they would be in the audience. But at least I knew he wouldn't be surprising me on stage.

A few minutes before seven Kristen and I returned

to dressing room one to change clothes. We were both wearing new dresses for tonight. Chase and his wife Yvonne were using dressing room two. The rest of the guys were using the two remaining dressing rooms. We met back in the green room for a prayer before heading upstairs.

Upstairs in the auditorium, the crowd waited in anticipation. The house lights dimmed and the crowd rose to their feet and started cheering. Loudly! The curtain opened and the stage was dark. Two of the local volunteer workers led the band to the stage. They got into position. Kristen and I waited just off stage left. We would move into position after the band had started playing. Upstairs in the tech booth, Yvonne communicated with the light guys. They were set and ready. Stuart Lederer killed the house music that had been playing. He was ready to go. Bruce was ready on the side of the stage to mix the monitors. Stuart began the intro music.

"Are you ready, Emmy? We are all set to go." I heard Yvonne in my IEMs.

"We are in position, Yvonne. Wish us well."

"You guys will do a great job."

As the intro music ended, Alan counted off the first song. Jeff hit the light cue right on time as the band began playing. Kristen and I held hands as we walked out onstage together and the crowd erupted with cheers.

"It seems louder than at the stadium, Krissy. I can't tell for sure, but it looks like the place is packed."

"They are sure making a lot of noise."

I waited until Kristen was in position before grabbing my wireless microphone. I sang the first few lines of "Majestic," and the band kicked it into gear for the chorus. The crowd remained on their feet for the first five songs, and I was having fun. I had plenty of room to move around, and I think I was more animated tonight than ever. I danced and really got the crowd going. After five songs, we slowed things down. I had everyone sit as we sang some slower songs. We even did an old hymn.

Most of the crowd was young, but they still appreciated the hymn. It was difficult for me to see the audience because of the lights, but the energy from the crowd hyped me up.

The highlight of the evening for me was when we did "Yolanda's Song." I usually sang the song with my eyes closed, but tonight I opened them after the first verse. I could see an ocean of cell phones being held aloft by most of the crowd. I looked over at Kristen and saw tears already running down her face. We ended the concert with two uptempo songs and then Chase talked to the crowd.

"We will be in the front somewhere by the merchandise table area. If anyone needs to pray, we will be more than willing to pray with you. We aren't rock stars or anything. We all have a love for Christ and want to share his message with those in need."

Chase prayed, and the crowd started filing out. Kristen and I headed downstairs to our dressing room. We changed into jeans and headed back upstairs.

We recruited some teens from the church to handle the merchandise table tonight. That freed up the team to talk to people. Kristen was amazed by the attention I received and by how many times she heard comments about how tiny I was and how young I looked. It took over an hour, but eventually the crowd was gone. The merchandise table was packed away and everyone headed downstairs. The caterers did an excellent job and the whole team ate until we were full.

Chase and Yvonne talked to their friends. "Thank you for everything you have done, Earl. You, too, Rose. I know how much Earl depends on you."

"Thank you, Chase. It was a fantastic concert and there were over twenty teens who accepted Jesus."

"That's great. I hope that someone can follow through and talk to them about finding a church."

"I think they all filled out my cards. We will make sure someone talks to them. It's important."

184

"It looked like a large crowd tonight."

"We sold over eleven hundred tickets and gave away all the rest. We came out in the black tonight. That doesn't always happen. You know that's not why we do this though."

"I know, Earl. You are allowed to make money though. That's not a sin."

The two friends laughed and shook hands.

"Have a safe trip home and thanks again for tonight. I hope we can afford to have your group back again."

"Why do you say that, Earl?"

"You guys are going to start charging more money. I don't know if I can afford what you will be asking."

"You know we would do this for nothing if we could."

"Yeah! It's too bad it's getting so expensive for everything. The rental of the venue, the cost of transportation. Everything is going up in price."

"At least gas is still cheap," Chase said as he laughed.

Emmy glanced up and saw two college-age girls staring at her. She closed her laptop and bit her lip.

"We're sorry, but is anyone sitting here?" one of the girls put a hand on the empty chair across from Emmy.

"No, please have a seat. I need to get going." Emmy noticed a lot more people milling around.

"Thanks, you look familiar for some reason. Do we know you from school? We go to North Park College."

Emmy gathered her stuff and stood up. "I graduated from North Park, but it was several years ago."

"We must have seen you on campus," one of the girls said. "Thanks for letting us use the table."

"It's okay. It's not my table," Emmy said. She smiled and thought about the booth at Darby's she usually shared with Kenny and her friends.

Chapter Eighteen

Emmy sat with her laptop on her thighs and looked up every time someone entered the waiting room.

"You need to be patient," Mona Robertson patted Emmy's shoulder. "This could take a while."

"I know, but this is her fourth kid. It shouldn't take forever." Emmy turned her attention back to her story.

Kristen had moved back home to her parents' house after Kenny and I got back from our honeymoon. I told her she could stay, but she wouldn't.

"I'm not going to stay here with you guys."

"Why not? It's a big house."

"Because you guys are gonna be having sex all the time. That's why."

I understood her point. After waiting until we got married, Kenny and I were making up for lost time. I love Kenny and sex with my husband is wonderful. Okay, that's all I'm gonna say about sex.

On May 28, Wednesday night, Kenny and I made plans to hear Dixie and Alan's new band at Larry's Uptown Grill. Dixie brought a couple of guys he knew up from Alabama. Wells Callaghan and Stuart Dengel. One of them played lead and the other switched back and forth between guitar and keys. I can't remember who did what now. I'll have to ask Kenny because he will remember.

Mr. Kesson, the owner of the Steward Music Group, met us there with his wife, but he didn't want Dixie or the band to know he was there. He wanted to hear the band without the pressure of them knowing they were auditioning for his label. The guys were having trouble coming up with a name, so I suggested a name I thought might be cool for the band. The Dixie Case Band. Hey, I didn't say it was original, but it fit.

"We tried to convince Dixie to use that but he won't." Kenny told me. "His excuse was 'We are a band. It's not just me and a bunch of sidemen.'"

"How about 'Dixie Case and The Plaintiffs' then?"

"That's kinda catchy, Emmy."

Mr. Kesson would have the final say since it was his company and his money.

I sat with Kenny, and we listened to the first set. Mr. and Mrs. Kesson sat in the back, so the band couldn't see them. Kenny was even more impressed with Dixie's band since his friends from Alabama were playing. The lead guitar player was fantastic.

"What did you think?" I asked between sets.

"I think they have some talent. Dixie is good and Alan is a good fit. Steve Van Zant was not, though. He's all right as a player, but he is not creative enough to go in the studio. I'm glad that Dixie and Jimmy Cronin are getting along so well. I thought Jimmy would be a good fit."

Jimmy Cronin played bass guitar. He had really long hair that flowed all over and the ladies loved him. My only problem with him was his mouth. Two reasons. He swore constantly, and he always had a cigarette in his mouth.

"Steve doesn't want to quit his job. He told Chase that he might do a tour in the fall but that would be it for him. I don't blame him at all. He has a family to support."

"Don't get me wrong," Kenny waved a hand. "I love Steve. He's a great guy. I can understand his decision, though. He's still going to play at church."

I excused myself to use the restroom. Dixie saw me leave the table and knew where I was going. He waited in the hallway.

"Hi, Dixie. Are you waiting for me?"

"Yes. Did Kenny say anything about us?"

"He really likes your new lead guitar player."

"All right! Did he say anything else?"

"I'll tell you, but you can't tell anyone, okay."

"Okay Emmy. I won't. What did he say?"

"He told me that... I have pretty eyes!"

Dixie shook his head as I giggled and ran away.

We stayed for all three sets. It was nearly one

o'clock before we left. Kenny had a chance to talk to Dixie backstage. I waited while he talked to Dixie.

"I like the changes you have made. Nothing against Steve Van Zant, but the other guys are a better fit."

"Yeah. I agree. I like Steve, but he doesn't have the same goals as Alan and I. Do you want to meet my friends?"

"I do but maybe another time. I need to get Emmy home before she falls asleep. She has to work in the morning. She only has seven more days to work at Robertson Industries. Mr. Robertson has been so good to her. He has allowed her to work part-time and even gave her extra vacation time to go on tour."

"All right. Thanks for coming out to see us." Dixie turned to face me. "Thanks for bringing Kenny."

"It was my pleasure. We both had a good time."

"You're leaving soon, right?" Dixie asked.

"Yes, a week from this Sunday. I get to be on the road with Kenny and the guys for the whole summer. I'm looking forward to it."

I waved goodbye as Kenny and I left. In the car I asked, "Are they really good?"

"Yes, Emmy, they really are. Mr. Kesson thinks so, too."

"I thought they were, but I wanted your opinion."

We arrived home and I asked, "Do you want some ice cream or something? I'm still too keyed up to go to bed."

"I guess that means the honeymoon's over, huh?"

"I didn't mean it like that. I meant I wasn't ready to go to sleep. We can still make love."

"Okay. I'm sure we have some ice cream in the fridge."

I dished out some ice cream and warmed up some hot fudge. "We don't have any whipping cream. Sorry."

"That's all right. I like it better without."

We sat close together on the couch so we could talk quietly.

"Mr. Kesson talked to me about Dixie's band. He wants to sign them, and he wants me to produce the CD."

"That would be so cool, Kenny."

"I listened to the teen worship band, Em. Those guys have a lot of talent. I could see them making a career of music."

"They are really good, and they're good guys, too."

"I know this might sound strange, but just hear me out."

"I'm listening."

I cuddled close to Kenny as I ate my ice cream and hot fudge. He was already finished with his.

"Since most of the other guys in your worship band have jobs, or families and commitments with the church, maybe you should think about using the teen band as your touring band. I should stop calling them the teen band because they aren't teens anymore."

"Except for Bobby," I added.

"They are all single."

"I should hope so."

"They are very talented. I know you like having Dixie along to keep you company, but he wants his own band. Chase doesn't like to leave his family any more than the other guys do. It's just something to think about. Steve and Hank are not really interested in traveling much."

"I never thought about using the younger guys. Are they really that good?"

"Given enough time to play together, they will be better than the older guys. I watched them, and they are more energetic than the older guys. The older guys just stand there and play for the most part. The younger guys are all over the place. Adam may not be as good on keys as Chase, and his voice isn't as strong as Chase's, but he is talented. He will get better as he gains experience."

"I'll think about it, Kenny. You're probably right. Is it difficult to live knowing that you are always right about everything?"

"It's a burden I have to bear, Em."

I poked him in his ribs as we both laughed.

"Mr. Kesson wants you to travel a little more and this might be just the way to accomplish that. He is looking at you as a long term investment. He knows you place God and our marriage ahead of any career as a singer, but he still thinks you could travel a bit and maybe release a CD every couple of years."

"I suppose I can see myself doing that."

"We should get to bed. It's getting late, and you have to get up in the morning."

"I still have some time before I need to fall asleep," I whispered. He kissed me and carried me upstairs to our bedroom.

Emmy closed her laptop, stood up and stretched. "Why is it taking so long?"

Mr. Robertson grinned. "It hasn't been that long ago that you had Kevin Michael."

"I know, but did I take this long with him? I can't remember."

"We've only been here for an hour," Mr. Robertson said.

"I hate you, and I never want to see you again," Diane screamed at Brady while squeezing his hand as hard as she could. "You know I don't really mean that, but it hurts."

Brady smiled. His shifted his attention back and forth between his wife and the doctor delivering their son.

"One more push, Diane. He's almost here," Dr. Terence Walsh said calmly.

Diane closed her eyes and almost immediately heard their son crying. A couple of minutes later, Brady held his son in his arms and showed him to Diane.

"He's got healthy lungs," Brady said as he smiled.

"Does he have any hair?"

Brady nodded. "He's got a bunch of dark hair, and he looks like a wrinkled red plum."

A few minutes later Diane handed him back to the nurse who took him away for a bath.

"I'm going to let everyone know it's over while they clean you up. Do you know what room you will be moved to?"

"No, but someone will let you know."

Mr. Robertson nudged Emmy and then stood up as Brady walked into the room with a grin as wide as the Mississippi River.

Emmy rushed up to Brady. "Is she okay? How's the baby?"

"Yes to both of your questions, Aunt Emmy," Brady said. "They are cleaning up, or whatever they have to do with Diane."

"I hated that part," Emmy said.

"They will move her into a different room, but you know all of that, right?"

"It shouldn't take too long." Emmy put an arm around Mr. Robertson. "Are you pleased?"

"I'm happy he's finally here."

Emmy looked at Brady and then Mr. Robertson and finally at Mona. "Well, is anyone going to tell me his name? Diane was being a snot and wouldn't tell me yesterday."

Brady smiled and put his hands on Emmy's shoulders. "I suppose it's okay to tell you now. We have decided on Conor William."

"I like it. How are you going to spell it?" Emmy asked.

"W-i-l-l... "

"You are so funny." She put her hands on her hips.

"One N," Brady said.

"So C-O-N-O-R, right?"

"I think so. How else would you spell it?"

Mona answered, "Some people spell it with an E. I like your way."

"I better check on Diane. I'll come and get you after she's settled."

He left and everyone sat down to wait.

"Is it all right if I call Kenny?" Emmy asked.

"Sure, Emmy. You can post it on whatever media sites you are using these days," Mr. Robertson said.

Brady returned while Emmy was talking to Kristen.

"I'll talk to you later. I think Diane is ready. I'll post pictures as soon as I can."

Brady led the way and Emmy sat on the side of the bed and watched as Conor nursed.

"He's got hair. That's a good thing." Emmy pulled out her cell phone and snapped a photo.

"Do you mind waiting until he's finished." Diane shook her head and tried to cover up.

"No one can see anything," Emmy said, but she waited to take more pictures.

Brady took Conor after he fell asleep. The proud grandparents took a turn holding him.

"Did you call Carson and Caden?" Emmy asked.

"Yes, and Bennett and Marissa are bringing them and Lily. They should be here soon," Diane answered. The boys can't wait to see their new brother, but Lily didn't seem all that impressed. She wanted a sister. She complained to Uncle Bennett, and suggested we trade babies with someone."

"Did she really say that?" Emmy asked.

"Em, she's a year-and-a-half old. She just jabbered about a baby and Bennett made up the rest."

"I've heard Lily talk."

"Yes, but not in full sentences," Diane said.

After staying at St. Bart's for six hours, Emmy headed home. Everyone was in bed asleep, so she headed to the den to unwind. She checked her email and then opened her story.

My classes at North Park College started August 25. I had three semesters to go before I earned my degree. I was taking eighteen hours, and the classes kept me busy.

Emmy flung herself back in her recliner. "That sucks, but I'll leave it there for now. Denise will tell me to either expand on it or cut it unless it's important to the development of the story." She read a few more lines, corrected some spelling mistakes but then deleted the section. *Might as well cut it now because no one cares about the classes at North Park.*

Emmy headed to the kitchen and made some hot tea. She added honey, grabbed a bunch of red grapes from the fridge and returned to the den.

Kenny and the band returned home from their summer tour on September 22. Two days later, Kenny and I were in the Steward Music Group studio to begin work on the next CD. We had been writing songs and had fifteen to choose from. Although it had been intended to be the second Crest Ridge Worship Band project, it quickly became apparent that this would be more like a solo project. Chase and the other guys in the band were either too busy, or in some cases, not professional enough to work in the studio. I hate to say that, but it was true. There's a big difference in playing at church, or on the road, from playing in the studio. As a result, Kenny started laying down the tracks himself. Dave Persching assisted on the drum tracks. Kenny played all the guitar tracks, with occasional help from Paul Joseph, formerly of The Notable Exceptions, who in 2005 became a member of Fridays At Five. Jeremy Lenhart, of Fridays At Five, and Sammy Demont, who was a part of The Notable Exceptions, played the keyboards. The guys would work on the tracks during the day while I was at school. I would hurry over to the studio after my last class of the day. I added guide vocals to the tracks while studying for my classes. It was not in my character to let my schoolwork slide. Consequently, I would often be up until midnight or later. With Kenny and the guys working throughout the day, the tracks were quickly finished. I added my vocals at night. Later, background vocals would be added by Kristen, Kenny, Chase Hillman and me. That was kinda weird to sing harmony with myself. I'm glad Kenny made me do it, though. He forced me to step out of my comfort zone and challenge myself. Sometimes I would get frustrated with him because he would criticize a certain section of a vocal track and make me record it

193

over. Looking back, part of what he was doing was training me to pick out subtle nuances that I wouldn't have paid any attention to earlier. He taught me how to be a better singer and not just rely on the God-given voice I had. Wait! I don't know if that came across right. I wouldn't be singing at all if God hadn't given me the ability in the first place, but just as Kenny has become a better guitar player, and singer, over the years by working on his skills, I've become a better singer, too. I hope you understand.

"What do you want to call this CD, Em? Do you want to name it after one of the songs, or something else? It's your choice." Kenny discussed this important step with me.

"I've been thinking about that. What would you think if we called it *The Only Hope*? That's kind of the theme of the songs."

"I like it! That song is probably the strongest one on the CD. We could make it track one, and it could be the title of the project."

Kenny and the guys left on Monday, October 27, to begin a two-month-long Fridays At Five tour. While Kenny toured, Stuart Lederer helped me finish my vocal tracks. The team at Steward Music completed the artwork and other steps involved with the release of a new CD. I was disappointed that the other members of the worship band would not be pictured on the front. I did convince Mr. Kesson to include three pictures of the band in the CD booklet. Kenny was shooting for an early 2004 release. The staff at Steward Music worked efficiently and the new CD appeared in stores on January 13, 2004, which is the girls' birthday, but they weren't born yet. This was the first CD to be released under my name alone. Mr. Kesson insisted, and he is the boss.

I agreed to do one, or at the most, two concerts a month on Saturday nights starting in February. The Prater-Saylor Agency, who booked Fridays At Five, agreed to keep the bookings close enough that it would not take more than four hours to drive to the venue. I insisted I be able to make it to church on Sunday mornings.

The difficult decision was made to change the touring personnel of the band. Kenny and I met with Chase to discuss the future of the Crest Ridge Worship Band.

"I want to let you guys know up front that I have talked to the other guys in the band, and we unanimously agreed with what I'm about to tell you. We appreciated the opportunity to record the first CD and to do that first tour, however..." Chase paused. "None of us are really cut out to be in a band that travels. Hank doesn't want to take a chance on hurting his back. Steve and John have families and jobs that really don't allow them to travel much. Dixie and Alan have their own band now. Skip is away at college. However, there is good news. Bobby O'Connor told me he would be thrilled to be a part of your band."

I giggled because Bobby was so young. "Kenny and I have talked about using the teen band. I shouldn't call them the teen band anymore. He thinks they are really talented. Since we are not going to be doing extended tours, they won't be away overnight except for an occasional Friday."

"I think the guys would love to be your band, Emmy."

"What about you, Chase?" Kenny asked.

"I will agree to travel for the first couple concerts, and I will help you whip the band into shape. I know Bruce Sutherland has expressed a willingness to run the sound for you. His friend Sean DelSasso would do the monitor sound. Jeff's son, Josh, could do the lights. Of course, Jess and Joe Zawaski will do anything you ask. They adore you."

"It sounds like this could work. The young guys have commented to me they would like to get some experience playing in other places."

So the switch was made. My new band would be:

195

Adam Vicini on keys and background vocals; Boyd Goldman on guitars and background vocals; Perry Johnstone on guitars and background vocals; Ryan Lederer on bass and background vocals; and Bobby O'Connor on drums. The tech crew was set. Gear was purchased and the new Crest Ridge Worship Band started practicing. I tried to convince Kristen to join. She agreed to give it a try, but wouldn't commit to a long-term commitment. I didn't hold that against her. She never really wanted to sing in the first place. I think she did it just to please me.

Emmy jumped as she felt a hand on her shoulder. "Kenny, you scared the crap out of me."

"Sorry, but I thought you heard me."

"How long have you been in here?" Emmy turned her laptop around so Kenny couldn't see it.

"Only a few seconds. I didn't read anything. Are you going to stay up much longer?"

"I don't have to." Emmy bit her lip. "Do you need me to come to bed?"

He raised and lowered his eyebrows and said, "I wouldn't mind having a warm body to cuddle with."

Emmy saved her work, shut down the laptop and set it on the desk. "Just any old warm body?" She stood up and moved close to Kenny.

He pulled her closer, put his hands around her and rubbed her back. "I kinda like cuddling with this old warm body."

"So you think I'm old, huh?"

"Old enough to be naughty with me." He kissed her, picked her up and carried her upstairs.

Emmy put her hands behind Kenny's neck and bit her lip. "What will you do when I'm old and fat and you can't carry me?"

He paused, tilted his head and said, "I suppose we could buy a house with an elevator."

Emmy frowned. "You're supposed to say I'll never get fat."

196

"No, I'm not home yet," Diane rolled her eyes. "I said I would call you when I get home. Can't you be patient for a little while? You are worse than the kids, Emmy."

"Sorry, but I want to see Conor," Emmy said.

"You've seen him every day. I should be home a little after one." Diane sat on the edge of the bed and held Conor William as Brady gathered up Diane's possessions.

"Should I wait for you at the house? I could make sure it's clean," Emmy offered.

"Fine! There might be some dirty dishes in the sink. You could make sure the kitchen is clean and check the laundry. I told Carson and Caden to pick up their rooms. You could check the upstairs. It might need to be vacuumed." Diane grinned at Brady.

He grinned back. "You know she will clean the whole house if you tell her to."

"I know," Diane said and then asked, "Do you remember the garage code?"

"I remember. I'll head over and make sure the house is clean enough for baby Conor," Emmy replied.

"We will be home around one." Diane ended the call.

Brady held up a plastic bag. "Are you taking this stuff home?"

"No, you can dump it. It's just lotion, and I have plenty of it at home."

"Do you feel guilty about taking advantage of your sister like that?" Brady set the bag in the trash. "She is a neat freak and you... well, our house is always a mess compared to hers."

"An operating room isn't as clean as Emmy's house, and I don't feel guilty. I'm not forcing her to clean up for me."

"Did you ever clean your room when you and Emmy were kids?" Brady asked.

Diane laughed. "Never had to. She never let it get messy."

"You should pay her for cleaning our house," Brady said.

"You can try, but she won't take the money. I'm ready to go. Will you call the nurse, please?"

Later, Brady hit the remote button and pulled into the garage.

197

"Emmy's still here." Diane noticed Emmy's BMW in the drive. "I wonder how much cleaning she's done."

"Stop it." Brady helped Diane bring the baby carrier inside.

Emmy dashed into the kitchen and slid to a stop just before running into Diane. "Where is he?"

"Who?" Diane asked with a straight face."

"Very funny." Emmy peeked into the carrier. "He is so precious."

"Have you been running around the house in your socks to dust the floors?" Diane looked down at Emmy's white socks.

Emmy lifted a foot. "Are my socks totally black?"

"Not totally. I do have someone clean once a week." Diane removed her coat and placed it on the island.

Emmy picked it up and headed to the mudroom. "I put the dishes in the dishwasher, but I didn't start it. I sorted the dirty clothes from the boy's rooms and started a load."

Brady shrugged and said, "You don't have to clean just because Diane suggested it."

"I don't mind. I've always been the neat one," Emmy replied.

Conor chose that moment to remind his mother he needed to be fed.

Emmy rushed over. "Are you hungry, Conor? I would take care of you if I could, but you need your mommy."

"Would you bring him into the family room, Em. I'll feed him in there."

Emmy brought Conor to Diane as Brady brought everything in from the car.

"What does Lily think of her new brother?" Emmy handed Conor to Diane.

"She took a look at him yesterday and tried to feed him with one of her baby bottles. She's next door. Bill and Mona are spoiling her."

"Has she tried to hold him?" Emmy sat next to Diane.

"No. Would you grab my blanket?" Diane pointed to the recliner across from the couch.

"Are you afraid to nurse him in front of me?" Emmy got

up, grabbed the blanket and covered Diane and Conor before sitting back down.

"I'm not like you," Diane said adjusting the blanket. "Carson and Caden wanted to hold him. I made them sit in a chair. Caden was a little afraid, but Carson asked if he could take Conor to school and show him to his friends."

"You should let him, "Emmy said.

Diane shook her head. "Get real, Emmy."

"Heather and Isa want to see him again." Emmy left and returned a moment later. "I put the clothes in the dryer and added another load to the washer."

Diane glanced at Brady as he stood in the doorway. "Thanks, Em. I'll take care of the rest."

"You're welcome. I should get back home. I need to work on my book some more."

"How's that going?" Brady asked.

Emmy shrugged. "I've gotten most of the first draft done, but it needs a lot of work. Call me if you need any help."

"Thanks for all you do, Emmy," Brady said as he walked her to the door.

"I don't mind. It gives me a chance to get a baby fix." Emmy waved and headed to her BMW.

Chapter Nineteen

"Is everyone completely satisfied with our discussion of the three bids?" Pastor Tyler glanced at the board members most of whom nodded. "I think it's time to vote. The building committee has recommended we accept the bid from the Bertucci and Keasling Construction Company. The motion has been seconded. All those in favor please raise your right hand." Tyler smiled as everyone raised their hand. "Those opposed please raise a hand." He waited a second. "The motion has passed unanimously. I will contact Dr. Schofield and inform him."

Tony and John high-fived each other the next morning as they talked to Pastor Tyler on the phone.

"Thank you for calling, Pastor. We will get everything ready so we can start as soon as we have the go ahead," John said.

"I will let you know as soon as everything has been approved by the district," Tyler said and then chuckled. "I have been in contact with Dr. Schofield, and he assures me he will do everything in his power to expedite the process. He was certainly impressed that we have the building project fully funded."

John glanced at Tony who shrugged.

"I can't wait until we move into the new sanctuary," Tyler said. "Then we can begin converting the old sanctuary into usable space for the teens and junior high group."

"That will free up additional space for the school, right?" John asked.

"Yes, I believe we can add four additional classrooms."

"We can help with those projects, too," John said.

"I appreciate the offer. I think the building and grounds committee will try to do most of the work ourselves, but we wouldn't turn down any professional help and advice."

"I believe we might have someone around who might know what they're doing," John said.

"I bet you do," Pastor Tyler replied as he laughed.

"Thank you for calling, Pastor Tyler. we will get started today. I think Garrick Winston already has a time schedule in place. He will be in charge of the project. He's built two or three churches, and really knows his stuff. We will do our best to finish under budget and as early as possible."

"Without cutting corners?" Tyler asked.

John laughed. "My father-in-law will be keeping a close eye on the project because Kristen told him how important it is. He won't accept anything less than perfection."

"That's good to hear," Tyler said and then chuckled.

That afternoon John, Tony and Daniel Keasling met with all the department heads involved in the project.

"We want to use our best people for this project," Daniel stated. "Pull them off of other projects if you need. This is our number one priority until it is finished. Does everyone understand that?" He glanced around the large conference table and noted the positive looks from his people. "There will be bonuses if we come in under budget and before the deadline. That doesn't mean we will accept cutting corners. Garrick and I will be checking everything."

Roy Posey chuckled as he smiled at the diminutive Garrick Winston. "I remember when Garrick first started. He got after a guy for using a piece of lumber that was slightly out of true by about an eighth of an inch."

Garrick adjusted his glasses and grinned at the man who towered above everyone in the room including Tony and John. "I admit I can be rather anal at times, but the company's reputation is at stake."

"I think you all understand how important this project is. Let's do our jobs, and then I can retire for good." Daniel smiled. "Maybe that way I won't have to have my knees replaced. At least not until I get really old."

Saturday afternoon Dr. Steve Borger and his wife, Carol pulled into the driveway of Dr. Herb Ausland. Pastor Herb and Carolyn walked outside and waited beside the Toyota Sienna. Steve opened his door and stepped out. Carolyn walked around the vehicle and waited for Carol Borger to step down.

"How was your trip?" Herb asked as he hugged his old friend.

201

"It's been a good trip so far," Steve said with a smile. "We've seen all the kids and grandkids. We've visited with some old friends, and I even took care of some church business."

"Please, come inside." Herb checked the gray sky. "I do believe we are in for some rain today."

Steve glanced up. "I agree." He turned his attention to the house. "The ivy on the wall reminds me of Wrigley Field."

"That's right. You've always been a Cubs fan." Herb patted Steve's back. "Don't give up hope. The Cubs could make it to the World Series one year."

Steve laughed. "Ever the eternal optimist."

Carol climbed down from the minivan and embraced Carolyn. "I love the color of the trees."

Carolyn looked over her shoulder. "One of the advantages of an older home, I suppose. Large trees and colorful foliage."

"But then you have to rake up all the leaves later," Carol added.

"Allow me to carry that in for you." Herb took the small piece of luggage from Steve. "Have you eaten lunch?"

"Yes, we stopped a couple of hours ago." Steve held onto his gray fedora as the wind picked up. "What was the name of that diner you took us to the last time we were in Illinois?"

"Darby's Dogs," Herb said over his shoulder.

Everyone headed inside as a few sprinkles of rain arrived.

"Is it still there?" Steve asked.

"It's in SoHam close to the river. We could stop there before you have to leave." Herb took Steve's hat and coat and hung them in the front closet. "I remember your father always wore a fedora."

"That's actually Dad's hat," Steve said. "It fits, so I wear it."

Carolyn took Carol's coat and handed it to Herb.

"Do we need to remove our shoes?" Carol took a step onto the polished wooden floor from the stone entryway.

"No need. We never do," Carolyn answered. "Come and sit. I want to hear all about the children and grandchildren." Carolyn led the way into the front parlor.

"I love this room." Carol glanced around. "I'd love a stone

fireplace like that. This reminds me of a cottage we rented in the English countryside a few years ago. Except your ceilings are much higher. Steve had to be careful in that cottage. The doors were short and he needed to duck under some of the wooden beams."

"Shall we join the ladies?" Herb extended an arm.

An hour later they finished catching up on family news. Carolyn took Carol on a tour of the house.

"The kitchen is smaller than in modern homes, but it's enough for us," Carolyn explained.

Carol ran a hand along the countertop. "It feels cozy and warm."

"So many of these smaller, older homes are being bought and knocked down. People like to live close to the train into the city."

"I suppose homes are rather expensive in this area."

Carolyn nodded. "We bought this over twenty years ago from one of the members of the church. It had belonged to his mother. We could never afford to buy a home in Wheaton now. We've been approached many times with offers to buy it, but this is home. We will stay here as long as we are physically able to navigate the stairs. All the bedrooms are on the second floor."

"Our place outside of Nampa has a bedroom on the first floor." Carol looked at the family photos lining the wall of the stairway. "Was this taken in the Philippines?"

"Yes, those are my parents, and that's me as a teenager." Carolyn continued up the stairs and opened the door to a bedroom. "I thought you and Steve could use this room."

Carol stepped into the room. "This is lovely. I love the window seat."

The ladies continued to explore the house while the men talked about church business.

"I'm looking forward to meeting your young pastor. How old is he, by the way?" Steve asked.

"He's twenty-nine and Liz is a year or two younger. They are expecting their third child in December, I believe."

"That's amazing. Crest Ridge is the largest Nazarene

203

church in Illinois and one of the largest in the entire country by attendance. Most other churches of this size are led by older senior pastors." Steve waved a hand. "I realize he inherited a very large church, but it has continued to grow according to the statistics I see."

"As one of the General Superintendents of the church, you must see a lot of large churches," Herb said.

"One of the largest churches I had the privilege of attending last year did not have an actual building. There must have been close to three thousand worshipers. Of course, the weather in that part of Africa is much warmer than here," Steve said and then chuckled.

"There is such a difference in the physical church around the world. Here in the states we have large buildings to accommodate our people. We are actually in the process of building a new sanctuary. We have outgrown our current one."

"I did receive an email from Dr. Schofield." Steve tapped a finger to his chin. "He mentioned the new building is fully funded."

"Yes, we have some very generous people in the church, but the funds for the new building actually came from outside the church membership." Herb explained more about the donation.

"God does work in amazing ways. Too often we place limits on what we think God can do. You will have to send me photos of the new sanctuary."

"Did I mention that Dr. Keck visited here last year?" Herb asked.

"Ed did mention that to me when I told him I would be in the area." Steve closed his eyes for a moment. "Ed hasn't shared this with everyone, but he has cancer."

"I'm sorry to hear that. I will make sure to add him to my prayers."

"Have you thought about retiring again now that the church seems to be growing under Tyler's leadership?"

"Carolyn and I plan to visit the Philippines again soon. I have agreed to teach for one semester at the Bible college, but I enjoy my role as a mentor too much to leave now. Actually, I'm not mentoring Tyler all that much, but I have taken on the duties of ministering to the more seasoned members of the congregation. That is Tyler's word for the senior citizens."

"He must do a good job of relating to the various demographics of the church. Many of our more experienced pastors struggle with that."

Herb smiled. "I do believe that is one of his strengths."

Herb drove to church the next morning and pointed out some of the new construction in the towns between Wheaton and Crest Ridge. "There are not clear divisions between the towns anymore. I find it difficult to tell the various cities apart."

"That is certainly not the case in Idaho," Steve said. "We can't see our nearest neighbor from our house."

Herb dropped the ladies off at the front entrance and parked in back. "This is closer to my office, and we need to save as many parking places as we can for people in the front. After the new building is finished, we will have to enlarge the parking lots." Herb opened the door. "We will lose a lot of parking once the construction begins."

"Where will the new building be situated?" Steve removed his hat.

"It will be connected to the front entrance where we dropped off the wives."

"At least the church has plenty of room to expand."

"The church purchased more of the field out back and to the south. One of these days we might surround the Methodist church," Herb said.

"How much time do we have before the first service?"

Herb checked his watch. "We have fifteen minutes. Would you like to meet Tyler and Darren now?"

"As long as that will not disturb them."

Herb located Tyler and Darren Eaton, the associate pastor, in the church's main office going over the order of service.

"Pastor Tyler, I would like to introduce an old friend if I may," Herb said. "This is Dr. Steve Borger."

Tyler and Darren turned around and stared.

"Good morning, I am sorry for interrupting, but I wanted to meet you. Carol and I are visiting our old friends."

"It's a pleasure to meet you, sir." Tyler shook Dr. Borger's extended hand. "This is Darren Eaton. He's the associate pastor in charge of everything I can pass off onto him," Tyler said and then chuckled.

Darren shook hands, too.

"I have heard some good reports about the church, and Herb has enlightened me even more."

"We are very fortunate to have great people and some fine staff members," Tyler said. "Other than Darren, that is."

"We should find our wives," Herb suggested.

"Is it all right if I introduce you to the rest of the staff later?" Tyler asked.

"That would be fine," Dr. Borger nodded.

"Would you like a few minutes during the service?"

"If that is all right with you? I promise not to take more than five minutes."

Tyler allowed Pastor Herb to introduce his friend during the service. Dr. Borger finished in just under five minutes as promised. As Pastor Tyler, Pastor Herb and Dr. Borger greeted people after the service, Darren gathered the rest of the staff in the main office.

"How many General Superintendents are there? Didn't one of them stop by last year?" Pastor Jonah Galves asked.

"I think there are six of them, and it's rather unusual for them to visit a church like this," Darren answered.

Fifteen minutes later Tyler and Herb arrived at the office with Dr. Borger. Tyler introduced Jake and Maddy first.

"I was very impressed by the teen group leading the service this morning," Steve said while shaking Jake's hand. "Is that something that happens often?"

"We lead service once a month," Jake answered and then explained about the different worship teams.

Tyler added, "Chase and Yvonne Hillman were the worship leaders here for a long time, but they left to go back to Toledo. We haven't replaced him officially, but we have a couple filling that spot temporarily. We will probably offer them the position soon."

"I think it's a great idea to include the youth in the service."

Tyler introduced Jeremiah and Mia Tolla. "They are in charge of the younger children."

Dr. Borger shook hands with Jeremiah. "I bet the children love your full beard."

Jeremiah grinned, "Some of them think I look like Jesus except I don't wear a robe."

Tyler explained that Pastor Williams taught a Sunday School class and Reed Shafer and his wife were on vacation.

"I would like to join a class if I may," Dr. Borger disclosed to Herb.

"I think Carolyn and Carol are probably in one of the adult classes. I'm sure I can find them."

Everyone left leaving Tyler and Darren alone in the office.

"Do you think there's something going on we don't know about?" Darren asked.

Tyler shrugged. "All I know is that it's rather unusual for a General Superintendent to show up, and we've had two in the last year."

"Maybe they are looking at you for a different position down the road," Darren responded.

"Liz and I are happy here. I don't plan to leave anytime soon."

"But what if you don't have a choice? God might have other plans."

Pastor Tyler sighed. "I try not to think about that."

Chapter Twenty

Emmy drove the kids to school and stopped at Sainsbury's to grab a few groceries.

"Hi, Emmy," the cashier smiled. "I loved that new song you guys sang a while back."

Emmy smiled. "Thanks, Paige."

"Was it one you wrote? I can't remember the title, but the chorus was about grace not working that way."

"It was one of mine, but Kenny helped."

"I wish you sang more often. I like how you sing better than the other singers." Paige finished ringing up Emmy's groceries. "It's $26.18, please."

Emmy used her VISA card and didn't comment about the other singers.

"I thought Pastor Jake and the teen band did a good job, but some of those older singers are too stuffy."

"Take care. I'll talk to you later, Paige," Emmy said and then smiled as she walked away. *One of these days the teens will think I'm old and stuffy, too.*

Emmy put the groceries away and headed to the den. She saw Isabella's stuffed lion on the hallway floor and picked it up. *I should take another look at those lion stories someday.* She carried the lion into the den and set it on the desk. She plopped into her recliner, opened her laptop and went to work.

In the summer of 2004, I went on tour for two weeks. We left on July eleventh and didn't get home until the twenty-sixth. I teased Kenny about this being payback for all the times he left me at home while he toured the world. He told me he missed me before I even left the church parking lot.

For the first time, I missed church on Sunday because of being on tour. By this time the younger guys had replaced the original worship band. They decided to use the name "The Only Hope" until they could come up with some thing better. They never did.

Using the younger guys to back me up changed the dynamics of the tour. The older guys were married, except for Dixie, and they were more settled if you get my picture. The younger guys had different priorities. Girls. They weren't wild like some rock bands, but they were definitely interested in the opposite sex. Since I was the only female on the bus, I needed to be careful. There were times when I couldn't tell if someone was flirting with me or not. Most of the time they treated me like a little sister, but there were occasions. I certainly didn't wrestle with anyone like I did that time with Ryan.

We used two buses and two semis this time. Each bus had a bedroom in the back. The larger bus had twelve bunks and two bathrooms. The other bus was smaller with only eight bunks, one bedroom and one bathroom. I used the bedroom and the band guys used the bunks on the smaller bus. Oh, Skip Mason handled the drums for us on this tour. Bobby O'Connor broke his arm while skateboarding and couldn't play. He tried to talk his parents into letting him come along, but they vetoed that plan. Skip had just graduated from Ohio State and would be starting his job as a teacher in the fall. Bruce Sutherland, our FOH mixer, Sean DelSasso, who handled the monitors, and Josh Morrissey, who handled the lights, traveled with us. The crew and tech staff used the other bus. After playing at New Life Church in Sumpter Park on Sunday, we hit the road to Pittsburgh.

After the concert, I hung out with the guys. I didn't have to work at the merchandise table tonight. The Zawaski brothers supervised loading the truck. The guys on our crew with help from some volunteers from the church did most of the work. We would use local volunteers quite a bit on this tour. Boyd and Perry helped out, too. Boyd made me promise to put that in the book. I'm not sure if he and Perry helped much, or just got in the way. A new guy had been added to the crew. Nelson Grapella was new to the church and needed a job so he was hired for this tour. Actually, I'm teasing. He worked

209

for Walker Management, Inc. He took over as the tour manager, which was the role Chase had always handled. Nelson's wife Belinda accompianed him on the tour. She handled the production office. We were big enough to need a production office on the tour.

I watched as the guys worked and even helped a little bit. I was still wearing the dress I wore onstage tonight. It was probably the shortest one they had ever seen me wearing, but I wore black tights so no one could see my legs. I was helping Boyd and Ryan roll one of the large speakers into the truck. The guys jumped down because more stuff was coming up the ramp into the truck. They turned to help me down, but instead, I jumped and Ryan grabbed me so I didn't hurt myself. Jess and Joe saw me jump down from the truck like the tomboy that I am and were upset.

"Miss Emmy! Don't you ever do that again. You could get hurt and we don't want to see that happen."

"I'm sorry, guys. I won't do that again."

"I'm sorry for yelling at you, Miss Emmy."

"It's all right, Joe. I shouldn't have been in the trailer to begin with."

"You should stay inside, Miss Emmy."

I learned my lesson, and didn't get in the way of the crew after that. I went back and sat on the steps outside the sanctuary reflecting on the concert. All the young guys were with me, and they started goofing around. I watched as they teased each other. Ryan came over and sat next to me.

"What are you thinking about, Emmy?"

"I was just going over the concert in my head wondering if there was anything I should have done differently."

"You are your own worst enemy, I mean critic. You did a fantastic job and should be proud of that."

"Do you know that pride is not a virtue, Ryan?"

"I know, but I don't see anything wrong with being pleased with something you do well."

As we headed to Pittsburgh, I talked to the guys in the lounge area. Skip and Adam were in their bunks. I sat on the couch with Ryan while Boyd and Perry sat across from us on the other couch. I think Bruce, Sean and Josh were watching a movie.

"You guys did a good job tonight. I'm so proud of you."

"Isn't it wrong to be proud, Emmy?" Ryan asked with a smile.

"I was thinking about what you said earlier. I guess it's not a crime to take some pride in what you do for God."

"Thanks, Emmy. You sounded great as usual."

I knew it wasn't my best concert, but it was all right.

"We need to get to bed. I'm getting sleepy." Boyd stood up.

"I'll see you guys in the morning."

"Good night, Emmy. Sleep well."

I went to the bedroom, but didn't close the door right away. I saw the guys look at each other and heard Ryan mention, "This is going to be a fun tour with Emmy on this bus with us."

"Yeah! She seems to act our age instead of someone with a husband." Sean glanced at me.

I was only a couple of years older than most of them. Sean was the same age as me.

"She probably misses Kenny so much. We need to be extra thoughtful and treat her with respect," Perry said.

"What? Can't we tease her all the time?" Ryan asked with a straight face before he started laughing.

"Maybe half the time," Sean said.

I grinned and then closed the door. Although Kenny and I had been married for over a year, I did miss him a lot. I had a bit of trouble falling asleep without him next to me.

We arrived in New Castle, Pennsylvania, shortly after nine. Ryan got up first. He headed up front to talk to Buck and his son Sutton, who was along for the first time.

"How are you guys doing?"

"We're fine, Ryan. This is Sutton by the way. He's helping me out this trip. We were beginning to wonder if we had left you all behind somewhere. It was too quiet back there. Are those other kids ever going to get up?"

"They were up late, so we probably won't see them for a couple hours yet."

Buck had pulled the bus next to the other one. Larry and his neighbor, Jack Wills, were driving the other bus. Carl Twilley and Cecil Parrmeister handled the trucks this trip. Jack and Sutton would help drive the trucks, too. The drivers would all catch a few hours of sleep, even though they would not be driving very far tonight.

Instead of playing at churches this tour, the Prater-Saylor Agency booked us into theaters and small auditoriums. We would be in the Pittsburgh area for two nights. Castle Productions of Philadelphia promoted the tour. We traveled through the eastern states for two weeks. Nelson called the promoter and arranged for someone to meet us in an hour to open up the venue, which was a refurbished theater called the Paramount. Most of the crew guys headed out for breakfast. Adam and Bruce were the only ones up from our bus. When I finally woke up, I looked for Ryan. Nelson left me a cell phone message explaining where everyone was going for breakfast. I changed into jeans and a sweatshirt since it was a little cool. The rest of the guys finally started getting up. I noticed they walked around the bus in their boxers or whatever they slept in until they saw me. Then they all grabbed shorts or jeans to wear. I think they got embarrassed having me around.

"Is there anything to eat, Emmy?"

"There is cereal and fruit, Ryan. I'm going to have that for breakfast. You guys should get dressed in case Nelson or Belinda come back to check on us. They will get after you for being in just boxers."

"Sorry, Emmy. We weren't thinking."

"It's all right. It doesn't bother me. I'm used to it."

The guys wondered what I meant by that. I meant Kenny walked around in boxers. Nothing else. The guys scrounged up food for breakfast as I checked my email.

"I'm going for a run. Anyone want to join me?"

"I will, Emmy!"

"Anyone besides Ryan willing to suffer some pain?"

"I'll go, too," Boyd answered.

"The rest of you guys stay on the bus," I warned them.

"Yes, Mom!"

I stuck out my tongue at them. The three of us headed out for a brisk morning run. They struggled to keep up with me, so I slowed the pace down a bit. The boys looked at me and noticed I wasn't even breathing hard. We were gone for a half hour. I was warm now, so I used the bedroom to take off my sweatshirt and jeans. I put on a t-shirt and shorts and sat on the couch just like I would at home. Nelson returned from breakfast, and told us to get our butts in gear because we had work to do.

Carl and Cecil moved the trucks to the loading dock, and all the guys pitched in to help unload. Actually, the volunteers did most of the work. Belinda and I supervised some guys unloading the merchandise from under the bus. I smiled at the guys to thank them. I learned that a smile went a lot farther than trying to boss the guys around. Besides, I wasn't the boss. We took our time setting up since there wasn't anything to do but the soundcheck, and then we faced the boredom of waiting. We finished the soundcheck by three o'clock. Josh Morrissey spent some time programming the lighting cues. Adam made sure his keyboards were set. I still can't understand exactly how he manages to program the midi stuff. I know it's not real easy. At least it wouldn't be easy for me. All the amps were in position on stage. We used risers belonging to the venue.

On this tour we had contracts with riders just like a *real* group. Most of it just specified what the promoter needed to provide for us to eat. There was stuff about the gear, but I didn't get into that. I liked to have fresh fruit and honey available. Most of the guys didn't really care—especially the crew. They would eat anything. I had a dressing room to myself, and the guys shared the other three rooms. Belinda didn't need a dressing room, but she hung out with me and helped me decide what to wear each night. That night we decided on a white dress with purple trim that looked very nice on me. It was one that Kristen picked out. I bought it because it was on sale. I wouldn't put it on until just before I had to sing.

After the soundcheck Nelson and Belinda met with the promoter to go over last minute details. So far there were no problems. The sold-out venue seated just over a thousand, or was it two thousand? Anyway, I headed back to the bus with Ryan. The guys followed, and Ryan told them the plan for getting ready. Ryan had kinda assumed a position of authority on our bus. The guys respected him, and he never really tried to boss us around.

"Since we only have one bathroom you guys can go first. Remember to conserve the hot water if you can. Emmy will need some for her shower. Emmy will stay in the bedroom while you guys are getting ready so you don't have to worry about her being in the way if you know what I mean. After you guys are ready, we will leave the bus so Emmy can have privacy. I would like for at least one guy to hang out by the bus just to make sure no one tries to break in. Any volunteers?"

They all volunteered.

"You guys can figure out who has the honor of guarding the bus. We will be gone for two weeks so everyone will have an opportunity."

The guys got ready and then I had my turn. Ryan was going to guard the bus today. Everyone else headed into the venue to hang around and eat. We still had two hours before the concert started. I talked to Kenny and then Ryan and I joined everyone. The guys waited for Nelson to pray because they figured he was like Chase. Nelson wasn't real comfortable about praying out loud in front of people, so Josh said the prayer. I realized that Josh was the oldest guy in our group, other than the drivers. After that Josh kinda took on more of a leadership role when it came to spiritual stuff. I thought about the older guys and Dixie. I wondered if I would regret traveling with guys who were my age and younger. Not because they weren't as good of musicians because they were, but because people might get the wrong impression about their relationship with me. I probably didn't help matters because I goofed around with them a lot. I sat with the guys in the band while we ate, and we clowned around like kids. The guys started teasing me about my loose-fitting jeans.

"I can't help it if I don't have a big butt like some people."

"There isn't any part of you that's big, Emmy!"

I looked at Boyd. He realized he hurt my feelings.

"I'm sorry, Emmy. I didn't mean that in a bad way. You look perfect. You're just petite."

I would often feel bad about being so petite. I wanted to look more like Kristen. She looked like a princess to me, and I felt envious.

A few minutes before seven The Only Hope started getting ready. The guys tuned their guitars, Skip warmed up on his kit, and I don't think the crowd recognized them. They looked like roadies. The house lights dimmed and a local radio personality came out to make some announcements before introducing us. The guys didn't show any sign of jitters at all. They played for a minute and I guess the audience finally realized these guys were the real band. The guys watched as I walked out. Ryan, Boyd and Perry looked at each other and smiled. I could read their lips and almost giggled.

"'Wow!''

"Yeah! Double Wow!"

215

I guess they really liked my dress. Boyd and Perry acted as their own guitar techs until they trained a couple of the crew members. One of Adam's keyboards quit working, and he had to make some adjustments, but I doubt if anyone in the audience caught on. Ryan was assigned to the merchandise table along with some local teenage girls. He enjoyed this assignment even though he was looking forward to seeing Jennifer Sinclaire again. They did get married in April of 2007.

Just before the last song, I talked to the crowd about why we were here. Since this wasn't a church, we didn't have an altar call like on the first tour. I realized I needed Chase with us just to talk to the crowd because he did a much better job than me. We did our last song and one encore before the house lights came up. Boyd headed back to the merchandise table because he heard there were a bunch of cute teenage girls helping Ryan. Most of the guys were free to head downstairs and just hang out. I went out to the merchandise table and talked to fans. I signed autographs and had my picture taken. I was eventually able to break away and go downstairs. Boyd, Ryan and Perry broke down the merchandise table and loaded everything back into the bus. Nelson took care of the money and receipts. That stuff would go into the safe on bus one.

The crew broke down the gear and loaded the trucks. With help from the locals. We stayed in the area that night, so Belinda arranged for us to stay overnight in a truck stop a few miles from tomorrow's venue. These days we would stay in a hotel, but back then we needed to keep our expenses under control. Everyone took advantage of the buffet downstairs. Those guys on the crew can sure eat. I tried to eat while talking to the promoters, but they kept asking me all kinds of questions. Some of which I didn't think appropriate. All of a sudden Chase walked up behind me.

"Emmy, would you mind having your picture taken one more time?"

216

"Of course not." I turned around and about keeled over. He surprised the crap out of me. "Chase! Why are you here? When did you get here? Are you gonna stay with us?" I rattled off a hundred questions.

"Please excuse us," Chase apologized to the promoters.

He took my arm and maneuvered me away from everyone.

"I missed you so much at the end of the show. You're so much better at talking to the crowd than me. Are you gonna stay?"

"Yes, Emmy."

I hugged him as hard as I could. "Who wants a picture?" I asked after I let go.

"No one. I just needed to get you away from those guys so you could eat."

"Thanks, Chase. I didn't think they were ever going to let me go. Maybe we should take a picture in case they are watching."

"Good idea."

"I'm so glad you're here. Are you gonna ride on my bus?"

He explained how he arrived at the airport and caught took a cab to the venue.

"Who's covering the service on Sunday?" I felt guilty about not being there myself and now Chase wouldn't be there, either.

"Dr. Behren's friend from Nashville, Brian Hanson is going to be there, so I have the week free. I thought you might not mind too much if I hang around."

"You can play keyboards, too, right?"

"I will if Adam doesn't mind."

Adam was thrilled that Chase showed up. They knew exactly how to complement each other.

Chase gathered some of the guys and took a couple pictures just for appearances. I fixed myself a plate and sat with Chase and Ryan.

"Nice job tonight, Emmy. You sounded better than

217

last night," Ryan told me as he bit into a slice of pizza.

"I know. Sunday wasn't one of my better nights. I'm not sure why."

"I think you sound great every night, Miss Emmy."

"Oh, thank you, Joe. I can always count on you to cheer me up."

I noticed that neither Joe nor Jess wore a suit tonight. I thought about asking why but decided not to pry. By one o'clock everyone had stuffed themselves. Chase talked to Nelson, and I could see a look of relief on Nelson's face. I didn't realize this was his first tour. Chase had called the promoter earlier to arrange a time to meet at tomorrow's venue. They agreed to meet at noon. That would give us enough time to unload and set everything up. Tomorrow's venue was a small auditorium in the suburb of East Stanton, which is a suburb on the south side of Pittsburgh.

Emmy took a break to eat lunch. She sat at the island to eat her soup and sandwich. She checked her email and saw one from Rory Porter. "About time you emailed me," she said out loud. "What have you been up to?" She took a moment to read the email while waiting for her soup to cool. *You've got a girlfriend? I thought I was your girlfriend. Not really, but I do feel a little jealous. I know I shouldn't, but I do.* Emmy continued to read the email. *You really met her in a bookstore? At least it's nothing too serious. I should call you one of these days. I do kinda miss you.* She finished her lunch and went back into the den to work.

Our caravan pulled out and moseyed over to the twenty-four hour truck stop. Some of the guys were ready to call it a night but a few of us, including me, remained wide awake. I changed out of my dress and into jeans and a sweatshirt. I now looked younger than the guys. The drivers headed to the area reserved for them. This travel center was large enough to have rooms available for the truckers. Larry booked three rooms since there wouldn't be any empty bunks on the buses until mid-morning. Chase just naturally took over the role as leader of our group which enabled. Nelson to concentrate on the crew and his other responsibilities. We found a bowling alley open all night and asked Chase if we could hang out there.

"I suppose so. Just remember that we have work to do tomorrow. Are you going with the guys, Emmy?"

"Yes, at least for a while."

"Keep an eye on her okay," Chase told Ryan.

"We will. We don't want anything to happen to her. Kenny would kill us."

Five guys and I went bowling. I bought Cokes for everyone. The sugar and caffeine would keep us going for some time.

Despite being a tomboy with good athletic skills, I had never been very good at bowling. No matter how hard I tried, I just couldn't improve. I finished last in every game we bowled.

"Guys, do you realize it is almost five o'clock? We need to get back and get some sleep."

"Yeah, we have to start working around noon."

"Who won? Who had the highest total overall?" Skip asked.

Skip thought it might have been him. Ryan did the math.

"Sorry, Skip, but Perry beat you by twelve pins."

"Shoot! I thought maybe I had won."

"Emmy, I'm sorry but you finished last."

The guys patted me on the back to console me though they were laughing at the time.

"I have an idea. Let's use the order we finished in bowling as the order we get to use the bathroom for showers. It should work out since Emmy needs to go last anyway," Boyd suggested as we headed back to the bus.

"Sure, why not? I get to use the most hot water that way."

Everyone was in bed and asleep by six. Chase woke

up shortly after seven and headed to the restaurant for breakfast. Some of the guys from the other bus were already there.

"Do you know what time the kids got back?" Nelson asked Chase.

"It was after five. Five thirty or so. They tried to be quiet, but I woke up."

"I hope they don't do that every night."

"I think it was just the excitement of the first tour and all. I don't think Emmy will want to stay out so late again."

Our caravan moved on to the auditorium in East Stanton. I didn't even wake up during the short trip.

I woke up right at noon and scrambled to get dressed. I came out of the bedroom and didn't see anyone else awake yet. I decided to play drill sergeant.

"Everybody up! It's noon and we are late for duty. Come on! Out of those bunks!"

Slowly the guys materialized from their bunks.

"Do we have to get up now?"

"Yes, Sean, get dressed and grab a piece of fruit. We're late for duty."

I left the bus to look for Chase or Nelson. I saw both of them outside the large overhead receiving door.

"Well, look who finally made it out of bed," Chase teased.

I knew they could tell I felt guilty about staying out so late by the look on my face.

"Sorry, Chase. It won't happen again. The guys are getting dressed and should be here in a couple minutes."

The guys emerged from the bus and apologized for staying out too late and oversleeping.

"Let's get to work. Emmy, you take Joe to help with the merchandise. The other guys are inside. They will help Bruce and Sean get everything set up."

"Belinda will help me get set up if someone carries the heavy stuff inside." I smiled at the guys, but they didn't respond to my flirting.

220

We were fortunate to have a crew along to do the heavy work. They unloaded the trucks, so none of the guys in the band had to worry about that. The guys in the band just needed to set up their amps and pedal boards and that kind of stuff. Everyone knew the drill and soon the trucks were empty, the PA up and running and the merchandise tables stocked and ready for tonight. Chase looked at his watch.

"Three hours. Not too bad for a bunch of half-asleep kids and a bunch of old men."

"Who says we're old? I don't feel old," Josh laughed.

"You will in a couple of days, Josh."

Chase gathered everyone to go over plans for the rest of the day. Belinda handed him a printout of the daily schedule. He read his copy.

"Okay. Soundcheck is at four. We can eat around five and the doors open at six. Belinda has the schedule for the tables, so check with her. I know you are on duty at six, Skip. The show starts at seven sharp. Any questions?"

"Are we going to be fed after the concert?"

"Yes, Sean. You won't starve."

"Anything else?"

Nelson had an idea. "I think we need to name the buses to avoid confusion."

"Okay, that sounds like a good idea. Do you have names picked out?"

"Yes I do. I think our bus should be called Alpha and the kids bus Omega."

The crew guys thought those names fit, but the band guys disagreed. Chase agreed with Nelson and so the buses now had names. I think Chase did it just to tease me and the band. Alpha-beginning. Omega-end. Do you get it now? Okay, kinda dumb.

Everyone in the band checked with Belinda for their assignments. The crew got everything they would need later off of Alpha. The drivers took over the bus for a few

221

hours of sleep and unwinding. By six everyone was anxious for the concert to start. We still had a couple of hours to kill before we would play.

After a few opening announcements, the opening act took the stage. They were a new band from the Pittsburgh area called The Reign. They would be with us for the next two nights. I met them, but didn't really have a chance to talk to them. They were allowed a full hour tonight, and I caught part of their set from the side of the stage. I headed back downstairs to my dressing room. I looked through my clothes and tried to decide what to wear. Belinda was busy somewhere, so I had to choose without her input. I missed Kristen because she always knew what would look good. The Reign finished, and I heard them as they congratulated each other in the catering area. I had about twenty minutes to prepare.

"Boyd, have you seen Emmy yet?" Ryan asked.

"No, have you?"

"She must be either on the bus or in her dressing room. I wonder what she is going to wear tonight?"

"We'll just have to wait and see."

I was in my dressing room, which was barely larger than a closet, and heard the guys. I didn't realize they noticed my clothes so much. I made my decision. I picked out a dress and some tight fitting black Capri pants. That way I could dance around all I wanted.

Just after eight thirty the house lights dimmed and the MC introduced us.

"Please welcome from South Hampshire, Illinois, Emmy Colasanti and The Only Hope Band!"

The auditorium held over two thousand people and most of them rose to their feet. We sang a hymn to start the concert. After that I prayed, and we kicked off the concert with our regular songs. We finished an hour and fifteen minutes later. An hour after that we were downstairs eating and socializing with some of the fans who were contest winners of a local radio promotion. I talked to everyone and signed some autographs. I had my picture taken too many times to remember. The crew did their job and shortly after one o'clock, we headed to Allentown. Tonight the Omega bus was quiet.

After getting the kids ready for bed the next night, Emmy decided to call Rory.

"Hey, Emmy. What's up? I haven't heard from you in ages. I thought maybe you had forgotten all about me."

"I've been trying to forget you, but without any luck," Emmy teased. "What's this about you dating some bimbo you met in a bookstore?"

"She's not a bimbo, Emmy, and we are just getting to know each other."

"What's her name? I forgot."

"Her name is Rochelle Nash, and you didn't forget."

"Should I be jealous?"

Rory laughed. "Isn't one of the ten commandments something about coveting your neighbor's wife?"

"And his house and servants and donkeys. Are you a donkey?" Emmy asked.

"Are you calling me an ass?"

She giggled for a moment. "Don't let Isabella hear you use that word."

"It's a word for a certain animal," Rory insisted.

"Yeah. Whatever. So describe Rochelle to me."

"She's two years older than me. She's taller than you by several inches, but then so are most children."

"Ha! Ha! You're a creep. What color hair does she have?"

"Brown and shorter than yours. Brown eyes. Red lips..."

"Does she have her own teeth? Two eyes? Ten fingers and toes like normal people?"

"I'll ask her," Rory said.

"Is she there now? Can she hear me?" Emmy shouted.

Rory laughed again. "I'm pulling your leg. She's not here."

"You are such a creep. I will hate you forever, and stop touching my body parts."

"I thought you liked it."

223

"Shut up, Rory."

"What have you been up to? How are the kids? The girls are in second grade, right?"

Emmy caught Rory up on news about the kids and then mentioned her book.

"Please tell me this isn't one of those tell-all books. Am I in it?"

"It's not that kind of book, and you might be mentioned at some point." She explained more about the book.

"So, it's mostly about you and the guys in the band fooling around, huh?" he teased.

"Can you tell I'm giving you a special salute?"

Rory laughed. "Are you going to let me read your book someday?"

"You can read it if you buy a copy."

"Would you sign it for me at least?"

Emmy sighed. "I suppose. Now tell me more about Rochelle. Does she go by Shelly or some other nickname?"

"Some of her friends call her Shelly but not me. She works as a nurse for one of the doctors who works in our facility."

"What's the name of the place you work? I forgot."

"Presence Medical Care. It's in Tampa about ten minutes from my apartment," he answered.

"How does Rochelle like your apartment?" Emmy asked.

Rory chuckled, "Do you really think I'm going to fall for that? If you want to know if I've slept with her, just ask."

"Have you?"

"None of your business, Olivia."

"Stuff it, Clarence." She used his hated middle name. "I don't care if you have or not."

"Christians aren't supposed to lie, Em."

"Anything else happening down there in the land of old fogies? You still got your old man SUV?"

"I still have my CR-V, and it runs great. It's a 2010, and I got a good deal on it."

"I bet I could blow your doors off with either of my cars."

"I bet I get better gas mileage, and I can use regular." He

224

opened the fridge and pulled out a microwavable pizza. "Are you going to tour again?"

"Nothing's scheduled now. I recorded a bunch of Christmas songs, so I stopped recording my other songs. I'll finish that CD up sometime. I might tour in the summer. If I do, should I book something close to Tampa?"

"Nah! No need. I've heard you sing before." He popped the pizza in the microwave, opened his fridge and grabbed a beer. "You do know I'm kidding, right?"

"You hurt my feelings, Rory. I'm going to cry."

He laughed. "Go ahead, you spoiled brat."

"The church is going to build a new sanctuary," she informed him.

"Why? Did something happen to the old one?"

"Nothing happened to it. We need more room if we want the church to keep growing."

"How are your pastor and his wife doing? Are they still doing the foster parent thing?"

"Liz is expecting, but they don't have any foster kids at the moment." Emmy thought about Avery and her brothers. "They don't want to know the sex of the baby and that bugs me. I want to know."

"In the old days mothers never knew. Your mother probably didn't know if you were going to be a boy or a girl."

"Daddy wanted a boy. I remember Mom telling that to someone," Emmy admitted.

"I'm sure glad you weren't a boy, Em."

"Is that because of what you... Never mind."

"So, how about Fridays At Five? Are they going to record now that the tour is over?"

"Duh! They finished their CD before the tour. It's supposed to come out in November, and it's going to be a two CD set. Do you think you can afford to buy it?"

"Might have to save up. Maybe it won't be any good, and I can buy it used on Amazon."

"Are my CDs available like that?"

Rory grinned. "Of course. I think you can buy yours for a

penny and just pay for shipping."

"I don't care. I would give them away if it meant someone would accept Jesus into their life," Emmy said.

Rory waited for several seconds. "I think you really would, Em. Oh, I went to a Nazarene church a couple of Sundays ago. They had a worship band, but they sucked compared to you guys."

"Rory! That's not nice."

"Sorry, but it's the truth. The singer sounded awful, and the band didn't start or end together."

"How would you know?"

"Hey! Are you forgetting you're talking to Tim Burine? I'm one of the best tambourine players in this whole apartment building," he joked.

"Does that mean you want to go on the road with me next summer?"

"I'll check my schedule. The Royal Philharmonic might already have me booked," he said and then chuckled.

"You are such a riot. I bet you don't even know what key your tambourine plays."

"Ha! Tambourines are like drums. They don't play in a certain key. You can't fool me, little girl."

"I better let you go, Rory. Let's Skype one of these days. I want to see Rochelle and tell her all of your dirty secrets."

"You might spill some secrets about you instead," he whispered.

"Shut up, Rory. I don't have any deep secrets."

"If you say so, Em."

Chapter Twenty-One

Less two weeks later everything regarding the new sanctuary had been approved by all the necessary committees and people. Tyler called the Bertucci and Keasling office again and talked with John Randolph.

"So, we are good to go, correct?"

"Yes, John. I would like to have a groundbreaking ceremony after church this Sunday."

"We will be there for that, and we should start excavating on Monday. Garrick Winston will be in charge of the entire project. He's the best guy we have, and I know he will make sure everything goes great."

"Thank you, John. I'll see you on Sunday."

Emmy grabbed a Dr Pepper from the fridge and checked the time. *I better stop now and review my work. The kids will be home soon.* She grabbed her laptop from the couch in the family room and walked into the den. She closed the door and sat down.

After an uneventful overnight trip, our caravan pulled into the rear of the Allentown Symphony Hall. The Hall is a historic twelve hundred seat facility which serves the entire Lehigh Valley area. I knew this because I looked it up online. After the routine of unloading and preparing for the concert everyone had three or four hours of free time.

I took Ryan with me and we did some sightseeing. I felt comfortable with Ryan, but I suppose to anyone who didn't know us, we looked like a young couple on a date. Trust me, we weren't. He treated me like a little sister even though I was older. We arrived at a small park and sat on a bench to enjoy the fresh air and sunshine.

"What are your plans for after college, Ryan?"

"I had hoped to go into teaching, but now that I have a chance for a career with the band, that idea is going to have to wait."

"It's taking me forever to earn my degree. I have one semester to go. I'm taking eighteen hours, but at least I'm not working. We're going to have a party when I finish. I'll make sure you're invited."

"Where do you go to school? I didn't even realize you were still taking classes? How on earth do you ever find the time?"

"North Park, but I started at Paul Frank Junior College. I took classes as I could. That's why it's taking me so long. After Kenny and I got married, I stopped working and started going to school full-time."

"Congratulations, Mrs. Colwell."

"Thank you very much, Mr. Lederer."

The hall was not quite sold out tonight. There were a few empty seats but not too many. The concert started a few minutes late because of all the late arrivals. I noticed more older people in the crowd tonight. I mentioned it to Chase, and we made adjustments in our set. The Reign did their set and then we went on. I still hadn't had a chance to talk to those guys, but Boyd, Perry and Adam did. They told me later that the guys in The Reign were all brothers or cousins. I thought that was kinda cool. They had been playing music together for ten years, but only in the last two years had they been playing Christian music. They had all been saved at a camp meeting and totally changed their focus. After the concert several older people come up to me. I couldn't tell by the looks on their faces whether they were happy or not. I bit my lip and hoped for the best.

"We just want to thank you for including some older songs even if you did play them too loud," the spokeswoman for the group informed me.

I smiled and let them hug me.

"Thank you for coming to see us. We appreciate it."

"You have a beautiful voice, young lady."

"And a pretty face, too."

I blushed as the older ladies make such a fuss over me. I noticed Ryan watching. I knew he would tease me later on the bus. Some of the teens walked over to talk to me, too.

"We really liked your show even if you sang some of those old fashioned songs."

A couple of them suggested, "You should play louder. We love it when bands play loud enough so we can feel it."

I realized that we would never please everyone. We just had to please God.

"Are you still in high school?"

I giggled and said, "Not anymore. I graduated."

I wasn't telling a fib because I did graduate. I didn't mention how long ago it was.

The next stop was Charlottesville, Virginia. It would be a six hour drive. The buses and trucks pulled out of Allentown a few minutes before one. Chase and Nelson were pleasantly surprised to be on the road ahead of schedule.

We would be playing in the John Paul Jones Arena, the home of the Virginia Cavaliers. Chase was a little nervous about the next four nights. We would be playing in large venues with two opening acts. Jennifer Sinclaire would be joining us and a group I didn't know anything about. The lights and sound would be handled by ClairShowco. This company is the major provider of sound and lights in the industry. I checked online. They would be handling lights and sound for the rest of the tour with the exception of the Lansing and Springfield venues. There was even a company called Stagemonkey providing labor. This was all part of the contract, but I didn't know it at the time. I didn't get into the logistics too much. I just wanted to sing.

The buses and trucks pulled into the area behind the arena. Already there were trucks at the dock and men unloading gear. Chase, Nelson and I headed into the arena after clearing security. We looked around and the guys seemed to be in awe of the place.

"Nice place, huh?" Chase said.

"You could say that," Nelson added.

I almost laughed at them, but I didn't.

"Just think we don't have to worry about setting up our PA."

"I'm worried about the lights. I've talked to the guys from ClairShowco, and they assured me that their guy can handle our show. I told them that we weren't a rock show and not to go nuts."

"I'm sure they will figure it out."

I had seen so many Fridays concerts that the large venue didn't faze me. All right, I confess I was excited to be playing in a place that big without Kenny around.

The guys were truly amazed by the activity and size of the arena. I acted like it wasn't a big deal around them. I didn't want them to be nervous later. Of course, I had been on stage in front of thirty thousand fans before. I reminded the guys of the Fourth of July gig from a couple years ago in SoHam.

"There won't even be half as many people here tonight as there was that day."

"Yeah, but that was a Fridays At Five show. Tonight we are supposed to be the headliners."

"I think Jesus is the headliner, guys. We are just a little ole band from SoHam." I know that sounds super corny, but I really said it. Something like that at least.

I managed to ease any nervousness the guys might have. I saw a familiar face and ran over to talk to him. He saw me coming and held out his arms to hug me. I jumped into his arms and he held me tight.

"It's so good to see you, cuz. How has the trip been so far?"

"It's been fantastic! I am so glad to see you, Andy. I told the guys that tonight was no big deal, but I'll admit to you that I am a little anxious. Now that I know you're here I can relax."

"You don't need to worry, Em. I will make sure everything runs as smoothly as possible. I have done this a couple times before."

I was so relieved to see Andrew Walker. He is the long time manager of Fridays At Five and a veteran of many years of major touring. He was here to check up on Nelson, too.

"Kenny said to say hi, but that he doesn't miss you."

I knew Kenny was missing me because he told me on the phone earlier that morning.

"I don't miss him, either. Is he keeping out of trouble?"

"He told me he has been busy in the studio. He's been working on some new tunes, but needs your help with the lyrics."

I felt so much better with Andy around. Of course, I would have felt even better had Kenny come with him. Oh, I promised not to mention sex anymore. Andy would be around for the rest of the tour if we needed him. He would not be traveling in a bus, though. He would stay for tonight's show and then fly into Asheville in the morning on his company's private jet. He had assistants already in Asheville making sure everything was set for tomorrow. He had been through so many worldwide tours that this was almost a vacation for him.

"Chase, it's good to see you. I'm glad you were able to make it after all."

"Yes, sir. I'm happy to see you, Mr. Walker."

"Please call me Andy."

"This is amazing! Look at all the people. It must cost a fortune to pay for this."

"You do realize that the ticket sales for tonight are over $250,000."

"You're joking, right?"

"Not in the least. The place is sold out, and so are the next three places. I know you are not doing this for the money, Chase, but the promoter does like to make a profit. They couldn't survive otherwise. You should be able to do a thorough soundcheck around three or so."

"What about Jennifer Sinclaire?"

231

"Normally, I would say that I don't care about the opening act, but since this is different, I will make sure she has an opportunity for a good soundcheck, too."

"Thanks, Mr... Andy. I appreciate it."

Chase noticed that if Andy wanted something done it happened right away. He didn't have to raise his voice or anything.

Emmy checked the time again. *Shoot! I need to get through this chapter so I can have the weekend free.* She sat at the desk and continued. *What did I write in the journal about this show?* She read the journal and remembered an unpleasant incident involving one of the guys from the Stagemonkey crew. *I forgot about that. I should have told Andy about it, but I didn't want to get the guy in trouble. He didn't realize I was married when he propositioned me.* She tried to picture the crew member, but drew a blank.

Later, we finished the soundchecks and the caterers began feeding the starving crew. I was hanging out with Andy. Did I mention he and I are third cousins, or something like that. He was telling me stories about Fridays At Five I had never heard. I was laughing so hard my side hurt.

I saw Ryan heading toward Jennifer Sinclaire. I pulled Andy in that direction so I could listen to their conversation. I felt like a matchmaker. We were standing behind Jennifer so she didn't see us.

"Hi, Jennifer. I'm Ryan Lederer. We met in Carbondale at that festival."

"I remember you. How have you been?"

"Doing good. I don't know if you are aware of it, but I'm in a band called The Only Hope, and we are playing tonight."

"For real! That's cool. I knew there was another band playing after me and before Emmy."

"Actually, we're Emmy's band now. The band she had in Carbondale decided not to tour anymore, so we're her band now."

"I didn't know that. Do you know where she is?"

Ryan grinned and nodded his head. "She was talking to Mr. Walker before. He's the manager for Fridays At Five."

"I knew that. Is he really here?"

I couldn't keep from laughing, so I put my hand on her arm.

"Hi, Jennifer. It's good to see you. How have you been?"

She looked surprised, but she hugged me.

"This is Andy. He's here to help make sure things run smoothly."

Andy stuck out his hand. "It's a pleasure to meet you, Jennifer."

"Yes, hi, Mr. Walker."

"You better call him Andy or else he will get mad," I told her.

"If there's anything you need for the show, please ask." Andy needed to take care of business so he left us.

"It's so good to see you." I hugged her again. "When did you get here?"

"We got to D.C. last night and came on down here this morning. Isn't this exciting? I have never played a place so big. Do you know how many people this place seats?"

"I think Andy said we sold over 12,000 tickets so I guess it holds at least that many."

"I know that isn't the largest crowd you've ever seen, but it is for me."

"Did you get anything to eat? Are your guys and crew being taken care of all right?"

"Yes, we've already eaten. Will I see you after the show?"

"Yes, let's get together and talk. It will be nice to have another girl around."

Soon it was time for Jennifer to head upstairs to play. After an initial problem with her IEM, Jennifer's set was flawless. Her band was getting better and better and

233

her voice was in good form. After a short change on stage, the second act took the stage. I didn't even catch their name. Maybe that's a good thing because I didn't really like their music. I thought they were way too loud and, I hate to say this, they didn't seem sincere to me.

It would be about twenty five minutes before the guys and I would be on stage. Jennifer came downstairs and I saw her.

"Jennifer, I listened to most of your set and you sounded super."

"Did you really like it?"

"Yes."

"I'm going to listen to you from the side of the stage. Is that okay?"

"Sure. Hey! Do you know the song 'I Will Be True To You' by any chance?"

"Of course I do. We sing it every night. We didn't sing it tonight because you are here."

"Would you be willing to sing it with me?"

"You want me to sing with you?"

"If you would, please. You could sing Kristen's part. It's right in your range."

"Okay! I will."

"Thank you, Jennifer. I'll tell Chase and the crew will make sure you have a microphone. I'll talk to you upstairs. I have to go change."

I figured Ryan and the guys would be curious about what I was going to wear. I had a comfortable pair of jeans I wanted to wear and had a long top that almost looked like a dress on me. Chase gathered everyone for a prayer, then we headed upstairs. The stage manager gave a thumbs up to Andy and he passed it along to Chase and Nelson. The house lights faded out and the crowd roared. The band moved into position and began to play the intro. I prayed as I waited for my cue. I calmly walked out and was stunned by the noise from the crowd. I began singing. Tonight the band was rocking hard. No hymns to start the show tonight. We had the crowd on their feet, and I did everything I could to keep them there. I danced all over the large stage. I used every bit of it. That's something I learned from Kenny. We only slowed down for a moment when I brought Jennifer out to sing with me. Jennifer did a great job, and I hugged her as she left the stage. After the crowd settled down, I walked to the front of the stage.

"You can sit down if you want. This next song is about a girl I knew..."

That's as far as I got because the crowd erupted and stood to their feet as one. I looked over to the side of the stage on my right half expecting, as I did every night, to be surprised by Kenny. I didn't see him and wondered why the crowd was reacting so, then I heard a voice beside me.

"Sorry to do this again, Em."

I hung onto my microphone, but Stuart had muted it already. Stuart had flown in with Andy to handle FOH for the large venues. He had a lot more experience than Bruce. Bruce was running the IEMs while Sean ran the monitor wedges.

"Where did you come from?"

"From the other side. Chase told me you always look to your right to see if I'm going to surprise you. So I thought I would sneak up on you from the other side."

"You are a real stinker, but I love you anyway."

I hugged him and the crowd kept screaming. It took a minute for them to become quiet again.

"As I was saying..."

The crowd responded with laughter.

"This song is about... Do I really need to introduce it?"

Chase hollered, "Just sing it, Em! They all know the story."

Kenny started softly playing his acoustic guitar and then the band joined in. I saw the cell phones light up all over the arena. With tears flowing down my face, I sang Kenny's song for Yolanda. I finished and Kenny hugged me again. Instead of leaving the stage Kenny took a place beside Boyd. Frankie Hanna waved at me. Then he handed Kenny his Stratocaster. I wondered how many other Fridays At Five guys had flown in with Kenny and Andy. I should explain again that Frankie is Kenny's cousin and guitar tech. He's had that job from the very beginning. Anyway, Kenny played for the rest of the set. We finished with our normal closing song and the crowd would not leave. We did two more songs. After we finished those songs the band moved to the front center of the stage and waved to the crowd. Kenny stayed back not wanting to interfere.

Chase took my microphone. "Thank you so much for being a great crowd. Thanks for Kenny Colwell joining us and for writing such a great song."

Chase looked around and didn't see Kenny.

"Where is he?"

Ryan saw Kenny standing back by the backline of amps and told everyone. The guys turned and waved for Kenny to join us. He hesitated and I had to go get him. I brought him to the front and he seemed shy for some reason. I hugged him and he held me close.

"Once again thank you for an incredible night. We'll see you soon!" Chase hollered.

We took a final bow and waved as we headed off the stage.

"Why were you standing back there trying to hide?"

"Because I didn't want to interfere. This is your band, Em. Yours and God's!"

"You are just as goofy as me sometimes. You know that."

"No one is as silly as you, m'lady."

"I saw Frankie and heard that Stuart is here. I saw Andy when we first got here. Did you bring anyone else?"

"If you mean Kristen or Tony or anyone, the answer is no."

"Who did you bring?"

"Nobody. Frankie wanted to come with me, and

Stuart volunteered to help out."

"Are you going home tonight?" There was no way I was going to let him leave, but I had to ask.

"I really don't have any plans for the next couple of days."

"Can you stay for real? Please stay!"

I sounded like a schoolgirl; I was so excited. Oooh! That's a Fridays At Five song.

"I'm going to fly to Asheville with Andy in the morning. Do you think you might have a spot for another guitar player in the band?"

I teased him the same way I did before. "I don't know. Are you any good?" I knew I wasn't going to get much sleep that night.

We made it downstairs, and I saw Jennifer already talking to Ryan. Kenny and I walked over to join them. Jennifer saw me and smiled. Then she saw Kenny and stopped talking.

"This is my best friend in the whole world. Kenny, this is Jennifer Sinclaire." I'm almost ashamed to admit that I enjoyed introducing people to Kenny at times just to see the look on their face. They see him as a rock star, and I see him as my dorky friend. When we're alone, I see him as my husband and lover. But I guess I already told you that.

"I'm pleased to meet you, Jennifer. I heard part of your set and I enjoyed it very much. You sounded so much better than that other girl singer."

I smacked his arm for teasing me.

Jennifer laughed and told Kenny, "You know Emmy is a much better singer than me, but thank you for the compliment."

Andy wandered over to talk to Kenny and me.

"We have room in the plane if you are interested, Emmy. You could stay at the hotel and get a good night's rest."

"I would like that, but I need to ask Chase first."

Andy shook his head. "I took the liberty of asking

237

him already, and he gave you permission. Emmy, you need to take more control of your career. You should be calling the shots."

"Oh, I don't want to cause any trouble. Did you really ask Chase?"

"Actually, I told him you were coming with me. That's the difference between you and me. You would have asked permission, and I told him how it was going to be."

I looked at Kenny and he grinned. "It pays to be the king, and Andy is one step above king."

I didn't need to introduce Kenny to the guys from the Omega bus, but I knew they wanted to talk to him. Andy saw some of the Stagemonkey crew hanging around instead of doing their jobs.

"I need to go kick some monkey butt. I'll be back in a few minutes."

Kenny spent a few minutes talking to the guys from Jennifer's band. They asked him questions about his gear and stuff, and he gave them honest, detailed answers. Later, I packed my suitcase with the necessary items and thanked Chase for letting me fly on ahead.

"You deserve it, Em. We'll see you in the morning."

I saw a funny look on his face.

"Did you know Kenny was going to be here tonight?"

Chase hung his head a little.

"You stinker! You should have told me."

"What? And miss the look on your face. Not a chance."

I rode to the airport in a limo with Kenny and Andy. Andy's staff was also flying into Asheville on the plane with us. I'm sorry if I disappointed the guys by not being on the bus that night, but I'd do it again in a heartbeat.

Emmy sat back and laughed. That was a fun time. She heard a commotion from the kitchen and closed her laptop. She headed to the kitchen and Kevin Michael came running past

238

followed by Heather.

"What's going on?" Emmy tried to grab Heather but missed.

Isabella walked up. "Kevin took Heather's story and ripped it."

"On purpose?" Emmy asked.

Isabella shrugged and sprinted up the stairs after her siblings.

Emmy glared at Kenny. "Do you know what your son did?"

"I have the paper. It can be fixed." He kissed Emmy's forehead. "How was your day? Did you get any work done?"

"I did, but I don't think I'm getting any better at this," Emmy said and then sighed.

"That's why you have a professional editor. What's for dinner?"

"I put a meat loaf together. I thought we could have that and baked beans and baked potatoes."

"I like cheesy potatoes better," he said.

"Baked potatoes are so much easier," Emmy replied.

"I could help. I'll watch the kids if you make cheesy potatoes." He hugged her from behind and nuzzled her neck.

She leaned back into him. "Fine, but you will owe me."

Pastor Tyler closed the second service with a prayer and then announced, "For those of you who can stay, we will have the groundbreaking ceremony for the new sanctuary."

Emmy tapped Tony on the shoulder.

He turned around to look at her. "What's up, Emmy?"

"Are you and John going to get your picture taken?"

"Yes, why?" Tony tilted his head.

"No reason. I just wondered if you know which end of the shovel to use," Emmy grinned.

"Such a comedian, brat." Tony shook his head.

Emmy and Kenny joined the group of close to three hundred in front of the building. Pastor Tyler prayed and then drove the shovel into the ground at the edge of the parking lot.

"Where are we going to park when they start building?"

Emmy asked Kenny. "I hope we won't have to park in the field."

"I think they will put in a temporary lot for now, but I think the main lot will be over there." He pointed to the area to the north of the building.

Daniel Keasling joined Pastor Tyler, and the photographer from the *SoHam Herald* continued to take pictures. Tony and John each took a turn with the shovel. John went first and then handed the shovel to Tony. He held it up and looked at it.

"The pointy end goes in the dirt, Uncle Tony," Heather hollered.

Tony laughed. "Thank you, Heather Rose. Did your mother put you up to that?"

"She said you wouldn't know which end to use," Heather answered and the crowd erupted.

By ten o'clock the next morning several earth-moving machines ripped into the parking lot and ground in front of the sanctuary and educational building. Mary Galves kept a close eye on her class as they watched the machines during recess.

Kevin Michael pointed to the machines. "Ben, look! There are diggers all over."

"Stay here, boys," Mary insisted.

"Can we watch the diggers again tomorrow?" Benjamin Bertucci asked. "My daddy said he might teach me how to drive one when I get older."

Mary grinned and replied, "We can watch them if the weather holds out."

Chapter Twenty-Two

"I will be back as soon as I can, Em." Kenny kissed her and patted her back as he stuffed his wallet into his pocket, grabbed his keys and got ready to head to the Steward Music Group building.

"Do you think anyone will show up for your press conference?" Emmy asked with a straight face.

"Stephanie texted a few minutes ago. Apparently the press room is packed with reporters and photographers."

"Really?" Emmy looked up at Kenny and shrugged. "I can't imagine why they would still be interested in your old band."

"Amazing, huh?"

"Try not to act like a dork, and I hope you guys sell a few copies. What is the name of the CD? I forgot," Emmy teased.

"Dangerous Circumstances," Kenny answered and then realized Emmy was joking.

"Always a dork," she said.

"Sorry, I'll trash a hotel room the next time I go somewhere. See you later."

Kenny backed his blue 2013 Civic EX-L out of the garage and actually drove five miles faster than the speed limit on his way to the press conference. *Too bad Emmy isn't along to see me speeding.* He pushed a little harder on the gas pedal, but then slowed down when he spotted a SoHam squad car. He sighed with relief when the car turned a corner and disappeared. *That was a close call.* He pushed his speed up to forty-five miles-an-hour. *Wow! Ten miles over the limit.* He checked the trip computer. *I'm still getting great gas mileage. Over thirty-three miles per gallon. Sweet!* He pulled behind the Steward Music Group building and parked. He wiped some imaginary dust off of the front fender and jauntily walked inside.

"Hello, Mr. Colwell. Everyone is ready in the press room," the new secretary said.

"Thanks," he smiled.

He met Stephanie Grachan by the door. "How are you and those boys doing?"

"They are growing up much too fast. I can barely keep up

241

with them. How are Emmy and the kids?"

"Same thing. Growing up too fast."

She tilted her head.

Kenny laughed. "Well, the kids are growing up, but Emmy isn't any different."

Jeff Rawlings and Paul Joseph entered the room.

"About time." Stephanie checked the time. "Are we ready to do this?"

The guys nodded.

Stephanie led the way and P.J., Kenny and Jeff joined Dave Persching and Adam Vicini at the table set up in front. Stephanie read the official press release and some instructions for the questions and answer session.

Thirty minutes later Stephanie ended the session. "The tour schedule is available online, and for those of you who are still in the dark ages, I have a printed copy. Thank you all for your cooperation, and you have five minutes to take photos. Please try not to blind the guys because then I would be out of a job, and I have to feed four growing boys."

Kenny leaned closer to Jeff. "Emmy didn't think anyone would show up."

Jeff laughed. "It's amazing they still do. I never would have thought we would still be doing this at our age."

"Jeff, you're only forty-three, and I'm a year older," P.J. said. "It's not like we're old men."

"Yeah, Bono is ten years older than you," Kenny replied.

"They don't tour as much as they did a few years ago," Jeff said.

Adam checked the tour schedule. "Juliana is not going to like this. I'll be gone for the best part of six months."

Dave posed for a few photos and then got up. "I'm out of here. I have to explain to Macy why we aren't touring the entire year."

"Is she still spending every penny you earn?" Adam asked.

Jeff's stomach shook as he laughed. "Yeah, but Dave still has her believing he's on a salary of a grand a week."

"Hey! If I told her the truth, I would be penniless."

"You could always sell one of those houses you own in England, Montana and Hawaii," Jeff suggested.

"Macy likes to travel and stay at our own place. She'll never let me sell them. She'd rather sell the place here in SoHam."

"Who would ever want to buy that place," Jeff teased. "It looks like some kind of futuristic spaceship or something. It's all steel and glass."

"It's a contemporary house. It's not a hundred years old like that place you and Frances live in." Dave referred to the house in Timberline Heights that Jeff and his wife spent years restoring.

"Our place actually looks like a house."

"Emmy and I are going to coordinate her tour with ours so one of us is always home with the kids. At least as much as possible," Kenny said. "We will probably both be gone some Fridays and Saturdays though."

"Good luck with that," Adam said. "I know what it's like to tour with both bands."

Since the kids were home Friday because of a teacher's institute day, Emmy took her laptop to the carriage house to work. She pulled into the alley behind Kenny's parents' house, got out and looked at the two-and-a-half story brick home that had been in the family for nearly a century and a half. *I hope our house still looks this good in a hundred years.* She walked up the sidewalk, climbed the back porch and let herself in. "Anyone home?" she hollered.

Mr. Colwell rose from his recliner and walked into the kitchen. "I didn't know you were coming over. Do you have the kids with you?"

She hugged her father-in-law. "I'm sorry, but I didn't bring them. They didn't have school today, so I thought I would come over here to work. Where's Mom?"

He yawned and stretched his arms over his head. "She is visiting her brother. She won't be back until late tonight."

"Were you taking a nap?" Emmy asked. "It's pretty early to be napping."

"I was up at six, so this is my morning nap," he answered.

243

"If I'm lucky, I'll take another one this afternoon. How's the book coming along? I don't think Kenny is working on his at all."

"I thought you were writing the official history of Fridays At Five."

"I suppose so, but I need his input to make it more personal."

Emmy sighed and plopped down onto one of the barstools. "I keep writing mine using the journals as a guide, but I think it sucks. I'm writing about the early tours, and it seems rather dry. I could spice it up with some of the stuff that happened on the bus, but I don't want it to be a tell-all thing."

He leaned against the counter next to her. "I'm not an expert by any means, but I do know that writing consists of rewriting over and over. This is your first draft." He patted her on the back. "You shouldn't expect it to be perfect."

"I guess so." She got up. "I'm going out to the carriage house to work. Maybe I can pick up lunch from Darby's since I'm so close."

"I'd like that. I cleaned up the carriage house a couple of days ago."

Emmy tilted her head.

Mr. Colwell chuckled. "Okay, the cleaning lady did the actual work, but I pointed out a few things."

She laughed. "That's what I thought. I'll be back around lunch."

"I'll buy."

Emmy walked back to the carriage house and glanced up at the second floor. *I've spent a lot of time in there. I still remember the first time. It was full of junk and spider webs and dust. I will always remember our wedding night.* She sighed. *This was the perfect place to spend our first night together. Our first night as man and wife.* She thought about the time she spent working on songs as she climbed the stairs. She opened the door, flipped on the lights and smiled. *I know that's not the same couch, but it's eerily similar to the one where Kenny first kissed me.* She adjusted the heat, sat down on the couch and went to work.

We arrived at the Asheville Regional Airport and were taken by limo to the Renaissance Asheville Hotel. Andy's assistant made all the room reservations but didn't realize I would be traveling with them. Kenny and Frankie were sharing a room.

"I'm sorry, Andy. I didn't know she would be with us."

"It's all right. Can't we just reserve another room for Frankie?"

"They are full according to the desk."

Kenny was listening to the conversation and whispered to Andy.

"We can tease Emmy about not having any room."

"Are you sure?"

Andy loved to tease me about as much as Kenny or Tony. I saw the look on their faces and knew something was up. I decided to play along with whatever scheme they were hatching. They walked over to where I had been waiting with some members of Andy's staff.

"Emmy, may I talk to you privately for a moment?"

"Of course, Andy. Is there something wrong?"

"My assistant did not book a room for you and the hotel is full."

I played along. "Does that mean I have to sleep outside?"

"Unfortunately, yes. Frankie and Kenny are sharing a room and hotel policy won't allow you to share their room. This is the South and they have some pretty strict rules about women sharing a room with a man who is not her husband."

I couldn't believe he could keep a straight face while telling me this malarkey, so I tried to look worried.

"However, they do have a sleeping bag you could use, but it is rather filthy and was last used by a homeless man."

I looked at Andy and managed not to laugh. He was so convincing.

"Could I at least sleep in the bathroom or in a

closet?" I pointed to a restroom.

Finally, Andy started to laugh.

"You weren't buying it for a second, were you?"

I shook my head. "I'm going to sleep with Kenny, and I don't care if Frankie's in the room or not."

Andy laughed. "Kenny, I think you're stuck with her tonight."

I could see some of the hotel staff hanging around but were kinda afraid to approach Kenny. I figured I could use that to get back at him and Andy for trying to tease me.

Andy's assistant made arrangements for a later checkout time and wake-up calls for all the rooms. Andy's and Kenny's luggage was taken up to their rooms by hotel staff. My suitcase was taken also which surprised me. Andy and Kenny are used to special treatment, but I wasn't.

"Do you always get treated like this?" I knew that would embarrass him because although he was treated like a celebrity, it always kinda bothered him.

"I suppose so, Em. It kinda goes with the job I guess. There is a downside. I have to tip well or else be thought of as a miser or something worse."

I raised my voice a little. "Do you mean like an ego tripping, son of a bitch, full of crap, booze guzzling, drug addicted, run of the mill, has been rock star?"

"That's one way of putting it, Em."

I made sure the staff could hear me. "Every rock star needs his groupies! Can I be yours? I know you're married, but I don't care."

I smiled at Kenny and took his arm and pretended to be his groupie.

"Frankie, I guess you'll have to share my suite for tonight." Andy had plenty of room for Frankie.

Frankie nodded.

I should explain that Frankie is a man of very few words. He probably doesn't say more than ten words a day. I'm kidding, but he is very introverted.

246

Kenny and I followed our luggage to his room. He always stayed on the top floor if at all possible. Andy stayed on the floor below him most of the time. This is because Fridays At Five rents out an entire floor for security purposes. Since this wasn't a Fridays tour, the whole floor was not booked. Kenny tipped the bellhop generously as I plopped down on the bed nearest the window. For some reason I decided to act like the young teenager I had been when we first fell in love instead of his horny wife. I was going to make him work for... you know.

"I want this one!" I teased him about sleeping in separate beds.

"Doesn't matter to me."

"Are we gonna stay up all night like when we were kids?"

"You might regret that tomorrow, sweetie."

"I want to take a shower. Do you mind?" I jumped off of the bed.

"Go ahead. I'll take one after you. Please don't use all the towels."

"Can't you always call for more? You are a big rock star after all."

Kenny moved over closer to me. I had my back turned and didn't see him until he was next to me. He put his hands on my shoulders and any thought of not sharing his bed instantly vanished.

"Do I need to remind you who the arena was cheering for tonight?"

"They weren't screaming for me like they did for you."

"I beg to differ but no matter. Are you going to take that shower, or can I go ahead?"

"I'm going first. Just give me a minute to get my pajamas." I don't know why I bothered with the pajamas.

I took my shower first. By the time Kenny finished and climbed into bed, I was sound asleep. He told me in the morning that he watched me sleeping for a few minutes before he turned off the light. He whispered good night and let me sleep.

Kenny woke up at ten, but I was still sound asleep. Kenny laughed as he looked at me. I was almost sideways on the bed on my stomach. Kenny chuckled and took a picture with his phone. I should explain. I grew up sharing a small bed with my sister, Diane. I had no room, so when I got my own place with a bed of my own, I developed a habit of wandering all over the bed as I slept. I was better now that Kenny and I shared a bed, but I still moved around a lot. He sent it to Kristen's email and then called home to talk to his parents.

"How are you feeling today, Mom?"

"I feel much better."

Kenny talked to his mom for several minutes and then my cell phone rang. He saw that it was Kristen calling, so he answered it.

"Did you surprise Emmy again?"

"Yeah! It was priceless. Chase told me she always looks to her right to see if I'm going to surprise her, so I snuck up on her from her left. She didn't see me until I was right beside her."

"Did she cry?"

"Of course. You know how she is. She did such a great job, though. She is getting better every night. Did you get my email message?"

"Yes. Something about the hotel being full and you and Andy teasing her. Did you guys stay up all night?"

"No. She took a shower, and by the time I finished she was sound asleep. She's still sleeping. Did you check your email this morning? I sent a picture of her."

"I can check it now. Did I tell you Tony called. He took Mama to the doctor."

"Is she all right?"

"Yeah. She was running a fever, but she's okay now. Don't tell Emmy she will just worry needlessly." Kristen paused then laughed and said, "Oh! I see the picture. Is she really sleeping like that?"

Kenny looked over at me. I guess I had moved again, so he took another picture and sent it along to Kristen.

"Nope! I just took another shot. She has moved."

Kristen opened the second email and looked at the picture. I was now on the other side of the bed and on my back.

"Does she still do that to you?"

"Not as much as when we were first married, but sometimes I end up on the edge of the bed with only a foot of space."

"That is so funny. Can you picture Emmy married to Tony? She would be taking up the whole bed and this gigantic man would be sleeping on the very edge."

"I can see that clearly."

I woke up just in time to hear the last part of Kenny's conversation with Kristen. I guess I fell back asleep because when I woke up again, Kenny was sitting at the desk working on his laptop. He heard me and looked over.

"Good afternoon, Sleeping Beauty. Did you sleep well?"

"What time is it?"

"Twelve fifteen."

"I am so late. Chase is going to kill me."

"Relax! I already talked to him. You don't have to be there for the soundcheck until three thirty."

"I can't believe I slept so long."

"Kristen said to say hi. I sent her a couple pictures of you in bed."

"Creep! Was I spread out all over?"

"Yep. I'll show you the pictures."

I sat up in bed as Kenny showed me the two pictures.

"Crap! I can't help it. I just move around. You know that."

"Come on. Get out of bed and get dressed. I'm hungry."

Kenny packed up both suitcases while I got ready. I added my toiletries bag to my suitcase and we were ready to leave. All the luggage would be picked up by a hotel employee and taken downstairs. The limo driver would pick it up later. We headed downstairs to the restaurant to order lunch. Andy was gone but had left a message for Kenny to meet him at the Civic Center. We ate lunch and decided to walk to the venue since it was so close. Less than half a mile away.

"Such a beautiful day, Kenny. Wouldn't you agree?"

"Yes indeed, my little sugarplum. A beautiful day indeed."

Kenny did his impression of W.C. Fields. I didn't have a clue who he was, but I always laughed when Kenny did his impersonation. We arrived at the Civic Center and were cleared by security. The first person we saw inside was Andy Walker and he looked upset.

"About time you got here. How is our princess today?"

"I'm sorry I overslept, Andy. I didn't want to wake up. I was having such pleasant dreams."

"Andy is just teasing you, Em. We are early and he knows it."

"Do you know where Chase might be?"

"He was talking to Stuart Lederer a few minutes ago. Jennifer was asking about you."

"I'll see if I can find her."

"You need to wear this pass, Emmy. Otherwise they might toss you out on your butt," Andy reminded me.

Although I should know better, I sometimes forgot I needed to wear a pass when I was backstage. I found Jennifer and told her about the flight and the stay in the hotel, but I didn't tell her I fell asleep before Kenny was even in bed. So much for a night of taking advantage of my husband.

I should tell you more about Jennifer Sinclaire. She was born and lived in Bryson City, North Carolina until she was ten. Then her family moved to Knoxville, Tennessee.

Although Asheville is only sixty-four miles from Bryson City, Jennifer was never in Asheville until the previous year when she sang at a local church without her band. Oh, she has a gorgeous southern accent and she's very pretty, too.

"What a difference a year can make, Emmy. Last year I sang at a small church in Asheville for forty-seven dollars. Tonight I will be singing in front of several thousand people and earning fifty-two dollars."

"You're making that much! I only get twenty-five, a cheeseburger and a Coke."

"I'll trade you some of my money for the cheeseburger."

"No way! I'd do this for free as long as I get my cheeseburger."

We kept asking everyone we saw if they knew where to get a good cheeseburger. Sometimes you get kinda slap-happy on the road and silly things seem a whole lot funnier than they should. Shoot! Now you're going to think I'm just as dorky as Kenny. I'll have to fix this in the next draft.

The afternoon was easy because all the team had to do was the soundcheck. We had our meal before the show, and I talked to the Omega guys. They told me they missed me last night. I promised I would be back on the bus soon. I listened to Jennifer from the side of the stage. So did Ryan Lederer. I wondered if Ryan still had a thing for Jennifer, or was I just imagining that. I knew they were dating, but because of where they lived they weren't together all that often. I decided to tease him.

"Ryan, do you have Jennifer's phone number by any chance. I want to be able to call her when we get home."

"What makes you think I would have it, Emmy?"

"Well, do you?"

"Yes, and I have her email address."

"You like her a lot, huh?"

"Maybe."

"It's all right. She is sorta nice and kinda pretty if you like that type."

"What type is that?"

"You know. Tall, slender, gorgeous eyes, lovely hair. All those things that some guys like."

"She is rather pretty, isn't she?"

I could tell Ryan was still crazy about Jennifer.

Jennifer and her band rocked the place that night. Their confidence and musicianship had improved since the festival in Carbondale. Jennifer was learning how to work the crowd better. She was used to small venues, but in a place this big you needed to get the crowd involved. They played for forty minutes and received a standing ovation when they left the stage. Okay, maybe half of the crowd cheered which for an opening act is doing all right.

There was a different band following her tonight. I liked this group a lot better. They were from Macon, Georgia, and called themselves The Apostles Creed. Kenny and I got to meet them and spent some time talking to them. The five guys in the group attended the same church. We caught part of their set from the side of the stage. They finished and came off the stage.

The lead singer asked us, "Are they cheering so loud because we stopped playing, or did they like us?"

He was such a down-to-earth guy that I felt I could get away with teasing him a little. "They're cheering because you're finally done."

"That's what I figured," he drawled, laughed and shook my hand.

After a thirty minute break to reset the stage and give the crowd a brief intermission, the guys took their places on stage. Kenny waited just offstage with me.

"Please welcome from South Hampshire, Illinois, Emmy Colasanti and The Only Hope Band!"

The announcer dragged out my name like you would hear at a sporting event. The band started playing and Kenny and I walked out together. Later he tried to tell me that all the cheers were for me, but I'm smart enough to realize they weren't. By this time, rumors had spread about him appearing with us. I'm sure that's why we sold out the larger arenas. We played our set and then Chase had a chance to talk to the audience. The band and I never wanted to lose sight of our main reason for singing in front of people.

Afterward, I had a chance to talk to some people backstage. I wasn't sure who all of them were, but Kenny told me that two of them were reporters for *CCM Magazine.* I guess they were interviewing me. I hope I didn't say anything mean or stupid.

The guys in the band were a little envious that I got to fly with Kenny and Andy, and they teased me, but they understood why.

"So the princess gets to fly in her own private jet again while the rest of us have to travel in these old broken down dilapidated smelly buses," Ryan teased.

I teased them back. "The buses wouldn't smell so bad if you guys would take showers once in a while and do your laundry more often than once a year."

"I suppose we will have to bow when you come on the stage now."

I laughed. "I think that would be appropriate. After all I am a diva."

I made sure I talked to all the guys before leaving. I hugged most of them. Some of the guys are not huggers, so I always respected that. Chase had to convince me it was all right to fly again. I genuinely felt bad about leaving everyone, but I couldn't pass up the opportunity.

"Emmy, you expend so much energy onstage. You need the rest, or else you are going to burn out. I know you don't get enough quality sleep on the bus."

"It's not fair to everyone else, Chase. They work just as hard as I do."

"They do more physical work, I'll give you that, but they don't have the stress of being the front man of the band. The kind of stress that you go through is much more taxing than a bit of physical labor. If you ever get to the place where you are actually doing this for a living, you will have to learn that you need to take of your body and mind as well as your spirit. If that means flying while everyone travels by bus, then so be it."

I flew into Atlanta on Andy's plane. We checked into the Atlanta Marriott Downtown hotel, and tonight I managed to stay awake longer than the night before. That's a sly way of saying... you know.

Emmy bit her lip. *I still remember that night. I didn't get a lot of sleep, but by the time I did fall asleep, I was totally relaxed. I guess if I am honest with myself, I'd rather fly than spend all night in a bus.* She checked the time. "I better see what Dad wants for lunch." She saved her revisions and headed to the main house. She found Kenny's father in the living room.

"What would you like for lunch, Emmy? I'm buying," Dad Colwell said.

"Are we going to eat there, or come back here?"

"Up to you. We could see how crowded it is."

Darby's was packed, so they placed their order to go. They sat in the breakfast nook to eat.

"Did you get some work done?" Dad Colwell asked.

"Yes," Emmy said and explained the setting for the chapter.

Dad Colwell laughed. "I remember Kenny telling me about a time when you stayed overnight. I can't remember why now, but you slept in the room next to his. You were around eight or nine, I think."

"I think I remember that night. Mom and Dad were at the hospital," Emmy said.

"He checked on you in the morning, and you were sprawled sideways across the bed."

"Yeah, I did that whenever I had a bed to myself. I loved sleeping at Grandma Isabel's because I had a big bed and didn't have to share."

"Times have changed, huh?"

"Yes, thank the Lord."

Chapter Twenty-Three

Emmy entered the Starbucks and looked around. *I don't see Denise anywhere.* She checked the time. *I am a couple of minutes early, but she's always here before me. I wonder if she got stuck at the office.* Emmy ordered a White Chocolate Mocha Frappuccino, and sat down at the table next to where she and Denise usually sat. Their regular table being occupied. Emmy opened her laptop, but then also pulled out some short stories she printed that morning. She read through the stories again and grinned. *I like these better than the chapters of my book. They're nice and short and kinda whimsical.* She waited fifteen minutes before spotting Denise.

"I'm sorry I'm late, but I had to put out a fire at the office." Denise sat across from Emmy and saw the look on Emmy's face and chuckled. "Not literally." Denise removed her long coat and floppy black hat. She spotted the printed pages on the table. "What do we have here?"

"These are those short stories I mentioned."

"May I read them?"

"Sure, but they're just fairy-tales I threw together."

Denise read the first page silently for a moment and then burst into laughter. She read the second page and laughed again. "This is quite good. I love how you have humanized your animal characters. Do you have more?"

Emmy handed Denise the second short story. Denise read it and asked for the rest of the stack. Emmy finished her Frappuccino while Denise read.

"Emmy! You need to publish these right away. They are excellent."

"Really?" Emmy's eyes opened wide.

"Yes!" Denise slapped the table top. "All they need is some illustrations."

"I have these drawings." Emmy pulled some illustrations from her bag and handed them to Denise. "They aren't real good, but they kinda fit."

Denise shook her head as she looked at the drawings. "These are perfect. I wouldn't make any changes. We could tighten up the stories a bit, but I wouldn't change these illustrations at all."

For the next few minutes they discussed Emmy's options.

"These would make an excellent book for children. Let me make a few calls, and then we can decide how to proceed."

"What should I call it?" Emmy asked.

Denise picked up the first story. "I like this title. Grandpa and the Three Lost Lonely Lions."

"The girls loved it when I read these stories to them."

"I can understand why. I will work on this later today. I have an old friend who works for a vanity publisher. I'll call her and see what she suggests. Since there isn't much editing to do, I think you could format these into an electronic book rather quickly and into a traditional book format in a few weeks or less."

"That would be so cool!" Emmy beamed. "I like these stories better than my other book. The real one."

"Speaking of your book. How is that going?"

"I'm trudging along. I'm hoping to have a first draft completed by December. I don't want to work on it during the holidays. I will be too busy to do justice to it."

"Sounds reasonable. Let's concentrate on the lion stories for now." Denise grabbed Emmy's hands. "I am so thrilled for you. You may have found your niche. Your true calling as an author."

"Mom! The filling is all stirred up. Can I have a bite?" Heather lifted the bowl and held it out for Emmy to see.

Emmy checked the oven temperature and then walked around the island to inspect the pumpkin pie filling. "That looks good, Heather, but I don't think you will like it until it's cooked. It's not like cookie batter."

Heather and Isabella sniffed the mixture.

Isabella pinched her nose. "It smells yucky. I'm not going to eat it."

"It will be good after it's cooked," Emmy said.

"What do we do now?" Heather asked.

Emmy placed two pie shells in front of the girls. "Fill these up, and try to make them even. Then we will put them in the oven."

"Can we eat some pie tonight?" Heather asked.

"Heather! Be careful! You spilled some filling," Isabella stated emphatically.

"Sorry," Heather apologized.

Emmy handed them a roll of paper towels. "You can clean up the mess after you're finished. And the pies are for tomorrow. You have to wait."

Isabella began smoothing out the filling in her pie. "Doreen from school said the Pilgrims didn't eat turkey or pumpkin pies at the first Thanksgiving. Is that true, Mommy?"

"No one knows for sure what they ate, Isa, but it's likely they didn't have turkey or pies. They probably ate corn or something they grew."

"Couldn't they shoot a wild turkey?" Heather asked.

"Maybe all the turkeys were hiding so they wouldn't get eaten," Isabella said and then giggled.

The landline rang and Emmy picked it up after checking the caller ID. "Hi, Denise. Happy almost Thanksgiving."

"Thank you, Emmy. Happy Thanksgiving to you, too. Do you have your laptop handy?"

"It's on the desk. Why?"

"Pull up Amazon and do a search for your name," Denise instructed and then began chatting about what she planned to cook for Thanksgiving.

A minute later Emmy opened Amazon and typed in her name. She ran down the list of CDs and came to something new. "Oh, my God! My little book is here. How did you do that? It's only been a couple weeks."

Denise laughed. "I pulled in a bunch of favors."

"So people can actually buy it now?"

"People are already buying it, Emmy. Once word gets around, you might have a bestseller on your hands."

"No way!" Emmy looked at the girls. "Come and see. The lion book is online already."

"Can we see?" The girls scampered down from the barstools and rushed over to Emmy.

"It's right here on the computer," Emmy pointed out.

257

"Is it like a real book, or is it just on the computer like your other big book?" Isabella asked.

Denise heard the girls and laughed. "Tell them it is a real book. You should have a few copies arriving soon, but for now if you want to buy a real book, you have to do it online."

"It's going to be a real book like the ones you read," Emmy said.

"Is it like our Junie B. Jones books?" Isabella asked.

"Sorta, but it will just be one book with all of my stories about the lions."

The girls scampered back to their pies.

"I'll let you get back to whatever," Denise said. "I wanted to let you know about the book."

"Thanks, Denise. I hope you and your family have a great Thanksgiving." Emmy hung up and leaned against the desk. "Can you believe it, girls? I am a real author now. Isn't that exciting?"

"Our pies are ready for the oven. Will you put them in for us?" Heather asked.

"Please, Mommy?" Isabella asked. "Heather and I are gonna write some more stories about the lions so we can be real Arthurs, too."

"Go ahead. Thank you for all your help," Emmy said, but the girls had dashed away already. She did a little dance and was pumping her fists when Kenny entered the kitchen.

"You seem excited, Em. What's going on?"

She put up a hand. "High-five me."

Kenny did.

"My lion stories are on Amazon already. Can you believe it? I am a real author."

"I knew you could do it." He picked her up and hugged her tightly. "I am so proud of you."

"Can we buy one?" Emmy asked.

Kenny kissed her, set her down and grinned. "I guess it depends on how much they cost."

"You are such a stinker." She frowned and put her hands on her hips.

"Okay, maybe one copy."

"Does anyone have room for dessert?" Emmy looked around the dining room table the next day.

"Not me." Kenny pushed back from the table and shook his head.

Dad Colwell rubbed his stomach. "I am stuffed. I can't eat another bite."

"Everything was delicious, Emmy," Mom Colwell said. "The turkey was moist, the mashed potatoes and dressing were scrumptious and I loved the ham. Did you buy it at that store by the video place?"

"Yes, all I had to do was heat it."

"It will make delicious ham sandwiches."

"I liked the sweet potatoes, Mommy," Kevin Michael said.

Emmy checked his plate. "You didn't eat the sweet potatoes. All you ate was the marshmallow topping. You should try a bite of the potatoes. You like potatoes."

Kevin looked at the sweet potatoes again.

"Try a little bite for me, please," Mom Colwell asked.

Kevin Michael took a small bite, chewed it up and then grinned. "I like the potatoes, too. Even if they are a funny color."

"Mommy, can we have some pie now?" Heather asked. "I cleaned up my plate. Look!"

"Good job, Heather," Kenny said and then checked the floor under Heather's chair. *I guess you did eat everything.*

Isabella turned to her grandfather. "Gra, Heather and I made the pies. Do you want some?"

He looked across the table at Emmy.

Emmy nodded. "It's true. Heather and Isa mixed the ingredients and put the pies together. All I did was put them in the oven."

"Then I think I have just enough room for a small piece of pumpkin pie."

Heather said, "We have whipped cream to put on top."

Emmy brought one of the pies into the dining room and cut slices for Gra, Kenny and the kids.

Dad Colwell took a bite and smiled. "This is the best pumpkin pie I have ever eaten."

259

Isabella took a bite of her pie. "Gra, do you know the Pilgrims didn't have pumpkin pie or even turkey?" She held out her hands palms up. "Why do we eat turkey now?"

"I'm not sure how that tradition started, Isa, but I'm sure glad we eat pumpkin pies now."

Emmy heard the front doorbell ring on Monday morning. "Who can that be? No one except delivery guys ever use the front door." She set down her coffee mug, walked out of the kitchen and opened the front door. She spotted a box from UPS. "Oh, my! This might be my books." She picked up the box. "It's heavy enough to be books." She brought it inside and set it down on the foyer floor. She dashed to the kitchen, found a pair of scissors, ran back to the foyer, got on her knees and cut open the shipping tape. She threw back the flaps, tossed some shipping material over her head and lifted out a book. She held it up with both hands and began to cry. "Thank you. Lord, for making this come true." She opened the book and turned the pages. *I can't believe it's real.* She stood up and raced downstairs to the recording studio, She burst into the control room and startled Kenny. He nearly fell over in the recliner as she jumped onto his lap.

"Look!" She waved her book in his face.

"Em, I think you just broke my legs." He grabbed her hands to hold them still and took a look. "That's just like a real book."

"It is a real book!" Emmy shouted and bounced on his legs. "Oh, sorry. Am I hurting you?"

"Just a little, but I'll probably survive."

Emmy stood up and handed her book to Kenny. "UPS just delivered a whole box full of these. What should I do with them?"

"You could try to sell them," Kenny suggested while rubbing his legs.

Emmy put a finger to her mouth and tilted her head. "I think I'll give them away to people at church."

"That's a good idea, Em. Could you help me up? I want to see if my legs will still hold me."

"Oh, hush. I didn't break your legs."

Chapter Twenty-Four

"Hi, Kristen. How are you?" Emmy answered her cell phone while sorting laundry.

"Why didn't you tell me you were doing a Christmas CD? I'm at the mall, and there is a big display in the window of the Christian Family Bookstore."

"There is!?"

Kristen rolled her eyes. "Don't tell me you didn't know about it."

"Of course I knew I recorded it, but I didn't know for sure Steward Music was releasing it today," Emmy explained.

"Have you started your Christmas shopping? I don't know why I even bothered coming to the mall. Christmas is still twenty-two days away, and this place is crowded already." Kristen kept walking and threading her way through the mass of people.

"I'm hoping I don't have to go to any stores at all. I'm going to try to do all of my shopping online. I know that kinda hurts local businesses, but I hate fighting crowds." Emmy added the laundry detergent and closed the washer lid.

"Guess what?"

"What?" Emmy asked.

"This other music place has your CD, too. It looks like people are buying it. You are selling your children's book and your CDs. Must be nice to be so talented," Kristen said.

"Are you being sarcastic?"

"No, I'm happy for you." Kristen dodged out of the way of two shoppers pushing strollers. "I wish I could do something like that."

"Kristen, you have other talents. You could be a very successful businesswoman if you tried."

"Maybe, but I'm content to stay at home with the kids even though they are in school all day."

Emmy leaned against the washer and felt the vibrations. "You could take on a larger role with the company. You could help the guys by running the office," Emmy suggested.

"That would be more responsibility than I want to take on. I could work part-time, but Gladys Posey works fifty hours a week. That's not for me," Kristen replied. "Are you still working on that other book?"

"Yeah, but I'm letting it slide until after the holidays. I had more fun writing the stories about the lions. The other book is like work."

"I'll talk to you later. I need to find something for my mother. She insists she doesn't need anything, but if I don't buy her something unique, she would be upset. You're lucky your mom doesn't even know it's almost Christmas." Kristen froze and put a hand over her mouth. "I'm so sorry. Here I am complaining about my mother, and you are dealing with your mother's Alzheimer's."

"It's okay, Krissy. I understand."

"I should know better. We are studying that book about attitudes and complaining on Wednesday nights. Who is the author? I can't think of his name."

"James MacDonald. He's the pastor of Harvest Bible Chapel."

"Right, and the book is *Lord, Change My Attitude*."

Emmy chuckled and added, "*Before it's too late*. That's the other part of the title."

"Before we started doing this book, I would have never thought of complaining as a sin. Now I'm trying to control my thoughts, but it's not easy."

"Tell me about it," Emmy sighed.

"You don't complain very much. Certainly not as much as I do," Kristen admitted.

"It's something we both need to work on," Emmy said.

"Tyler, my mom says it's time to go." Liz rubbed her belly as she talked on the phone.

Tyler checked the time on his laptop "I'm almost through with my sermon, and I thought we were supposed to meet the Briggs at six. We have time..."

"No! It's time to go to the hospital!" Liz handed the phone to her mother. "You talk to him."

"What's going on?" Tyler asked.

Liz's mother calmly said, "Tyler, you need to come home now. Liz needs to get to St. Bart's."

Tyler jumped up from his office chair. "Right! I'll be right there." He grabbed his keys from his coat on the rack by the door, forgot the coat and dashed out of his office. "Mrs. Millner, I'm going home so I can take Liz to the hospital. If you see Darren or Jake let them know I left," he shouted while running past the main office.

Mrs. Millner, the longtime church secretary nodded and kept typing. She paused and then stood up. "Did you say the hospital?"

But Tyler couldn't hear her because he was sprinting across the parking lot. He opened the car, jumped in, started it and floored it. The Prius slowly gained some momentum. *Shoot! I should buy a car like Emmy's Civic Si.* He made it home in three minutes and rushed inside using the front door. "Liz, where are you?"

Dany Kimmerle walked out of the kitchen. "She and Mom are upstairs getting ready."

"My God! Is she going to have the baby here? At home?" Tyler shouted while scampering past Dany and racing up the stairs three at a time. "Wait. Liz! We need to go to the hospital." He bounced off of the door frame and into the bedroom. "Wait!"

Liz and her mother turned to stare at Tyler.

"I'm pretty sure the baby's not going to wait, Tyler," Liz said.

"But I got a call that's it's time, and Dany said you're getting ready."

"I am getting ready. I needed to get dressed. Will you grab the suitcase, please?" Liz pointed to the ready-to-go-to-the-hospital bag.

"So the baby's not coming right now?"

"We have enough time to get to St. Bart's," Mom Kimmerle assured Tyler.

Tyler wiped the sweat off of his brow. "Thank God for that. Where are Natty and Grayson? Do we need to take them with?"

Dany shook her head, grabbed Tyler's arms and looked up at him. "They are staying here with me. You need to take some

263

deep breaths, so you can drive Liz and Mom to St. Bart's. Don't leave without them like Kenny Colwell did to Emmy."

Tyler took a few deep breaths. "Okay, I'm ready. Do you need help getting down the stairs?"

"I can still walk," Liz smiled.

"I'll carry the bag for you."

"Mommy, can I come to the hospital with you? I want to see the baby," Natalie asked.

Dany intercepted Natalie. "You and Grayson are going to stay with me. We will have lots of time to see the baby later." Dany looked at Liz. "I will be glad when this is over. I am tired of calling it the baby because we don't know if it's a boy or a girl. If I ever have a baby, I will want to know the sex as soon as possible."

Tyler helped Liz into the Ford Flex. Mom Kimmerle got in back, and Tyler backed out of the driveway and slammed on the brakes as Liz moaned. "Do we still have time?"

"Yes, Tyler, but we won't if you keep stopping like that."

"Sorry, Liz, I'll get us there. I promise."

True to his word, Tyler made it to St. Bart's without further incident. Liz was quickly admitted and transported to the fourth floor.

Emmy picked up her cell phone and asked, "Hey, Dany, what's up?"

"Tyler, Liz and Mom just left for St. Bart's. I thought you might want to know," Dany answered. "You should have seen Tyler. I think he's more nervous now than with Natty and Grayson."

Emmy laughed. "Dany, are you sure he didn't leave them behind?"

"I watched Mom and Liz get into the car. I've heard the story of Kenny leaving you behind. That must have been hilarious."

"Are you watching Natty and Grayson?"

"Yeah, I'm going to spend the night here. Who knows how long Liz will be in labor?" Dany shrugged.

"Do you think Liz would mind if I go over to St. Bart's to wait?"

"I don't think she'll mind at all. Are you sure you want to do that? It could take several hours."

"I'm betting that it won't. This is her third time. They still don't know the sex, right?"

"No, but I think they have names picked out for a boy and a girl."

"I tried to get the names out of her, but she wouldn't tell me," Emmy complained. "Do you think Liz will want more kids, or will this one be the last?"

"Liz still insists she wants six kids. Darian and I talked about kids. I might want four, but no more than that. Darian wants a son and a daughter in that order. After that, he doesn't care."

"I'm glad Kevin Michael was a boy. Kenny wanted a son to carry on the family name, and he was going to be our last baby."

"He is all boy, Emmy," Dany said with a laugh. "He caught a snake in the woods back in August and showed it to me."

"Please tell me he didn't bring it in the house."

"He had it in a box, but I convinced him to let it go. I was afraid to touch it."

"I remember catching snakes with Kenny when we were kids. I'd be afraid to catch one now, but I didn't know any better back then. I'm going to tell Kenny and then head up to St. Bart's. I'll talk to you later."

"Keep me posted, Emmy."

After telling Kenny and the kids about the news, Emmy headed over to St. Bart's. She parked her Civic Si and almost sprinted inside. She shifted her weight from one foot to the other as she waited in line to get a pass for upstairs. *Hurry up, people! I want to get there before the baby is born.* Finally, the older couple in front of her moved on.

"May I help you?" the volunteer asked.

"I'm here to see Liz Hammond. She's on the fourth floor having a baby," Emmy explained.

The volunteer took her time checking the computer.

Any day now. Emmy rolled her eyes.

"Ah. I see it now." The volunteer handed Emmy a pass. "Do you know how...?"

265

Emmy didn't hear because she was racing away.

"... to get to the maternity ward?" The volunteer shrugged and looked at the next person in line. "How may I help you?"

Emmy hit the up button on the elevator again.

"It won't get here any sooner, sweetie," the elderly lady waiting with Emmy said.

"Sorry, but my friends are having a baby. I should learn to be more patient."

The elevator door opened and Emmy allowed the older lady to step inside first. "Which floor?"

"Number eight, please."

Emmy stabbed eight and then smacked four.

"You look familiar," the elderly lady said. "Do I know you?"

Emmy looked at her. "Maybe. I'm Emmy. What is your name?"

"Mrs. Miriam Wallace. I'm here to see my husband. He had a mild heart attack."

"I'm so sorry. I will say a prayer for him."

"Thank you, dear."

The elevator started to slow for the fourth floor.

"Did I mention I used to teach school?" Mrs. Wallace said.

"That's nice," Emmy replied as the doors opened. She dashed out and raced away before slamming on the brakes and stopping. Emmy turned back to the elevator just as the doors closed. "Oh, my God! That might have been my first grade teacher. Her name was Mrs. Wallace." Emmy waited a moment and then hurried down the hall and around the corner to the nurse's station.

"Hello," a lady behind the counter smiled.

"Hi, could you tell me which room Liz Hammond is in, please?"

"She's in 4012. Are you family?"

Emmy nodded as she crossed her fingers behind her back.

"It doesn't matter. You can go ahead. Do you know how to get there?"

Emmy uncrossed her fingers. "Oh, yeah! I've been there before."

She hurried to room 4012 and knocked on the open door.

Tyler turned, saw her and waved. "Come on in, Emmy. We've been expecting you."

"You have?"

"Dany called."

Emmy stepped inside the door. "Is it all right for me to be here?"

Liz waved. "Of course. It might be a couple of hours, but I'm glad you're here."

"Hi, Mrs. Kimmerle. I mean Dr. Lindower." Emmy moved closer to the bed.

Mom Kimmerle put an arm around Emmy. "Liz is doing fine. The baby is doing fine, and I think she is ready to see us."

Emmy grinned. "It's a girl. I knew you guys were holding back."

"Mom!" Liz shook her head. "You're just hoping for a girl. Em, Mom doesn't know the sex," Liz said.

"I'm just guessing based on my experience as a doctor," Mom Kimmerle said while checking Liz's pulse.

Emmy shrugged. "Sometimes I think you should have a girl, but then I think you should have a boy. I guess I'm just happy everything is going all right."

An hour later Emmy stood up from her chair in the corner. "Would you mind if I run upstairs for a moment? I think there's someone here I should go see."

"Go ahead, Emmy. We'll let you know if anything happens," Tyler said as he wiped some sweat from his forehead.

"I have my cell phone with me." Emmy left the room and walked over to the elevators. *Should I bother her? What if she isn't who I think she is?* Emmy hit the button for the eighth floor. *How will I even know what room is his?*

The doors opened and Emmy turned to her right. She inquired at the nurse's station and learned which room was Mr. Wallace's. She walked down the hall, found the room and peered inside. *Here goes.* She waited a few seconds but then knocked and stepped inside.

Mrs. Wallace turned to look.

267

"I'm sorry to bother you, but I think you were my first grade teacher. I'm Emmy Colasanti, and I went to Robert T. Colwell in Raynor Park."

Mrs. Wallace smiled. "I taught there for over thirty years. When did you start?"

Emmy thought about it for a moment. "I started first grade in 1986."

"Colasanti, huh?" Mrs. Wallace tapped her chin. "Did you have an older sister?"

Emmy noticed the age spots on Mrs. Wallace's hand and nodded. "Diane."

Mrs. Wallace closed her eyes for a moment. "Yes! I remember both of you. Diane was loud and boisterous. You were as shy and quiet as a church mouse. You were a tiny little thing." Mrs. Wallace looked at Emmy and grinned. "Some things haven't changed."

"I'm not quite as shy as I used to be. Should I leave? I don't want to bother you."

"Nonsense! Pull up a chair and talk to us. This is my husband, Irving, but everyone calls him Ike."

"Pleased to meet you, Mr. Wallace. I hope you're feeling better."

"It's Ike, and I feel fine. I am ready to go home. The food here is enough to make you sick."

Emmy laughed. *I'm glad you have a sense of humor.*

"Tell me about yourself," Mrs. Wallace insisted. "Do you still live in SoHam?"

Emmy mentioned a few things.

"Wait a minute! I picked up a book for my great grandkids last week. It's about some lions. Did you write that?"

Emmy bit her lip. "I did. Did you like it?"

"Of course, your picture is on the back. That's why I recognized you. It was wonderful. I wish I could take credit for your talent, but you were just learning how to read in my class."

"I remember your class. You were so nice to us."

"I wasn't nice to all the kids, but there were some who deserved more kindness than others."

268

Emmy stayed and talked to the Wallaces for thirty minutes. She prayed for them before leaving. As she turned the corner back on the fourth floor, she nearly bumped into Dr. Walsh.

"Dr. Walsh, I'm sorry. I didn't see you."

"It's all right, Emmy. How are you? How are those girls? They must be six or seven by now."

"They will be eight in another month. I can't believe it. Kevin Michael will be six in March. I'm here because my friend Liz is having her third."

"Really? Liz Hammond?"

"Yes. Are you her doctor? I didn't know that."

"Small world. I've known her parents for years. Professionally."

Emmy bit her lip and then asked, "Do you know what they're having? I bet you do, but they won't tell. They claim they don't know. I'm just dying to know. Can you tell me? I won't tell a soul. Promise." Emmy crossed her heart with both hands.

"Well, since she will be delivering rather soon, I suppose I can tell you."

Emmy bounced on her toes, clapped her hands together and grinned. "Please, tell me."

Dr. Walsh leaned close to Emmy's ear. "They are having... a baby... human."

Emmy stomped her foot. "You're a stinker, Dr. Walsh."

He laughed and shook his head. "You will know soon enough, Emmy."

"Do you think it will be much longer?" Emmy asked.

Dr. Walsh checked the time. "You might need to wait a couple of hours, Emmy. Do you think you can be patient that long?"

Emmy sighed and said, "I suppose I'll have to." She returned to Liz's room.

"Would you stay with Liz and her mother while I take a quick break?" Tyler asked.

"No problem. Take your time."

"I'll only be a minute or two," Tyler assured them. "I'll hurry."

Forty minutes later the nurse asked Emmy to leave the room.

"I'm not leaving the hospital," Emmy held Liz's hand for a moment before leaving.

Mom Kimmerle walked Emmy to the door. "It shouldn't be too much longer, and I still think Liz is having a girl."

"To be honest, so do I," Emmy said and then grinned. "Would someone text me when I can return, please?"

Mom Kimmerle nodded and said, "Certainly, Emmy."

"One more push, Liz," Dr. Walsh said.

Tyler held Liz's hand as she scrunched her face.

"Just a bit more," Dr. Walsh said softly as he shifted his position and adjusted his hands. A few seconds later he looked up and smiled. "Congratulations! Are you ready to know?"

Liz and Tyler grinned at each other and then nodded.

"You should take a look," Dr. Walsh said as he handed the baby to Tyler.

Tyler took a quick look, did a double take and looked again. "We have another daughter," he said with a smile.

Later, Liz held the baby on her chest with Tyler and Mom Kimmerle leaning in close.

"Do you think she looks like me?" Liz asked her mother.

"She has cheeks like Dany had."

"I'm glad she has some hair," Tyler lifted the pink cap to check again.

"I have to call your father," Mom Kimmerle took out her cell phone. "Do you have the name picked out?"

Liz nodded. "We decided on Phoebe Grace. We had kinda decided on Phoebe a while back, but it wasn't until a couple of days ago we decided on Grace as the middle name."

"I will call your father and give him all the details. Do you want to call Dany or your brothers?"

"I'll let Tyler take care of that," Liz said as she watched Phoebe sleeping peacefully.

Tyler called home, told Dany the news and she passed the news along to Natalie and Grayson.

"Good. I wanted a baby sister," Natalie said. "When will

270

Phoebe and Mommy come home. I want to hold her."

"It might be as early as Sunday, Natty," Dany explained.

"Maybe Mommy can have a baby boy the next time," Grayson said. "I need a little brother."

Within ten minutes news of the birth began circulating on social media. Tyler took a selfie and pasted it on Facebook. Comments appeared almost instantaneously.

"Have you called Emmy?" Liz asked as Phoebe began to stir.

"Shoot! I forgot to let her know."

"She will be so disappointed if she sees it on her phone."

"You're right. I should find Emmy and tell her," Tyler said while sitting on the bed next to Liz.

"Okay, and tell her it's all right to tell everyone."

Tyler saw Emmy hanging out in the hallway by the nursery. Though he tried to approach silently, she turned and noticed him.

"Is the baby here?" Emmy ran toward Tyler.

Tyler nodded but then didn't say anymore.

Emmy poked his arm. "You have to tell me!"

"We have another... daughter," Tyler chuckled. "Her name is Phoebe Grace."

"I'm so happy. Are Liz and Phoebe all right? Kristen will be thrilled you named her Grace."

"Liz and Phoebe are doing great. You can see them now if you want."

"Of course I want to see them," Emmy raced down the hall, grabbed the railing and slid into the room.

Chapter Twenty-Five

"Kenny, will you help me carry my books out to the van, please?" Emmy hollered from the den.

Kenny walked toward the den and paused in the doorway. "Do you mean will I carry them for you? It would be rather difficult for both of us to carry that box."

"Yes, please. It's rather heavy for me, but I'm sure you can carry it."

Kenny sighed and said, "You don't have to make that face. I'll carry it. What are you planning to do? Are you going to sell them? You could say it's a school project, and you're trying to raise money for a band trip."

"I'm not selling them." She closed the four flaps of the box. "I'm giving them away to families with kids."

"Are you going to order more to give away?"

"I don't know. Maybe."

Kenny lifted the box and grunted. "There goes my back."

"It's not that heavy. I lifted it without any trouble." Emmy rolled her eyes.

"Figured as much." Kenny took the box out to the van, and they got ready to leave.

Pastor Darren, would it be possible for me to set up a small table in this corner?" Emmy pointed to an area of the church foyer. "I have some books to give away."

"I don't see why not. There's a small table in this storage room. I'll get it for you." He brought out the white plastic table. "Would this work?"

"Perfect! Thank you, Pastor Darren."

He situated the table for Emmy and then picked up a copy of the book. "I thought you were writing an autobiography."

"This is something different." Emmy explained about the children's book and showed him the poster she made.

"Free, huh? I might be able to afford that, but we don't have any kids," he said and then laughed.

Emmy and the girls manned her display after the second service.

272

Heather and Isabella held up copies of the book and hollered, "Free lion books!"

Soon, Emmy found herself explaining to a group of mothers and kids why she was giving her book away for free.

"Would you autograph it for me, please?" a lady asked politely.

"Of course," Emmy agreed. *I'd rather sign copies of my book than my CDs. I wonder why.*

Within fifteen minutes all the books had been distributed except for two.

"How is the book sale going, Emmy?" Pastor Tyler asked.

"It's not a sale, and I have two left. Would you like one?"

"Yes, please. I think Liz would like to read it to the baby."

"She does have a name, Pastor Tyler." Heather looked up at him with her hands on her hips.

"You are correct, Heather. I need to stop referring to her as the baby."

"When are Miss Liz and Phoebe coming home from the hospital? Mommy said me and Isa stayed at the hospital for two weeks."

"I'm heading to St. Bart's as soon as I leave here. My mother-in-law and Dany are with her now," Tyler explained.

Emmy handed Pastor Tyler a book and gave the last one to Isabella. "Isa, would you give this to Pastor Darren for me?" Emmy pointed to where he stood. "He and Jody might have a baby one of these days."

Isabella dashed away.

"All done. Thank you for your help, Heather."

"Are we going to buy more books to give away, Mommy?"

Pastor Tyler chuckled.

"Not now, Heather. Maybe later. Daddy wants me to sell some of them."

"If Isa and I write a book, can we sell it for a dollar?"

"It would have to be a very good book to sell it for that much," Emmy said. She handed the empty box to Kenny, who had just wandered over. "I think I'll save the poster."

He shook his head. "Are you going to make the girls sign it,

273

so you can sell it on the Internet?"

"I'm not going to sell it. I want to keep it."

Kenny pointed to the hand-drawn poster. "They misspelled for free."

"Did they?" Emmy folded the table and replaced it.

Kenny and Pastor Tyler checked the poster again.

"Aw, four free."

Emmy sipped her coffee the next morning after Diane had picked up the kids for school. *I know I didn't think I would look at my other book until after the new year, but I have some time. I am going to work on it every day this week. That is my early New Year's resolution, or maybe revolution. I'll see which later.* She finished her coffee and set the empty mug in the sink.

Chase decided there was enough money in the budget to splurge a bit. He told Belinda to reserve some rooms at the Castleberry Inn and Suites hotel in Atlanta. It was less than two miles from the arena. Plus it had free parking for the buses and the trucks.

"We have plenty of rooms and a late checkout time of three o'clock," Chase informed the guys. "It was very generous of the hotel to arrange that for us. I think one of the managers is a Christian and has heard of us."

"Cool!" the guys responded.

"Please, remember we are representing the church, and try not to destroy your rooms."

Chase knew the guys would behave, so I'm not sure why he bothered with that.

"This might be a good time to get some laundry done also," he added.

The buses and trucks pulled into the parking lot just before four. Belinda handled the registration and sorted out the room assignments for everyone.

By one o'clock everyone was up, dressed and fed. Some of the guys did some laundry while others decided to wait until their day off in Knoxville. The boys cleaned up the Omega bus because I would be back tonight. Chase made sure everyone was accounted for and checked out. He thanked the people at the registration and left ten tickets for the concert.

The caravan headed over to the venue. Philips Arena was built on the site of the old Omni. It is a modern arena, and the seating is a little different than older venues. The club seats and the luxury boxes are all on one side. Chase got the passes for everyone and told them they were free until three thirty. Jess, Joe, Nelson and the younger guys tried to help unload the truck, but the union guys told them to get out of the way. They didn't argue because the union guys looked pretty tough. Andy's staff set up a production office to handle the details for tonight. It didn't take long for the crews to build the stage and get everything is set for the tech guys.

Andy, Kenny and I arrived, and Andy immediately met with the stage manager. Andy was not happy with a section of the stage and raised his voice and became very animated. He waved his hands around and might have even shoved someone. Almost immediately five guys appeared on the stage and worked feverishly to please Andy. Thirty minutes later Andy inspected the stage, gave his approval and the soundchecks proceeded without any further delay.

I had a chance to talk to Jennifer after the soundcheck.

"What was it like to fly in a private jet?"

"It was okay," I replied rather nonchalantly. Like I flew on a private jet everywhere I went.

"Come on, Emmy! Tell the truth."

"It was fantastic. It was just Andy and his staff and Kenny and me. The seats are so comfortable. I guess it's like flying in first class except it's your own plane."

"Are you flying again tonight?"

"No, Andy and Kenny are going home. His staff in staying with us, but they will have to fly commercial after tonight. Andy will drop them off in Knoxville before he and Kenny go home."

"It's sure been nice to have Andy and his people around. They make everything go so smooth."

"Yeah, Now we kinda know what it's like to be real rock stars."

"I'll talk to you later, Emmy. I gotta go do my soundcheck."

I watched Jennifer walk away, saw my guys standing around by the stage and skipped over to see them. Literally. I skipped like I was jumping rope or something. They saw me and laughed, but I didn't care. I was as happy as could be.

"Hi, guys! Did you miss me?"

"Hello, Mrs. Colwell. How was your flight?"

"What's with the Mrs. Colwell?"

"We thought since you are a diva now we have to be polite and respectful," Ryan said.

"Very funny! I'm going to be on the bus tonight, and if it's a mess I will be upset with you guys. Did anyone sleep in my bed?"

"No! We were afraid of getting girl germs on us."

Like I said before, Nelson and Belinda used my bedroom until they arrived at the hotel. I made a face at the guys and Ryan started laughing.

"Okay, we missed you, Emmy. Tell us about your flights."

I told the guys everything I could remember about my flight and the hotels. I even told them about sprawling out on my bed.

"Was Kenny mad about that?"

I giggled and then answered, "No, he's used to that."

We headed to catering, and the guys got in line with the crew and some of the tech people. The people from ClairShowco and Stagemonkey ate in a different area, so this catering room belonged to us.

Boyd was the first of us to get in line. "Holy cow!

Look at all this food. Hey! They've even got pizzas."

"You can't eat it all, Boyd."

"I don't plan on it, but I want to stuff myself," he answered.

"Better take it easy. You have to play in a couple hours. There will be more food after the show, too."

I enjoyed teasing the guys since they were all good-natured about it. The guys were eating and goofing around when they noticed me sitting at a table with Andy Walker, Kenny and four other people they don't know.

"Hey, Chase, who are those people with Emmy and Kenny?" Skip asked.

"You know Andy Walker, right?" Chase asked. "Well, that couple across from Emmy is Max Kesson and his wife, Sheila. He's the owner of Steward Music Group. The other two guys are executives from Castle Productions."

"Big shots, huh?" Ryan stared at them for a moment.

"You could say that," Chase said with a chuckle. "I wasn't supposed to tell you guys, but Mr. Kesson is here to check you guys out again. There's a possibility he might be interested in signing you. A remote chance but still a possibility. You guys might want to give it your best shot tonight."

"You mean we shouldn't screw up, huh?" Boyd laughed.

After we finished eating, Jennifer Sinclaire started playing, and I was still downstairs with the big shots as the guys called them. I wanted to listen to Jennifer but didn't get a chance. Tomorrow would be her last night with us. Jennifer finished her set and the crew prepared the stage for The Apostles Creed. Celia Black from radio station WFSH in Athens introduced the different bands.

"I heard these guys a couple nights ago and I was blown away. Let's have a big Atlanta welcome for The Apostles Creed!"

They kicked off the first song, and for forty five minutes they rocked the house. They pulled out all their

277

best tunes, and the crowd wanted more. They did one encore and then ran off of the stage.

Chase greeted them, "Great job, guys. The crowd loved your set."

Over the years there have been plenty of bands that opened for Fridays At Five or my band. Some were really good. Others not so much. Some I got to know a little bit, but there were a few bands that I stayed away from. One band in particular that I won't name was rather obnoxious. The lead singer put a move on me. He knew I was married, but he didn't care. They never opened for us after that week, and I really don't know what ever happened to them. I could do some research, I suppose, but the truth is I don't care. Anyway, the guys in The Apostles Creed were some of the nicest guys that ever opened for us. This is a plug for them. They are still together, and still travel extensively. If they ever come to your town, spend a few bucks and show your support. Buy one or two or three of their CDs. I've got them all, and I highly recommend them.

Now back to Mr. Kesson. By now you probably know he did sign The Only Hope to a recording contract, but back in Atlanta that night he listened to them as they backed me up. I remember the guys were awesome that night. Since we played the same songs most every night, the guys would do a little improvising. Nothing too radical, but just little things that kept the music fresh. I remember one night when they started jamming, and I forget to come back in. I was like the fans in the crowd. I listened, and I even clapped. Then Adam told me I could start singing whenever I felt like it. It was funny.

Okay, I saw Jennifer as I came upstairs to hear the end of the Apostles Creed set and we talked behind the stage where we could hear each other.

"Oh, Jennifer, I'm so sorry I didn't get to hear you. I was tied up downstairs and couldn't get away."

"That's okay, Emmy. It wasn't our best set."

"I promise I will listen tomorrow night."

Jennifer and her four piece band traveled in a minivan and pulled a trailer behind them. She did have one roadie who did her sound and helped set up gear. She told me they would hire a couple of local guys to do the heavy lifting. She needed someone like the Zawaski brothers, but I wasn't about to give them up. Jennifer and the guys stayed in cheap motels overnight and traveled during the day. They shared the driving and tried to limit the hours on the road each day by carefully booking their shows as close together as possible. Life on the road was not easy for her and the band. Compared to Jennifer, I am a pampered princess. I asked her to ride on the bus with me.

"If I decide to go with you, I should take the bunk so you won't have to give up your bed."

"We can work that out later. Will you ride in the bus with me?"

"All right. I'll tell the guys."

That night we played for an hour and a half; a little bit longer than our normal set. Kenny joined us for the last half of the set. We played a new song that featured Adam on vocals. I sang harmony with him, and the crowd seemed to like the song. Later, it ended up on their first CD. Chase preached for ten minutes at the end of our set. I rushed out to help at the merchandise table because the guys were swamped. The crowd stuck around for over an hour and we came close to running out of merchandise. Luckily, we had more waiting in Knoxville. The crowd finally thinned out enough to allow Belinda and Nelson to finish up. The guys and I left to go eat. I made time to talk to Jennifer again. We sat together and snacked on some fresh fruit.

"The guys told me to go ahead and ride with you. They told me they were tired of having a girl in the van."

"Do the guys in your band tease you a lot?"

"Like all the time! They are great guys, and I love them to death, but sometimes I need a break. I need to do girl stuff, and it's hard with them around all the time."

279

"I get teased by all the guys. Not just the older guys in management, but the young guys, too."

"What is Ryan like when he's not onstage or whatever?"

"He's a good guy. I know he likes you."

"I kinda like him, too. I know he has one more semester of college to go."

"The band has a chance to sign with Steward Music." I explained more to Jennifer about my deal as a solo artist. I felt kinda bad after she told me about her recording contract.

"That would be great. I wish I had a better deal. I owe one more CD to my label and then I'll be looking for another deal."

"How long have you been singing professionally?"

"I'm not sure what you mean by professionally, Emmy. I've been singing at church and playing guitar since I was ten. I started singing other places my last couple years of high school. Then I got signed by my label. They helped me put this band together."

"Didn't you have a band before that?"

"No. I just played my guitar and sang. I write my own songs, and I do control my publishing. My father knew an attorney who helped set everything up. I was lucky in that regard. Anyway, after I graduated I spent a year at the local junior college."

"I know someone else who did that." I meant Kenny, but I didn't tell her.

"Then we hit the road, and I've been doing that for the last two years. I did have time to record two CDs, and I am grateful some of the radio stations play my songs."

"How often do you get home? And where is home?" Our conversation wasn't exactly like an interview, but I'll fix it later.

"I'm usually gone for two months at a time. I live with my parents in Knoxville. All the guys in the band are from the Knoxville area, but I never knew any of them before. We are together all the time on the road, but we

280

don't really see each other when we're home other than to rehearse."

Kenny had been looking for me, and he finally caught up to me. I knew he had to leave, so I was putting off saying goodbye for as long as I could.

"Em, we have to head out. I wanted to say goodbye before I left."

"It was so good to have you along. Thank you so much." All right, that's not even close to what we said to each other, but this book might be read by young teens and grandparent types, so I can't tell you exactly what we said. Or did.

"Oh, did Mr. Kesson say anything about The Only Hope?" I really did ask this.

"He was impressed to say the least. I think there's a good chance he will try to sign them soon."

"Where's Andy? I should say goodbye."

I spotted Andy with Mr. Kesson and Kenny and I walked over to join them. Andy saw me coming and held out his arms to hug me. He even kissed the top of my head.

"Thank you for everything, Andy. I appreciate being able to fly. I was able to catch up on my sleep."

"You're welcome, Emmy. It was my pleasure to have you on board. Just because I'm leaving doesn't mean I won't be keeping tabs on the rest of your tour."

"It was nice to see you and your wife again, Mr. Kesson."

Mrs. Kesson hugged me. I admit I really didn't know her all that well. She didn't travel very often and never really got too involved with the business. She spent most of her time with the grandkids.

"It's always good to see you, Emmy." He hugged me. "It's bands like yours that make it all worthwhile. What you are doing is more important than the bottom line. Though I am making money with your projects," he said and then chuckled. "Did you happen to see the latest *Billboard* issue."

"No, I don't really read it." I didn't back then, but I read it more often now.

"You should check it out sometime. 'Yolanda's Song' is in the top five on the Hot 100, and it's still in the top ten on the Christian music chart. It was on the country chart for the longest time, too. Both CDs are still on the Billboard 200 chart. That's the chart for albums."

"That's good, right?"

"Yes, Emmy, that's very good. That's partly why you are playing in larger venues now."

"We need to get going. We have to make a stop in Knoxville before we head home."

There were more hugs and kisses before they left for the airport. The kisses were all from Kenny in case you were wondering.

About "Yolanda's Song." It was first released to radio in December of 2002, I think. It took several months to gain any chart action. It did okay for a time and then slipped off the charts. About a year later some stations put in back in rotation and it made the charts again. Regular rock stations played it. I couldn't believe the response from people. Even now whenever I go on tour, people request it.

The buses and truck were ready to roll out by two o'clock. It was only a four hour trip to Knoxville. Jennifer was thrilled to be riding on the bus with me and a certain guy from the band. Ryan was excited to be able to spend some time with her, too. Jennifer, Ryan and I stayed up until five.

Ryan finally got tired. "I'm going to bed. Are you going to stay up all night?"

"I think we already have," I answered.

I convinced Jennifer to use the bedroom, and I took an empty bunk. I didn't mind sleeping with the guys. Shoot! That didn't sound right. I meant I didn't mind sleeping in the area of the bus where the bunks are located. We didn't have to be at the venue until around three tomorrow, so we could get a few hours of sleep.

Chapter Twenty-Six

"Hey, can you meet me for lunch?"

"And good morning to you, too, little sister."

"Sorry. Good morning, Father James. How are you today?" Emmy rolled her eyes.

Father James nodded to a couple walking past as he poured some salt on the icy steps of the rectory. "I'm very well. Thank you so much for asking."

"Oh, hush. I need to talk to you. Can we do Darby's?"

"I could hear your confession at the church."

Emmy shook her head. "No chance in hell. You just want to hear about how naughty I've been," she said and then giggled. "Can you meet me?"

"Are you buying?"

"Come on! You know Danny never makes you pay."

"Ah! Young Mr. Darby is a fine lad."

"Oh, knock it off. You're about as Irish as the Pope."

"Is he Irish?"

Emmy laughed. "I better pray for you. Hey, can you wear one of those fancy robe things and a hat so everyone knows you're a priest. The blue jeans and Fridays At Five sweatshirts don't cut it."

"What hat?"

"You know. One of those big fancy hats that popes and big shots wear."

Father James shook his head. "I did steal the Cardinal's biretta. I could wear that."

"Did you really?" Emmy stared at her cell phone. "Why am I even asking?"

"What time?"

"Noon thirty."

He laughed. "I'll see you at twelve thirty. Give or take. I'll be the one wearing a crown."

Emmy walked into Darby's a few minutes late. She looked into the open kitchen behind the counter. *I remember how my clothes used to smell like grease when I worked here.* She looked around and spotted Father James at her favorite booth. She walked up as he took a bite of his chili dog. She removed her coat, tossed it onto the bench and slipped into the red booth across from him. "You couldn't wait for me?" She looked at the baseball cap he wore. "A crown, huh?"

"I thought my regular crown would be too ostentatious. Nice stocking cap. Is it new?" he asked facetiously.

"Hush. You know it's almost as old as me."

Danny Darby walked over with a basket of fries and a chili dog. "Father James took the liberty of ordering for you. You want root beer?"

"Yes, thank you, Danny." She poured ketchup on her fries.

Father James watched with disgust. "You should try eating fries with your ketchup."

"Ha! Ha! I didn't know you were a Sox fan."

"I'm not. I found this at the lost and found at the mission." He said and then dipped one of his fries in her pile of ketchup. "To what do I owe the pleasure of your company today?"

She held up a finger as she finished chewing a bite of her chili dog.

"You've got chili running down your chin," he said.

She wiped her mouth. "I need your opinion about my book."

"Am I in this tell-all book of yours? I can't be associated with any scandal."

"You're a priest!" she said with a grin. "Need I say more?"

"Am I?"

"I might mention you at some point which brings me to my point." She paused to take a drink of the root beer Danny placed beside her elbow. "I don't know where to end the story."

Father James tilted his face down as if he was peering over his glasses, which were not in sight. "You are kidding, right?"

"No. It's supposed to be about traveling with the band, but should I keep writing up to the present, or end it much earlier?"

"Do I look like an expert?"

"No, you look like a homeless man. Do I need to buy you a new sweatshirt? Is that a coffee stain?"

284

He shrugged. "I have taken a vow of poverty."

"Whatever. I'm serious."

"How long is your book supposed to be?" he asked and then stood up. "I need another dog. You good?"

"I'm fine."

Father James returned a couple of minutes later with a chili dog and more fries.

"I don't know. The computer keeps track of how many words and stuff like that." She grabbed one of the fries. "Shoot! These are hot."

"Ah, you can learn new things."

She took another sip of root beer and glanced at the photograph on the wall above her. *I was really young in that picture.* "I don't want it to be too long."

"Have you finished the first draft?" He looked at his hot dog. "I wonder where they get their chili?"

"I could tell you because I used to work here, but then I'd have to kill you. Then I'd have to go to confession."

"Don't talk with your mouth full."

She waited until she could swallow her chili dog. "Denise suggested I write an ending chapter to summarize where things stand now. I should do that then I could go back and flesh out more of the middle."

"Sounds like a plan to me."

"You are so helpful. Why do I bother talking to you?" She stole more of his fries. "Don't you have any helpful suggestions?"

"Yes, say ten Hail Mary's and stop stealing my fries. Buy your own."

She crinkled her nose at him. "You didn't pay for these."

"A matter of semantics."

"Are you coming to our house for Christmas?"

"Will your mother and sister be there?" He swirled his Styrofoam cup around and tried to suck more Coke out of it.

"Mom won't be there, and we'll probably get together with Diane and the kids on Christmas Eve. You could come with us. Diane doesn't hate you."

"No, but she only tolerates my presence on this earth."

"She doesn't know you as well as I do. You're not a total jerk once one gets to know you." She grinned and then stuck out her tongue.

"Thank you so much. I'll think about it. Can you give me a ride home?"

"How did you get here?"

"The generosity of mankind."

"You took a cab, right?"

"More reliable than hitchhiking at this time of year."

"Did you pay him with cash, or did you bless him?" Emmy shook her head.

"The heathen insisted on cash."

"I'll give you a ride, but only because you've been so helpful."

"Doesn't your Nazarene church consider excessive sarcasm a sin?"

"Stuff it." Emmy gathered the trash, dumped it and returned the plastic baskets to the counter. "Thanks, Danny. See you around."

"Take care, Emmy. Say hi to Kenny and the kids."

She nodded. "Merry Christmas to you and Karen and Malinda."

Father James walked up behind her and waved to Danny. "I'll get her out of your hair now."

Danny laughed. "Thanks, Father."

Emmy poked Father James in the side. "If I didn't love you so much as a brother, I would hate you."

Emmy dropped Father James off and thought about her book on the way home. *I'm going to keep writing and let Denise decide how long it should be because I've got no clue. At least the lion stories are quick and easy.*

Jennifer Sinclaire calls Knoxville, Tennessee, home. Her parents and brother still live there. Jennifer has two older sisters who live in Texas now with their husbands and children. Her brother James is currently a senior at the University of Tennessee and still lives at home instead

286

of on campus. He is two years older than Jennifer. Tonight Jennifer would be performing after The Apostles Creed. Those guys graciously agreed to swap spots for the night. Jennifer knew there would be more people here to see her tonight than anywhere else on her tour. She mentioned she hadn't played in Knoxville for over a year and always at small venues back then. I really found it strange when she told me her parents and brother had never seen her play with her band before. She explained that they saw her play hundreds of solo sets though. Jennifer was understandably nervous about tonight.

The union guys unloaded the trucks earlier, and our drivers parked them across the street from the loading dock. The crews got busy with getting everything ready. The two buses and Jennifer's van and trailer parked under the Pratt Pavilion which is attached to the Thompson-Boling Arena. We still had two hours to kill before soundchecks while the finishing touches were being done to the stage and gear. Jennifer called her brother, and they made plans to meet.

"Do you want to go with me, Emmy? You could meet Jimmy, and he can give us a tour of the campus."

"That sounds like more fun than hanging out on the bus."

We arranged to meet Jimmy Sinclaire in front of the arena. He snuck up on his sister from behind and touched her shoulder.

"Jimmy! You nearly scared me to death."

"How are you, Jen? How is the music biz going?"

Jennifer talked to Jimmy for a couple of minutes about the tour, and then she grinned at me. I kinda knew something was up, but didn't know what.

"Oh, Jimmy, this is my friend Olivia... Bertucci."

I looked at her but kept my mouth shut. I wanted to see where this was going.

"Hello, Olivia. Bertucci, huh? I've heard that name before. I remember now. There is a football player with that name on the Bears. Are you a fan by any chance?"

287

"Not really," I lied through my teeth. "Are you?"

"Yeah. I played in high school, and I go to all the games here."

Jennifer asked, "Are you coming to the show tonight, Jimmy?"

"Wouldn't miss it. Mom and Dad and everyone they know is going to be there."

"I have some backstage passes for you."

"Cool! I want to meet that singer from the other band. I can't remember her name. Mom told me, but I forgot. I've never seen her before, but I've heard her songs on the radio. She has a nice voice."

"I think I might be able to introduce you to her if you want. You have to be careful around her though."

"Why is that?" he asked.

By now I knew Jennifer had something up her sleeve, so I played along and kept my mouth shut.

Jennifer continued, "She's... Uh... How can I put this tactfully?" Jennifer tilted her head back and forth a couple of times. "She's a real diva. She acts like a star and expects everyone to cater to her every whim."

"That sucks big time! And you have to deal with that. Too bad." Jimmy shook his head as he discretely checked me out.

"I try to stay away from her as much as I can. Had I known what a witch she was, I never would have agreed to be her opening act."

Okay, Jennifer used a different word than witch, and I think you can figure it out. By now I was having trouble keeping a straight face, but I did.

"We want you to show us around campus before I have to get back for my soundcheck," Jennifer said.

Okay," Jimmy answered. He smiled at me and then turned his back to lead the way.

While Jimmy had his back turned, I stuck out my tongue and made a face at Jennifer. We grinned at each other, and we both wanted to see how long we could keep Jimmy in the dark about my real identity. We walked past

288

Neyland Stadium where the football team played. Jimmy pointed out other buildings as we walked along. He stayed in between Jennifer and myself, and I could tell he was still checking me out. I figured I would go along with the ruse as long as possible.

"So, Olivia, how do you know Jen?" he asked.

Normally, I wouldn't lie, but I hope God will forgive me this time. I thought I would stick to a partial truth to make it easier to remember. "We met at SIU in Carbondale in late spring. I was a fan of hers, and I saw her with her band. We've sorta kept in contact since then, and I'm on a little vacation of sorts so we hooked up today."

"SIU, huh. That's a real party school. I've never been there but that's what I heard."

"I like the campus and the kids are nice."

Jennifer interrupted. "It is a party school, and I met this guy Olivia was hooking up with."

I didn't respond at first. I was kinda shocked that Jennifer would tell that to her brother. Jimmy grinned at me, and I knew he was thinking I might be easy like a groupie.

He put his hand on my arm. "Do you have tickets for tonight, too?"

I looked at Jennifer and regained my voice. "I was hoping to see Jennifer play again."

"Maybe Jen can get you a backstage pass, too."

Jennifer nodded. "I made sure Olivia will be backstage. I want her to meet everyone."

Jimmy still had no clue who I was as we kept walking around campus. I got over the comment Jennifer made about me hooking up, but Jimmy didn't.

"What time do you need to get back to the arena?" Jimmy asked his sister while standing in front of me and grinning.

"I need to be there at three thirty."

"What are you going to do to kill time, Olivia?"

"I was going to just hang out... "

289

Jennifer interrupted me. "Olivia is going to stay with me until the show starts. I put her name on the list so they think she works for my band as an assistant. Pretty sneaky, huh?"

"You always were a little devil, Jen. Olivia, just remember to avoid that other singer."

Jimmy put his hands on my shoulders, and I thought he was going to kiss me. I wasn't about to let things go that far.

"Oh, I will. Jen warned me about her." I took a couple of steps back.

"If you guys meet me at 6:30 out front, I will bring you backstage. I only have six passes though."

Jimmy nodded at Jennifer and grinned at me. "Okay. I'll make sure Mom and Dad are here early. See you later, Jen, and it was nice to meet you, Olivia. Maybe we can get together later. We can find something to do to kill time."

"Okay," I answered shyly. Now Jimmy was a good looking guy and most girls wouldn't hesitate to go out with him. Obviously, I couldn't, but he didn't know that.

"Hey, Jen, can I talk to you for a second?" He pulled her to the side.

"Sure. Just give me a sec, Olivia." Jennifer grinned at me. "What's on your mind, big brother?"

He glanced over Jennifer's shoulder at me. "I know Olivia goes to SIU and she's pretty."

"I'm not sure if she still has a boyfriend if that's what you're asking."

"Even better. She seems nice but kinda quiet."

"Maybe you can talk to her later."

"Yeah, talk to her," Jimmy said with a weird grin.

I was close enough to hear him, and I knew he wanted to do more than talk. We said goodbye to Jimmy and headed back to the arena.

"You are devious, Jen! Do you often tease your brother like that?"

"He has teased me my whole life. This is just

getting back at him for what he deserves."

"How long do you think we can keep this up?"

"I don't know. Do you want to keep fooling him?"

I thought about it for a moment. I was caught between wanting to help Jennifer keep up her practical joke on her brother, but I didn't want Jimmy to think I was flirting with him. "I'll play along if you want. For now."

"I think it would be great if we could keep it up all night and then see his face when you go onstage."

"Maybe we can." I sincerely doubted it. I didn't speak for a moment as we walked along. Then I asked, "Do you really think I'm a diva?"

"Oh, Emmy! You are the farthest thing from a diva that anyone could possibly be."

I was relieved to hear that. I talked to the band about Jimmy Sinclaire and Jennifer's plan. They agree to go along with the deception as long as possible. Jimmy had met the guys in Jennifer's band, but didn't know them all that well. He was clueless about me and The Only Hope.

Jennifer met her family as planned at 6:30. I stayed backstage and talked to the guys from The Apostles Creed. I would miss them when they left the tour.

"Hi, Mom! Hi, Dad! It's so good to see you." They hugged each other and Jennifer counted fifteen relatives and friends with them. "I'm sorry I can't get you backstage right now, but after the show I have passes for whoever wants to stick around."

"That's fine, dear. Your father and I would like to meet your friends, but not everyone can stay that late."

"I have to get back, Mom. I want to take Jimmy with me. I want to reintroduce him to the band."

"Okay, you do what you have to do. We will see you after the show."

"Did I tell you that I'm singing a duet with Em... with the singer from the other band. So make sure you

291

stay for everything, okay?"

"We will."

"Come on, Jimmy. You can talk to the guys, and I think Olivia might want to see you again."

"Cool!"

He actually said something else, but because of his southern accent, I didn't catch it. Jennifer brought Jimmy backstage, and they made their way downstairs.

"You know Peyton and I might get back together, right?" Jimmy replied.

"That's so sweet. I really like her. I hope you guys do get back together. Does that mean you aren't interested in seeing Olivia?"

"I'd like to talk to her again, but I'm not interested in a relationship with her."

He didn't elaborate, but I'm sure you can guess what he really wanted from me.

"She is sweet, and she seems to like being around you. Maybe you could hire her as a real assistant someday after you become famous like that diva from the other band. Does Olivia know how to sing at all?"

"I think she sings a little bit," Jennifer answered.

Jimmy laughed. "I can't imagine Olivia onstage in front of a lot of people. She's just too shy. She would probably just stand there and freeze up."

Jennifer saw me and waved. I walked over as Jennifer reintroduced Jimmy to her band. I grinned at Jimmy, and I'm sure he interpreted it as flirting.

"Hey, guys! Remember Jimmy? He goes to school here."

They said hi and smiled because they were in on the practical joke.

"This is Chris Henry. He plays guitar. This is Floyd Alcott who plays keyboards and guitar at times. This goofy looking guy is Brian Vogel who tries to play bass."

"Nice to see you again, Jimmy. I'm sorry your sister is such a dweeb," Brian said.

Jennifer smacked Brian's arm and then continued.

"Last but not least is Ted Riggs. He's the drummer."

Jimmy hung around with Jennifer and the guys. He tried to talk to me, but I was acting as shy and quiet as I possibly could. Jimmy asked the guys about that other singer. "Is she really as bad as Jennifer claims?"

"You better believe it."

"Where is she?"

"Oh, she's in her dressing room. She never comes out to mingle with us common folk," Brian said.

Jennifer added, "I heard that she barely even talks to her own band and then it's usually just to yell at them for making mistakes."

"Yeah and she's kinda fat, too!" Floyd grinned at me.

I made a face at him.

Chris spoke up, "And not very pretty either."

"I heard she eats a whole pizza by herself every night before she sings."

I could barely keep a straight face as I listened to the guys describing me.

"How is it that she's such a star then?" Jimmy scratched his ear. "Doesn't her band play like Christian music or something? You'd think she would be a better person."

"You'd think so!" Brian laughed.

"What do you think, Olivia?" Jennifer asked.

"I try to see the best in everyone. Not everyone is all bad or all good."

"Too bad you can't be a singer, Olivia." Jimmy moved closer to me and tried to grab my arm.

"We should get going." I scooted back. "I think The Apostles Creed is already playing."

Jimmy turned to Jennifer's band. "It was nice to see you guys. Please take care of Jen. I know she's a pain in the butt sometimes, but I still love her."

Brian grinned and said, "She is that at times."

"Let's go listen to the band. I want you to hear them," Jennifer said.

"Okay. Are you coming with us, Olivia?"

"I really can't, Jimmy. I'm not supposed to be..."

Jennifer pulled Jimmy away from me. "Olivia has to pretend to be getting things ready for my set."

He took this as the truth. Jennifer took Jimmy upstairs and they listened to The Apostles Creed from the side of the stage.

"They're pretty good, huh?" Jennifer hollered into his ear.

"Yeah. So?"

"I think the lead singer is cute."

Jimmy laughed and said, "He's not really my type."

She smacked his arm because she knew he was teasing her. Jennifer needed to get ready for her set, so she took Jimmy back downstairs.

"Just hang out with the guys for awhile. I need to talk to Olivia."

Jennifer found me, and we went to her dressing room.

"What about 'Shout To The Lord'? Are we still going to do it?" she asked.

"Why don't we do it in our set, Jennifer? I'm sure the guys all know it and that way we won't spoil the surprise."

"Good idea."

"I wish I could see his face when I start singing."

I stayed away from Jimmy and soon it was time for Jennifer's set. She took Jimmy with her and told him to stay on the side of the stage. Jimmy watched and listened to his sister. Jennifer told me later she imagined she was playing for her family the way she had since she first learned to play a guitar at the age of ten. She saw her parents in the crowd and embarrassed them by making them stand up. She finished her set and received a standing ovation. At least from part of the audience.

"Wow, Jen! You are really good. I guess I never realized that before."

"Thank you, Jimmy. It means a lot to me. Come

294

on. We have to get out of the way so they can get the stage ready."

"For the diva and her band, right?"

"Yeah! The diva."

Jennifer took Jimmy downstairs and tried to spot me. She saw me and the band and steered Jimmy in the other direction so he didn't see us.

"Let's see if there is any food left. Are you hungry?" Jennifer grabbed his arm and pulled him away.

"I'm starving. I didn't have any supper."

"Didn't Mom make supper?"

"I stayed on campus and studied at the library."

They grabbed some food and sat at a table. Jennifer knew I would be be entering the stage from the same side that she did for her set. She tried to think of the best way to keep Jimmy from seeing me until I made my entrance. She had an idea and slipped away from Jimmy for a minute to tell me her plan.

"That will be so cool!" I said.

"Do you think it will work?" she asked.

"As long as Jimmy doesn't notice and wonder why I have on a dress and tights." I laughed and for the first time thought we could actually pull this off.

The stage was set and the crowd was hollering and stomping their feet getting restless. Jennifer watched my guys head upstairs. I walked over and joined Jennifer and Jimmy. The curtain stayed closed as the guys tuned up while the MC made some announcements.

Jimmy checked me out and said, "You look very pretty, Olivia. That's a nice dress."

"Thank you. I just wanted to change into something nicer than my jeans and t-shirt."

He accepted my answer and didn't give it a second thought. I take that back. He did have a second thought because he whispered something in my ear. I can't tell you his exact words, but it was along the lines of seeing me without the dress. I couldn't get mad at him because for all he knew I was a party girl from SIU.

Jimmy turned back to Jennifer. "When does the diva make her entrance?"

"Not until the last moment."

"I bet she's not half as good as you were, Jen."

"She might be better than you think. Sssh. We need to listen to this." Jennifer poked him in the side.

Jennifer stood between Jimmy and me. I stepped away as the house and stage lights dimmed and the crowd erupted. Jimmy didn't see Nelson come over and hand me my microphone. He led me out to the stage with a flashlight as Chase prayed. The curtains opened and the band began playing the intro music softly. The MC was now out of sight on the other side of the stage. The arena was almost totally dark.

"Is everyone ready!" The MC knew how to get the crowd going because they got even louder. "Please welcome to the stage from South Hampshire, Illinois, Emmy Colasanti and The Only Hope Band!!!"

Skip counted off the first song and stage exploded with light. Lights and lasers were shining and moving in every direction. I couldn't see much of anything because of the spotlights shining in my eyes. I started singing, and I don't think Jimmy even realized it was me at first. He looked at Jennifer, and saw that I wasn't beside her. He looked out at the stage and suddenly realized he had been had. He leaned down and yelled into Jennifer's ear.

"You stinker! You got me! I had no idea at all. I guess this is payback for all the years of me teasing you."

"Are you surprised for real?"

"Yes! I never would have guessed."

Jimmy put his arm around Jennifer's shoulders as they watched me working. He told me later how he shook his head and wondered how in the world I could be so shy and unassuming and then do what I was doing now. We got to the part of the set where I needed Jennifer to join me.

"Jimmy, I have to sing this next song with Emmy. Will you wait here?"

296

"Where else am I supposed to go?"

I waved my hands and quieted the crowd down to introduce Jennifer.

"I want to bring out my friend, Jennifer Sinclaire." Jennifer walked out to join me. "She's going to help me with this next song. Please feel free to sing along if you know it. It's called 'Shout To the Lord,' and tonight I want to dedicate it to my new friend Jimmy. I hope he forgives me."

For the next five minutes Jennifer and I took turns with the verses to a song the whole crowd seemed to know. In the middle of the song Boyd did a screaming guitar solo, and then Perry took a turn. Jennifer and I watched as the band showed off their talents. Jennifer rejoined her brother, and they watched the rest of the concert from the side of the stage.

After the encore Chase talked to the audience for a few minutes about Jesus and prayed for anyone who might want to accept Him tonight. I wanted to join Jennifer at the side of the stage but didn't know how Jimmy would react. I bit my her lower lip. I do that a lot I'm told. I slowly approached them. It was quiet enough now to actually talk to one another.

I put my hands behind me and sort of moved back and forth a bit. Kind of like a little kid might do. "Do you hate me now, Jimmy? That was a pretty mean trick to play on you."

"I don't hate you one little bit. I've teased Jen all her life, and she's always been a good sport about it. I admit that I was totally blown away by you, Olivia. Or should I call you Emmy now?"

"All my friends call me Emmy."

"I need to find Mom and Dad somehow. I promised to bring them downstairs," Jennifer said.

"I'll take Jimmy with me. He will be all right as long as he's with the diva!"

I saw Ryan rush over to Jennifer shouting her name. He didn't care who knew he had a thing for her.

"You are something special, Emmy," Jimmy said.

I couldn't be sure, but I think he blushed. He took my hands and I looked into his eyes.

"Oh, crap!" he swore. "I'm sorry for what I said before. I guess you aren't interested in what I asked."

I knew it was wrong, but I couldn't resist one final tease. "Who knows, Jimmy. Maybe I am a wild girl from SIU."

He looked at me for a moment and then grinned. "That's not true, but you are really pretty."

"Jimmy, there is something else I should tell you. You asked about Tony Bertucci before."

"Yeah."

"He's my friend. I used to date him in high school."

"Get out! For real?"

"Yeah, and I'm married to Kenny Colwell."

He stared at me and didn't speak for a moment.

"Are you all right, Jimmy?"

He shook his head. "I can't believe I made a play for the wife of a famous rock star. You must think I'm a total loser."

I grinned and couldn't resist. "You're not a total loser, Jimmy." I emphasized total.

We laughed as I led him downstairs. I kept Jimmy with me until we saw Jennifer coming toward us with a whole bunch of people.

"Get ready, Emmy. It's time to meet the parents."

Jennifer walked up. "Mom, Dad, this is Emmy Colasanti."

"It's nice to meet you, Mrs. Sinclaire and Mr. Sinclaire. Didn't Jennifer do a great job tonight? Of course she is always great."

"I was so proud of her tonight." Mrs. Sinclaire hugged Jennifer. "What a thrill to see my little girl onstage singing for all those people."

Jennifer hugged her mother back, and then Jimmy told their parents about the practical joke Jen played on him.

"So you were with Emmy this afternoon and didn't even realize who she was?" Mr. Sinclaire asked and then laughed.

"No, I'd never seen a picture of her before and these two stinkers never let on. Emmy is shy and quiet when she's not singing, and Jen described the other singer as this diva and made her sound like a monster."

Eventually, Jennifer's family left and the bands were ready to call it a night. Chase and Belinda arranged for hotel rooms for everyone, since we were staying in Knoxville tonight.

"Emmy, would you like to stay with us tonight?" Jennifer grabbed my arm. "We have plenty of room, and I would love to have you stay."

"As long as Jimmy doesn't try to pull any jokes over on us I'd be happy to stay with you, Jen." I grinned at him, and I know he thought I was flirting.

He grinned back and whispered something to me. I can actually share this. He said, "I won't make any promises, Olivia."

I received permission from Chase to stay with Jennifer and her family tonight and the next day. Yeah, I can hear Andy Walker telling me to tell Chase and Nelson what I wanted to do instead of asking like a kid. Jimmy waited around to take Jennifer and me home. I grabbed some clean clothes while Jennifer said goodbye to her band and they scattered. They were glad to be able to be home tonight as well.

"Emmy, why did you ask that guy for permission to stay with Jen?" Jimmy asked.

"That's Chase Hillman. He's the boss. He's our worship pastor back home, and I just always ask him whenever I do anything different."

"But you're the diva. Shouldn't you just tell him what you are doing, and he has to accept it?"

"Very funny, Jimmy." I rolled my eyes. *Are you going to get on my case too? Maybe I do need to be more assertive.*

299

I have to admit I still ask permission when I'm on tour. I can't help it. It's who I am.

It only took fifteen to twenty minutes to arrive at the Sinclaire home. Jennifer showed me a room I could use. We were all rather tired so we went to bed right away.

When I woke up, I could smell breakfast cooking in the kitchen. I got dressed and wandered downstairs to find Mrs. Sinclaire in the kitchen.

"Good morning, dear. Did you sleep well? Jen and Jimmy are still sleeping. I hope you like bacon and eggs. If you don't, I could make pancakes or something."

"Bacon and eggs are fine, and I slept very well thank you. You have a beautiful home."

"It's nothing fancy but it's been our home for about fifteen years now."

"Where is Mr. Sinclaire?"

"He left for work already. I took today off since Jen was in town. I think Jimmy is skipping his classes today. Those two will never admit it, but they miss each other."

"I could tell."

Jennifer woke up and made it downstairs and a few minutes later Jimmy made an appearance.

"That smells good, Mom. What is it?" Jimmy asked.

"If I have have to tell you, how good could it be."

"I'm just teasing you, Mom! I love French toast."

Jimmy had a weird sense of humor.

"Why aren't you at a class or something?"

"I decided it was more important to stay home and entertain Emmy."

"How do you know she wants you to entertain her?" Jennifer asked. "Maybe she wants to spend the day with me."

"Why on earth would she want to do that when she could enjoy my company."

"Maybe because she's not a dork like you."

"Maybe you can both spend some time with Emmy. Did you ever think of that?" Mrs. Sinclaire suggested.

300

"But that would mean spending the day with her." Jimmy pointed to Jennifer and she smacked his hand.

"I would like to spend time with both of you as long as you are nice to each other."

Mrs. Sinclaire ignored the kids teasing each other. She must have been used to it.

"Is there anything you want or need to do today, Emmy?" Jennifer asked after breakfast.

"I would like to go for a run. I need to get back on track. I hate to ask but I need to do some laundry, too. Just the clothes I wore last night."

"I don't really do that but Jimmy does. Running, I mean," Jennifer said. "He would enjoy going with you."

"What would I enjoy? I heard my name." Jimmy walked up behind me and put a hand on my shoulder.

"Emmy wants to go for a run. She should have someone with her."

"Sure! I'll go with you, Emmy. When did you want to go?"

"Maybe in thirty minutes. I want to finish my emails first."

"That's a nice laptop."

"Kenny got it for me so I could stay in touch."

At the mention of Kenny's name, Jimmy jerked his hand away. I thought it was funny that he still thought of me like that.

"If you show me what you need laundered, I will take care of it for you while you have some fun. I won't take no for an answer, either!" Mrs. Sinclaire exclaimed.

"Thank you. I really appreciate it."

Chase called to check up on me. I didn't mind because it was part of his job. Or Nelson's job. One of them was supposed to keep track of me.

"I'm fine. I was just checking emails. How are you? Are you enjoying your day of rest?"

"I'm relaxing by the pool at the moment."

"That sounds like fun. Do you know what time we are leaving yet?"

"I need to talk to Larry, and see what he wants to do. It will take at least eight hours to get to Toledo."

"Let me know when I need to be back."

"Will do. Have a good run, Em."

Jimmy and I went for a run, and I surprised him with my supreme athletic ability. He couldn't keep up. Later, I realized he might have been enjoying the view from behind me. We got back to the house after thirty minutes, and my cell phone rang.

"Hey, Chase. What's the plan?"

"We are going to leave at two. We should arrive in the Toledo area between ten and midnight. Belinda made reservations at a motel for the night. I decided to reward the guys with another night in a motel with a pool. They deserve it, and we will still be under our budget."

"Cool! That means I can go swimming, too."

"I'm sorry this cuts your time with Jennifer short."

"That's okay. I'm sure I will see her again soon."

"Can you be back here by a quarter till two?"

"I think someone will give me a ride."

I let Jennifer know about the travel plans.

"I thought we would have more time together. I'm sorry I have to leave so soon."

"I'm sure we will see each other soon, Emmy. Jimmy and I will give you a ride to the hotel."

"Thanks."

"Do you have time for lunch before you go, Emmy?" Jimmy asked.

"Yes, that would be nice." I wondered if he was up to something because he asked so politely.

We ate lunch and I said goodbye to Mrs. Sinclaire, and Jimmy and Jennifer took me back to the hotel. They hugged me and promised to keep in touch. I'm pretty sure Jimmy wanted to kiss me, but I never gave him the opportunity. They hung around until the buses pulled out for the long trip to Toledo, Ohio.

"Are you crying, Jen?"

"No, I got some dust in my eye, dorkbrain."

"How long am I gonna have to put up with you in the house?"

"I'll be here all week. We leave on Saturday morning. So I have to see your ugly face until then."

"And I have to put up with you pestering me every night."

"You better not skip any more classes."

"I won't. Not if you're gonna be around."

Jennifer told me this was the way they normally treated each other. It reminded me of the way Tony and I get along.

Later that night Emmy slipped into bed beside Kenny. "Are you awake?"

"No, I'm reading this book in my sleep."

"I bought some more clothes for the kids. I don't want to buy any more toys. They've got so much stuff even after I cleaned out things that Kevin Michael doesn't play with anymore. I took a whole box of toys to the mission."

"I am in total agreement with you, Em." Kenny closed his book and set it on the nightstand. "How was your lunch with Father James? Did he help?"

Emmy pulled the covers over her head. "About as much as Kevin Michael. He wants me to write about his firetrucks."

"Father James has a firetruck?" Kenny grinned.

Emmy threw the covers off and sat up. "No, you goof."

"Gotcha."

"You are such a dork, but I love you anyway. Are you finished with your book?" She moved closer and kissed him.

"I guess I am for tonight," Kenny responded to her kiss.

Chapter Twenty-Seven

Kenny pulled the Odyssey into the parking lot at church and turned around to smile at the kids. "We're here. This is the end of the line. Everyone out of the train."

Emmy shook her head. "You are such a goof." She turned to look at the construction site. "They're making progress."

"Other than that one little snow, the weather's been cooperating." Kenny got out of the van and helped Kevin Michael.

"Do you think Liz will be here with Phoebe? She was going to bring her last week but didn't because of the colds going around.

"I haven't heard anything, Em. There's Kristen. Maybe she knows." Kenny pointed to Kristen, Zachary and Grace.

"Will you get the kids inside?" Emmy rushed to Kristen.

"Sure, Em. I'll watch out for them," Kenny said.

"Hey, Krissy," Emmy hollered.

Kristen stopped and waited for Emmy.

"Is Liz here today?" Emmy asked.

"I don't know, but she should be."

Emmy and Kristen walked into the foyer together and saw more people than normal crowding into the space.

"What's going on?" Emmy stood on tiptoes to try to see over the crowd.

Kristen walked around the edge of the crowd. "There's Tony and Sloane. Maybe they know."

Emmy dodged around a few people and reached Tony. "What's going on? Why aren't these people leaving or going to Sunday School?"

"They're trying to see Liz and the baby," Tony said.

Emmy smacked his arm. "They're here!?"

"Duh! Isn't that what I just said." Tony rubbed his arm and grinned. "Haven't you seen the baby yet?"

"Just at the hospital. I haven't had a chance to get over to their house. Did you see them?"

"Not yet. We just got here a few minutes ago.

Sloane held onto Coby's hand. "People are making a bigger

fuss over Liz and Phoebe Grace than when Prince George was born a few months ago."

"That's because this is more important," Emmy said.

Eventually most of the crowd dissipated. The people from the early service left to go home, and other people headed to their Sunday School classes. Emmy, Kristen and Sloane stood with Liz and Tyler.

"Can I hold her, please?" Emmy begged.

"Okay, but you can't keep her, Emmy," Liz said as she smiled at Phoebe.

Dany Kimmerle and Darian Michaelis walked up and Emmy grinned. "Are you guys going to start a family right away?"

"I think we'll wait until after we get married," Darian said with a straight face.

Emmy made a face at him. "That's what I meant."

Kristen tried to take the baby away, but Emmy wouldn't let go.

"You have to share, Emmy," Kristen said.

Emmy held onto Phoebe Grace for a little longer before passing her over to Kristen.

"I love her hair, and she has your eyes, Liz," Emmy said.

"You can't tell that. It's too early," Liz said.

Dany put an arm around her sister. "I agree with Emmy."

Kenny approached after getting the kids to their classrooms. "Congratulations, Pastor Tyler." Kenny shook his hand. "You've got as many kids as us now."

Emmy grinned and said, "But they've got a long way to go to catch Tony and Sloane."

"I don't think we'll catch them." Tyler shook his head.

"You never know," Liz said. "I want a large family."

"We better get to class," Kenny suggested.

"I think I'll go to the nursery with Liz," Emmy said.

Tony looked at Sloane. "Can you get your tubes untied after they've been... you know?"

"I'm not going to have another baby, Tony." Emmy stuck out her tongue.

305

Heather tugged on Emmy's covers. "Mommy, you should wake up because I think Santa Claus was here."

"No, it's too early. Go back to bed." Emmy pulled the covers up to her neck.

"But Daddy said you need to get up," Heather insisted.

"What time is it?"

Heather shrugged. "How should I know? I'm just a kid."

"You know how to tell time when your favorite TV show is on." Emmy threw back the covers and sat up. "Give me a few minutes to get dressed."

Heather walked away. "And remember to brush your teeth."

Emmy used her hand to check her breath. "It's not that bad." She glanced out the windows. "It's snowing! Two days ago it was in the sixties. Goofy weather."

Two hours later Kenny cleaned up the last of the wrapping paper. "So much for a simple Christmas." He carried the garbage bags out to the garage.

Mom Colwell handed him another bag. "I'm sorry, son, but I couldn't resist buying more gifts than I should."

"It's all right, Mom. They won't be kids forever."

"What are we having for lunch?" Kevin Michael rubbed his belly. "I'm hungry."

"You should have eaten your breakfast instead of throwing a fit. Lunch will be ready in an hour." Emmy stirred the pot of chili. "Go to your room and play with your new toys."

"Do I have to give away more toys?" He tried to look into the pot of chili.

"You know the rules. When you get new toys, you have to share some with children who don't have any."

"Okay, Mom, but no firetrucks."

"You can keep your firetrucks, Kevin."

"Am I in time for lunch?" Father James walked into the kitchen and stood behind Emmy. "Before you say anything, Kenny let me in. I know better than to walk in unannounced."

Emmy turned around and waved the spoon at him. "Shut up! We don't do that anymore."

He jumped back to avoid being splattered with chili. "Do what? I'm a priest, remember?"

"Never mind. Did you bring anything?"

"No gifts as you insisted." He held out his hands. "See? Empty."

Kenny walked back in from the garage. "Where should I put these?" He carried two bags with him.

Emmy shook her head at her half-brother. "Lying is a sin even for you."

Later, Heather and Isabella played dress up with their dolls in their room as Kenny tried to convince Kevin to take a nap. Emmy talked to her brother in the family room.

"I could use a nap," Father James yawned.

"Why? You haven't done anything strenuous."

"I am mentally drained from caring for my flock."

Emmy rolled her eyes. "Fleecing your flock is more like it."

"I depend on the generosity of the church for my survival. Was there any chili left?"

"I saved some for you to take home."

"Cornbread?"

"Yes, there is cornbread, too." Emmy sighed.

"Bless you, my child."

"You have to stop buying stuff for the kids. They have plenty. Buy stuff for the mission if you need to spend your money."

Father James rose from the couch. "I should get back. I have to prepare a sermon about being grateful for God's gifts to us."

"Ain't working," Emmy said.

"Worth a try. Thanks for the chili and cornbread." He waited for her to get up.

"Fine! I'll get it for you. I should have given it to Kenny's parents."

"Where did they go?"

"To visit Kenny's aunt and uncle." Emmy took the chili from the fridge. "I want my Tupperware back. It's not cheap."

"I wouldn't dare keep it. Give me a hug." He opened his arms.

"Merry Christmas, James." She hugged him. "Don't forget the cornbread."

He kissed the top of her head. "Thank you, Emmy. You are special."

"Go on with you."

"You're not Irish, either." He laughed and then walked away.

Emmy's cell phone buzzed and she pulled it out of her pocket. She smiled and boosted herself onto the countertop. "Merry Christmas, Rory. What are you up to?"

"Just got back from Rochelle's parents, and before you even ask, it's nothing serious. We ate lunch with them. How are you and the kids?"

"Everyone is fine. Father James just left. Kenny's parents were here earlier. The girls are playing and Kevin Michael better be taking a nap."

"Did everyone spoil the kids?"

"Of course. Uncle Andy came over yesterday with stuff. Father James brought gifts. Did you get anything in the mail?"

"Yes, Emmy, thank you. I'm sorry I didn't get you anything," Rory said.

"I don't expect anything. Hey, I saw that Warren Sanders got promoted. He's deputy police chief or something."

"That's nice," Rory said.

"Shoot! Maybe I shouldn't have mentioned that. Does it bring back bad memories?"

"Yeah, but at least he got the guy who murdered Amy."

Emmy thought about the day his sister Amy was murdered, and she was able to provide an alibi for Rory because he was at church with her. "I shouldn't have said anything."

"It's all right, Em. Anything new going on? How's the book coming?"

Emmy groaned. "I'm beginning to hate it."

"I thought God told you to write it."

"Don't make fun of me, Rory."

"I'm not. I know this is serious. Hey, guess what I saw the other day."

"What?"

"A book about lions."

Emmy jumped down. "Where?"

"In a bookstore. There was a big display and I bought one. Will you sign it for me someday?"

"Very funny. Did you really?"

"Sure. I thought the plot had a few holes in it, but overall I give it four stars," he said and then chuckled. "Lions and cats who talk in English. Go figure."

"You do realize it's a book for children, right?"

"Then why was it in the non-fiction section?"

"What?" Emmy asked.

"Just kidding. When are you going to come and see me?"

"I'm not touring until April or May."

"Not what I meant," Rory whispered.

"I suppose we could come down to Florida after the holidays."

"You're always welcome, but I'd have to get a hotel room for you guys. My place isn't big enough for the whole family." Rory opened the fridge and pulled out a Coke.

Emmy talked for a few minutes about the book.

"I have been thinking about writing a chapter about my childhood." She bit her lip.

"Would that be wise?"

"I wouldn't include everything, Rory."

"That's good. I should go, Em. I just wanted to wish you guys Merry Christmas."

"Merry Christmas to you, Rory. Thanks for calling. I'll talk to you soon."

"Are you sure you don't want to go for a ride?" Kenny asked Emmy two days after Christmas. "You haven't been on the snowmobile for over a year."

"No, you and Tony can take the kids out. Just be careful. I don't want to have to search the woods for you. And don't let them freeze to death."

"We won't freeze, Mommy," Isabella said.

"What are you going to do, Em?" Kenny adjusted Kevin Michael's snowsuit.

"I'm going to make some hot chocolate and work on my book. That's all I ever do anymore."

"We will help you when we get back, Mommy," Heather replied.

Thank you, sweetheart." Emmy watched as the kids scampered out to the garage and then filled the kettle with water. *I should go snowmobiling again one of these days.*

I got back to the bus, and the guys appeared happy to see me.

"You missed it, Emmy. Boyd and Perry bought some of those Super Soaker water guns. We were running all over having water fights," Ryan informed me.

"Isn't it too cold for that?"

"No, it was all right. It might be colder in Ohio and Michigan, but we can still use the guns."

"I heard you guys went swimming, too."

Skip high-fived Perry. "Yeah, that was cool. There were these two girls and I got names, numbers and email addresses."

"Now why doesn't that surprise me, Skip."

"Nothing wrong will being sociable is there, Emmy?"

"Did you guys do your laundry?"

"Yes, Mom! We got all our laundry done and we even took showers," Boyd said.

"The bus looks clean and it smells better, too."

Soon we ran out of things to talk about, so I went to my bedroom for a nap. The guys listened to their iPods. Except for stops to change drivers and fill up with fuel, the buses kept rolling along. They kept in touch with the truck which was still ahead of them.

We finally arrived in Toledo after a long boring trip

of nearly ten hours. The drivers headed right to the hotel and dropped us off. I walked inside and saw Bobby O'Connor talking to one of the ladies at the registration desk.

"What are you doing here?"

He turned around and grinned at me. He held up his arm. "Nice to see you, too. I thought you might need an extra percussionist."

"Do your parents know you're here?"

"Ah, come on, Emmy. I'm not a kid anymore."

"How did you know we would be here?"

"Boyd let me know. Could you explain to this lady that I'm a member of the band. I need a room."

"What's your name? Do I know you?" I couldn't pass up the opportunity to yank his chain.

Eventually, everyone was assigned a room. Most of the guys shared a room. Bobby ended up alone. I teased him about being afraid to stay by himself. He pretended to be afraid and wanted me to stay with him. He's certainly a lot more grown up than when I first met him.

I can only think of one thing that happened in Toledo. For some reason I didn't make an entry in my journal. Yvonne and the girls surprised Chase and myself by showing up at the venue. I take that back. They surprised me. Apparently Chase knew they were coming but didn't tell anyone.

I really don't remember much about the show that night. I do remember having a water fight later with the Super Soakers. That was fun.

Emmy drained her hot chocolate and returned to the kitchen to fill her mug. She opened the cabinet next to the fridge, reached up for a bag of marshmallows and squeezed it. *Shoot! These are like rocks.* She tossed them in the garbage, walked into the pantry and spotted an unopened jar of Marshmallow Fluff. She strained to open it but finally managed. She scooped some into her mug and returned to the den.

311

After the relatively short hop from Toledo, about two hours, we arrived in Lansing, Michigan. Yvonne Hillman booked us at The Ramada Lansing Hotel because she had stayed here before and remembered it had a restaurant and a pool. The price fit our budget, too. We got a discount because we reserved nine rooms. Belinda arranged for a three o'clock checkout time, which meant we had the rooms for over twelve hours. The truck was already parked in the back of the lot. Rooms were assigned and Nelson convinced the drivers to use rooms and not stay on the bus. They were worried about someone breaking in. Jess and Joe absolutely refused to stay in the hotel. They stayed on the buses to act as security. Chase did convince them to come in for breakfast at least.

Belinda offered to let me share a room with her and Nelson but I declined with a smile. I couldn't imagine sharing a room with Nelson. He's a super nice guy and all, but I do like my privacy. Instead the guys and I got ground floor rooms with a connecting door. They were at the end of the hallway away from the other guest rooms. A perfect location! Now we could stay up all night if we wanted and not bother anyone. I staked my claim to one of the beds and agreed to let Bobby have the other one. The other four guys would double up on the two queen size beds in the other room. If you're counting, Skip and Bruce shared a room on the third floor. We left the connecting door open all night. Unlocked, I mean. Now, if you think it's weird that I would share a room with one of the guys from the band, it wasn't. Remember, we shared living quarters in a bus. We had more space in a hotel. And despite what Bobby had said earlier, I felt safer with him than any of the other guys. Except for maybe Adam, but he would never have shared a room with me. He and Juliana were serious about their relationship. Bobby and I hung out with the other guys in their room. I sat on one of the beds with Ryan and Boyd while the other guys sat on the other bed or the chairs in the room. They talked about the trip, and I was pleasantly surprised they talked about how many people they had seen come forward to pray. I realized these young men were serious about what God had led them to be doing with their lives. They weren't saints by any means. They were still guys and sometimes could be a little gross, but they were my guys. I think we stayed up until three that night after the concert. They wanted to get up early, have breakfast and then go swimming. Bobby waited in the other room while I got ready for bed. It wouldn't have mattered. I wore an old sweatshirt and gym shorts to bed most nights on the bus.

Getting up early for the young guys meant ten o'clock. I woke up at eight and ate breakfast in a room by the lobby. Fresh fruit, a donut and about a gallon of coffee. I don't function well on five hours of sleep. I hung out there for over an hour and didn't see any of the other guys. If they didn't make it to breakfast within the hour, they would go hungry. I headed back to the room and woke everyone up.

"It's too early, Emmy!"

"We want to sleep longer."

"I just got to sleep!"

I heard all kinds of excuses, but then reminded them. "There is a pool, and we can only stay until two."

The guys grudgingly got out of bed and grabbed some breakfast. I had packed a one piece bathing suit and a bikini. I tried them both on while the guys were eating. I decided on the bikini because the one piece just didn't fit me right. It revealed more than my bikini. I didn't count my belly as being something sexy. I wore running shorts and a t-shirt on over my bikini. I waited until the guys got back from breakfast, and I headed to the pool to let the guys change in private. Soon I heard them coming. I listened to the guys as they teased Bobby about being so skinny. I looked at the guys. None of them were wearing shirts. I thought about Tony and his muscular body for some reason. The guys jumped into

313

the pool. We had the place to ourselves. I sat on the edge with my feet in the water. Ryan and Bobby swam over to me. I think Bobby grabbed my foot and tried to pull me into the pool, but I kicked him.

"Are you gonna join us, Emmy? Or are you going to just sit and watch?" Bobby asked.

"I'm going to join you, but not if you're all gonna stare at me while I take off my top and shorts."

The guys turned away and let me get in the pool. Now I felt more comfortable. I swam around in the deeper end while the guys were horsing around at the other end. They finally joined me, and we had fun playing keep away with a soccer-size ball. I had a blast goofing around with the younger guys. Chase stopped by to see how we were doing.

"We're going to try to get checked out before three and then have a late lunch at the restaurant."

"Okay, Chase. We will be ready," Ryan replied.

"Thanks, Ryan. See you guys later. Make sure Emmy doesn't drown, okay?"

At that moment Bobby and I were trying to pull each other under the water. Probably not the best thing for a married woman to be doing, but nothing happened. I didn't drown. Bobby didn't drown. And we had fun. It's important to be able to unwind even on a two-week-long tour.

We stayed in the pool until one o'clock, give or take, and then headed back to the rooms. Bobby joined the guys in their room so I could shower and change. I hurried and then let the guys use the room. I waited in the lobby while the guys finished up. We met and walked up to the registration desk.

Ryan talked to the clerk while Bobby and I goofed around. "We would just like to thank you for allowing us to checkout later than normal."

"You are most welcome. You were all so well behaved and not a problem at all. We've had some trouble with other bands who have stayed here before."

After lunch we boarded the buses for the trip to the church. The truck had already left and had arrived. Jess, Joe and Nelson went with Carl so they could start unloading the gear.

The Lansing United Nazarene was in a new building, and this would be the first time they had a group come in for a concert. Ryan and I went inside to take a look around. The other guys wandered over to help unload the truck.

"Wow! This is a beautiful sanctuary, Ryan."

"Thank you. We like to think so."

Ryan and I turned around to see who was talking to us.

"Hi, I'm Pastor Quinn Mannfried."

"Hello, Pastor Mannfried. I'm Emmy Colasanti and this is Ryan Lederer. I guess we are a little early."

"That's quite all right. I was just working in my office. I talked to the guys with the truck and showed them where they could unload. We don't have a loading dock."

"That's all right. We are used to churches that don't."

The other bus didn't arrive for an hour.

"We had a flat tire and it took a while to get it fixed," Chase explained.

"We were beginning to wonder if you had deserted us."

"We would never do that. I see the truck is unloaded."

"Yes, everything is inside and ready for Stuart and Bruce to hook it all up. We would have gone ahead and done that but we know how protective Stuart is about his cables."

After the normal routine of soundchecks, eating and getting dressed for the concert, the doors opened and people began filing into the church. By the time the local worship team moved onto the platform, the place was nearly full. There were more people entering, so the

315

ushers began bringing in chairs. I think they ran out of chairs.

"Good evening. I am Pastor Quinn Mannfried, and I would like to welcome you to our new sanctuary. I would like to be able to tell you that we are always this full but we aren't. If I could ask everyone to move closer together so we can squeeze in just a few more people I would appreciate it."

Eventually, everyone had a place to sit and the program began. We cut our normal set down because the entire program was only supposed to last ninety minutes. After I finished the last song of the night, Chase took a few minutes to thank everyone for coming. He quickly mentioned they would be in the foyer if anyone would like to talk to them or pray for a moment together. He had the feeling that an altar call was unnecessary.

The crowd cleared out early, and the guys were able to load-out the gear and load the truck and buses. By midnight we were on the interstate heading to Lexington, Kentucky.

Emmy saved her work, closed her laptop, set it on the desk and walked toward the door She jumped out of the way as the door flew open in her face.

"Mommy! Uncle Tony let me ride with him, and we went so fast," Kevin Michael shouted.

"You did." Emmy looked up as Tony walked toward her. "Did you endanger the life of my son?"

Tony chuckled and said, "We were going about ten miles an hour."

"Yeah, it was super fast!" Kevin Michael exclaimed again.

Chapter Twenty-Eight

"You need to wear a hardhat, guys." Tony handed yellow hardhats to Emmy and Kenny as they entered the the new sanctuary. "It's required in a construction zone."

"Do you have one that fits better?" Emmy's hat was several sizes too large. "I can barely see where I'm going."

Tony laughed. "Sorry, brat, but I don't have any that would fit a child."

Kenny pointed to the roof. "Are these beams going to get covered?"

"Actually, no. The plan was to keep the framework exposed."

"Where are we standing now?" Emmy asked.

"This is the foyer area. There will be two sets of doors." Tony pointed to the entryway. "Double doors for protection from the weather. This whole front wall will be glass. There will be a wall separating the foyer and the actual sanctuary. Stairs going up to the second level will be at either end."

"I didn't know there would be a balcony," Emmy said. "Will it be for seating, or just the tech area like in the current building?"

There will be seating, but the tech rooms will be up there, too. Of course with the new technology, the sound guys can use tablets from anywhere in the building."

"Cool!" Kenny smiled.

"The sanctuary will be through here. Chairs like now. That raised area up there is the platform." Tony walked around some stacks of building materials. "Be careful." He made sure they didn't trip. "Behind the platform will be some rooms. A new music suite. Some bathrooms. Some rooms which could be used as dressing rooms."

"This place could be a music venue," Kenny said.

"That's the goal. It will be state-of-the-art as far as the lighting and audio stuff. There is going to be a loading dock on that side. Trucks will be able to back right up to it. The parking lot will extend behind the building."

"It looks huge." Emmy turned around to take in the view.

Tony grinned, "Yep! It's bigger than the current building including the sanctuary and all the offices."

"What about Pastor Tyler's office? Will that be in here?" Emmy wondered.

"No, they wanted to keep their current offices."

"How tall is the ceiling?" Emmy looked up.

Tony pointed. "See how the roof goes up in the middle?"

"Yeah."

"I think at the highest point it's fifty feet above the floor. Something like that."

"The roof in the foyer doesn't look as high," Emmy said.

"It's not. There are rooms on the second level. A TV production room and other spaces. Pastor Tyler could move his office up there later. There's plenty of room."

"How about the furnaces and stuff?" Kenny asked. "All the mechanical systems."

"All on the roof. The main utility room is on the second level. There's another utility room by the bathrooms in the back," Tony explained.

Emmy walked closer to the platform area. "This is humongous."

"Do you think you'll have enough room, Em?" Tony smiled. "You do like to move around a lot."

"I suppose so."

"When do you think we will be using the new building?" Kenny asked.

"The goal is to have the dedication ceremony in November."

"That's fast."

"We have twice the crew working in here as a regular site would have. So many hours of planning went into this. Garrick Winston is a genius when it comes to the details. So far we are a few hours ahead of his plan. That should increase as we go along."

"It looks like we are going to have an amazing sanctuary, Tony," Kenny said and then shook his hand.

"What color will the inside walls be?" Emmy asked.

318

"Everything on the platform will be black. We weren't going to paint the rest of the walls. They will just be steel and concrete." Tony winked at Kenny.

"Mr. Robertson will not like that." Emmy poked Tony in the side.

"Then I guess you need to buy some paint and a few rollers, brat."

"What about the baptism area? Where's it supposed to be?"

Tony rubbed his jaw. "You know. Uh, come to think of it. I think we forgot about it."

Emmy smacked him harder than before. "No, you didn't. Where is it?"

"At the back of the platform. Can you kinda see those areas that kinda look like risers?"

"Yeah," Emmy used her imagination.

"The baptism thing will be in the center, but it will be covered most of the time. It will blend in with the stage. Any other questions?"

Kenny shook his head.

Tony looked at Emmy. "Are you crying?"

"Hush, I can't help it. God has blessed this church with so much."

"I think it says something in Luke that to whom much is given, much is expected. I think that means the church will be held accountable for using this building right," Tony said and then put an arm around her shoulders.

Emmy looked up at Tony. "Since when did you learn anything about the Bible?"

"Hey! I may not know as much as you, but I can remember some verses."

"Are you guys coming over this afternoon?"

"Yes, Sloane said around four."

"Yeah, that will give the younger ones time for a nap," Emmy said and glanced at Kenny. "And some of the older kids, too."

"Can you believe they are eight already," Kristen said to Emmy as they watched the girls open a few presents later.

319

"I remember the day they were born like it was yesterday," Emmy said.

Kristen watched her kids sitting quietly on the floor of the family room. "We all remember that day, Em. Your labor took forever, and then... you had some complications. We were so worried about you." Kristen hugged Emmy. "Everyone did a lot of praying that day."

"Actually, I don't remember parts of that day. I guess I was pretty doped up."

"Do you remember how Kenny took off down the driveway without you?"

Emmy grinned. "I remember that part. He did that twice while Mom Colwell and I waited in the garage."

"John got lost taking me to St. Bart's," Kristen added.

Emmy looked around the room and then back at Kristen. "Sometimes I feel this is all a dream, and I'll wake up back in our little house and be a kid again."

"We have been very fortunate, Em." Kristen smiled as she watched John and Tony sitting together on the couch. "One of these days we will be grandmas and be watching a new generation of kids opening gifts."

Emmy nudged Kristen's side. "Hey! We are too young to even think about that." Emmy walked over to the love seat and put her hands on Mama Bertucci's shoulders.

Mama reached back and patted Emmy's hand. "The girls are so pretty, Emmy. They look like you," Mama said without looking back.

"How did you know it was me?"

Mama laughed. "Because I know everything, dear."

Emmy massaged Mama's shoulders. "I went to see Mom last week."

"How is she doing?"

Emmy shrugged. "She's as healthy as a horse, but she has trouble remembering my name now. She still knows I'm her daughter, I think, but she thinks I'm still a kid."

Mama squeezed Emmy's hand. "It's not easy to see someone go through that. I will say an extra prayer for you."

"Thank you, Mama."

Heather and Isabella held up identical dresses to show everyone.

"Mommy! Look! Someone forgot the rule," Heather said.

Isabella added, "It's all right. We can dress like twins once in a while, and these are very pretty."

Emmy took some time that night to work on her book.

Lexington was 400 miles away, and the trip took seven and a half hours. By eight o'clock we pulled into the parking area of the famous Rupp Arena—the home of the Kentucky Wildcats basketball teams. Chase checked in with security, and he and Stuart Lederer were allowed into the arena, Chase looked around in awe at the many banners hanging in the rafters. The stage was ready as were the lights and sound system. The labor crew and the ClairShowco guys finished late the previous night. Chase found Andy's team already at work in the production office. Marianne Lowenfield was Andy's production manager, and she needed to talk to Chase and Nelson.

"I'm glad you're here. We have one small problem. The band that was supposed to open for you guys had an accident last night."

"Are they all right?" Chase asked.

"They are fine, but their bus was totaled. It seems a fire broke out in the engine compartment. They were in the middle of nowhere, and by the time the fire department arrived it was too late to salvage anything. All their personal effects, their instruments, PA. They lost everything."

"The important thing is that they are all right. Is there anything we can do to help them?"

"Not right now. They are heading home. I called Andy, and he called Jennifer Sinclaire. She is flying up here to open for you guys. We will pick her and her brother up at the airport. Unfortunately, her band won't make it tonight. They will meet you guys tomorrow in Cincinnati. Jennifer couldn't get in touch with them quick enough to drive up here from Knoxville, and they can't afford to all fly. Andy would have covered the cost, but Jennifer told her guys to get on the road before we had a chance to talk to her again."

"I think we know enough of her songs to help her out."

"That's up to you guys."

"Hi, Chase, Nelson. I'm Joel Kinnaman. We met in Charlottesville."

"Hi, Joel, I remember you. You were a great help those nights you were with us. It's good to see you again."

"How was your little trip to Lansing and Toledo?"

"It went all right except for a flat tire on one of the buses. I guess we should considerate ourselves fortunate and blessed because we've had a safe trip so far."

"The stage is ready and so are the ClairShowco people. You can pull your truck right into the building, and the local guys will unload it. You can do your soundcheck as soon as they get everything set up."

"Thanks, Joel."

I confess I was getting spoiled by having so much of the work done for us. I knew that's how it happened for Fridays At Five, but we were just a relatively unknown band.

We finished our soundcheck, and I was on my way to the bus when Jennifer and Jimmy arrived. I rushed over to them and hugged Jennifer. Jimmy waited for a hug, but I didn't want him to get the wrong idea.

"Thank you so much for filling in, Jen. I know you were on vacation."

""I can always take a vacation, Emmy. When would I get another chance to play in Rupp Arena in front of a packed house?"

I turned and looked up at Jimmy. "Hi, Jimmy. It's good to see you again."

"Hey, Emmy. I hope it's all right that I tagged along with Jen."

"I'm glad you did."

"She made me carry her guitar so I earned my way."

I looked up at Jimmy and then Jennifer. "We are staying in town tonight. Maybe we can share a room unless you already have one."

Jimmy grinned and I poked his side.

"Marianne told me that she would take care of that," Jennifer said.

"Let's go see what the plan is. I know where the production office is located."

We talked to Marianne, and she arranged for Jennifer to share my room. Jimmy would share a room with one of the guys. They would both ride up to Cincinnati on the Omega bus with me. Did I mention that the bus my guys rode on was still called the Omega bus? The crew rode on the Alpha bus. I thought it should be the other way around, but no biggie.

Jennifer and I met with Chase and Ryan to come up with a plan for Jennifer's set. Jennifer would do some songs on her own, and the guys will back her on the rest. Jennifer would open with two songs with the band and then do her solo stuff. They practiced for thirty minutes and Jennifer was satisfied.

The afternoon went quickly and before we realized it was time for Jennifer to sing. Chase explained what had happened to the other band and led the crowd in a prayer. Jennifer did her set and the crowd showed their appreciation for her filling in on short notice.

Emmy's cell phone chirped, so she checked the text message.

"Call me now!" Diane had texted.

This might be important. Emmy set her laptop on the desk and called.

"What's wrong?"

"I just got a call from Mom's nurse. She was being difficult and they had to sedate her to get her to go to bed. You need to go see her. She was complaining that she never sees you."

"The last time I went over there she didn't know my name," Emmy explained.

"She knew it two days ago. I was over there, and all she did was talk about you. She rambled on about how you were going to college. She pulled out some photos and showed them to me. She didn't realize I was in the photos too."

Emmy sighed and then took a deep breath.

"I know you're busy, Em, but could you run over there soon?" Diane asked.

"I'll try. Do you think I should bring her to the birthday party?"

"No, Em. She doesn't remember any of the grandkids. A room full of loud kids would just set her off."

"I'll see her sometime this week, okay?"

"Just be prepared for a surprise." Diane ended the call.

What kind of surprise? I hate it when you do that, Diane. Emmy returned to her laptop.

The guys started playing and I came out to start the set. There were 19,000 fans on their feet and making so much noise I could barely hear even with my IEMs. I looked at Chase and let him know I couldn't hear so the band kept playing and Chase was able to give me a visual cue. The crowd quieted down enough so I could hear and the rest of the set went on without a hitch. It was the largest crowd of the tour and the loudest by far.

Shortly after one o'clock, Jennifer and I were in our hotel room, in bed and already asleep. Ryan, Boyd, Adam and Perry were downstairs in the lobby. They were too wound up for sleep, so they were talking about the arena and the loud crowd. Bobby and Jimmy found an arcade at the hotel and spent their time playing games. Skip and Bruce decided to check out the area, so they wandered around. I hate to say this, but they ended up at a bar. They were both of legal age so that wasn't a problem. Let me explain a little background. I grew up in a house where alcohol was consumed on a regular basis. My father drank at Miller's Bar a lot. Mom drank but more as a social thing. I would have a glass of wine at dinner when I was a bit older, but I used to sneak some of Daddy's beer when I was too young to be drinking. I never drank enough to get drunk, but I will never let my kids get away with it. The Nazarene church as a denomination frowns on the consumption of alcohol, tobacco, drugs. You get the picture. They used to forbid movies and dancing, too, but I think they have relaxed their attitude about that. As a representative of the church I try to avoid any semblance of moral misbehaving. Let me clarify that a little. In the beginning the church helped support the worship band when we toured. That isn't the case now. My band is totally separate from the church. Yeah, we go to church there. Most of us anyway. But we don't receive any financial support. I still try to behave in a way that would not reflect poorly on my church. Basically, I don't want to do anything Jesus wouldn't want me to. I'm not perfect, so I fall short. Now back to the alcohol thing. On occasion I will have a beer at home. Not very often but once in a while. Tony and John don't see anything wrong with having a beer. Tony was brought up Catholic but is a Nazarene now. John is still Catholic, and he's very sincere about his faith. I grew up in the Catholic church until we stopped attending mass. Different story. Skip and Bruce might have had too much to drink that night. That's where I was going with this. They didn't know when to stop. Chase found out and he sent them home. Bobby would have to take over on drums, and one of the crew filled in for Bruce. That was the only time we ever had to discipline anyone in the band like that.

The truck was on its way to Cincinnati as well as the other trucks carrying the stage and all the ClairShowco gear. They would arrive overnight and early in the morning the labor crew would begin the job of building the stage and preparing for the show again.

The ride to Cincinnati was short. About eighty-five miles and should have been just over ninety minutes. We pulled out of Lexington right at eleven. Jennifer and Jimmy hitched a ride on the Omega bus. Because of an accident on the interstate the trip took twice as long as planned. It was after two when we pulled into the U.S. Bank Arena parking lot. The stage was finished and the sound and lights were being line checked. That means the guys were testing all the connections to make sure they worked. All of our gear was onstage and ready.

Jennifer looked around for her band.

"I don't see them, Emmy. I hope nothing happened to them."

I looked around and spotted Chris Henry and Brian Vogel. "There they are, Jen."

"Oh, good! I was worried about the van. It's got so many miles on it. It seems like something needs to be repaired on it every week. I wish we could afford a new one."

She told me some stories about the van. She was still using the Dodge Grand Caravan I had seen in Carbondale. It didn't look all that great back then. I knew right then that Jennifer would get her wish. I didn't want my friend to be traveling around the country in an unsafe van. I called Andy and explained the situation. He called a dealership in Cincinnati. To make a long story short, we bought Jennifer a new van. Easy as pie.

Okay, it was a little more complicated than that, but Andy handled it. I didn't tell Jennifer about the van yet. I would tell her when it actually arrived if there was time, otherwise, I planned to mention it after her set. When the new van finally arrived there wasn't enough time to tell her. She was getting ready to go on stage. I had the guys park the van inside where I could show it to her as soon as she finished her set. I was so excited for her. As soon as she left the stage, I grabbed her.

"You need to come with me. I have to show you guys something."

"What is it, Em?"

"You'll see! I need all of you guys."

I took them downstairs and into the area where the trucks pulled into the building to be unloaded. The van was parked on the other side of a truck. I walked around the truck holding Jen's hand. I was a stinker and made her close her eyes. The guys in the band saw the van first.

"Oh, wow! Is that what I think it is?" Floyd said.

"You can open your eyes now, Jen."

She did and looked at the van, then at me. She looked back at the van.

"Do you still like the color white?"

"Yes, but I can't afford a new van, Emmy."

"I know that's why we got this one for you."

"What do you mean?"

Jen thought for a moment as I grinned.

"No! You didn't, Emmy. Tell me you didn't buy us a new van."

"Actually, Kenny and I bought it. Well technically it was Andy. I'll explain it later."

"I can't let you do that. I mean I appreciate the gesture but... Oh, Emmy! How can you afford to buy me a van?"

"Trust me, Jennifer. I can afford it. If it makes you feel better, I have a financial guardian angel who helped me and Diane. So now I'm helping you."

Kenny made more money than we could spend. Jennifer hugged me and let the tears flow.

"Emmy, you need to be getting ready."

"I'll be right there, Chase."

Jennifer stopped crying, and I let go of her.

"Somehow I will pay you back for this, Emmy. It make take forever, but I will pay you back."

By the time we started our set everyone in the band knew about the new van.

"I think I will tell the whole arena about the new van," Chase said.

327

"Don't you dare, Chase. Then I'll have to buy one for everybody, and I can't afford to do that."

"I won't say anything, Em."

I wasn't sure I liked the way Chase phrased that, but I knew him to be a man of his word. In the middle of our set Jennifer was brought out to sing with me. The band started playing softly as if it was background music. I looked at Chase wanting him to pick up the band. He smiled at me and shook his head. I tried to use my microphone but it was muted. I signaled to Stuart, but he ignored me. Now I knew what Chase meant. I slumped my shoulders and shook my head at him.

"Hi! My name is Jennifer Sinclaire, and I'm the singer for the band that opened the show."

The crowd cheered because they remember her. She waited until they settled down.

"My band and I have been traveling in an old Dodge Grand Caravan. It's got over three hundred thousand miles on it for which we are grateful. However lately it has been falling apart. To be truthful it was a hunk of junk. My band and I have been praying for a replacement for months. I just happened to mention our van trouble to a dear friend of mine and not two hours ago a brand new Honda Odyssey was delivered to us. Bought and paid for! I want to publicly thank God for answering our prayer."

The crowd cheered wildly as Jennifer raised her hand to the sky. I discovered that my microphone was working again. I made a face at Stuart, but he couldn't see from where he was.

"We should shout our praises to God for answering our prayers. Not just when we get something we want but even when he answers our prayer with a no. He always knows what is best for us so let's all stand and 'Shout To The Lord'."

Chase kicked the band into the intro and I began to sing. Jennifer joined in and most of the crowd sang along. We did most of the song again as I signaled Chase to

328

keep it going. More people joined in. It felt like the whole crowd of close to 15,000 people were on their feet singing and waving their arms above their head. As the song finished Jennifer hugged me. Her microphone was still on as Jennifer said, "Thank you for your generosity, Emmy."

"You're welcome, Jen."

After the concert Jennifer and the guys had a chance to really check out the new van.

"This thing has leather seats and a navigation center."

"These vans are supposed to be the best in the class."

"Who gets to drive it first?"

All the guys volunteered. Only Brian really liked to drive.

"I think Brian should have that privilege. He has driven the most miles in the old van," Jennifer suggested.

"Yeah! You're right, Jen. Let's let Brian drive first."

It didn't take too long to load the trailer and hook it up to the new van. Brian took it for a spin around the block.

"It handles like a race car with new tires!"

We hung out at the arena for a while and then caught a ride to the Millennium Hotel in downtown. Jennifer and I shared a room again.

"Are you going to ride in the van tomorrow or go with us on the bus?" I asked.

"I suppose I should ride on the bus, Emmy. After all, I will be riding in that van for many years to come."

"Plus there is that one guy who will be on the bus."

"There is that to consider!"

Jennifer and I giggled like teenage girls.

Okay, now let me explain about the van. I'm not Elvis! I don't give away cars and jewelry to strangers or on a whim. Jennifer had a real need, and Kenny and I are blessed financially. We could easily afford the price of the minivan. Especially after Andy negotiated it down a few grand. I felt the Holy Spirit leading me to buy the van for her. Nothing else. And just for the record, Jennifer did pay us back. Just a few days ago I got an email from her and Ryan. It was a sonogram. Is that the right word? You know, an ultrasound. Jen and Ryan are having a baby. A daughter. She said they already have a name picked out. They're going to name her Emmy Rose. Jennifer's grandmother was Rose. I think that's way better than a minivan.

Emmy paused and opened the email again. *It's about time you guys start a family.* She looked at the ultrasound and remembered the one that revealed she was carrying twins. She prayed for Ryan and Jennifer and then returned to her book.

The trucks were loaded and sent on to Indianapolis. This would be the last stop on the tour for Andy's team and the ClairShowco guys. The guys and I would be on our own for the last stop in Springfield.

Jennifer and I got up with the sun so she could see the new van. We threw on some clothes and ran outside.

"Do you still like it, Jen? Would you have rather had a different color?"

"No, I like white. It's easier to keep clean."

"Do you have to drive very often?"

"Not really. The guys don't trust me enough. Especially when we're pulling the trailer. If we're just driving around town, they will let me drive."

"Let's go see if anyone else is up. I'm not sure if we're going to have breakfast at the restaurant or go somewhere else."

I called Chase to see what the plans were.

"We're going to eat here, Emmy. If you and Jennifer are hungry, go ahead and eat. Just charge it to your room."

"Okay. Thanks, Chase. I'm sorry if I woke you up."

"I was awake, Em."

I don't think he was because he sure sounded groggy.

330

By eleven everyone had eaten and was ready for the short hop into Indianapolis. Jennifer warned the guys to be careful with the van.

"Just remember this one has to last even longer than the last one. Treat it with respect. I'll see you guys in a couple of hours."

"Does that mean we can't eat in the van?"

"You can eat in the van just try not to spill stuff everywhere and clean up the mess. Don't just toss it in the back and let it pile up."

Emmy closed her laptop and sat back in the recliner. *I remember that van. Jennifer and the guys used it for several years. Kenny's right about Hondas. They do last a long time, but they can be boring to drive.* She got up and set her laptop on the desk. She opened the blinds and stared out the window. *It's snowing again. I wonder how much we'll get this time.* She turned off the light as she left the den, but instead of going to bed, she walked into the mudroom. She grabbed her coat, put on a stocking cap and walked outside. She stood in the driveway and lifted her face to the sky. *I love feeling snowflakes on my face. I remember how much fun Kenny and I had building snowmen when we were kids.* She spun in a circle like a ballerina with her hands above her head while humming "Clair de Lune."

Suddenly, she staggered as something struck her in the chest. Again she felt something. She touched the front of her coat and felt something wet and cold.

"What are you doing out here, Em? Why aren't you in bed?" Kenny asked.

She looked at Kenny just as Tony threw another snowball at her. This one missed.

"What are you guys doing?"

"Tony and I went for a ride. We were sitting on the deck having a conversation when we heard you singing."

Emmy grinned. She bent down, smashed some snow together and threw it at Tony. "You're gonna get it."

Chapter Twenty-Nine

Emmy brought the kids to school Monday morning. She dropped them off at the door and then parked the van. She carried cupcakes into Ms. Redmon's classroom.

"Oh, thank you, Emmy." Ms. Redmon took the cupcakes. "Let's put these away. Do they need to be refrigerated?"

Emmy shook her head. "They weren't at the store."

"We will wait until this afternoon to have a party for the girls."

That afternoon Ms. Redmon stopped her normal routine to help celebrate another birthday. "This is a special day. We have two birthdays to celebrate..."

Emmy watched a few minutes later as the children ate their cupcakes and drank punch. *You are identical twins, but you are so different. You are almost like the two sides of a coin. Your personalities have been different from the start, but now they are even more.* She watched as Isabella cleaned up the crumbs from her cupcake while Heather ignored the mess. Emmy chuckled.

"What are you thinking, Em?" Kristen asked.

"They are so different yet they are so alike. Does that make any sense?"

"Totally. Which one is more like you at that age?"

Emmy shrugged. "Can't say. I see myself in both of them. I was shy and quiet around people like Isa, but I would be like Heather with my friends. Heather is fearless. She's not as much of a tomboy perhaps, but she's more physical than Isa."

"Definitely!" Kristen laughed. "She's more aggressive than Zach, and he's twice her size."

Emmy glanced around and then whispered, "I kinda dread when they reach puberty. Heather might turn out like me."

"Do you mean Diane?" Kristen knew about Diane's early sexual activity.

"No, me." Emmy bit her lip and didn't elaborate.

Kristen waited for Emmy to continue and then realized she wouldn't. "Aren't you glad the kids are in a Christian school? We could never do this in a public school. Too many rules."

"I am grateful." Emmy thought about her grade school only a couple of blocks from her childhood home and named for Kenny's grandfather, Robert T. Colwell. *You will never know how grateful I am for this school.*

Emmy talked to Denise later that afternoon.

"So I should include something about my childhood, huh?"

"Yes!" Denise exclaimed. "You want to personalize your story. Think of something that maybe no one knows about, or something that meant a lot to you."

"I might know just the thing, Denise. Thanks for your help. I really appreciate it."

"You're welcome. Let's get together again soon. I want to read more of your story." Denise ended the call.

"Kenny, would you might watching the kids until dinner? I really need to work on something."

"No problem, Em." Kenny looked up from his recliner. "Heather suggested pizza. Could we order out?"

"Sounds like a plan to me. Thanks."

Emmy locked herself in the den and opened her laptop.

I remember a pleasant spring day when I was nine-years-old. I was playing at the park over by the school by myself. There were a couple of little kids with their mothers, so I wasn't completely alone. Anyway, I was having fun, and these two older boys appeared out of nowhere. I didn't pay any attention to them at first, but they walked over to me and started asking questions. They wanted to know where I lived, my name and stuff like that. I told them my name, but not where I lived. They were quite a bit bigger than me, and I was scared of them. I thought about running home or over to where the mothers were sitting, but one of the boys grabbed my arm. He squeezed it hard enough to hurt and pulled me over to a bench on the opposite side of the park from the little kids. The taller boy began to talk about some stuff that I didn't understand. You get the picture? I remember wrapping my arms around my knees on the bench. I closed my eyes and felt a hand on me. I think I started crying, and then I heard someone yell. I opened my eyes in time to see Rory Porter yanking both boys off of the bench. I will never forget the look on his face as he pounded these two bigger boys with his fists and he kicked them. Within a few seconds those boys ran away like rabbits. Rory sat beside me and used his shirt to dry my face. We really didn't say anything to each other but we sat there for a few minutes. Then he took my hand and walked me home.

A couple of weeks later, those boys came back with two other friends. They beat the crap out of Rory. I wasn't there, but I learned about from someone at school. I talked to Rory about it, and he shrugged it off as no big deal. I wish I could say he didn't retaliate, but he did. Over the summer he sought out those boys, and took them on one at a time. Rory never lost another fight in his life.

Maybe you can understand a little better the special relationship I have with him. I confess that sometimes I have wondered what would have happened if he hadn't left SoHam that year. Kenny was gone most of the time during my last years of high school. Rory disappeared in my junior year, and I didn't see him for years. I found out what happened from his mother, so I knew where he lived. Not his address, but I knew the state. Would things have turned out differently? Maybe. Maybe not. God has a plan for our lives, and His plan for me was to be with Kenny. It took a while for me to realize that, but I don't regret it.

Emmy closed her eyes and sat back. She let the tears flow down her cheeks for a moment. Then she opened her eyes wiped away her tears, double clicked a folder, opened a JPEG file and stared at it. *I think I was fourteen when someone took this.* In the photo she stood in front of Rory while looking over her shoulder at him. He had his hands on her shoulders with his head turned to the side. *I wonder who he was looking at. Probably some girl.*

334

"Mommy!" Heather hollered from outside the door. "It's locked. I want to see you."

Emmy closed her laptop, got up and opened the door.

"Mommy! What do you want on your pizza? I want pepperoni, but Isa wants mushrooms. I don't want mushrooms. They're yucky." Heather folded her arms across her chest. "Are you all right, Mommy?"

"I am fine, sweetie. Maybe we should order two pizzas," Emmy suggested.

They walked into the kitchen and saw Kenny and Isabella. Emmy walked up behind Kenny and wrapped her arms around his waist.

He glanced back over his shoulder. "You okay, Em?"

"Perfectly! Have I told you how much I love you lately?"

Kenny spun around and rubbed his jaw. "Not that I remember."

"Well, I do. I love you very much, m'lord." She pulled his face down to hers and kissed him.

Heather and Isabella looked at each other and giggled.

"We can have pepperoni," Isabella said.

Heather shrugged, "I can pick off the mushrooms, Isa."

Before going to bed a few hours later, Emmy read a chapter she had written the day before.

"We're ready to roll out, Emmy."

"Thanks, Buck."

Since hearing about the misfortune that befell the band that was supposed to open for us in Lexington, I started each trip with a prayer.

"Dear Lord, please grant us a safe journey so that we might be able to sing for you. Amen."

"Emmy, are you trying to lay a good old fashioned Catholic guilt trip on God?" Adam asked.

"Why do you think that?"

"Because you make it sound like it will be God's fault if something happens, and if he wants his word spread then he better take care of us."

"I don't intend to do that but if it works."

I felt a little guilty that I didn't start each journey with a prayer before the fire happened to the other band's bus. Better late than never, I guess.

"What are you going to wear tonight, Emmy?"

"I don't know yet. I'll have to see what's clean."

"You mean you haven't done your laundry! Shame on you, Emmy."

"No wonder it smells so funny in here. It's Emmy's dirty clothes."

"Do they always tease you this much, Emmy?" Jimmy laughed while he smiled at me.

"Oh, we're just getting started, Jimmy," Boyd said.

I rolled my eyes to show them how immature they were. "Yes, they are impossible sometimes."

"They are just like my band. At least you have a bedroom to escape to." Jennifer thought about what she said. "Emmy, I didn't mean to sound ungrateful because you travel in a bus and I travel in a van. I love my new van."

"I didn't take it that way at all, Jen. I know you are grateful for the van. I'm grateful that God has blessed Kenny and I so we were able to help you."

The guys looked at each other and grinned. I kinda knew what they were going to say.

"Emmy, can I have a new car. My old one has over thirty thousand miles, and it needs new brakes."

"Emmy, I need a new boat. Mine is only forty feet long and it's too slow. I need one of those huge yachts."

"Don't listen to those guys, Emmy. They can get by with what they have. I, on the other hand, desperately need a new Lear jet."

I shook my head. "And what do you need, Bobby?"

He thought about it a few seconds. "I could use a new bicycle. My old one is rusty."

"Listen to Bobby. He's just trying to get on Emmy's good side. Don't listen to him, Em. He wants something expensive, too."

"He'd ask for a car, but he doesn't has his driver's license," Ryan teased.

I looked at Jennifer and shrugged my shoulders. "At least I will be home by Sunday morning. You are stuck with your band all year long."

The trip to Conseco Fieldhouse was uneventful, which was a good thing, and everyone arrived on time. Brian drove the new van and stayed behind the two buses. Once again the work crews had done their job and the stage and gear were ready to go. After the soundchecks Jennifer took me, Jimmy and Ryan for a ride around the city of Indianapolis.

Jennifer was a happy camper as she took the stage. She considered herself very fortunate to have her band on stage with her and a new van in which to travel. She felt relaxed and it showed in her performance. Jimmy and I watched from a spot off stage out of sight of the crowd.

I moved close to him and shouted in his ear. "Jennifer sounds more at ease tonight. Probably because she has her band back."

"She's not playing her guitar on every song either. She's moving around and getting the crowd more involved. I wonder where she might have picked up that little trick. Do you have any guess, Emmy?" He leaned close and talked right into my ear.

I could feel his lips brush against my ear. "What do you mean?"

"She has been watching and learning from you."

"Do I do that?"

Jimmy looked at me. "You don't even know exactly what you do onstage, do you?"

"Most of the time I do, but sometimes... I just let God take over."

Jennifer finished her set and ran off stage and over to us.

I hugged her. "That was great, Jen!"

"Thanks, Emmy. I just felt better. I didn't have so

337

many thoughts running through my head so I was able to focus better."

"Jen, I think maybe you should get back out there." Jimmy pointed to the stage where her band was waving at her.

Jennifer realized the crowd actually wanted more.

"Come with me, Emmy! You can use Brian's microphone."

"What are we gonna sing?"

Jennifer hollered out the name of a song as she pulled me with her. I didn't even think about the fact I was wearing old jeans and a Fridays At Five t-shirt. I sang with Jennifer, and only the fans close enough to the stage even recognized me. We did one more song and then ran off of the stage.

"Thank you for everything, Emmy. Not just the van but letting me join you guys on tour and for showing me how to be a better performer but most importantly, a better person."

Jennifer hugged me and squeezed hard.

"I can't breathe, Jen!"

"Sorry, Emmy. I forgot how tiny you are."

Someone from one of the local radio stations walked out on stage and did about a ten minute plug for Compassion International. Then the crew got the stage ready for me and the guys.

The Only Hope took the stage to do a couple of songs, and then I came out to thunderous applause. Not really. I just put that there to see if you were paying attention. I'm talking about Kenny, in case you couldn't tell. He gets thunderous applause. I get polite clapping if I'm lucky. No, that's wrong. I hate false modesty. I won't lie to you. I get goosebumps whenever I hear the crowd hollering at me. I feed off of it. I suppose it goes with the job. You have to have some kind of ego to perform in front of people. I would pray for the wisdom to know I was just a conduit for God's word. At least I always tried to be.

Boyd and Perry loved the openness of our stage. They had a ramp which enabled them to run all the way around the back of the stage. They took advantage of their wireless rigs and roamed around during the songs. Adam was handling more of the harmony vocals so that freed Boyd and Perry. That was important tonight because there were people sitting behind the stage.

Maybe I should describe our stage arrangement. Even though Chase was playing with us, we still used our regular positions on stage. Since I'm the lead singer, my microphone is in the front center of the stage. I always use a wireless Shure SM58. To be honest, when I first started I couldn't tell the difference. Now I can. Whoever is running the sound knows how to set the EQ on my microphone and the SM58 gives them a consistency. No, I'm not getting paid to plug Shure mics. They are as reliable as a hammer. Sure, there are more expensive mics out there, and we use them in the studio, but for live performances, I'll take a 58 any day. We all use IEMs, but there are floor monitors, too. The drum riser is in the middle behind me and wherever possible we use smaller risers for Adam and Ryan. Adam has streamlined his keyboard gear. Most nights he uses two keyboards, and I'll have to ask him what models they are. One is a Yamaha. I think the other is a Roland. He also uses an old Korg thing at times. He knows exactly which setting to use to get the right sound. Since Chase was here, he was across from Adam on a riser where Ryan would normally be. Ryan could roam around if he wanted since he's wireless, but he usually stays by Bobby so they can communicate visually. Tonight he kinda wandered around more than normal. He would be back by Bobby and then walk over to Adam and Chase. There are two guitar players in the band. Three really. Adam can play guitar too and he does occasionally. Boyd Goldman is to my right and Perry Johnstone on my left. Just the way we've always done it. No particular reason that I know of. They use Shure wireless rigs and are free to roam around except when they have to sing harmony. I'm the one who runs around the stage the most. I can't stand still. Oh, another thing. I never, never use prerecorded tracks for my vocals. You can tell because sometimes I run around so much I get out of breath. The guys know how to cover for me if that happens. A lot of times the crowd is singing so loud, it doesn't matter if I sing or not. I consider myself very fortunate to have three guys who are great singers in their own right. Four when Chase is along. Once in a while this other guy comes along and plays guitar and tries to sing, but the guys running sound know to keep his microphone at a really low level. He tries, but... you know.

Tonight Chase and I switched things around a bit. We started off slower with some of the well known worship songs we do. The crowd sang along, and I was almost moved to tears at times because of the presence of the Lord that filled the arena. Jennifer came out to sing 'Shout To The Lord' and 'Yolanda's Song' with me. From there we picked up the pace. For the rest of the set we rocked it. All concerts are loud. If you went to hear a string quartet, they would be loud. We are no exception. At church we keep the sound pressure level down to just over a hundred decibels, or just under. I can't remember. I should ask Stuart about it. In a place like this, we crank it up. We 'tear the roof off the sucker' so to speak. That's a song. I can't remember who sings it. Since this was the last night for Jennifer and her band to be with us, I brought them out for the last song. For over eight minutes we played 'I Will Be True To You' as the crowd sang. There was no encore tonight.

We headed backstage, and I was wiped out. I felt so gross and yucky from sweating like a pig. I wanted to take a shower in the worst way, but I had to wait.

"Emmy, you guys were awesome tonight. The change in the set was just perfect." Jennifer tried to hug me but I held her away and explained why. She understood.

340

"Chase suggested it and it did work out nicely."

"Did you guys hear Bobby singing?" Ryan asked.

"No, why? Was he really singing?"

"Not into a microphone, but I was standing next to him most of the time and he was actually singing. He sounded good."

I walked up to him and poked him in the chest. "Is that true, Bobby? Were you actually singing?"

"Yeah, so."

"We didn't know you could sing. Why haven't you sung before tonight?"

"No one ever asked me to sing. I never told anyone I couldn't sing."

"Do you want to sing?"

"I would like to sometime. I like playing the drums, but maybe I can sing something sometime."

"Maybe we can figure something out. You wanna sing tomorrow night? It will be a smaller crowd."

"That might be harder."

"Oh, so you only want to sing in front of thousands of people. Maybe thousands of teenage girls, perhaps!"

"That would be awesome!" Bobby grinned.

"Ain't gonna happen." I shook my head and walked away.

I managed to sneak away and shower. I changed into comfy jeans and a t-shirt. I remembered to wear my pass because I didn't look like I belonged. Jimmy saw me and wanted to sit with me while we ate. I let him, but a couple of times I needed to remind him about Kenny.

After grabbing a bite to eat, Jennifer and her band loaded up their trailer. They had about a six hour trip ahead of them to get home to Knoxville. I followed them outside.

"Jimmy, I must say it was a real pleasure to meet you and see you again. I'm sorry I was such a diva."

"You are hilarious sometimes, Emmy. Jennifer is lucky to have met you."

"I hope the van works out all right for her. By the

way, what did they do with the old one?"

"Brian and Ted found a junkyard that would give them three hundred dollars for it, so they took the offer. It needed a thousand dollars in repairs just to make it home to Knoxville. Your timing was perfect, Emmy."

"I think it was the Lord's timing, Jimmy."

"You are right, Emmy. We sometimes forget that He knows what is best for us."

Ryan was talking to Jennifer, so Jimmy and I let them have a few minutes together. The guys in the bands were saying their goodbyes. They had become friends in the short time they were together. I noticed Ryan kissing Jennifer and she smiled. They seem to be meant for each other. Jennifer looked over at me and we walked toward each other.

"I will miss you so much, Emmy!"

"I will miss you more, Jen. We can stay in touch by email and maybe Skype once in a while. I have a feeling that we will run into each other again. Who knows what the future will hold for us."

"We've gotta go. The guys are anxious to get home."

Jennifer hugged me and this time I didn't mind being squeezed too hard. I even let Jimmy hug me and then I headed to the bus.

A little while later Chase clapped his hands to get everyone's attention. "All right, guys! It's time to move out. The days of being pampered rock stars are over. We have one more stop and we are on our own. No more fancy arenas or sound companies or dozens of roadies. It's up to us."

"We can handle it, Mr. Chase. We have been getting lazy the last few days. We are ready to work hard."

"Thank you, Jess. I know you and Joe are always willing to do whatever it takes to get the job done. We appreciate that. I know you all are anxious to get home. I know I am."

"Are we forgetting anyone?" Nelson asked.

Chase and Belinda looked around to make sure everyone was accounted for.

"Where is Emmy? Has anyone seen Emmy lately?"

"Is she on the bus already?"

"I think I saw her get on the bus a few minutes ago, Chase."

"Come on, Belinda." Nelson said. "Let's check the bus. The rest of you guys look around. Jess and Joe will you stay here in case she comes back."

"We will, Mr. Nelson."

Nelson and Belinda checked the Omega bus to see if I was on board. The bedroom door was open and Belinda looked inside. It was empty, so Belinda checked the bunks.

"Nelson, be quiet but come and look at this!" she waved.

Nelson moved quietly and peered into my bunk. He saw me curled up and sound asleep.

"I'll go tell everyone Emmy is safe and sound."

Belinda reached in and placed a blanket over me. I didn't wake up or even move. I was totally zonked. I'm glad I don't snore.

"Did you find Miss Emmy?" Jess asked Nelson.

"Yes, she's asleep on the bus."

"That's a relief! I would be heartbroken if anything ever happened to Miss Emmy."

"I know you would, Joe. We should let everyone know Emmy is on the bus already."

Everyone returned from their search and Nelson told them I was sleeping.

"Shoot!" Bobby exclaimed. "I guess that means we can't party all night long tonight."

"When have you ever done that?" Ryan asked.

Bobby shrugged and said, "Well, never, I guess but I thought we might tonight."

"You are a doofus sometimes."

"No, I'm not."

Chase rolled his eyes. "Okay, let's get this show on

343

the road. Everybody on board."

"Springfield! Here we come." Bobby ran for the bus.

"See what I mean? You are a doofus," Ryan hollered.

Springfield was about four hours away. We would arrive early in the morning if all went well. Larry knew a travel center where we could park and stay until noon which was the time Chase arranged to meet with the pastor of the church.

One note of explanation. Nelson and Belinda were using the bedroom on the Omega bus. My old bedroom. They were having a difficult time riding the Alpha bus because the crew was rowdy. I suggested they use the bedroom because they were the only married couple on the tour. Well, Chase and I were married, but our spouses were back at home. I didn't mind sleeping in a bunk. The guys didn't care one way or another. They treated me like a little sister most of the time. A bratty little sister Bobby reminded me once. They did tone it down with Chase around, but they still teased me a lot. It made sense to have the whole band together. We could rehearse and go over any changes to the set list. So, six people in the band. I'm counting on my fingers. Chase and Stuart Lederer took the other two bunks. Remember, Skip and Bruce had been sent home. Whatever. Denise, please help me!

Chapter Thirty

With school in session Emmy had the opportunity to work on her book again. She skimmed her journals for a time, and then sat at the desk. She read an entry about Larry Twilley. *I remember the night he helped that lady change a flat tire and then refused to accept any money. I need to write about him.* She sat at the desk and thought for a moment. Then she smiled and began to write.

There is a group of guys that are invaluable to any tour. The drivers. We take them for granted, but they are responsible for getting us from one gig to the next, and they do a great job. Thanks, guys.

Larry Twilley and his crew of drivers did a fantastic job of making sure the buses and trucks arrived safely and on time at our destination every day. They pulled into the Griffin Brothers Travel Center a few minutes after five. Everyone was asleep except for the drivers. They headed inside to the restaurant and ordered coffee and breakfast.

"Larry, do you ever drink anything besides hot coffee?"

"Sure! Sometimes I drink iced coffee."

"I would hate to be your stomach."

"Have you come up with a schedule for the next couple weeks?"

"Yeah, I hooked Buck and Sutton up with this band from Milwaukee. They're heading west for a month long trip."

Larry had assignments for all the guys. His business was growing, and he was able to keep all six drivers busy for the next few months. I know all of this because I talked to him and inquired.

"How is Leonard doing?" In case you don't know, Leonard Twilley is the legendary driver for Fridays At Five. Even when they fly to gigs, Leonard is there to drive a truck or something.

"He's doing better. The doctors told him to slow down and cut out the crappy food."

345

"Do you think he will?"

"Not a chance! He's too bull-headed and more stubborn than a Missouri mule."

"And you're just like your father." I grinned.

After breakfast the drivers spent the rest of the morning in the driver's lounge killing time. They spent many hours doing just that.

Back on the buses everyone slept late. They were all wiped out. No one got up before nine thirty except me. I got up early and did my morning run. Nelson and Belinda woke up, showered and got dressed. By the time they finished, all of the guys on the Omega bus were up. Belinda stayed in the bedroom making phone calls and checking her email. She didn't like being around the guys in the morning because they were... guys. I didn't mind.

"Morning, guys. Everybody get a good night of sleep?" I asked.

"Not too bad. I miss Hank's snoring though," Chase said. With Nelson handling the tour manager duties, Chase could relax and just be one of the guys.

"I think I heard Emmy snoring last night," Bobby teased.

"I don't snore!" I smacked his good arm. "Good morning, Adam. Are you awake yet?"

"I don't think so. I need some coffee."

Nelson walked through the lounge area. "You guys need to get ready. We are supposed to be at the church at noon."

"Do you have any idea how far away we are?" I asked.

"Larry told me we are about thirty minutes from the church. It's 10:21 now. You guys know how long it takes to get ready, so I'll see you later. We need to pull out by 11:30."

I assumed my role of drill sergeant and rousted the guys into action. Then I headed to the restaurant. The guys could get ready without worrying about me being around.

It only took twenty-eight minutes to get to the church on Shaler Road. Chase, Nelson and Stuart hopped off of the bus, walked inside and were greeted by the pastor.

"You must be Chase Hillman. I'm Pastor Frank Hanson. Did you have a safe trip over here?"

"I am and we had a good trip. We were in Indianapolis last night. We stopped at the Travel Center outside of town." Chase introduced Nelson and Stuart and Pastor Hanson shook their hands.

"I'm sorry to leave you, but I need to make an unexpected pastoral call."

"I understand. Is there someone here who could show us where to unload our gear?"

"My associate is in the building somewhere. He can show you everything you need. I should be back in about an hour. You guys are probably hungry."

"We will be after we unload and set up. The guys all like to eat."

"We will take good care of you in that regard."

They found Pastor Jacob Nordyke. He looked like an Amish guy because he had a big bushy beard. Are Amish the ones who don't shave? I'll have to look it up. Anyway, he showed them where to unload and answered all their questions about the church. Pastor Jacob showed Stuart Lederer their recently updated tech booth.

"Very nice. Someone has put a lot of thought into the selection of gear."

"Thank you. Do you guys need any assistance setting up?"

"Thanks, but we can handle it. Would it be all right if one of our guys takes a look at your light desk?"

"Certainly! I know we have the lights programmed for Sunday already. I think Myles is here somewhere. He can show you more than I can."

Stuart and Tobias met Myles. Myles looked like the typical computer geek. He wore thick glasses and had one of those pocket protector things in his shirt pocket. He showed Stuart and Tobias the cues they had programmed. Stuart only needed a few minutes to become familiar with the light desk. He explained it to Tobias who would operate the lights manually so he didn't mess up any of the cues. It is an easy task for him. Oh, Tobias Wouters is now the FOH mixer for my current band. Back then he was one of the crew, but he stuck with it and now is responsible for my sound design. He actually has a college degree in that field.

Cecil Parrmeister moved the truck into position. After the crew guys got what they would need for later off of the Alpha bus, the drivers commandeered it for a few hours of sleep. I could never survive on the sleep those guys get. A few hours now and maybe a few more later. I wouldn't last a week, but those guys do it all the time. We paid them a bonus after we got home.

The Zawaski brothers and the crew soon had everything unloaded, brought into the sanctuary and up and running.

"Who needs all those roadies and union labor guys?" Jess pushed a stack of travel cases into the church.

"We might if we were building a stage and setting up all the lights," Joe admitted.

"We could handle it now," Jess said.

I heard their conversation before I took off for my run. "We might need a couple more guys, Jess."

"We do have a couple cousins who live in Cleveland, Miss Emmy."

I grinned. "You might have to give them a call for the next tour."

Pastor Hanson returned from his meeting.

"I'm sorry I had to rush out so quick."

"It's okay. We understand. I hope everything is all right."

"Yes. One of our young couples is having some difficulties. Are you folks ready to eat?"

"If you give us maybe thirty minutes, we should be

348

ready to go. Emmy and one of the guys are out somewhere getting in their daily run."

"I'm anticipating meeting her. My daughter Hannah was playing one of your CDs at home. She has a lovely voice."

"Yes, but she doesn't realize it. I think you might be surprised when you meet her."

Ryan and I returned from our run and got ready to grab an early dinner. Chase found Pastor Frank and let him know.

"Are you guys ready to eat?" Pastor Hanson asked.

"Yes, we're ready. Is there somewhere you would recommend?"

"There is a nice place about a mile away," Pastor Hanson paused. "Unfortunately, we don't have any way of getting everyone there."

"Oh, don't worry about that. Does this place have somewhere close where we could park the bus?"

"Yes. They have an area out back where trucks often park. Let me give them a quick call. How many people are going?"

Chase made a quick calculation. "Fifteen all together. The drivers and some of the other guys are catching up on their sleep. Seventeen, I guess counting yourself and Pastor Jacob."

"This place has a nice buffet if that appeals to anyone."

"I think the restaurant will lose money on our crew. The younger guys can eat a lot."

"I think they are used to healthy appetites around here."

We piled into the bus and Chase had to drive since the drivers were still sleeping. He had driven buses before and had the proper license. I tried to talk him into letting me drive, but he wouldn't. Most everyone was sitting in the lounge area, but Ryan, Bobby and myself had taken over the bedroom to play a game of hearts. We would often play card games to kill time. Pastor Frank looked around but didn't see any females except Belinda, so he assumed she was me. He didn't have an opportunity to talk to her though. Pastor Jacob sat up front with Chase to give him the directions to the Country Kitchen Buffet. Once inside everyone decided to have the buffet. The restaurant didn't have a table, or an area, large enough to accommodate all of us, so we were scattered at three different tables. The two local pastors sat with Chase, Nelson and Belinda. I grabbed a seat with Ryan, Bobby, Boyd, Perry and Adam close to the wall. The rest of the guys chose a table between the other two.

"How long have you been together?" Pastor Hanson asked.

Nelson assumed Pastor Hanson was asking about he and Belinda since he was looking at the two of them. "We met at college with one of the college sponsored outreach groups. We have been together ever since we graduated."

"So you are used to traveling then."

"I suppose," Nelson answered.

I saw Pastor Hanson looking at us, so I told the guys to cool it. They had been teasing me and Bobby about something.

"Now who are those kids at the table closest to the wall?" Pastor Hanson asked.

"Those kids are the members of The Only Hope," Chase answered and assumed Pastor Hanson understood who we were. "We plan to do two forty-five minute sets with a break in between."

"So all together, counting the break, it will be around two hours. Correct?"

"Yes, if you feel that is too long we can always cut it back."

"I don't think that will be too long. I expect most of the crowd to be young people. We probably won't have a lot of senior citizens in the crowd. Although, we do have some seniors who are here every time the doors are open."

"We have a few of those at our home church, too," Chase said with a chuckle.

"Every church needs prayer warriors, and we go out of our way to take care of our seniors."

"We will try not to get too loud tonight."

"Oh, don't worry about that." Pastor Hanson waved a hand. "Some of our seniors are almost stone deaf. They wouldn't hear it if a jet took off from the parking lot."

"We'll keep that in mind."

Chase watched the guys going back for more food. He watched as Bobby came back to the table with all desserts on his plate. Chase shook his head as Bobby grinned. Some of the desserts were for me.

After a few minutes Pastor Jacob mentioned to Chase, "I really like that song you sing about the young girl who was killed."

"'Yolanda's Song.' Emmy helped lead her to Christ just before she was killed and her friend wrote that song the night..." Chase paused. "I should let Emmy tell you the story later tonight."

Both of the local pastors nodded at Belinda.

Pastor Hanson noticed me sitting next to Ryan. "What does the young girl sitting at the other table do? She and the young man sitting next to her seem to share a family resemblance. Is she his younger sister by any chance?"

Chase frowned at us because we were getting loud. "No, Emmy is older than Ryan, and they aren't brother and sister."

"So you have two Emmys in the group."

Chase, Nelson and Belinda looked confused.

"No, we just have one Emmy. That's more than enough," Chase said and then laughed.

Now both the pastors look confused. Belinda noticed and began to smile.

"Chase, I think we have another case of mistaken identity."

"I don't understand." Pastor Hanson tilted his head.

Pastor Nordyke rubbed his beard.

Belinda tried to explain. "I am Belinda Grapella, Nelson's wife. The young lady at the other table is Emmy Colasanti."

Pastor Hanson pointed a finger at me. I saw that and figured I was in trouble for goofing around.

"But... but... but she looks like a kid! I assumed you were the singer."

"She gets that a lot," Nelson replied.

Chase hollered over to the other table.

"Emmy! Would you please stop what you guys are doing and come here."

"You're in trouble now for sure, Em," Bobby teased.

I smacked his shoulder, told him to stuff it somewhere private and walked over to Chase. "They started it. I was just minding my own business."

"You aren't in trouble yet, young lady. I just want to introduce you to Pastor Hanson and Pastor Nordyke."

"Hello, I'm pleased to meet you. Thank you for inviting us into your church. I pray that we can be a blessing to someone tonight." Something like that anyway. My normal speaking voice has been described as childlike on occasion, and right then I happened to have something going on with my throat, so I'm sure I sounded like a kid. That coupled with Chase disciplining me, the braids in my hair, the jeans and t-shirt I wore made me appear totally adolescent. I turned a deep shade of red.

"I'm sure you will be."

"You can go back to your table, but I'm keeping an eye on you, young lady."

"Yes, Daddy," I said to get back at Chase.

Both pastors looked at Chase and then watched as I walked back to my table. The guys were pointing at me and laughing. So I did what came naturally, I stuck out my tongue and smacked whoever I could reach.

"She's not really my daughter," Chase explained. "She just likes to tease everyone, and we tease her back.

352

How old do you think she is?"

This was in late July after my twenty-fourth birthday.

"She looks a bit younger than my daughter Hannah. Hannah is a freshman in college and just turned nineteen, so I would guess she is seventeen."

Pastor Nordyke shook his head. "But that young man sitting next to her is younger. Remember, Pastor Frank?"

"I forgot about that, Jacob," Pastor Hanson said. He looked at me and smiled. "I give up. I have no clue. How old is Emmy?"

"She had her twenty-fourth birthday earlier this month," Chase said as he grinned.

"Amazing! I'm sure I'm not the first person to be fooled by her appearance."

"You aren't. It happens almost every night."

"I'm sorry for making the wrong assumption."

"That's quite all right. I think you will be amazed even more when you hear and see Emmy tonight."

At times it bothered me that I looked so young. I was married, earned good money and didn't blow it the way some people my age did. I didn't help matters by wearing faded jeans and t-shirts and acting like a teenager. I suppose I will be thankful when I get older. Of course, I might actually look old then.

Anyway, Pastor Hanson was amazed when he heard me. He told me that after the concert. At first I wasn't sure if he meant it as a compliment or not. The band had gone back to our roots and played as if we were in our own church. I still danced around but not as much as in the big arenas. The whole group didn't feel the need to perform tonight. Chase talked to the crowd for a few minutes at the conclusion of the service. I went to the large foyer and talked to people for close to an hour. I signed some autographs and had my picture taken with teenage girls, as usual. When the crowd thinned out the guys started loading out the gear. The truck and buses were soon loaded, and we were ready to head home. Everyone was anxious to get back to their families, or in some cases just back to their own place. I admit I needed to sleep with my husband. Hey! We were still newlyweds.

Kenny walked up behind Emmy later that night and rubbed her shoulders. "They are asleep. Got time to do something?"

Emmy closed her book and grinned over her shoulder. "Always."

"Good. I've been messing around with that track, and I think I have the perfect solution."

Emmy let her shoulders slump. "Oh, that's nice."

"Come with me, and I'll play it for you."

She followed him to the basement and took a seat in the studio control room.

"Listen to the difference." Kenny played the track twice. "Do you hear it?"

"I can hear the difference. What did you do?"

Kenny spent several minutes explaining the technical details.

"I just got that plug-in and it works great."

"Is that track finished now?"

"I'm satisfied with it. We really should finish in the next couple of weeks if you want this CD to be out before summer."

"I'm willing to work on it during the day."

"I think this is going to be your best CD ever, Em."

"It's certainly been the most difficult to finish."

Chapter Thirty-One

Emmy sipped her coffee and listened as Diane left a message on the landline.

"I know you're home, and I'm coming over in five minutes. We are going to Sunrise Garden to spent time with our mother. No excuses! You are coming with me."

Emmy drained her coffee and set the mug in the sink. *Shoot! I've been putting it off and I feel guilty. I know I should go see Mom, but what if she doesn't remember me?*

Diane arrived and honked the horn. Emmy walked outside and got in.

"We don't have to stay long, Em. She doesn't like deviations in her routine." Diane waited until Emmy had fastened her seatbelt before heading down the driveway. "Why do you have barrettes in your hair. It makes you look like a kid. No wonder Mom still thinks you're in high school. Can't you wear something besides old jeans and that old army coat."

"Sorry, but my hair is a mess, and this is a new old army coat. I like it. It's comfy and keeps me warm." Emmy removed the barrettes, put them in a pocket and stuffed her hands in the pockets of the coat. "Happy now?"

Diane shook her head.

They arrived at Sunrise Garden and took the elevator to the second floor. Diane keyed in the code and they walked down the hall to their mother's apartment. Diane knocked and they entered. Patricia Colasanti sat in her chair staring at the TV and didn't acknowledge their presence for a moment.

"Good morning, Mom. How are you today?" Diane stood in front of her mother but didn't block her line of sight to the TV. Emmy stood behind Diane.

"You're my daughter. I need to eat breakfast soon. I'm getting hungry."

Diane pulled on Emmy's arm. "Don't hide behind me."

"I'm not hiding," Emmy insisted.

"Mom, it will be time for lunch in about an hour. Look! Emmy came to see you." Diane pushed Emmy closer.

"Hi, Mom. How are you feeling?"

"I'm hungry. Why aren't you in school? Isn't this a school day?"

"It's Wednesday, Mom, but I don't go to school anymore. I graduated already."

Patricia stared at Emmy for a moment and then shifted her attention to Diane. "I wrote a letter to my sister, but I don't have any stamps. Will you take it to the post office for me?"

"I'll take care of it, Mom. Aunt Betty will be thrilled to hear from you."

Emmy bit her lip. *Aunt Betty's been dead for almost a year.* Emmy glanced up at Diane. *I guess it doesn't matter.*

"How has the food been, Mom?" Diane asked.

"Pretty good, but I don't leave a tip. I don't have any money."

"That's all right. You don't need to leave a tip," Diane explained. "The carpet looks nice. Have you been using your Bissell Sweeper?"

"I use it every day." Mom pointed at the sweeper. "I even use it in the hallway."

"That's good. It keeps you in shape."

Mom stood up. "I need to eat lunch now. You better go home, and make sure your sister goes to school tomorrow. I know she's not old enough to be out of school, but I used to skip days, too."

Diane and Emmy left. "Now that wasn't so bad, was it?" Diane pulled out of the parking lot. "A few minutes is all it takes, and you won't have to feel guilty about not going to see her."

"I don't feel guilty," Emmy insisted.

Diane looked at her and laughed. "The hell you don't."

"Fine! I feel guilty, but why should I go? She doesn't remember."

"The nurse suggested we visit more often but keep the visits short. Make it part of Mom's routine."

"I'll try, Diane. Once I finish the book, I'll have more time."

"How's the book going, anyway? Are you ever going to let anyone read it?"

"It's about finished. The first draft at least, and no one can read it until it's done."

Diane dropped Emmy off. "Thanks for going with me, Em."

"Let me know when you're going back."

"You can go by yourself, you know."

Emmy shook her head. "No way! That place freaks me out. See ya." Emmy walked into the house. She fixed herself a sandwich, plopped down in her recliner in the den and opened her laptop.

It was three in the morning on Monday when we arrived at the church. Three hours ahead of the time I told Kenny we would arrive. Most of the guys had parked their cars at the church. Some were giving each other rides. I didn't know if I should call Kenny. No one really lived close to the Timberline Heights neighborhood area where we lived. The guesthouse in Bristol Ridge was close to being finished, but we hadn't moved yet.

"Do you need a ride Emmy?" Chase asked.

"I told Kenny we were arriving around six. I hate to call him and wake him up so early. I could just wait in the church."

"Don't be silly, Emmy. I can give you a ride."

"Are you sure, Chase? I know you want to get home to see your girls."

"They will be asleep. We won't see them until morning anyway. Get in and I'll give you a lift. That way you can surprise Kenny."

"Okay, thanks, Chase."

I knew the perfect way to surprise Kenny, and I think Chase knew it too. Chase dropped me off, and helped me unload my luggage. I did have to take some clothes with me on tour. I couldn't wear the same thing every night although it would have been easier. We dumped my suitcases and backpack in the kitchen. I thanked Chase, and he grinned at me and left. I ran upstairs and into the bedroom. Kenny was sound asleep. I undressed in record time and climbed in next to him. I cuddled up close, and he wrapped his arm around me. He realized I was there and reacted the way any guy would. In fifteen minutes I was happy and sound asleep.

Emmy leaned back and stretched her arms over her head. *I remember that night, and I remember how Chase teased me the next time I saw him. I should email him. The worship team isn't the same without those guys.* She scratched her nose and read her journal for a few minutes before she started writing again.

I left out a tour I did with The Only Hope back in February through May of 2004. It wasn't a real tour because we only played on Friday and Saturday nights. The gigs were fairly close, so we didn't have to spend hours and hours on the road. That's good because we traveled in a large van and pulled a trailer behind us. I was still finishing up my degree at North Park College. That's why we only traveled on the weekend. I would finish class on Friday morning, and we would drive to the gig. I should confess that these gigs were different. We didn't play in churches at all. Prater-Saylor booked us into small clubs to expand our fan base. That's how they got me to agree to it. I sincerely thought it would be a way to reach people who would never be caught dead in a church.

This was at a time when I went through a rough period in my life. Not in February but later in March. A man I knew from Robertson Industries died in a plane crash. He was a man I knew for a short time while Kenny and I weren't together. Anyway, I was supposed to be on the plane. It really freaked me out, and it took a long while to get over it. We even sold the house in Timberline Heights because of the memories of that man.

Back to that little tour. Skip was the drummer because Bobby's parents wouldn't let him travel during the school year. He was still in high school, and wasn't old enough to get into some of the venues anyway. We played in clubs and stuff. Yeah, some of the places were bars. We did some cover songs and some of our our material. We didn't do the more preachy songs if you want to call them that. Some Christian groups record songs without ever mentioning Jesus. I'm not saying every song has to be about Him, but some bands never mention God at all. Some of my songs are like that now, but I'm rambling. We played the shows, and I got really close to a couple of the guys from the band. Nothing physical! Close in a friendship way. They kept me on track at a time when things could have fallen apart. After that tour I told the guys at Prater-Saylor I didn't ever want to play in those kind of places again. As it has turned out, I've never had to. We don't always play in churches anymore, but we play in venues where people can go without feeling uncomfortable. I confess that I got goosebumps at times when we played in really big places. But when it all comes down to reality, I'd rather play in churches. I guess I've experienced enough of the rock-star-type tours. I love the intimacy of smaller places.

Kenny knocked on the open door of the den and stood in the doorway. "Sorry to bother you, Em, but are you going to get the kids?"

Emmy closed her laptop and jumped up. "Sorry, I got kinda busy. I'll leave now."

"I could pick them up if you want. I'm not doing anything important," Kenny said.

"I thought you were working on my CD." Emmy made a face at him as she wiggled past him. "Isn't that important?"

"I suppose so, but I'm almost finished. I'll let you hear the final mix tonight if you want."

"Maybe after the kids go to bed. I'm sure it will sound amazing."

"I happen to think it does, Em." He shook his head. "You still don't even realize how talented you are."

359

Emmy closed the dishwasher after dinner Thursday and heard the landline ringing. She looked at the caller ID and didn't recognize the name. Only when she heard the message did she realize who was calling.

"Hello, Marley. How are you?"

Emmy and Marley Menconi talked for a time.

"The reason I'm calling, and I totally understand this is a last minute thing, but this Saturday is the women's meeting, and the speaker I had lined up called early today and canceled. Her father is ill, and she had to fly to the Philippines. I'm looking for a replacement, and Liz Hammond suggested you. Would you be interested?"

"What would I have to do?" *Shoot! I've never been to one of these meetings. I know Kristen has gone, but I thought they were for the old ladies in the church.*

"I'm looking for someone to speak to the group for maybe thirty minutes," Marley explained.

"I don't think I could speak to a group of people for that long. What would I talk about?"

Marley chuckled, "You could talk about your book, or your life as a singer. I think you could easily find something to talk about."

"Really? I don't know. How many people are usually there?"

"The largest crowd we've ever had was around a hundred ladies. I'm sure you've spoken to much larger groups before."

"Thirty minutes, huh?" Emmy bit her lip.

"It doesn't have to be thirty minutes," Marley replied and then waited for an answer.

"Okay, I guess I could talk about my book."

"Thank you, Emmy. I really appreciate it. We'll see you Saturday at nine o'clock." Marley hung up before Emmy could change her mind.

Emmy stared at the phone for a moment.

"Who are you talking to, Em?" Kenny grabbed a bag of chips from the pantry. "We should stop buying these because I'm eating too much junk."

"You are never going to believe what I just agreed to do," Emmy sighed.

"What?"

Emmy explained.

"Wow! What are you going to talk about?"

Emmy shrugged. "You got me."

"You could talk about the kids," Kenny suggested.

"I'm going to call Kristen. She went to one of these meetings. I'll ask her what she thinks."

Emmy talked to Kristen a few minutes later.

"What should I talk about?"

"Em, you could talk about lots of stuff. The band. Your books. Meeting Kenny. Meeting me," Kristen said and then laughed.

"Do you think anyone would be interested in that stuff? I don't want to bore people."

"Trust me, Em. You will not bore anyone."

Kristen picked up Emmy Saturday morning. She waited until Emmy fastened her seatbelt before asking, "Are you nervous?"

"Seriously?" Emmy stared at Kristen. "You're really asking. I almost puked up my breakfast. I can't stop sweating, and my voice is cracking like a guy going through puberty."

"Oh, come on. You've sang in front of thousands of people, Em." Kristen pulled out of the driveway and headed to Crest Ridge.

"Not the same and you know it."

"Have you got anything written down?"

"Kenny helped me with a few ideas." Emmy pulled some index cards out of her army coat pocket and held them up. "Should I have worn a dress?" Emmy noticed Kristen's bare legs under her coat.

"You might be the only person there in jeans, but it's all right."

"Crap! Stop the car and take me back home."

Kristen shook her head. "You look fine. Just take off that

jacket when we get there."

"Why didn't you tell me to wear a dress?" Emmy whispered to Kristen as they walked into the church. "I look like a homeless person." Emmy took off her army jacket and hung it up before anyone could see it.

"Oh, hush. You look fine." Kristen adjusted the collar of Emmy's top. "There. Now you look adorable."

"Will I have to wait long before I have to talk? If I have to wait too long, I'm going to puke."

"When I was here before, they spent about thirty minutes talking and eating before Marley introduced the speaker." Kristen led the way to the gym where tables had been set up. "Wow! There are more people here than the last time."

Emmy froze in the doorway, and then turned around to leave.

"Em, where are you going?" Liz Hammond asked as she grabbed hold of Emmy's arm. "The meeting is in here."

"I'm scared," Emmy whispered. "And under dressed."

"Nonsense! Why on earth would you be scared? You know most of these women. They won't mind that you're wearing jeans. You can sit in the back with me and no one will notice."

"They might notice when I get up to speak," Emmy responded.

"What?"

Kristen explained to Liz.

Liz waved a hand. "Ah, you'll be fine, and don't worry about the jeans. At least you don't have any rips in the knees."

Forty minutes later Marley tapped on the microphone to get everyone's attention. "In case you haven't heard Maria Juneau had to fly home because of her father's illness."

Emmy closed her eyes. *Lord, help me say something that isn't stupid or boring. I can't do this without you.*

"We are fortunate to have Emmy Colasanti-Colwell with us today." Marley glanced around the room. "Emmy, I know you're here."

"Em, you need to go up there now," Kristen whispered.

Emmy stood up and didn't hear the applause as she made

her way through the tables to the podium. *Shoot! I left those cards in my jacket. Lord, I really need your help now. Why on earth did I ever agree to do this?*

"Take it away, Emmy." Marley hugged her and then sat down.

Emmy moved behind the wooden podium and looked at the crowd. She took a deep breath and began. "Hi, I'm Emmy and this is my story."

She talked about her background for a couple of minutes.

"I suppose most of you know I'm part of the worship team, and do some singing with my husband and my band. Some of you might have seen my lion book." She bit her lip for a moment and then continued. "Would anyone like to hear how I came to accept Jesus into my life?"

Almost everyone in the room clapped.

"Okay, I'll tell you. When I was in high school, I came to this church a few times with Lynette Jefferson. She was Lynette Rosas back then. I began working a job on Sundays and didn't come back for years." She paused for a second. "I couldn't decide who I wanted to marry. I was in love with two different guys, and they both had girlfriends. Just my luck." Emmy shrugged and the crowd laughed. "I knew about one of the girlfriends but not the other one. I chose one of the guys, and did everything I could to win him back. Well, almost everything. He didn't take me up on my offer. I worried so much about this and made myself sick. I talked to Mama Bertucci, and she told me to pray about my relationship. Ooops! Now I guess you know who one of the guys was."

The crowd laughed again.

"Mama told me to pray, so I did. I prayed that Tony would want me again. I prayed selfishly like that for a week or so, and then one night I got out my old Bible. I hadn't opened it for a long time. There was an old bookmark in it, and I opened it to John 3:16. I read it and then turned to First Corinthians. I read about love. God's love. I read to the end of the chapter and kept going to the end of chapter fifteen." Emmy closed her eyes and bit her lip to fight back the tears. "I fell to my knees beside my bed and grabbed

363

my pillow, buried my face in it and sobbed. Then I lifted my head and looked up. I talked to Jesus just like I would talk to a friend because I didn't know any better. I prayed these words. 'Forgive me, Jesus, because I am a sinner. I don't understand everything, but I realize that I need you to be in my life and guide me. I want to make the same commitment to you that Kenny did. Show me what to do. Please.' As I uttered this simple plea, a peace came into my heart. I stopped sobbing and knew something had happened but was pretty clueless. I remember going to bed that night and sleeping peacefully for the first time since Tony left to go back to school. I figured I should go back to church, so I did. I ran into Paul Jefferson and told him who I was looking for. The sneaky guy didn't tell me Lynette was his wife." Emmy waited for the crowd to stop laughing. "Anyway, he took me to Lynette's Sunday School room, and I told her what happened. Paul went to get Aunt Doris." Emmy pointed to Doris Smith. "Auntie Dorie took over the class, and Lynette and I went somewhere to talk. She explained stuff to me, and I learned so much from her. She would always listen as I vented about my boyfriend trouble. Eventually, I realized who God wanted me to marry, and he realized it, too." Emmy paused for the laughter. "We got married, and a couple of years later God granted me a miracle. Two miracles." She held up two fingers. "That was over eight years ago, but it seems like yesterday. You see my doctor had told me I would never be able to have a baby. I thank God every day he was wrong." Emmy revealed how Kenny left for the hospital without her and the crowd laughed again. "I was in labor a long time, and," Emmy looked at Kristen. "Should I tell them?"

Kristen nodded.

"I guess everyone was quite worried about me because of the difficult labor. I guess I was real close to having a C-section to save my life, but God brought me through okay. My son came along two years later, and then I had my tubes tied." Emmy put a hand to her face. "Sorry, maybe I shouldn't have said that."

"It's all right, Emmy," Marley assured her."

"Kristen has always told me I don't know how to filter my thoughts and comments."

Emmy talked for a few more minutes and then stopped. Many of the ladies stood as they applauded.

"Would you be willing to answer a few questions, Emmy?" Marley stood beside Emmy at the podium.

"I guess so," she said as she shrugged.

Emmy answered a few questions about her inspiration for writing and other similar questions.

One of the ladies raised a hand and asked, "Where do you see yourself in twenty years?"

"Geez! I've never thought about that." She paused for a second. "I could be a grandmother in twenty years."

Before Emmy left one of the ladies approached her.

"Hi, I really enjoyed your talk. I don't normally come to this church except to help my sister clean."

"Hi, I'm Emmy," Emmy held out a hand. "I'm glad you had a good time."

"My name's Barb Hannon, and I'm a grandmother of twins."

"Oh, congratulations. What are their names?"

Liz Hammond saw Emmy talking to Mrs. Hannon and raced over and stood behind Emmy.

"Their names were Harper and Luna. They would have been a year old on March twenty-ninth."

Emmy felt hands on her shoulders.

Liz whispered into Emmy's ear. "The twins were born prematurely, and did not make it. Jesus took them to be his little angels."

Emmy wrapped her arms around Barb, and they both cried.

Chapter Thirty-Two

Emmy grabbed Kenny's hand as the worship band left the platform after finishing their set of songs for the second service.

"Should I tell them now?" Kenny asked.

"Might as well," Emmy replied. "He knows you guys are going on tour, so I don't think it will be a major shock."

Most of the team walked around the hallway and returned to the sanctuary, but Kenny guided Robby and Regina Collins into their office in the music suite.

"I take it you need to talk to us, huh?" Robby said.

"Yes, Emmy said you would probably know why."

Regina sat in one of the chairs against the wall as Robby leaned against the front of the large wooden desk. Kenny stood close to the door stood facing Robby.

"I know the band is going on tour. Should I take you off of the schedule until you are finished touring?" Robby asked.

"Yes, please." Kenny nodded but then he sighed. "There is more, and this isn't a rash decision but something I have thought and prayed about for at least the last year."

Regina sucked in her breath and put a hand to her mouth. A glimmering shine of sweat began to cover Robby's shaved head.

"Today was my final time playing with the worship team," Kenny said quickly.

Neither Robby nor Regina said anything in reply.

Kenny waited for several seconds before continuing, "There are numerous talented musicians on the team now, and I feel I've become a distraction. I overheard a comment a couple of weeks ago along the lines of some teens only coming to church to see a celebrity, and they didn't mean Emmy. Please don't think this is an ego thing. It isn't. Emmy deflates my ego on a regular basis."

Robby smiled. "She has a way of keeping all of us in check."

"Yes, she does. I haven't told her yet," Kenny said. "Not about the permanent part, I mean. She knows the other part."

"Am I correct in assuming you don't want this to become public knowledge?" Regina asked.

"You can tell the teams I am not on the schedule because of the tour. They will get used to me not being a part of the team, and then after the tour they might forget about me."

"Yeah, that's likely," Robby said in jest.

"They will be used to not having me on a team."

Robby stood up and extended a massive hand. "It's been a pleasure having you on the team. Should you ever change your mind, there will always be a spot open for you."

Kenny shook hands. "I appreciate that, Robby. I will still be a part of the church, and if you ever need a new song, I'll make Emmy write you one."

On the way home Emmy stared at Kenny.

"What?" he asked.

"Did you tell them?"

Kenny slowed to a stop at a red light. "I told them, and I need to tell you something."

After a few seconds of silence, she turned to look at him. "Well, are you going to tell me?"

He looked in the rearview mirror at the girls as they sang one of the songs the worship team sang that morning. "Uh... I told them this was my last time playing with the team."

"Yeah, you're going on tour. You can't be in two places at once."

"No, I'm talking about after the tour. I said I wouldn't be returning."

Emmy stared at him for several seconds. "Serious?"

He nodded.

"You didn't tell me. When did you decide to quit?"

"I've been thinking about it for a year or more." He drove through the intersection. "I should have told you."

"Maybe I should quit, too."

"No way, Em. You like singing at church better than on the road."

"I see a digger and a concrete truck." Kevin Michael pointed at a construction site.

"It won't be the same without you." Emmy glanced over her shoulder. "I see them, buddy."

367

"Mom," Heather hollered from the back row of the van.

"What, Heather?"

"Can we stop and get nuggets for lunch?"

"I have some in the freezer at home," Emmy answered.

"Those aren't as good. Can we stop, please?"

Emmy looked at Kenny, and he shrugged.

"Your call, Em."

"Let's stop. I don't feel like cooking all of a sudden."

Kenny laughed and said, "You just have to turn on the oven to heat the nuggets."

"Do you want to eat those generic nuggets?"

"You got a point. There's a Burger Bob's on the way home. We can stop. What do you want?"

Kenny got in line with the other cars and eventually placed his order. At the first window, the cashier took his money and smiled. "Have a nice day, Mr. Colwell."

"Thank you," he responded.

The cashier spotted Emmy and waved. "Hi, Emmy, I love your new CD. I'm still playing it even though Christmas is long gone."

"Thank you," Emmy answered as Kenny moved up.

"Do I look like an old man?" Kenny ran a hand through his hair and checked the mirror.

"How old do you mean?" Emmy kept a straight face for a few seconds before laughing.

"Ha! Ha! One of these days you will start looking your age."

They moved up to the next window, and Kenny handed Emmy the bag of food.

"Can we eat our nuggets now? We're starving," Heather complained.

"I don't think you'll starve before we get home," Emmy answered.

"There goes a police car!" Kevin Michael pointed. "He's probably after bad guys."

Kenny pulled into the garage and the kids raced into the house.

368

"So, do you plan to keep coming to church?" Emmy sat next to Kenny on the family room couch.

"Of course. Why wouldn't I?"

"Well, you quit the worship team."

"Doesn't mean I'm going to quit going to church. There are plenty of other musicians on the team. No one will miss me," he assured her.

"I got a call from Nelson yesterday. He wants to know if he can talk to Prater-Saylor to start booking my tour."

"What did you tell him?"

"I said I would talk to you and then call him back."

"Our dates are already set, Em. We really can't change them."

Emmy pulled her knees to her chest and wrapped her arms around her legs. "I know. I think it would be best for the kids if we weren't away at the same time. Sofia could handle them, but I'd rather not have to resort to that again."

"What would you suggest?" Kenny put an arm around her and pulled her close. "Are you still sad about Harper and Luna and their grandmother?"

"I cry every time I think of them, but we need to decide what I should do."

"Well, it would be unusual, but you could book your tour on the nights we aren't playing."

"I have thought about that. Do you honestly think we could draw a crowd on Sundays through Tuesdays?"

"Em, I think you could schedule your gigs in the morning, and people would skip work to see you."

She poked him in the side. "Get out! No one would come to a show in the morning. I would insist on being here for church."

"You could fly to the shows, Em. I'm sure that could be arranged."

"Are you guys going to fly everywhere?"

"That's the plan. We would fly out on Wednesday and return after the Saturday shows. That seems to work for everyone."

"It would cost a fortune for me to fly everywhere."

"Now who's a goof? Do you think Mr. Robertson is going

369

to charge you to use his plane?"

Emmy bit her lip. "I can't use his plane all summer."

Kenny kissed her cheek. "You won't have to. He asked me about it, and I said you might need to use it. He said Mona wants to stay home this summer to spoil Lily and Conor."

"Can you believe Lily will be two in a few weeks? It doesn't seem possible." She snuggled closer to Kenny.

Heather and Isabella walked into the room. "Mom, we want to go over to play with Dotty and Noemi. Can we?"

"Did you ask Uncle Tony if you could?"

Isabella nodded. "Dotty asked him. He said we could come over if he could come over here and pester you. Can he?"

"No way!" Emmy laughed. "You can play with them, but Tony can't come over here."

"Thanks, Mommy. We'll be home in time for dinner."

"Be careful crossing the road," Kenny hollered.

Emmy looked at him. "Can you believe they are old enough to walk over there by themselves?"

He pulled her even closer. "You used to come over to my house all the time when you were eight. Sometimes you didn't even tell your parents. At least the girls let us know where they're going."

"You lived down the alley. I didn't have to cross a big street."

"Springdale Lane may be a wide street, but there was more traffic in the alley behind our house than out here," Kenny said and then grinned.

"I still don't like the idea of them roaming around the neighborhood alone."

"They aren't alone. They have each other."

"Yeah, you can say that now, but you'll change your tune when they get old enough to date."

Kenny shook his head. "Nope! You're wrong, Em. I will be happy to let them date," he paused. "When they turn thirty-five, and I let them out of the closet."

"I hope they cause you as many gray hairs as I caused my father," Emmy said as she moved onto Kenny's lap.

Chapter Thirty-Three

"I think the artwork looks great," Mr Kesson told Emmy.

"Are you sure? Wouldn't you rather have a photo of something besides me?" Emmy asked.

"No, and since I have the final word, I like it the way it is." Mr. Kesson owned Steward Music Group, so he normally got his way. "Emmy, it's a very good picture of you."

She bit her lip. "I look fat."

Mr. Kesson laughed. "You don't look any different than you did for your first CD, and you are definitely not fat."

"Okay, I guess it's all right with me."

"Thank you, Emmy. Now, if you'll excuse me, I'm going to take my wife out for brunch." Mr. Kesson rose from his desk and left the office.

Emmy turned to Peggy Rainier the head of the art department for Steward Music and whispered, "I look fat."

Peggy shook her hand and chuckled. "You look beautiful in that shot. I love your dreamy expression. Do you remember what you were thinking about?"

Emmy smiled. "I do, but you can't tell anyone."

"Our secret," Peggy promised.

"I was thinking about when Kenny walked me to school for my first day at Roosevelt High. He held my hand as we crossed the street in front of the school."

"Ah, that's so sweet. The only time my husband holds my hand is when he's taking money from it," Peggy laughed so hard her chin shook like Jell-O. "Of course we've been married for forty years, and I wouldn't trade him for anything."

"That's sweet," Emmy said.

Peggy tilted her head. "I might trade him for a free trip to Alaska. I've always wanted to go on one of those cruise ships and watch the whales." She laughed again.

Emmy returned home and found a note on the kitchen island. *Oh, you took the kids over to see your parents. Are you going to go to Darby's for lunch? I should call you and make you bring me something home.* She fixed a salad for lunch and decided to read the part of her story she wrote about her and Rory. She read through it once while she ate. *It's not too revealing.* She wiped some dressing off of her lips. *Should I mention that one kid's name? It's not like he is going to ever read the book. His brother's probably still in jail somewhere.* She closed her eyes and thought about it for a moment. *No, he doesn't deserve to have his name mentioned. I'm sorry, God, but he was a worthless piece of crap, and I'm not sorry for what happened to him.*

"Mommy, we're home!" Isabella rushed into the family room. "Gra and Daddy took us to Darby's for lunch. We brought you a piece of chocolate cake. Do you want to eat it now?"

"That was very thoughtful of you. I love their chocolate cake. Would it be all right if I wait a while to eat it?"

"That's okay. Daddy can put it in the fridge, and you can have it later. Come on, Heather. Let's write another story about tigers and bears who can talk."

Emmy checked the date on her laptop. *How can it be the end of February already. This year is going too fast.* She turned on a light and sat in her recliner in the family room. *Okay, Denise suggested I write a closing chapter to update the reader about some of the characters in the book. I made a list like she advised. I might as well start at the top.* She checked her list and began to type.

It's Friday night. February 21, 2014. The kids are asleep. Kenny left a couple of hours ago to check out a new band with Andy and Father James, so I have the place to myself. I'm going to update you, the reader, on some of the things the people in my book are doing now. I'm going to start with the original worship band that did the first tour in 2003 just before Kenny and I got married. That seems like an eternity ago.

Chase, Yvonne and the girls are living in Toledo, Ohio. Chase is doing double duty as the worship pastor and associate pastor at Toledo Trinity United Nazarene. Yvonne is helping in the youth department at church and working in a legal office. This is unbelievable but Anna is nineteen and going to Olivet. She was so little when I first met her and Jada. Jada is sixteen and in high school. I can't imagine my girls being in high school.

Hank Lysenko, John Patterson and Steve Van Zant are all retired. Hank and John live out of state, but Steve is back in the area. He still plays for the worship band at church but with a different team than me. I see him once in a while, but rarely get to talk to him.

Now the drummers. When I joined the worship band back in 2002, Bobby O'Connor and Skip Mason shared the position. Later, Alan Vicini joined the group. Mr. Vicini did the first tour. He became a grandpa last month. Adam and Juliana had a girl. Kinsey Alyssa. She is adorable. Mr. Vicini still owns a music store in SoHam, but he doesn't come to church anymore. I wish he would.

Skip is still a part of the worship team. You might remember he had that one incident. He told me he still likes a glass of wine now and then, but that's it. He teaches fifth grade at a school in Platteville, which is a little town west of here. West of SoHam. He's technically single, but I hope that changes soon because he and Jenara Ribiero are living together. I don't understand why so many of the young people today are doing that.

That leaves Bobby O'Connor. Bobby, Bobby, Bobby! I can't get away from that young punk. He is still the drummer in my current band. He's... Oh, my gosh! He's twenty-seven now, or he will be later this month. He was like fourteen or fifteen when I met him. Bobby and I have always gotten along. In the early days, we teased each other a lot. As we got older he became more of a guy I leaned on to vent and stuff. I've always wrote about him as being girl crazy. He still is, I guess. He was briefly married to Maria DeGott the keyboard player in the Katie Hollins Band. It only lasted two or three months. I hope he finds someone soon. Oh, I should tell you about his latest tattoo. He showed it to me. It's a drum kit and it's on his hip. He's got a bunch of ink on his arms. They're colorful, but I'm glad Kenny doesn't have any tattoos.

Dixie Case joined the touring band in 2003. His real name is Martin, but no one calls him that. He moved back to Alabama a few years ago. He's still got a band, and they did record a couple of CDs. One of them for Steward Music Group. I always liked Dixie, and we were good friends for a time, but not now. I suppose it's all right to mention this. He did a stint in rehab for drug and alcohol abuse. He claims to be clean now. I pray he is.

Over the years I shared the stage with countless bands. I opened for some, and then later these bands opened for me. Kenny once asked me if I had a favorite. Two bands come to mind. The Reign and The Apostles Creed. I've gotten to know the guys in these bands over the years, and I can tell you they are for real. I'm glad to have been a part of their careers. Not that I had anything to do with their success. I still buy every CD they release, and we run into each over once in a while. So buy their music. It keeps them on the road.

"Hey, Em, I'm home," Kenny said. He walked into the family room but stopped when he saw Emmy working on her laptop.

"I didn't expect you home this soon. How was the band?"

Kenny shrugged. "They definitely need some work. Maybe a new singer, but they're young. I'm beat. I think I'll head upstairs. Are you going to be up late?"

"Another hour at the most. I want to finish this chapter if I can."

Kenny headed up the stairs. Emmy continued to work on her story.

That brings me to the guys from The Only Hope band. I mentioned Bobby and Skip. Ryan and Jennifer are expecting. Emmy Rose Lederer. I can't wait to meet her. Adam and Juliana are still in SoHam with baby Kinsey. Adam is a member of Fridays At Five, and Juliana works for the church's school, or she did. She might go back to work when the baby is older. Sean DelSasso, who replaced Ryan after he married Jennifer, manages his father's music store DelSasso Sound. He was married, but it didn't last. Boyd Goldman married Bailey Hammes. They both work for the city of SoHam. No kids yet. Perry Johnstone and Kaylie Kendall are married and live in the same neighborhood as Boyd and Bailey. They have a little girl named Sadie. Perry works for an insurance company whose name I can't reveal because I'm mad at them for denying a claim my mother had. Kaylie works part-time in an Edward Jones office. No gripes against them.

Who else is there? I'm not including the people on the worship team at church who never traveled with me. Kristen threatened to murder me if I wrote anything about her. Too bad, Krissy. Kristen Keasling Randolph and I have been best friends since I literally ran into her in one of the bathrooms at Roosevelt High. There! Take that, Kristen.

I mentioned the current guys in the band earlier, so nothing has changed with them. Some of the crew and tech guys are still around. A lot of them work for Fridays At Five and me. Frankie Hanna talked about retiring and moving to Canada, but he was probably joking.

Speaking of Fridays At Five, Kenny and the guys are going to tour for most of this year. I have to say that we are in a much better place in our relationship than the last time they did a long tour. That year nearly ruined our marriage. We were both to blame. I was just as guilty. Maybe more. Now, we are more in love than ever. And, yes, I still... we... okay, the sex is still great! There you had to wait until the end, but I did talk about my sex life.

I don't know what the future holds for me as an artist. Duh! No one knows the future except God. But I will continue to do whatever God tells me to. I'm writing this book after all. I do know that much. Maybe if I live to be a hundred like Grandma Isabel, I will look back on this period of my life and wonder how in the world I ever survived my life on the road. The end!

Emmy shook her head. *Denise will tell me that's the worst ending she's ever read. I just know it, but I'm too tired to change it now.* She saved her work, shut down her laptop and headed upstairs to bed. *I'm glad Kenny didn't stay out too late. I don't want to miss out on that great sex life.* She bit her lip but then giggled as she ran up the wooden stairs and heard a creak. Her blue eyes sparkled as she opened her bedroom door.

Check out these other titles by the author. Visit the website:
kennethleemcgee.com

The Emmy's Story Series

1. We We're 'posed to Get Married
2. One Of The Guys
3. A New Friend
4. Did You Like the Ravioli Tonight?
5. Completely and Forever: A Wedding
6. It's Time To Go!
7. How Difficult Can It Be?
8. Forever... Isabella... Forever
9. The Forgettable Year
10. Turning Thirty
11. Hello, I'm James
12. Remember The Struggle

The Annie Mercer O'Dell Series

1. Roosevelt High
2. North Park College
3. Smoky Mountain Summer

Stand Alone Books

1. Growing Up In Kinmundy Junction
2. Grandpa, Lions and Kitty Cats: A Collection Of Short Stories For Children Of All Ages

www.ingramcontent.com/pod-product-compliance
Lightning Source LLC
Chambersburg PA
CBHW021432240626
47153CB00001B/123